THE SCRIBE OF THE SOUL

PATRICIA MARSH

The Scribe of the Soul
Published by The Conrad Press in the United Kingdom 2018

Tel: +44(0)1227 472 874
www.theconradpress.com
info@theconradpress.com

ISBN 978-1-911546-35-1

Book cover design and typesetting by:
Charlotte Mouncey, www.bookstyle.co.uk

The Conrad Press logo was designed by Maria Priestley.

Printed and bound in Great Britain by Clays Ltd, St Ives plc

For Goran, Igor and Jana

'Memory is the scribe of the soul.'
Aristotle

Ever since I read about the generous provisions the philosopher Aristotle made in his will for a woman called Herpyllis – a woman about whom nothing else is known – she has intrigued me.

Herpyllis was clearly someone who held a special position in the great man's life, a woman from Stagira, the city of his birth. Once I knew the dire fate of that city and how Aristotle may well have played a part in the tragedy, I found Herpyllis's story gradually coming to me.

I saw her as a victim of the crazed territorial ambitions of King Philip II of Macedon (Ancient Macedonia), taken as a slave to his capital, a witness to the upbringing of his son, Alexander the Great, and to the people and forces which shaped him. Through Herpyllis, I could examine the key themes of so many women's lives: coming to terms with a patriarchal society's war-mongering and suppression of women; a yearning for the company and solidarity of other women; and the lifelong search for identity and self-knowledge.

We can never know what Herpyllis was really like, but this is how I imagine her.

Patricia Marsh

Note: All quotations used as chapter headings are attributed to Aristotle.

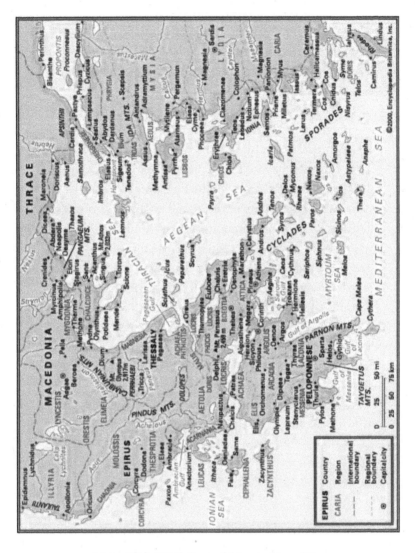

Map of the Greek world in Ancient Times
(Stagira is marked as Stagirus, Troy as Ilium, Dion as Dium, Macedon as Macedonia, etc.)

LIST OF CHARACTERS

Characters followed by (f) are fictional.

STAGIRA

Agathias (f), chief magistrate

Antheia (f), his wife, high priestess of the sanctuary of the Great Goddess

Theron (f), their elder son

Aristion (f), their younger son

Herpyllis, their daughter, narrator of the novel

Linos (f), freedman, steward of the household, later chief magistrate

Chloe (f), his wife

ARISTOTLE'S HOUSEHOLD

Aristotle, philosopher

Pythias, his wife, daughter of **Hermias**, ruler of Atarneus, a Greek city in Asia Minor

Pythy (Pythias), their daughter

Nicky (Nicomachus), their son

Nicanor, Aristotle's nephew and adopted son, officer in the Macedonian army

Callisthenes, Aristotle's great-nephew, historian

Theophrastus, philosopher, Aristotle's friend and colleague

Cassander, Macedonian nobleman, son of Antipater

Ambracis, Pythy's nurse

Myrmex, ward of Aristotle in Chalcis

Simon, Tycho, Philo, Pyrrhaeus – servants/slaves

PELLA

Philip (II), King of Macedon

Olympias, his wife, Queen, formerly known as **Myrtale** and as Polyxena, daughter of the King of the Molossians of Epirus

Alexander, their son, later Alexander III (the Great), King of Macedon

Cleopatra, their daughter, later wife of King Alexander I of the Molossians

Charis (f), one of Olympias's ladies, friend to Herpyllis

Xanthe (f), **Berenice** (f), **Hippolyta** (f), **Philylla** (f), **Eudoxia** (f) – ladies of the court

Audata, Philip's wife, daughter of the King of Illyria

Cynane, their daughter

Arrhidaeus, later Philip III, Philip's son by his wife Philinna, a former dancer

Thessalonica, Philip's daughter by a deceased wife

Antipater, Macedonian nobleman, King's counsellor and later regent

Alexander, Olympias's brother, later King Alexander I of the Molossians of Epirus

Amyntas, Philip's nephew, son of King Perdiccas III, Philip's elder brother and predecessor on the throne

Adea, daughter of Amyntas and Cynane

Leonnatus of Lyncestis, hostage, later officer in Alexander's army

Perdiccas of Orestis, hostage, later officer in Alexander's army and regent after his death

Leonidas, relative of Olympias, tutor to Alexander

Ptolemy, reputedly Philip II's illegitimate son, army officer, later Ptolemy I Soter, pharaoh of Egypt

Attalus, Macedonian nobleman and general of the army

Cleopatra/Eurydice, Attalus's niece, Philip's last wife

Hephaestion, Alexander the Great's favourite and officer in his army

Theopompus, historian

Iollas, Antipater's son, Cassander's younger brother, Alexander the Great's cup bearer

Polyperchon, Macedonian general

Roxana, Alexander the Great's wife

Alexander IV, their son, King of Macedon

PROLOGUE

'To write well, express yourself like the common people, but think like a wise man.'

My name is Herpyllis. I'm an unremarkable woman, but I've known remarkable men and women and lived through extraordinary times in exceptional places. Now I'm fifty years old, my thick wavy hair dull and grey – though once it shone like a black stallion's coat – my blue-green eyes, once so admired, strained and dim.

After a life spent mainly in Macedon and Athens, I find myself back here in Stagira, where I was born, living in the house Aristotle left me in his will when he died, eighteen years ago.

I'm sitting in this small room he must have known as a boy, the three windows high in the stone wall letting in the light, but not the glare and heat of the midday summer sun. The furniture is sparse, just this simple wooden desk and chair and, against the opposite wall, the long couch with its grey woollen upholstery and black-and-white striped cushions.

I see Aristotle sitting there as I look over at the couch now, those cold grey eyes behind the narrowed lids, their penetrating gaze fixed on me, his long straight nose in between, his huge brow framed in grey curls cleft by a deep frown, his thin lips set in a line above the neatly trimmed grey beard. I know exactly what he would be saying:

What are you doing outside the women's quarters, Herpyllis? How dare you sit there and use my precious papyrus for your scribblings? Do you know how much that cost? What do you know that could possibly be worth writing down for posterity anyway?

Well, Aristotle, there are many things I know and will record for those who will read it all when I am long gone. I will tell them who you really were, the man behind the famed philosopher, what it was that haunted your nights and troubled your days, why you adopted me as your ward, why you put up with me, the woman who never knew her place.

And I will write, too, of that other man who marked my life, who destroyed what I held most dear, whose name strikes terror into the peoples of half the known world – Alexander, King of Macedon, he who slaughtered and plundered his way across all the lands to the very Ends of the Earth and died far away in Babylon, the year before you, his teacher, joined him in the Underworld.

I've read much of what you wrote and I've thought about how it applies to our lives. I'm going to tell my story quoting from your works, so I can consider where you were right and where you were wrong.

Fear not, Aristotle. These scrolls won't be read for years; indeed they may never be read at all. I care too much for two particular people still living who would be harmed by the truths I tell here: your daughter Pythias and your pupil Cassander, the man I call my little brother. I shall keep my scribblings secret and hide them well. And if no one ever finds them, it is no great matter. At least I will have unburdened my soul and can live more at peace with myself for the few years I have left on this Earth.

1
CHILDHOOD

*'Give me a child until it is seven and I will show
you the adult.'*

So where shall I start, unknown reader?

With Macedon, I think. When I write that name I
still feel an icy hand grip my heart. Yesterday a flash of
memory came to me of the first time I heard it. I was
sitting in the little cove down the winding path from the
square, the one I often went to with my father, Agathias.
He was getting on in life when I was born. I must have
been about five that day in the cove, so he would have
been in his early fifties. He was an enormous presence by
my side, a brown robe hanging heavy round sandalled
feet, a nutty smell. A rush of that same feeling I had then
comes over me now as I recall the complete trust and
assurance I felt when his large warm hand held mine.

Suddenly he is crouching beside me, stroking that
speckled prickly beard of his that tickled my cheek when
he kissed me, his crinkled brown face with its smiling
hazel eyes on a level with mine. I have no idea what I
had asked him, but I remember how he took a stick from
among the brushwood on the beach and started drawing
in the sand with it. He outlined a kind of claw with three
fingers and drew a line joining the left-hand side of the

claw curving down until he reached my feet as I looked on. Next he drew a baby dragon alongside the lower part of the line. Father straightened up a little and then pointed to the right-hand side of the third finger.

'Here we are,' he said, 'here's Stagira, where we live.' And he stuck the end of the stick in the sand and made a little hole, almost exactly where the finger joined the claw.

'Macedon to the west here,' he said, outlining a big circle to the left of the claw. 'Thrace to the north,' he added, making another big circle above. 'Here's Chalcis down here on the island of Euboea far to the south,' he continued, making another hole in the sand in the side of the baby dragon. 'That, Herpyllis, is the city our ancestors left hundreds of years ago to find a new home and make a new life in the land they named Chalcidice after their old home. They built our city here with the natural defence of the sea on three sides, and they soon protected it with stout walls and towers to landward,' he went on, pointing over my shoulder. 'They made us prosperous, working the metal from the hills over there, making our bright silver coins with the boar of Stagira on them, the boar of the Goddess.'

And he held out one of the coins for me to play with. I loved that boar, I loved our Goddess. She lived in the sanctuary behind the high walls with the great wooden gates. It stood in a hollow near the cliff edge, the jagged rocks far below with the white foamy sea swirling round them. A place of awe and mystery, its gates locked to me.

Another two long years pass before I finally walk through those gates. It's my seventh birthday. I stand face-to-face with the Goddess, a huge stone figure looming up out of the smoke. There's a rich heavy scent in the air and it makes me dizzy. Suddenly I see sharp teeth in snarling mouths – two lions at the Goddess's feet. I scream and fall backwards. Mother's face is above me. I can hardly make her out in the shadow. She has a strange tall hat on her head and a veil over her long wavy black hair.

'Herpyllis!' Mother whispers. 'The Goddess is waiting. Where are the wheat stalks you brought for her?'

I gasp, I panic. Where are the wheat stalks, my gift for the Goddess? I was clutching them tight in my right hand, but now my hand's empty. Mother feels around on the floor under me in the gloom.

'Here,' Mother says, and I can hear the relief in her voice matching my own, 'here they are. Take them and get up now. Lay them on the fire before our Great Mother.'

I scramble to my feet, the damp stalks clutched again in my right hand. I am shaking now. A little push from behind. I take a step forward, keeping my eyes on the fire flickering ahead, dreading those teeth appearing again out of the shadows. A hand on my shoulder, a few more steps. The heat from the fire strikes my chin, making me draw back. The hand raises my arm.

Great Mother, receive this gift from your daughter Herpyllis. Look with favour on her and guide her to womanhood in your service.

I fling the stalks onto the fire as if they are burning my hand and step back, afraid they're going to burst into flame, but there is only a slight crackle. The hand on my shoulder again, pushing gently down. I drop to my knees, the cold earth floor a shock.

Suddenly a deep booming sound, followed by another and then another, a drum reverberating in the small chamber. Then chords on a lyre and women's voices ringing out behind me.

Mother, Mother of us all, keep Herpyllis, guard her, take her in your loving arms, Mother of us all, and make her yours forever.

How often since then have I heard the simple stark melody of that song sung for an awe-struck girl? Every single time it moves me, takes me back, has me kneeling there again. I can feel Mother's arms raising me to my feet, kissing each cheek and smiling, the firelight catching the tears in the corners of her eyes. She holds me to her and I am overwhelmed by elation.

That same look was on her face when I played my lyre and sang for the visitors one afternoon, not long after my first sight of the Goddess. I don't know who they were, but the words one of the ladies said to Mother have stuck in my mind all these years:

'You've taught Herpyllis well, Antheia, very well. Why, she's good enough to entertain the men in Athens!'

I had no idea why they all laughed at that, though I could see my mother only joined in for the sake of politeness.

The memories are flooding back now. There she is again, the basket she carried to collect herbs on her arm, her big floppy straw hat on her head. I am standing watching her as she kneels on the ground.

'Here it is,' Mother says with satisfaction. She holds up a sprig of green leaves. I love her hands, the thin fingers with their prominent knuckles. I love the way she moves, the earthy smell of her. I love her melodious voice. And now for the first time I hear her speak about Aristotle.

'When Aristotle and I were about the same age as you, Herpyllis, he showed me the little see-through dots on the leaves of the goatweed,' she says, beckoning me to her. 'That's how you recognise it.' Mother holds the sprig up to the light. 'Look.' And there they are suddenly, tiny silver ants spaced out evenly along the leaves.

'Goatweed's good for melancholy,' Mother says. 'Aristotle's father was our physician. He knew which plants cure which complaint. Aristotle's family used to live next door,' she continues. 'But they all went away after his father died. Aristotle's in Athens now. I don't suppose he'll ever come back.'

I remember Mother sighing and I wondered what she was thinking about behind those deep blue eyes, the colour of my favourite cornflowers. We moved on to look for camomile with its happy bright yellow centres fringed with delicate white petals, slanting strangely downwards.

I was eager to learn everything my mother taught me. And I knew I had to excel at it all, to make up for being her only daughter, the only one left. My two elder sisters had died of fever within ten days of each other, a couple of summers before I first saw the Goddess. Once a week we would walk up to the cemetery near the temple and Mother would stand before their statues, lost in thought, but those marble figures meant nothing to me. What I remembered about my sisters was their chatter and their giggles, the shivery sensation when they combed my hair, the painful tugs when the comb got snagged in a knotted tangle, the tight feeling round my temples when they did my plaits and wound them round my head. There was a place where they were, but it was empty now. So I tried to be a boy and do everything my brothers did.

My eldest brother Theron liked playing teacher. He was ten years older than me and quite the scholar. I was about five the first time he let me write on his wax tablet with the thin iron stylus. I was sitting on his knee and he put the stylus between my finger and thumb and held my hand in his. I pressed the metal point into the wax and Theron guided my hand to make a slanting mark.

'How does that feel?' he asked, a strange emotion lighting his face. 'I love that sensation – don't you?'

I nodded enthusiastically. With that one act he passed his love of writing on to me. Mother taught me to read and write, and gave me my own tablet. I loved the weight of it, the feel of the wood and the pungent smell of the wax when we put it on top of the cooking pot over the fire. Mother would tell me to keep away from the fire, but I would beg her to let me watch the magical way my writing would disappear and the wax would be transformed from that cloudy solid to a clear liquid. We would remove the tablet carefully so the wax wouldn't spill out, and put it on a stone to cool and set.

'Haven't you got anything better to do?' my other brother Aristion would ask if he saw me squatting by the tablet and watching transfixed as it slowly clouded over, until I had the smooth wax in front of me again without a mark on it.

Aristion was six years older than me. I see him in the square, one of a dozen or so boys of all shapes and sizes, half on one side of a white line, the other half on the other side. They're shouting and sprinting up and down without crossing the line, jumping to catch a pig's bladder they're throwing around. I have no idea what they're doing, but I want to join in. I can't be more than four years old; I've somehow got away from my nurse. I run in among them, calling Aristion's name. Suddenly I'm in a fog of dust and sweat, legs suddenly rushing out at me. I go on calling my brother's name 'Aristion! Aristion!', turning from side to side, trying to find him. Then the smelly pig's bladder hits me on the head and I fall to the ground and burst into tears. The next thing I remember is my brother's almost unrecognisable red face close to mine and the words he says between gritted teeth:

'Herpyllis, in the name of all the gods, stay out of our way! You're a *girl* – you can't play with us! Go home!'

And he picks me up under his arm and roughly sets me down on the edge of the square before running back to his game. I watch him stride back, his body already thick-set and powerful. Not at all like his father and brother. They're both tall and wiry. Mother says her second son takes after her own brother and she despairs of him.

'Aristion will never be good for anything but soldiery,' I remember her complaining to my father.

'Oh, he'll find his place in the world, Antheia,' he replied. 'He only wants to be different from his brother.'

22

As for my wanting to be one of the boys, Father said his teacher at the Academy in Athens, the great Plato himself, recommended educating a girl in everything a boy would do, so he taught me to swim and run, though he drew the line at wrestling.

What I loved doing most with Father was archery. We would always go to the same spot on the hill near the temple where he'd set up a target on a tree with the high city wall behind it. He explained he did this because, if I missed the target by any chance, nobody would get hurt and we wouldn't lose the arrow. I can still feel him standing behind me that first day, pulling the bow back with me, getting the right position for the arrow, angling my head correctly so I could aim right. *Slowly now... No hurry... Keep it steady... Pull a bit harder... That's it... Take aim... When you're ready...* I can hear his voice quite plainly in my ear as I write, and now I'm clenching my lips together as I did then to concentrate hard on my shot.

There was another man who sometimes took care of me when I was growing up. His name was Linos and he had been a slave. He was in his mid-twenties, tall and slim with black hair and deep brown eyes. My father had freed him the year I was born so he could be steward of the household. I was infatuated with Linos and wanted to please him in everything. I must have been six the first time he took me fishing with Aristion – I was so happy I couldn't speak. I just nodded at everything he said with a silly smile on my face, or so my brother told me. I was given a line to hold and sat with Linos, Aristion at the front.

Soon my brother was catching mackerel and throwing them into the bottom of the boat, where they flopped about until they gradually stopped moving. A dozen dark blue dots surrounded by golden circles stared up at me from among the shiny silver, streaked on the top half with those crooked dark blue lines. I sat there trailing my line in the water and looking down at the dead fish with a mixture of horror and fascination. Suddenly there was a great tug on the line – Linos just managed to catch me round the waist before I went overboard. He pulled me back, still clutching the line, and told me to put one hand in front of the other to gradually pull it in. He was holding the end and helping, of course. You can imagine my surprise when a huge turbot emerged out of the waves. It was bigger than me, and Linos had to pull it over the side of the boat for me. It thrashed about frighteningly for minutes before Linos's blows finally took effect. My brother looked on with undisguised envy. Linos beamed at me. We paraded through the city with Linos helping me carry my prize, and everyone who saw us smiled at me and said '*Well done, Herpyllis!*'

Another day sticks out in my memories of childhood. We went to the island of Kapros across the bay. Father had decided to get to the bottom of a legend about the island's inhabitant, a fisherman whose fate was a strange one.

This fisherman had been born in the harbour village outside Stagira fifty years earlier and had grown up apart from the other boys; they considered him odd and mocked him, so he avoided them and preferred to be alone. But one day, when he was a young man, he saw a neighbour's fourteen-year-old daughter at her mother's funeral. From that day on, he nursed an all-consuming passion for her. The girl's father allowed them to marry when she was fifteen, but the fisherman became convinced that all the other young men were just waiting for the opportunity to carry off his wife while he was out in his boat. He took her to Kapros and kept her there, gradually building a house with a high wall around it from the ruins on the island.

The ringleaders of earlier torments for the fisherman tried to land on the island's small beach several times to play tricks on him, but each time they encountered a hail of stones and had to retreat. Others who managed to land in later years said cacti and thorn bushes barred the way. They had only been able to glimpse the top of the wall around the house but found no path or gate to gain access. From the temple hill of Stagira the walls and roof of a mansion inside were clearly visible. Most Stagirans scared their children with stories of the crazed fisherman coming over to eat them if they misbehaved.

It was a calm sunny day in early autumn when my father set out for Kapros with us, Linos rowing the boat. He took all three of us children to show there was nothing to fear on the island. That was the kind of man he was. He hated superstition and irrational folk tales; he was determined to put an end to the rumours which had made a mythical monster out of a sad, obsessive man.

In retrospect, Father was taking quite a risk. Something must have convinced him that the man posed no danger, though Linos carried a long knife – for cutting a way through the vegetation, he said – and a shield to hold up if we were met with flying stones. Aristion and I were bubbling with excitement; for us the trip across the sea seemed endless and we could hardly sit still, but Theron was more sober about the whole affair and gave us supercilious looks. We finally landed, and the men pulled the boat up onto the beach. My father ordered us to wait there while he and Linos cautiously walked up to the first line of defence. My heart was in my throat and I could hardly breathe.

Linos started cutting down the bushes to make a path up to the wall surrounding the house. The only sounds were the regular slash of the knife and the gentle lapping of the waves on the shore. We were all alert for the slightest movement from above. It was not long before Linos and Father were both at the wall and one went left round it and the other right, disappearing into the trees. After several minutes Linos came back into view to beckon Father to join him. Then they both set off together the way Linos had come. It was Aristion who finally broke the silence.

'Where've they gone?' he asked.

Theron gave him a withering look and said:

'They're looking for a gate or some way in, stupid.'

'I'm *not* stupid – I knew that,' replied Aristion indignantly. 'But why can't we go and help?'

'Just shut up and do as you're told,' was Theron's response.

We stood and stared for ages at the newly-made path. Aristion was pacing around in circles and sighing loudly throughout. Eventually Linos appeared again and waved us up. We all ran to join him and followed in single file round the wall, which was built very close to the cliff edge on the other side of the island, with a really nasty drop down to the rocks below; there was just enough room to walk sideways along it. I was determined to be as brave as my brothers and forced myself to look ahead instead of down, as Linos told me, and edge along slowly.

Just when I thought I could stand it no longer, we came to a gap in the wall, hidden by a bush. It was just big enough for a man to get through, doubled over. I still remember the relief of standing on the solid ground inside, Linos giving me that proud look. Theron's face was whiter than usual when he came through the gap, but he managed to regain his superior smile as soon as he saw Aristion looking at him. In front of us was a little wood, and Linos led us through.

The sight that greeted us was a complete surprise. There was a shady garden beyond, well-tended and watered. My father was sitting on a stone bench with a bearded man, who had a few wisps of white hair on his head and was dressed in a strange outfit, apparently made of seaweed and fishing net. The man looked to me like one of the creatures on the big fruit dish at home, dancing round the sea god Poseidon. His legs and arms were pitifully thin and his face gaunt and wrinkled. On seeing us, the man jumped up and looked frantically around, then let out a high-pitched wailing sound. My father stood and put an arm round his shoulder, gently sitting him down again.

'These, Pelagios, are my children,' Father said. 'Theron, my eldest, Aristion, and my daughter Herpyllis.'

We were staring open-mouthed at the man, who nodded to each of us as our name was given, and we each nodded back, remembering our manners and behaving as if this were the most normal of visits to a neighbour. There was an awkward pause and then Father said:

'So, you see, there's no need for alarm, my friend. No Stagiran wishes any harm to you or to your wife.'

Pelagios nodded and said: 'No, no harm to my wife,' in a voice as resonant as that of a tragic actor. It was a shock to hear it coming from that wasted body.

'May we meet her?' pursued my father.

'Meet her?' the man repeated in the same intonation, as if he were learning his lines, his eyes vacant.

'May we?' repeated Father.

There was a long pause and then Pelagios stood up and bowed. He made a theatrical gesture towards the house, turned and led the way inside. A wooden gate led us into the courtyard of the house with its two storeys, the upper floor surrounded by a wooden balcony. We followed Pelagios straight ahead into a small room, lit by two windows high in the stone wall. It took a while for my eyes to adjust to the scene inside, but then I saw there was a low square table with two makeshift couches made from driftwood on either side. The table was laid with dishes of fish, bread and cheese. As my eyes got used to the dim light, I noticed a figure on the couch. She was wearing a dark robe with a silver brooch at her left shoulder and a veil over her head.

'As you see,' said Pelagios suddenly in that deep voice of his, making me jump, 'my wife wants for nothing. Can I get you anything else, dear?' he asked, lifting the veil from his wife's face.

I gasped and took a step back, treading on Aristion's toes. He gave me an angry push forwards and then I heard him catch his breath too. The face was a skull, the figure a skeleton propped up on the couch, the thin white bones of the hands standing out against the dark wood.

There was complete silence as we all gazed in horror at the scene before us, Pelagios standing beside his long-dead wife with a look of pride and satisfaction. Finally Father found his voice.

'Well, thank you, Pelagios,' he said. 'We'll take our leave now.'

Father looked at us. We all muttered Thank you in the customary way and filed out of the house after him and back through the garden. It was only when we had negotiated the narrow path outside the wall and got back to the boat that Father spoke again.

'Well, poor Pelagios is completely mad but seems harmless. He let me in without question when I told him I was chief magistrate, and said he had a complaint to make against his fellow citizens. They were always trying to break in and steal his wife. But he'd made her such a beautiful house and garden she didn't want to go off with anyone else. I assured him I'd make sure no one bothered him again. I wonder when his wife died. Poor woman.'

After a pause he looked at us and said we should tell our friends not to be afraid of the man on Kapros, rather to feel sorry for him.

'He's an excellent example,' he added, 'of what happens when a man takes things to excess. Remember the old teaching of our ancestors: *Nothing in excess*. That applies to love as to everything else. You must never let it take you over to make a prison for your beloved and a constant torment for yourself. Jealousy and possessiveness are terrible things, which leave you a shadow of a man, like Pelagios.'

There are other images from my childhood which suddenly come to mind, but no other events like our visit to Kapros. Sometimes I see Mother's gentle smile as I look up from my lyre, hold out a bunch of thyme or rosemary I have picked, hand her my tablet with the letters scored into it. I can still see that despairing look Theron used to give me when I asked him something, as if it was the stupidest question in the world, and hear Aristion's grunts of excitement when he was running and chasing me, inevitably catching me and tickling me mercilessly.

As for Father, I mainly see him now with that constant furrowing of the brow he developed after the letter came from Aristotle the following mid-winter. I didn't know then what it said. I was only seven years old and had little understanding of what it was all about. Something to do with Macedon and King Philip, husband of my mother's friend, Myrtale. My mother had named her after the white, star-like myrtle flowers she had worn on her initiation day. Her name was Olympias now, but my mother always called her Myrtale. I little expected I was soon to meet her.

My father was rarely home during those last weeks; he spent most of his time with the men in the big colonnade by the square, all so serious. I heard cities mentioned around the dinner table: Potidea, Acanthus, Olynthos. They meant nothing to me. I only knew they made my parents worry and look anxious. My brothers spent every day training with the men. No more fighting games for Theron or Aristion. Now they were getting ready for war in earnest. Theron was nearly seventeen and looking forward to going to Athens; he was to study with Aristotle from the autumn. His face was pale and set every evening when he came home, but Aristion's was shining with excitement. He could hardly wait to take part in real combat, though he was only thirteen.

It was getting dark the day we heard the galloping horse stop at our gate, followed by an insistent knocking. My brothers had not yet come home. The slave opened the gate to an exhausted man bursting in to tell us the Macedonians were on the march and that Stagira, like as not, was their destination.

My father's furrowed brow was suddenly flat as his face fell and went grey. My mother sat down very suddenly. They both looked at me. That was when I first felt it was all somehow my fault. Then Father excused himself to the man, told him to sit, drink, and ordered food for him. Father turned to say something to Mother but she anticipated him.

'Yes, you must call the men to the square,' she said. He left. I had long been in bed when I heard him return, hushed voices, and then silence.

2
THE ANTICIPATION OF EVIL

'Fear is pain arising from the anticipation of evil.'

My mother wakes me just before dawn. She is in blue and tells me to dress in my best long white dress. I know where we're going. The sky is a rosy pink when we arrive at the sanctuary, and I shiver in the cold spring air. All the others have assembled in a few minutes. We go inside. The Great Goddess's face is in darkness – only the snarling lions on either side of her glare malevolently back at me. But I am used to their sharp teeth now and the way they seem to be striding towards me.

Mother leads the prayers:

'O Great Mother, hear us and protect us in our hour of need. We, who have honoured you all the days of our lives, beseech you not to turn your face away from us now that great peril threatens us...'

This is not what I was expecting. I feel none of the wonder that usually comes over me in this place. I am confused and lost. I want Mother to make it right again, say the thrilling words, talk about the Goddess and how she leads us through the important moments of life. I am biting my lip; it feels cold and dry. The bewilderment lasts and lasts. Then Mother's hand on my back, guiding me outside. She takes a dove from the cage as we pass, and nods to me to do the same. We assemble in a circle round the lifelike statue I love so much in the courtyard, the girl gently holding the bird between her cupped hands, just as we are all doing now.

'Mother of us all, shield us and keep us, and grant us your peace.'

Heads go down and then up; we all release the white birds together into the transparent azure of the lightening sky. They gain height and then break away, flying in all directions. Part of me wants to follow them, soaring up and out.

Some minutes go by before small groups of women start leaving. When we are alone, my mother folds me into her arms. We stand like that for a long while. Then she holds me at arms' length, her hands on my shoulders, a look of infinite sadness on her face.

'Promise me you'll never forget what I've taught you. Whatever happens, you'll always be true in your heart.'

That's what she says – I remember the exact words. I can't say anything. Finally I manage to stammer:

'But... you... ?'

She forces a smile.

'Who knows? Stagira's walls can keep them out for many months and they may soon give up. The Athenians did in our grandfathers' time. We've got supplies to last us. Your father's seen to that.'

'But he said the harvest wasn't good last year and our stores are low. And Philip's a clever strategist and Cleon the Athenian was a fool.'

I'm repeating what I've overheard in snatches over the last few days. I only know Philip is the husband of my mother's friend and that he is King of Macedon.

Mother turns now, a proper smile on her face as she puts out her hand to take mine and lead the way home. My father has already gone to the citadel to organise the defence of our city. When I go to get my bow and arrows, Mother shakes her head sadly.

'No,' she says. 'We'll both stay here until he sends news.'

Father returns himself at noon. It is a sunny day, the sky clear and the white cherry blossom dazzling against it. On a day like this in other years my father has swept me up from my lessons and chased me out to run and play, my mother half-heartedly tut-tutting behind us. But today he only manages a gentle stroke of my cheek and a distracted smile before he sits down wearily.

'They'll be here in five days,' Father says, 'if they keep up the same pace. They've got siege towers and catapults.'

'Our walls are strong and high, and in good repair,' Mother replies. 'You've seen to that yourself.'

'Yes, my love,' he concedes, 'but we haven't got the men to guard the entire length of them.'

'You've got women and girls, too,' I pipe up. 'I can shoot my arrows and we can throw stones!'

Father gives me the same half-smile as before. 'We'll discuss these things later,' he says. 'Now let's eat.'

We eat in silence, my parents busy with their own thoughts, none of the conversation I'm used to around the table. Father leaves for the citadel after a short talk with my mother beyond my hearing. I feel guilty again, helpless. I want everything to go back to normal.

Any hopes we have that Stagira is not the King's target are dashed in the late afternoon four days later. The road round the bay is slowly growing black as the approaching troops fill it, a giant snake slithering inexorably towards our gates to devour the city whole. They stop at the end of the bay and one lone horseman comes on up the hill towards the citadel. The magistrates have assembled on the wall to face him, my father at their head. Mother is there as high priestess and we children are at their side, Theron holding me in his arms so I can see over the wall. The Macedonian looks up at us, then turns his gaze to the sky as if checking the weather. Finally he fixes his eyes on my father.

'I bear a message from King Philip,' he shouts. 'Open your city gates immediately, Agathias, and swear an oath of fealty to him, you and all the magistrates. You will pay a tribute of one hundred talents of silver to your king and make him a gift of Stagira's silver mines, which he will allow you to lease back from him for three quarters of their annual output. Those are King Philip's terms. If you accept them, no citizen will be harmed. If you reject them, no mercy will be shown. I will come back for my answer in one hour.'

But as he turns his horse, my father calls down to him and he looks back. Father's voice rings out firm and clear:

'Tell your king the citizens of Stagira are free men who will never be subject to him or any other. Our walls have kept us safe from invasion for hundreds of years and will shield us for many hundreds more. We have no quarrel with Macedon. Tell your king to leave us in peace, or he will waste much time and many men in a futile endeavour.'

There is a short pause before the horseman turns his mount again and rides back to the army without another word. Then everyone starts running, taking up their battle positions. But the snake slithers slowly back; the Macedonians pitch their tents and prepare for their evening meal and a night's rest. We return to our homes, leaving the guards and the watchmen on the walls.

My father is more like himself again. The furrow has left his brow and he steps more lightly.

'The Macedonians have left us no alternative but to defend our city,' he explains to my brothers. 'Their terms were deliberately unreasonable. Philip has no intention of leaving Stagira intact to switch allegiances as soon as his back is turned. Even if we'd accepted his terms, they would have destroyed our city and taken us away as slaves.'

He pauses and then continues with a grim smile: 'We mustn't lose heart. Our walls have never yet failed us. I'll be spending most of my time at the citadel from now on. I've got the best view from there of what the Macedonians are doing on all sides. I can send reinforcements to any part of the walls where they might concentrate their attack.'

Aristion is brimming with eagerness. But Theron is grey, his jaw set rigid. My father turns to Mother and me.

'I want you both to stay in the house and courtyard,' he says in his voice that means... *and that's final.* I can't hide my disappointment.

'But, Father,' I say. 'I nearly always hit the bull's eye on the target with my arrows and you call me your little Amazon, and...'

He holds up a hand.

'No, Herpyllis,' his expression is deadly serious – no little upturn of the mouth, none of the crinkles round his eyes. 'The best way you can help is to do as you're told swiftly and obediently.'

I feel the tears pricking my eyes and hang my head so Aristion won't see. Then Father comes over and picks me up. He hugs me for a long time, much as Mother did at the sanctuary.

Our house is on the other side of the hill from the city gates; we hear little of the fighting the next day. Linos badgers us to let him go out from time to time to bring us news, as Father has instructed. Each time he goes, Mother and I sit anxiously waiting for his return, both pretending to be busy with our music, writing or sewing. Each time he comes back, he simply tells us our men are resisting the Macedonian attack bravely.

It is dark when Father comes home, looking tired and worn. All he will say is that the enemy has been repulsed, but that they far outnumber us and there is no limit to how long they can stay camped in the foothills.

The very next day Linos rushes back into the courtyard to tell us the Macedonians have somehow broken into the city – he thinks from the western wall. So my father was right. Too few Stagirans to man the length of the walls; but it puzzles me that he didn't see the danger from his vantage point and send reinforcements as planned.

'Why didn't Father...' I begin, but Mother isn't in the mood for a discussion of strategy.

'Quick, Herpyllis,' she interrupts, 'go and get your bundle – *now*!'

Mother has made me a bundle of food, clothing, my lyre – just in case. I run and get it, my father's words fresh in my ears about doing as I'm told, my face hot with shame again.

When I come back, Mother is in the courtyard with our cook and two maids, all holding their own prepared bundles. Her face has taken on an expression I've never seen before, as if she is no longer present in her body. As if she is already elsewhere. It is the face I still see today in sharp relief, all these long years later. She looks at me like that for several seconds, and then she comes to life again and takes my hand, guiding us all out of the gate, up the road and down the hill to the sanctuary. Most of the women and children have already assembled and she unlocks the great gates to let us inside, waiting for the stragglers before locking them again behind us.

We are all squashed into the courtyard, shuffling around to make room, children whimpering, babies crying, women muttering together. Mother pushes through the throng to unlock the sanctuary doors and some of us squeeze in, others entering the adjoining rooms, many still in the courtyard. We are all waiting for her to take charge. She summons up that commanding voice and begins the prayer:

'O Great Mother, hear us and protect us in our hour of need. We, who have honoured you all the days of our lives, beseech you not to turn your face away from us now that great peril threatens us...'

It is a comfort to join in. But I can't control the trembling in my voice and soon my throat is so dry it refuses to produce any sound at all. All I want to do is fling myself into my mother's arms and feel her wrapped safely around me, telling me one of the old stories of the Great Goddess and her lovers, lulling me to sleep. How can she stand there, upright and composed, as if it is any other day in Stagira, the birds singing in the trees, the servants sweeping the floors and the doorsteps, the slaves pulling the fresh bread out of the ovens, the smell wafting over to us, the expectation of breakfast quickening our step on the way back home?

But I must be worthy of her, I mustn't break down. I'm shaking, my breath fast and shallow, my palms sweating. At the first test, the girl her father described as a little Amazon has become a weak, cowardly creature, longing for her mother, impatient only to retreat into the warm secure world of childhood.

The rite continues, but in the silences we can hear the women and children in the courtyard becoming restless and alarmed; soon even inside we can hear shouting, screaming, loud thuds and crashes. The panic spreads like a huge wave dashing the shore. Even Mother is overcome. She hesitates and looks around in agitation. When she sees me, she opens her arms wide and I push through the others, trembling no longer, to be folded into her embrace. Her heart is beating fast but she seems to be as reassured as I am by holding on tight to each other. After a minute or two she has regained her authority. With her arm around me, we jostle our way outside and go over to stand by the gates.

'Come now, women of Stagira,' she shouts above the hubbub. Many anxious faces turn to look at her and listen. 'Let us not shame our men or our grandmothers. We are made of sterner stuff. We may still prevail. The enemy has breached our walls but not beaten us yet. Our husbands, brothers and sons are fighting for our city, and that gives them each the strength of ten men. Do not despair. Pray with me now.'

But just as some order has been restored and there is relative quiet, a loud knocking on the gate startles us all and a deep male voice calls out:

'Open up. Don't make us burn you out. We won't harm you. You'll be taken to Pella.'

We all look to my mother. She remains still and silent. Then the man calls:

'Antheia! Open the gates! Queen Olympias greets you. I swear you won't be harmed. She told me to find you. You can trust me to take you to her.'

My mother's expression changes. I hear her catch her breath, see a leap of hope in her. After a short pause she calls out:

'Do you bear a token from the Queen?'

There is a pause. Then the man's tone changes:

41

'She says she is your Myrtale, still, in her heart.'

Mother hardly hesitates. She takes the great key and unlocks the gates. A huge figure in a shining breastplate and helmet sits astride his horse facing us, his short greying beard standing out against his weather-beaten skin, his bright blue eyes calm and intent. There is a small cavalry unit behind him, each man holding a lighted torch. Their leader nods to Mother and draws his horse to one side, indicating that we should walk out, his men parting to form a guard on either side.

We all come through the gates in silence and then the leader rides to the front to conduct our ragged procession back to the square. It is as if we are in a different time and place from the one where we heard fighting and screaming. But, as we leave the sanctuary, I turn to see three horsemen go in, tossing their burning torches inside. I cry out, but Mother grasps my shoulder and moves my head away, staring straight ahead herself, her mouth and her jaw set hard. She is in that other place again.

As we come down towards the square we glimpse our men and boys standing in a large group, surrounded by Macedonian soldiers. It is only when we enter the paved area in front of the colonnade that I see the King with his captains at the top of the steps. I know him immediately. His polished helmet and greaves catch the afternoon sun and the gold on his breastplate glitters. He is not the tallest of the men but the most stocky and commanding, his beard still black. There is something strange about his face, but at that distance I can't make out what it is. The leader of our group rides over and dismounts, taking up a place near the King. It seems they have been waiting for us before they start the grim proceedings.

'Agathias!' the King bellows. It is only then that I become aware of the six men kneeling in front of the steps below, my father in the middle. 'You were warned. Now you and your fellow magistrates will be punished in accordance with our customs. Proceed.'

The last word is not in Greek. It is directed at the guards behind the kneeling men; they now step forward, each holding a short spear. As one, they draw their spears back, and it is then I realise what they are going to do. I duck between the soldiers' legs and run towards Father, screaming *Daddy!* over and over again. The spears are plunged into the men's backs, but I keep running and throw myself down beside my father's body, where he lies on the steps doubled over in agony, struggling for breath. I take his face in my hands, still screaming *Daddy!* – but his eyes are wide and empty. He doesn't see me. He is staring at the yawning gates of the Underworld.

The soldier who has killed him is startled by the sound of someone running up behind him. He spins round, his spear still up. Mother is not far behind me and runs straight onto it. I turn from Father's black lifeless eyes to the look of astonishment on her face as her left hand goes up to the gaping wound in her chest and she slumps to the ground in front of me. She just manages to reach out her right hand to me and say my name before she dies. I grab her hand and start frantically stroking it, willing her to get up and take me in her arms, soothe me and wake me from the nightmare. But she just lies there.

I am left kneeling on the ground between my parents, groaning and swaying backwards and forwards, the grief overwhelming. That's all I remember. Except that somewhere in the background I hear another muffled command, followed by volley upon volley of dull thuds, women and children shrieking and wailing a long way away, in some other world. The soldiers stoning the defenders of our walls to death. Theron, Aristion – my brothers.

I can't tell you how long I stay on the ground there by the steps. The child in me is still there. In this world we call reality I gradually become aware of the huge face of a man leaning over me. I recognise him. He is the one who gave Mother the Queen's message, the one she seemed to trust. He picks me up and places me on his horse, swinging up after me. I am completely numb. I think I am still groaning. I don't know.

As we ride, I see soldiers going into houses, coming out with full, lumpy sacks. They throw burning torches in behind them. We come to Melissa's house. My mother's sick friend is lying on the ground. A soldier is holding her arms pinned back while another jerks brutally backwards and forwards on top of her. Her mouth is wide open, but I can't hear her screams. Her white-haired father is struggling with another soldier, trying to get to his daughter, trying to stop them hurting her. As I watch, he falls to the ground. The soldier leans down and pulls his knife out of the old man's stomach, casually wiping it on his clothes. Flames are licking through the roof of the house behind them.

One Macedonian is standing to the side, holding a piece of bread, rhythmically tearing off and chewing each mouthful. Like him, I am completely removed from it all. I look on, impassively observing the scenes in a floor mosaic like the one in the temple on the hill. The smoke makes my eyes smart but I don't blink. I can't.

In the following dreary days on the road I am surrounded by blurred images of my childhood playmates, my mother's friends, our neighbours, the boisterous children of Stagira, trailing along after the soldiers, dazed and hopeless, slaves now to the masters who have chosen them. The smell of soaked leather on the horse, of wet wool on the cloak round my shoulders, the heat of the man behind me, the cold of the nights huddled in a corner of his tent.

I am in a ghastly world between sleeping and waking, where the same hideous scene keeps being repeated over and over again: Father kneeling, the King's command, the guard stepping forward, the spear being plunged into his back, his body doubled over on the steps, the look in his eyes, Mother's face as she sinks down, reaches out her hand and says my name. My groans. A jolt. The same sad scene around me. I hug my bundle more tightly to me, the lyre sticking into my ribs. I lean into it, making it hurt as much as I can. It is a distraction, a kind of reassurance in the pain, holding close all I have left of my former life, of my home, of my family.

3
DARK MOMENTS

*'It is during our darkest moments that we
must focus to see the light.'*

Olympias, Philip's Queen, never ceased to remind me
how fortunate I had been the day Stagira fell. Yes, fortunate that terrible day of death and destruction because
the man who took charge of me was Antipater. Antipater,
her friend, the King's trusted adviser.

I still remember coming into the Macedonian capital
of Pella on his horse in the rain as if I've just woken from
a ghastly dream. All my senses were dulled and I was
incapable of thought, but the images must be etched
indelibly on my mind. I still see the huge carved wooden
gates of Pella and my first view of the main street of
that modern city, glimpsing the enormous marketplace,
its throng of people bustling about, continuing on up
the hill towards the palace, the mythical building ahead,
its towering portico in the centre of a row of soaring
columns, stretching out endlessly either side in the mist
of the rain. We dismounted in front of the entrance
and Antipater steered me up the steps, through a high,
brightly coloured hall with swirling frescoes, and into
the colonnade behind.

As we entered, a woman jumped up and darted towards us excitedly. But then she came to a halt just as suddenly. The memory is vivid. That billowing red-gold hair, those astonishing green eyes, that grace of movement and presence. How could she fail to make an impression at first sight, whatever the circumstances? Olympias, the Queen. My mother's friend Myrtale.

'Where is Antheia?' she demanded.

'I'm sorry, my lady,' Antipater said in his gentle voice, the one he had used to Mother to give her the Queen's message.

'I told you to take care of her. I told you to bring her to me,' said Olympias accusingly, her eyes shining with anger.

Antipater gave no reply. Instead he put his hand on my shoulder and said:

'This is her daughter.'

'I can see that,' she said. 'What happened?'

'There was nothing we could do. When Agathias was executed, she rushed forward. The soldier who killed him span round. She ran onto his spear.'

He didn't say she was running after me. He didn't say it was all my fault.

'She killed herself?' asked the Queen, a horrified look on her face.

'I don't think so, my lady. It was an accident.'

Olympias has told me since how she turned away to try to regain control of herself and heard the heavy thump as my body hit the floor. She turned back to see Antipater pick me up and follow Charis, one of the Queen's ladies,

47

who quickly led the way out. Apparently they laid me on a bed and Charis rubbed my wrists and my cheeks until I regained consciousness. She asked my name but only got an empty stare in reply. She felt how cold and wet I was and covered me in blankets, ordering a slave to prepare a warm bath for me. When it was ready, poor Charis had a struggle to take my bundle from me. I had not let go of it from the moment I left the house with my mother in that other life in Stagira.

The only thing I recall from that time is the feeling I had of being in a tightly fitting cage with invisible bars. Thoughts and images raced through my head but my mouth was incapable of forming words. I had forgotten how to speak. Charis told me I hardly blinked, reacted to nothing and no one. Everyone began to assume I was deaf and mute. They explained to me slowly and carefully, making signs with their hands, that I was now the Queen's slave and must be ready to do her bidding as soon as she called for me. I couldn't really understand what they meant. Our slaves at home fetched water, prepared food, swept the courtyard. But nobody told me to do anything like that. Most days they sat me in a corner of the back garden out of everyone's way.

It was there in the garden of the palace in Pella that I met Alexander for the first time. I couldn't have known then he would become the conqueror of all the lands to the Ends of the Earth. That afternoon I had no idea who he was. He was just a boy of my age playing with a wooden sword, thrusting and parrying. I heard him careering down the path as if in pursuit of the enemy.

Then, to my horror, he came to an abrupt halt in front of the bushes partly masking my seat. There was some rustling and suddenly the sword point was almost touching my nose. Behind it was a grotesquely contorted face, the eyes wide and staring. I let out a scream, mainly from the strangeness of those eyes – one blue, the other brown.

'Surrender, or I'll run you through!' he declared in as manly a tone as he could manage.

But just as he pulled the sword back, the Queen's voice rang out across the garden.

'Alexander! You must be kind to Herpyllis. She's the daughter of my best friend, and she's come to live with us.'

Alexander looked at me warily, then let down his sword and walked over to his mother. She beckoned me to join them, which I did quickly, remembering what I had been told about doing the Queen's bidding. I wondered if she'd tell me to sweep the floor, or fetch water. I looked around desperately to see where the broom was and the water bucket. When I stopped in front of her, she moved to put one arm round me and the other round her son.

'Herpyllis is from Stagira,' she said to him, 'the city your father's just taken. It had strong, high walls but now lies in ruins, like Troy. The women and girls have been brought to Pella as slaves, like Hecuba, Andromache, Cassandra. Herpyllis's mother was the Great Goddess's high priestess, her father chief magistrate of the city. Her family was like Trojan royalty, but now she's the only one left, and she's the same age as you. You must make her feel at home with us. You must be a good and generous prince, like Achilles, like your ancestor. Remember that Achilles treated his Trojan slave girl well.'

Alexander's expression changed completely. He drew himself up and assumed a lordly kind of smile. He reached over and took my hand. Olympias gently pushed me forward and I let the boy take me out of the garden. He was half a head shorter than me. I glanced back nervously to see his mother smiling happily after us. This wasn't what I thought being a slave meant.

The prince led me into a courtyard where other children were playing. They all turned to watch us as we approached, eyeing us curiously. Alexander stopped in the centre of the space and looked round with satisfaction at the attention he was being given.

'This is Herpyllis,' he said. 'She's from Stagira – it's like Troy. My father's taken her as a slave and we should be nice to her. She's a kind of princess.'

I was surprised at this description of myself, but gratified by the looks of approval which were coming my way. One boy stepped forward with a grin on his face. I liked him before he even opened his mouth. He had black hair and green eyes like me, and we were the same height.

'I'm Leonnatus of Lyncestis,' he said, 'Alexander's cousin. I came here a couple of years ago. I'm not a slave – I'm more of a hostage. My father still rules in Lyncestis but he'd better not do anything the King doesn't like, otherwise I'll be for it.'

He still had the same cheery look on his face as he said this. The word 'hostage' was new to me, but he had explained the notion well. He then introduced Perdiccas of Orestis; he was another hostage. I didn't like the look of him at all. Perdiccas had a contemptuous expression in the cold blue eyes staring at me from under a shock of curly blond hair. But I didn't spend much time considering him. To my amazement, an Amazon maiden had appeared behind him, wearing a sleeveless dress shockingly pulled up above her knees and tucked over a belt at her waist. She had a quiver of arrows over her shoulder and a bow in her hand. I felt Alexander shrink slightly as she approached. She was a head taller than him and her light brown hair was pulled back from her face, falling in a long cascade down her back; her hazel eyes had a golden sheen about them. A lithe, sleek lynx.

'I'm the King's daughter Cynane,' she said, 'and that's Cleopatra, Alexander's sister.' She gestured towards a dark-haired little girl hanging back shyly from the circle around us. She looked about five. Another Cleopatra. I'd already met two Cleopatras. Unlike us, the Macedonians seemed to use the same names for everyone. Alexander made a scoffing kind of noise next to me. He had his mother's looks except for his curious eyes, while his sister's colouring was her father's. I couldn't understand why Cynane called Cleopatra Alexander's sister, rather than her own sister. She'd just said she was the King's daughter, too. The princess looked me up and down and then asked in a bored voice, clearly not expecting a *Yes*:

'Can you shoot a bow?'

I felt a great rush of gratitude to my father for teaching me. I nodded. Cynane looked me over sceptically but made a sideways gesture with her head to indicate the target area.

'Here,' she said, giving me her bow and quiver. 'Let's see what you can do.'

I knew this was a decisive moment. On it depended whether I would be accepted, ignored or victimised in my new home. I drew a deep breath and focussed on Father's voice as I drew an arrow from the quiver, placed it carefully against the bowstring and slowly lifted the bow, drawing back the string as I did so. Luckily the bow and arrow were very similar to the ones I had practised with and nothing distracted me from the instructions being given in my head: *Slowly now... No hurry... Keep it steady... Pull a bit harder... That's it... Take aim... When you're ready...* I loosed the arrow and watched its seemingly endless trajectory to the target. To the centre of the target marked by the bull's eye.

'Well,' said a man's voice, 'impressive.'

I froze. It was a voice I had last heard in Stagira, giving the order of execution. It was the King. There was a pause.

'Who's this?' he said. He must have been looking at Cynane for it was she who replied.

'Herpyllis of Stagira, Father.'

Another pause.

'Let me look at you, child,' he said.

I had no choice but to turn to look at him. He was standing right behind me; and now it was obvious what had made the King's face look strange at a distance that day in Stagira. Where his right eye should have been, there was just dark puckered skin. I gasped audibly and quickly put my hand up to cover my mouth. A Cyclops from *The Odyssey* towering over me, about to grab and eat me, head first. I closed my eyes.

'Antheia's daughter,' the King commented. 'I suppose the Queen's taken you in. Well, make yourself useful and earn your keep.'

I opened my eyes, but he had already turned away and was walking towards the women's apartments. The man who had caused the death of my parents and brothers, the man who had destroyed my city. I should have put another arrow in my bow and shot it into his back while I had the chance. I bet Cynane would have done, had she been me. But I was still trembling from seeing the Cyclops. Anyway, Cynane tapped me on the shoulder and said:

'Watch *me*.'

She shot her arrow right next to mine, though she didn't split it. Leonnatus commented:

'Glad to see you've got some competition now, Cynane.'

'Unless it was just a fluke,' she countered, but she gave me a friendly look before bounding inside after her father, followed by the others.

It was then I caught sight of another boy in the courtyard, sitting in the corner. He was making a kind of droning noise which I had been aware of for some minutes, without registering where it was coming from. He was staring at me and making a kind of beckoning gesture with his left hand over and over again, so I thought I should go to him. But when I got closer I realised his eyes were completely vacant and his arm movement was a kind of tic he couldn't control, any more than he could stop making that strange noise. He was a simpleton like Simonides in Stagira, who my mother said must be pitied and not mocked – it wasn't his fault he couldn't play with us or talk to us. He wasn't stupid, just simple, she said, and couldn't learn like the rest of us, but we should be kind to him.

'I'm Herpyllis,' I said to the boy. 'Hello.'

His expression didn't change but his left hand began to move backwards and forwards much faster and the dribbling coming from his mouth made a big bubble as he grunted at me. Perhaps he was trying to tell me his name, or say *Hello* back. I didn't know what else to do, so I just gave him a smile and went back to my bench in the garden.

And that night, as every night, the terrible scenes in Stagira returned in my dreams and had me wake up screaming. Charis came and held me until I calmed down and fell asleep again. It was she who took me to the Queen the next morning and showed her the lyre I had in my bundle when I arrived. The Queen turned to me and then gave a little wave of her hand. This clearly meant something, as Charis handed me the instrument and nodded encouragingly. Suddenly I was back in the happy times. I took the lyre, tuned it quickly as Mother had taught me, and picked up the plectrum hanging on its ribbon on the side. It all happened automatically as if I had set it down only yesterday. I began to play and, right on cue, my voice emerged from my mouth as it always had when I played that song, my mother's favourite.

Awake, fair maid, come follow me,
Leave childhood things behind.
Your life awaits you here today
Come grasp it by the reins.
The springtime calls you, hear its voice,
The blossom fills your hair.
Choose worthy swain to take your hand,
To bring you joy unbound.
Your body aches, your heart leaps up,
The blood within you pounds.
Come join the round of Gaia's dance
Surrender to Her power.

There was a long silence. The Queen was looking into the distance as if trying to make something out. Finally she turned to me and said:

'Antheia lives on in you, Herpyllis. May our Great Mother grant you will become as excellent a lady as she was.'

From that day on the Queen kept me near her. I had passed some kind of test which meant she would give me her protection, even replace my mother. Olympias, too, grieved for her friend Antheia. She told me how they had met eight years earlier, the year before I was born, on Samothrace, a sacred island a day's sail from Stagira across the Aegean Sea.

'It's where all young men and women of noble birth go to be initiated into the rites of the Kabeiroi,' she said.

I must have looked blank. 'Divinities born of the Great Goddess,' she explained. 'Your mother was priestess in Stagira. She was already renowned. They invited her to be my mentor – I was just seventeen. My father, you know, was King of the Molossians of Epirus and my name at that time was Polyxena.'

Olympias paused for a moment and then continued: 'What a woman your mother was! Such quiet authority, such charisma. I drank in everything she said and believed it implicitly. Her dedication to the Great Goddess was unquestioning and complete. The women of my country have always been devout followers. I sat at your mother's feet and worshipped her as if she herself were the Goddess! In the initiation ceremony she gave me a wreath of myrtle to wear on my head. I'll never forget the moment she raised me from my knees and told me: *From henceforth you shall be called Myrtale!* and she kissed me on the lips. I can feel that kiss now, sweeter than any my husband has ever given me.'

And the Macedonian Queen lifted my chin as I sat beside her and gently kissed my lips with hers. In that moment she cast her own spell on me as Mother had on her.

Olympias's voice took on a dull note when she related how the young, newly-elected King of Macedon, Philip himself, later came to the island for the rites. She told me with a rueful laugh about the dancing and drinking involved in the celebrations afterwards, and how men and women came together, touching all ten fingers. Philip had fallen in love with Myrtale and they were married at the end of the summer. Myrtale kept in touch with my mother, who visited her at Pella twice. The year after her marriage, the new Queen took the name Olympias in honour of the victory of Philip's horse at the Olympic Games, the same month their son Alexander was born – three months after I was born.

The Queen asked me to play and sing for her often; she loved my pure young voice. Perhaps I reminded her of herself as a child, before the loss of innocence. I was Koré, daughter of the Great Goddess, the green corn. Olympias told me the story more than once. It was the old myth, different from the one men tell.

'Our Great Mother taught men to plough the fields and sow the corn,' she began. 'They did her bidding and every year in the autumn she would drink the nectar her priestesses made with barley water, mint and sacred mushrooms. Then she would choose a consort and lie in the thrice-ploughed field with him, taking her pleasure. Koré, her firstborn daughter, was her dearest child and she kept her close.

'Koré grew in wisdom and in beauty. One day, Hades, the ugly god of the Underworld, saw her and fell in love with her. He followed her until he found her alone one day, picking cornflowers in the fields of Eleusis. He snatched her up, threw her over his shoulder and ran with her until he reached the gates of his terrible underground kingdom. Koré screamed for her mother, but her voice was gradually muffled and finally lost as Hades sprinted with her deeper and deeper below the earth. When they came before his black throne, Hades threw Koré to the ground and ravished the Daughter of the Earth.

'Meanwhile the Goddess was sporting with her consort in the fields; their sighs and groans of pleasure had drowned out her daughter's cries. But her ecstasy soon turned to horror as she called and called for her beloved Koré and no answer came. She wandered the fields and forests, mourning and desperate. The wheat stopped growing, its ears shrinking and drying up, the fruit rotted and fell to the ground, the leaves on the trees turned yellow, the flowers withered and died. As they saw the Goddess pass by, the people beseeched her to make the land fertile again, but she ignored their pleas, still calling out her daughter's name, weeping and wailing. At last Grandmother Sun took pity on her and told her what she had seen from the heavens, how Koré had been abducted by the King of the Underworld.

'The Goddess ran to the gates of his dread realm. She rolled a pomegranate down into the depths, where it landed at Koré's feet as she sat on her own black throne, her belly just beginning to swell with child. The grief-stricken girl leaned down and snatched up the sacred fruit, the fruit of life. She split it open and began to eat the seeds, but only nine had passed her lips before Hades realised what she was doing and knocked the pomegranate from her hands.

'The seeds revived Koré; she ran to the gates of the Underworld, which burst open before her, and threw herself into her waiting mother's arms. At once green stalks of wheat burst up out of the soil, new leaves and buds sprouted on the trees, blades of grass and wild flowers from the ground, and people saw their world reborn with the return of the Goddess's daughter, the return of her joy.

'Five months passed and Koré was delivered of a child, her own daughter, the nymph Melinoë, who brings nightmares and madness and cannot live in the light. So the young mother and her baby returned to the world of darkness and the land died again as the Goddess mourned for her daughter once more.

'Finally it was agreed that Koré would stay with Hades and Melinoë for three months of the year, when she would rule the Underworld as dread Persephone, she who brings death. For the rest of the year she would return to her mother's side, giving her love and joy so the land could flower and bear crops for people to harvest and eat. So it was decided. And that is why for three months of the year nothing grows, for the Goddess is pining for her daughter, for her Koré.'

Did Olympias curse me by calling me her Koré? Did she foresee part of my fate? Or did I decide the role I was to play myself? I'm still not sure.

The Queen would stroke my face and kiss me. She would hum the songs I played and let me dress her hair. I was fascinated by those red-gold curls, enchanted by those eyes, as sparkling a green as the emeralds in the comb she wore. I became her favourite when she wanted to be entertained, her young companion and protegée when she wanted to reminisce about my mother. Then there were the rites of the Great Goddess at court. Olympias had me help her every morning, act as bearer, even play my lyre and sing on special days. The familiar words and chants had lost none of their magic and reassured me in the new world I had come to inhabit. I could close my eyes and imagine nothing had changed, that it was really my mother leading the rites back in Stagira.

But the Queen could not have been more opposite in character from Mother. Even when impatient or angry, my mother had been level-headed and controlled. Olympias, on the other hand, was like the active volcano on Methana my father had described to me, constantly sending out sparks and flashes, overflowing with burning rock at irregular intervals. A drinking bowl might be hurled across the room at a servant's head for the slightest offence, a resounding slap administered for a word out of place, a stream of abuse for an opinion expressed out of turn. At such times there was no reasoning with her; we all avoided her as far as possible until the eruption was over. Kindness, justice, moderation were all forgotten in her fury. She was indeed Olympian, a goddess raging from the heights of those great peaks on the borders of Macedon, which I was soon to see.

4
THE LOVERS OF MYTH

'Therefore, even the lover of myth is a philosopher;
for myth is composed of wonder.'

Often in the afternoons, when we were supposed to
be resting, Alexander would seek me out, and we would
go and sit in the garden together. He would call me his
princess and ask what he could bring me, what service
he could do me. And I would ask for a sprig of rosemary, thyme or lavender, fruit or berries, and he would
scramble up treetrunks, along branches, through the
undergrowth, to fetch me my heart's desire.

'Here, Lady,' he would say, bowing and holding out
his gift, which I would graciously take.

But he was a boy and we were seven years old. We were
both soon bored with this game. It wasn't long before
he held out the sprig of rosemary I had sent him to find
and then pulled it away as soon as I put my hand out to
take it. He did this a few times, sniggering when I failed
to grab it. This had been one of my brother Aristion's
tricks, so I played along and chased him when he ran off,
waving the sprig at me and taunting: *Come and get it!*
We were both giggling and shouting at each other as we
rushed around. This was much more fun than playing at
being a captive princess. I managed to snatch the sprig

of rosemary out of his hand and raced off. At once he sprinted after me and soon caught up, pushing me down onto the hard baked earth, grazing my knees. He pinned me down and tickled me under my arms, just as Aristion used to do. I did my best to keep hold of the rosemary as we writhed on the ground, shouting and squealing. And I was secretly disappointed when his nurse came and pulled him off me, boxing his ears.

From that day on we played together with much more rough and tumble than we had before.

'I'm going to begin training as a warrior soon, Herpyllis,' Alexander told me one afternoon after he had got the better of me once again. 'I'll be as great as Achilles. The world will marvel at me!'

His mother often told him stories of Achilles, great warrior of the Trojan War, who slaughtered his enemies by the hundreds and could only be slain himself by the arrow to his heel, the place where his mother had held him as she dipped him in the waters of immortality. Tears would come to Alexander's eyes as the Queen described that fatal wound from Paris's bow. I was surprised to hear that the great hero Achilles had really been his ancestor, a prince of Epirus.

One day Olympias beckoned me to join her and Alexander. She told us both the sad story of how Penthesilea, the Amazon queen, had come to fight on the side of the Trojans, seeking an honourable death as a warrior after she had accidentally killed her sister while out hunting. She fought and slew many of the Greeks, but finally met her death at Achilles' hand. When he removed her helmet and realised he had slain an Amazon maiden, he was filled with remorse.

Alexander and I soon invented a game of Achilles and Penthesilea. In our version of the tale they did some fighting, but also ran around much of the time and lay under trees in the afternoon heat, their heads together, and told each other stories and sucked pieces of grass and sometimes just kept quiet, content in each other's company.

Who knows what it was that drew us together? It was something instinctive, unquestioning, animal-like. Can children be in love? If so, we were. Most of what I remember now is the warm, happy feeling I had whenever I played with him. After my mornings serving the Queen, I looked forward to the afternoons, hoping he would come to find me. I can still remember the disappointment when he didn't, the elation when he did. Looking back on those early days in the palace, I see Alexander and me together much of the time. But that can only have been for a few short months; Alexander was about to leave us women and start his education as soldier and future king.

It happened on one of those late summer days in Pella when we children were playing in the large dusty front courtyard under the still blazing sun. Alexander and his Amazon sister Cynane were fighting with wooden swords. She soon had the upper hand and sprang at him, hitting him in the face with the sword. He fell to the ground, screaming, his left hand clutched over his left eye and cheek. I was terrified Cynane had taken his eye out. I rushed over and threw myself down beside him.

'Alexander,' I gasped, trying to pull his hand away so I could find out what had happened. 'Can you see? Has she put your eye out?'

My first remembered sight of his father's face had flashed before me and I thought Alexander would be transformed into another horrifying Cyclops like the King.

And suddenly there was Philip himself looming over us.

'What're you whimpering about, boy?' he boomed. 'Stop being a cry-baby. Get up and meet your tutor.'

The effect of that gruff voice on Alexander was immediate. He jumped to his feet, hurriedly wiping his face. Now I could see there were just tears on his left cheek, no blood. I breathed out with relief. There was a scarlet bruise under his eye, but the eye itself was open and unharmed. His father noted the bright red mark and glanced at Cynane, but said nothing.

'Well, Leonidas,' – Philip was speaking to a thin, balding man beside him – 'I was hoping to show you my son sweeping all before him, but it seems his swordsmanship leaves a lot to be desired. But then that's not your area. My men will knock him into shape somehow.'

He paused and looked Alexander up and down.

'Come, boy,' was all he said, and he led his son away from us and into the men's wing of the palace, which women and girls were strictly forbidden to enter. I could only gaze at the closed door leading into it across the colonnaded passageway.

I was shocked to see the effect on Olympias of this sudden separation from her son. It was as if he had dropped dead before her very eyes that afternoon. It was impossible to comfort her. She hardly ate or slept, and nothing could distract her from her grief, not even the songs she had loved hearing.

The effect on the Queen's daughter Cleopatra was just as dramatic; now she knew for certain that her brother Alexander was the only child their mother loved. Whenever she could, Cleopatra would stand as close as possible to her mother, in vain reaching out her little hand in the hope of feeling her mother's take it. Occasionally Olympias would pat the girl's hair absent-mindedly before taking my hand and heading for the gallery along the back of the palace, where we could spy unobserved on the dozen or so boys receiving their instruction in sword-fighting and wrestling on the wide dusty training ground, Alexander the smallest among them. We would watch them lunge at each other or grapple together, each trying to get a hold on his opponent and pull him down, all the time egged on by the shouting officers training them.

I missed Alexander and was pleased when Cleopatra attached herself to me. Feeling sorry for her, I had asked her one day if she could shoot a bow, as Cynane had asked me. I couldn't think of anything else to say. She shook her head, looking at the ground.

'What do you like doing?' I asked, wanting to put her at her ease. I sympathised with her, the little girl treated with contempt by her elder brother.

Cleopatra started swaying from side to side, still looking at the ground.

'You must like something,' I continued. And just as I was about to give up, I heard her say very softly:

'Stories.'

'Ah,' I said. 'I love stories, too, and I know lots of them. Which ones do you like best?'

'Andromeda,' she replied, sneaking a glance at me.

'Andromeda!' I repeated. 'The princess whose parents chained her to a rock for the sea monster to eat. Why do you like that one?'

No answer. She must feel like a victim too.

'Now, let's see,' I continued. 'Did the sea monster eat Andromeda? I can't remember.'

She looked up straightaway.

'No,' she said emphatically. 'Perseus came and rescued her and they got married and lived happily in a palace by the sea.'

'That's right,' I said. 'But first Perseus showed the Gorgon's head to the man her parents had betrothed her to, because that man still wanted to marry her, and he was turned to stone.'

She looked at me wide-eyed. Obviously this part of the story was not included in the version of the myth she had heard.

'What's a Gorgon?' she asked.

And that was how it started, Cleopatra and I. Now I had a little sister to tell stories to and look after, someone else to take my mind off everything that had happened in Stagira. I amused myself by putting in new details. But she would interrupt and say:

'That's not in the story!'

Then I would say it *was* and she had forgotten. We would exchange many a *Yes, it is! – No, it isn't!* until I added something so incongruous we would both collapse in giggles. So we had Andromeda eating a hundred pomegranates at one sitting, or Helen's impossibly elaborate headdress falling off and hanging tangled in her hair the first time she met Paris, or Achilles tripping over his spear on the battlefield before Troy.

Any kind of preposterous behaviour on the part of Achilles pleased her most. Though she loved her brother and was overawed by him, it was a release to ridicule him at one remove, through the hero he emulated. I knew how she felt. My brothers had belittled and mocked me so often; there had been a kind of satisfaction in seeing them reprimanded by my father or mother from time to time. Olympias never upbraided Alexander, at least not in our hearing. Cleopatra, on the other hand, was constantly reproached for something: chattering too loudly, giggling, fidgeting, singing flat, sewing badly. Her daughter's very presence seemed to irritate the Queen. It all seemed unfair, especially when Olympias treated me so kindly.

We saw Alexander in his new place beside his father the following year in late spring, in Dion, below the peaks of Olympus in the presence of Zeus, Father of the Gods, celebrating the King's latest victory. Philip had sacked Olynthos – another city looted and burned, more men killed, more women raped, more citizens enslaved.

Alexander's face was drawn and serious, there among the King's retinue as they entered the sacred grove of

Olympian Zeus. We all sensed Olympias's heart leap when she first glimpsed him, the corresponding lurch in Cleopatra's stomach. The girl was standing unnoticed beside the Queen and I was behind her. I reached out and squeezed her right hand.

The men filed in, forming rows behind the King and his captains, Alexander on his right. As they took their places facing the cloud-covered peaks, the boy kept looking straight ahead. But when his father turned to speak to my rescuer Antipater, Alexander took the opportunity of glancing over at Olympias, a shy smile on his face; I saw her head move slightly as she smiled back.

At the far end of the sanctuary was a colossal stone altar and in front of it three rows of eleven slabs each, their bronze rings gleaming in the early morning sun. A seemingly endless procession started as priests and acolytes led in the one hundred oxen to be sacrificed to the Father of the Gods. Three animals were tied to the ring on each slab and the rows gradually filled from back to front until the largest animal of all appeared bringing up the rear; it was tied to a ring in front of the altar.

The chief priest began intoning the prayers. At first the beasts were quiet and docile but, as the ceremony progressed, barley meal being sprinkled on each in turn, they became more restless, pulling on the ropes and lowing. Before the prayers were done and the sprinkling of meal was over, the oxen had set up a deafening noise, their eyes rolling, the smell of their fear overwhelming.

Cleopatra looked round at me, now squeezing my hand tightly as I had hers, and I slowly pulled her back towards me, turning her head to my chest and holding it there, gently stroking her hair. Olympias seemed transfixed; she was not aware of the princess leaving her side.

Suddenly, the chief priest threw up his arms and shouted above the din:

'Father, we offer to you this sacred sacrifice, in earnest of our thanks for your boundless beneficence. Pray look down on us in your mercy and grant us your favour again in the days to come.'

As his arms sliced back down through the air, the throat of each beast was slit with one slash of the ceremonial knife each priest was holding. The proficiency with which the men had manoeuvred the oxen into position and pulled their heads back so that the slaughter could take place in unison on that signal was so impressive that it seemed to happen in a dream. The hundred huge animals slumped to the ground. A stunned silence ensued for a few moments before the loud cries went up from all around:

'Mighty Zeus, we praise you!'

The priests and acolytes were soon knee-deep in blood, their clothes and hair splattered with it. They had started skinning the animals, cutting them open and removing their entrails. Cleopatra whimpered; she must have turned to peep through the space in front of us and seen enough to terrify her before hiding her face in my chest again. And by now the smell was simply overpowering. I turned, retching, the smaller girl still pressed against me, and moved to the back of the wooden platform in search of fresh air.

It was then that Alexander came into full view on the central platform. His eyes were wide and his face showed complete exultation. Years later I would remember him like that when we heard of him sacking yet another city; I needed no description of him from Callisthenes.

Fortunately the Queen started leading us away from the grove soon afterwards. Cleopatra and I stumbled along behind her and sank onto a couch back in the women's tent. Even though we had come through woods and were camped close to the Great Goddess's precinct at some distance from the sanctuary of Olympian Zeus, the dreadful stink hung in the air around us, or perhaps it had burrowed inside our noses.

The princess and I quickly fell asleep on our couch and did not wake till late afternoon. We crept outside to find all was quiet. Not a sound coming from the stadium up the hill, though the roars from the spectators had reverberated for hours on the previous day as the riding events and chariot races had taken place and the men had competed in the pentathlon. Today, it seemed, was for worship only.

We walked over to the Queen's tent, hoping that, as usual, she had not missed her daughter. The guards nodded us in. And there, resting his head against her breast in the old way, sat Alexander on the couch by his mother. They looked peaceful and content. And the Queen actually smiled when she saw us.

'Well, my daughter, Herpyllis,' she said, 'have you heard about my son's exploits? Tell them, Alexander.'

He lifted his head and pointed to the crown of oak leaves lying among his red-gold curls.

'See this?' he said with a triumphant grin. 'The victor's crown. You should've seen me run. I was right out in front. No one could catch me. And I'm the youngest! Mother says I'm truly the son of Father Zeus!'

He jumped down and started strutting about to his mother's delight. Cleopatra stared at him. Then she ran up and hugged him until he shook her off in disgust. She retreated to her mother and hotched up onto the couch to take Alexander's place. Olympias pushed her aside and opened her arms to her son.

'My Achilles,' she crooned.

There was something shocking in her tone and I was not the only one who felt embarrassed. I caught Charis's eye and she looked away. At dusk the prince went back to the men's tents and we made our way to the Goddess's sanctuary to pour the customary evening libation and say the prayers. The Queen was more animated than I had seen her for months. She even kissed Cleopatra and held her hand as we walked back; the joy on the girl's face was heartbreaking to see. Olympias told her daughter how originally it was girls and women who competed at games such as these. At Olympia the race winners had become priestesses of the Great Goddess.

I lagged behind them, then turned and went back, making my way up the mountain. I wanted to feel the magic of the place all by myself. There was a full moon so I could see where I was going. I headed for a clearing in the forest, halfway up the slope. My heart jumped every time there was a sudden rustling in the undergrowth, a desperate flapping in the trees. But there was such excitement and elation in what I was doing that I never once thought of turning back. I just had to be alone in that awe-inspiring home of the gods. The moonlight threw the mossy sides of rocks into sharp relief, aged bronze memorials to forest nymphs, whose daughters watched me from the deep shadows among the trees.

Suddenly the moon was covered by cloud and the magic was lost. I started groping my way along, the unseen beings around me now a threatening presence. I tripped on a tree root, shrank from a branch looming out of the blackness, cried out as a bramble scratched my arm. Panic overtook me. Where was the clearing I had seen so clearly from below? Was I still heading for it, or had I lost my sense of direction in the dark? Was this a charmed forest where I was doomed to wander forever? How could I have been so thoughtless as to tread blithely into the realm of the new gods without fear of punishment?

I stopped with a gasp, filled with amazement. The moon had re-emerged and there before me myth became reality – a unicorn, gambolling in the clearing ahead, its gleaming white form tracked by the moonlight. I watched enthralled and then started creeping up to the treeline, blinking hard. Could I trust the sight of my own eyes? Just as I came to the edge of the clearing, the unicorn turned into a child in a white tunic, dancing on the grass. A boy. Alexander. My heart leapt. I was about to run and join him, but something held me back. He was rolling his head around as he moved and his arms were stretched out towards the peak above us. It was a wild dance, in a state of ecstasy, a trance, a delirium. Alexander was touched by the god, his father Zeus. I stepped back and softly walked away, feeling I had committed blasphemy. I had seen what I should not have seen.

That night remains in my memory as a time of enchantment, when reality was frozen and a glimpse of some other world was revealed. As I came out of the forest again, the sea appeared to be standing up straight in front of me where the horizon and the sky should have been. The moonlight on the water was facing me head on. An effect I had never seen before and I've never seen since. Not strange, then, they say the gods live there. And in that altered reality it seemed I had not been missed in the tent. They were all asleep and I slipped in unobserved.

5
CHILD'S PLAY

*'Learning is not child's play; we cannot learn
without pain.'*

I gradually became accepted at court very naturally, as
if I were some distant relative, not a slave in the sense
I understood it. I became an elder sister to Cleopatra. I
found a role in teaching her what my mother had taught
me and, in so doing, the pain of losing my parents slowly
receded.

A year or two after Alexander had started spending
most of his time with the men, the Queen was also
deprived of her brother's company. He was called Alexander, too, and had lived at the Macedonian court since he
was a boy. As the son of a ruler of Epirus, a neighbouring
territory, he had been brought up in Pella as a hostage,
like Leonnatus and Perdiccas.

This Alexander was a special favourite of Philip's and
was now rewarded with his father's throne in Epirus,
which had been usurped by his uncle. He was in his early
twenties, some four years younger than Olympias, but
anyone seeing them side by side would immediately see
the family resemblance. Sister and brother would often
talk together in their own language and it must have been
a great loss to her when he left court.

Some weeks later, Olympias was brought a letter from him. To my amazement, she threw the tablet down and marched back into her apartment. I turned to Charis and asked why she would do such a thing.

'Oh,' she said, 'now she'll have to get Leonidas to read it to her. And there might be something she doesn't want him to know about.'

'You mean, the Queen can't read?' I said in astonishment.

'Of course she can't!' answered Charis. 'What woman can?' And then it dawned on her. 'You can read?' she asked.

'My mother taught me to read and write when I was very young,' I replied. 'I thought everyone could – I mean, everyone like us.'

'This is wonderful!' exclaimed Charis. 'We must tell the Queen. *You* can read the letter to her!'

Without more ado, Charis grabbed my hand and took me to Olympias, picking the tablet up on the way. The Queen still had a look of irritation on her face as she listened to Charis's revelation. But then her face, too, lit up for a moment before she frowned at me severely.

'Read it to me,' she said impatiently. 'Read it!'

She thrust the tablet into my hands and I glanced nervously at the writing. Luckily, it was written in formal Greek and in a fine hand.

My dear sister, I read. Olympias and Charis looked at me as if I had performed some astounding magic trick.

My journey home was uneventful. Uncle Arybbas has fled to Illyria, but Philip says he will find no welcome there.

I have been crowned king with great feasting and merry-making, which lasted for seven days. Our father's adviser Antenor has returned to court and will be a great help to me.

I miss you and all my dear companions in Pella. Write to me and tell me all the news from Macedon.

Your loving brother, Alexander

There was a long silence. Olympias snatched the tablet from me and looked at it searchingly.

'This says Alexander,' she said in a combative tone, pointing to the last word.

I nodded.

'Where does it say *Philip*?' she asked angrily. I showed her. '*Pella*?' she demanded.

Again I pointed, my finger trembling.

'You will show me everything,' she ordered. 'It can't be so difficult if you can do it. *Now*,' she said, sitting down and pointing to the floor beside her.

I knelt down. Suddenly I was perspiring and my face felt hot. The Queen was glaring at me as if I had just committed the most heinous of crimes. Then, from somewhere deep inside my head, I heard my mother's voice. *This is Alpha, it makes the sound 'A'...* And so I began with Alpha for Alexander, Alpha for Arybbas, Alpha for Antenor. The Queen's frown slowly disappeared and she gave me one of her rare smiles.

'Alpha,' she said, as if the greatest of all mysteries had finally been revealed to her.

She proved the most apt of students and I discovered a tact I had never known I possessed. I was nine years old by then and old enough to understand that Olympias must never be shown to be wrong in anything, and I became the most artful of teachers in ensuring she was always right. Charis started treating me with a new admiration and respect. By the end of the following spring, I had taught the Queen to read and write, although these new-found skills were kept secret from the rest of the court. Olympias would sit impassively while Leonidas read letters and documents to her in his patronising tone as before. We had both found something to occupy the time when her son was absent. And I became the Queen's shadow, always at her side.

On a swelteringly hot day towards the end of summer I was fanning Olympias as she lay on the couch in her apartment. It was late afternoon but we had eaten nothing since breakfast. Charis brought some pomegranates, the first of the season, and the Queen smiled at me.

'Ah, Herpyllis, my Koré,' she said, 'the fruit of life to revive you. Break one open and let's share the sweet seeds.'

I put down the fan and did as she ordered. She watched me and then whispered something to Charis, who went over to the large wooden chest where the Queen's most treasured possessions were kept. I concentrated on peeling the fruit and removing all the pith, dropping the seeds with their juicy red flesh into my favourite bowl, the one decorated with Amazon maidens running, their bows and quivers on their shoulders. When I finally looked up, my task accomplished, I glimpsed Charis putting something into the Queen's hand. I held out the bowl and Olympias gestured for me to place it on the low table.

'Come here, little maid,' she said softly, 'I have something for you.'

I went and stood in front of her and she leaned forward, telling me to bow my head. I did as I was told and felt the Queen fasten a fine chain round my neck. I looked down at the amulet hanging from it. It was a small gold box with star shapes cut into it and a clasp on the lid.

'Inside is the most precious thing of all,' Olympias whispered in my ear, her hands on my shoulders. 'See what it is, my Koré.'

I held the amulet in my left hand and took the clasp between the thumb and forefinger of my right hand. I was afraid of breaking it, but it lifted easily and I raised the little lid. Instead of the sparkling gem I had expected to find, I saw a dry head of wheat, its delicate beard intact on either side. I must have looked disappointed for the Queen gave a light laugh. Then she took my hands in hers and looked deep into my eyes.

'This is the most precious gift of our Great Mother, Herpyllis, of more worth than any jewel or metal to be found in the rocks. We sow it in the soil and it sprouts and shoots up again and again in an endless cycle. It is the secret of eternal life. Never forget that.'

I treasured my amulet with its precious contents as carefully as my lyre, and kept it safe with my few belongings, wearing it only for the morning ceremony.

Looking back over my other memories of growing up in Pella, it is, of course, Alexander who sticks out. Although I had already realised there were many Alexanders behind those mismatched eyes, the only one I saw in those years was *my* Alexander, my love. He would still seek me out as often as he could, and we would go to a secret grove we had found in the forest.

One day – a couple of summers after I came to court – he greeted me with a smile as usual, but it was half-hearted and he was clearly feeling dejected. I asked him what the matter was.

'Ah, Herpyllis,' he said. 'What if I'm not good enough? What if the King fathers another son who's better than me? I can't bear the thought of not being king. I must be king! I must be the greatest king Macedon has ever had! What will I do if...' His eyes filled with tears and he bit his lip.

'Alexander,' I cried, 'of course you'll be king! Who could be better than you? You'll be the greatest hero there has ever been! Everyone will love and admire you!'

'But Cynane can throw a spear further than me,' he complained, 'and she's much better with a bow and arrow.'

'You said yourself that bows and arrows are not weapons for real warriors! Anyway, she's two years older than you. Just wait till you're her age. You'll be unbeatable.'

'Perdiccas beat me in wrestling today. He really hurt me, too. My neck and shoulders are still throbbing.'

'Oh, Alexander,' I said, and I kissed his neck where it met his shoulder. He gave a kind of shudder, but said nothing. Then he took my hand and kissed it, and we sat for some time, holding hands on our branch.

Alexander became obsessed with impressing his father. He made up for his lack of height by developing his muscles and becoming the strongest of all the boys. He spent as long as he could on the training ground each day, speaking the Macedonian language of the soldiers. Kings of Macedon always spoke to their men in that tongue.

Once he practised making a speech to the army in front of me. He strutted up and down, blustering like Philip. He wanted to make me laugh, I think, but he reminded me too much of that day in Stagira I wanted to forget. He soon stopped when he saw I didn't like it.

Alexander was an actor, playing to an audience. If the audience were not entranced, he changed the performance. And soon he was learning *The Iliad* with Leonidas, Homer's epic poem of the tale of Troy with its hero Achilles. When he recited that, his conviction was such that no audience could have failed to be captivated.

> *'My mother, divine silver-footed Thetis,*
> *Tells of two fates which may be mine:*
> *The first to fight before the walls of Troy*
> *And never see my home again,*
> *Yet live forever in high renown;*
> *The second to journey home*
> *And live to ripe old age, unsung.'*

It was hard to ignore the extent to which Alexander identified with Achilles. His whole life was ruled by the overwhelming desire to imitate that most famous of heroes. How could I know then, listening to Alexander in our grove, what vital importance that quest of his would assume in my own life, not to speak of the lives of thousands upon thousands of others?

As the months went by in Pella and turned into years, it was clear Alexander was becoming more and more bored with the classroom. He only became animated when he talked of some wrestling bout he had won, or of the praise his tutor had given him for his swordplay. He revelled in hunting and often recounted to me in great detail what had happened during a hunt he had been on with the older men. This was the world Alexander loved, not the world of learning and music. When I heard him tell his mother he considered his lessons with Leonidas unnecessary, she laughed and said nothing, but the same complaint to his father brought a swift rebuke.

'If you are ever to be king, Alexander,' he boomed, 'and I stress the word *if*, you'll need to know a lot more than how to use a sword and shield.'

Alexander winced at the 'if', and I realised his fears that he might never be king might not be completely unfounded. Although Olympias was acknowledged as Queen, I discovered Philip had four other wives. This was why Cynane, the Amazon maiden in the courtyard, had said Cleopatra was Alexander's sister, not her own sister, though the King was father to them all. Only one other wife had a son and he was older than Alexander, but this boy was the dribbling simpleton I had met that day in the courtyard – Arrhidaeus, named after his grandfather.

Even though none of the other wives or their children posed a real threat to her and Alexander, Olympias never failed to take the opportunity of slighting or spiting them, all except Audata, daughter of the King of Illyria, mother of Cynane. She was a fellow initiate in the rites of the Great Goddess and a proud warrior in the traditions of her people.

'Better to have Audata as an ally,' Charis explained to me in hushed tones one day after I had commented on the fact that Olympias treated her differently from the other wives. 'She would make a formidable enemy. And, you know, Audata knows she's got to be nice to Olympias unless she can bear Philip a son.'

In the meantime Audata trained her daughter Cynane in all the military skills she had herself mastered. Cynane had adopted me as her companion because I could shoot my bow as well as she could. When I was ten and old enough, they persuaded the Queen to allow me to go hunting with them.

But first I had to learn to ride. This was one skill my parents had not taught me – our horses were only used to pull carts. My mount was a supposedly docile mare. First she bolted through a copse with me lying flat against her back and clinging to her mane, terrified of being swept off by a branch of the low-hanging trees. When we rejoined Audata and Cynane on the other side, the mare had slowed down to a gentle trot as if nothing had happened. Next she leant over in the middle of a stream, expertly dropping me into the water at the deepest point. Cynane laughed so much she nearly fell off her own horse. Finally, my mare reared unexpectedly, throwing me sprawling onto the ground, again much to the princess's amusement.

It was fortunate I wasn't badly injured in any of these incidents; they made me realise I had to assert my authority with the animal if I was to regain my dignity and avoid broken bones. Audata showed me how to use my legs to great effect and, though I never really felt one with the horse, as I could see she and her daughter did, I succeeded in controlling the animal and having my way with her.

As I gained confidence, I slowly grew to love teaming up with Cynane in the hunt to corner a deer or boar, but the first time the princess brought a hind down with her arrow, sprang from her horse to stick her knife in its stomach and rip it open, my stomach heaved. Scenes came back to me from Stagira; I was on my knees, groaning. Audata took pity on me and told Cynane she should deal with her kill herself and not expect me to take part in it.

And what of the King? What of the man who had casually destroyed all I held dear in the span of a few hours? Where was he during those years when I was growing up with his children? He spent most of his time campaigning. That year when I started hunting with Cynane and Audata, he was fighting an Illyrian tribe and was brought back to Pella with a serious wound in his right leg. The King's injury took several months to heal.

We always knew when he was in the feasting hall. The dinners were uproarious, the shouting and laughter punctuated by drinking songs. The noise carried all around the palace and went on into the early hours. Although

I longed to fall asleep to get away from those terrifying sounds of men giving vent to their rawest emotions, I knew what dreams I would have. I knew I would see them again on the loose in Stagira – more frightening than a pack of wolves bringing down their prey.

They were so different from the men I had known back home. I couldn't remember my father or Linos ever shouting, or singing a raucous song. Now I lived in a world where men were in an endless competition with each other, where women had no part to play, other than making sons to continue the rivalry. Luckily, the male world rarely impinged on ours. Philip sometimes came to the women's colonnade to see his wives and children, complaining as often as not about some aspect of the household, how expensive it was to keep everyone fed and clothed. I always made sure I kept out of his way.

It was during that time when he was recovering from his leg wound that I came face to face with him again. I was playing my lyre and singing, a strange Illyrian melody Audata had taught me. She and Olympias were sitting together in the colonnade that day. Suddenly Philip loomed up in front of me, not an arm's length away, that hated, disfigured face from my nightmares staring at me. I screamed and nearly dropped the instrument. I fumbled in my lap to right it.

'Aha!' exclaimed the King, that deep gruff voice making me jump again. 'Let's see now – Antheia's daughter, isn't it? My, my. She's becoming a pretty one!'

He leaned forward, supported on the thick stick he was using to hobble about, and grabbed my chin, pulling up my face. I tried to avert my eyes, but he pulled my head back until his one good eye was boring into them and I had to look straight at him, only my blurred nose between us. The evil eye. My heart stopped. I was cursed. He dropped my chin and adjusted his stick under his arm.

'Yes, yes,' he said, almost to himself, 'she'll do very nicely in a couple of years.'

There was the sound of his stick striking the floor, his leg being dragged across the marble floor, the same noises repeated again and again, gradually receding into silence.

6
THE FATE OF EMPIRES

*'All who have meditated on the art of governing
mankind have been convinced that the fate of
empires depends on the education of youth.'*

After that day I lived in terror of the King noticing me
again, but most of the year he was far away, waging an
endless war. I discovered that he had in fact snatched the
crown from his nephew, Amyntas, the son of his elder
brother. Amyntas had been a small boy when his father
died, so Philip became regent and was soon elected king
in his own right.

Amyntas still lived at court. He was a young man now
and we caught sight of him from time to time at ceremonies. He kept himself to himself and said little. His
hair was light brown and his features unremarkable; he
had somehow found the knack of going unnoticed in
any company. He had failed to distinguish himself in
any way and been discounted as a potential successor to
Philip, much as Arrhidaeus the simpleton was. The first
time I pointed him out to Charis in an assembly she said:

'Who? That? Oh, that's just Amyntas.'

There was one thing Amyntas loved, however, and that
was horses. I caught sight of him once in a cloud of dust,
cantering around on a beautiful animal he had bought

from Thessalian traders and trained himself. They came to court twice a year, having reserved the finest beasts for the Macedonians who now ruled their land. Alexander and I were about twelve that momentous year when they brought Bucephalus. He was a magnificent black creature, already large enough to be a warhorse, although only a three-year-old. He had been named after the white mark shaped like an oxhead on his nose. Women didn't usually attend the horse trading, but Cynane wanted a faster horse for hunting; the King had told her to come and take her pick. She had brought me along as her hunting partner, so I was there on that day when Alexander met Bucephalus. The King had promised his son a new horse too.

The traders were putting the horses through their paces in front of the Macedonian officers and courtiers. All eyes were on Bucephalus. The stallion would not be led and kept rearing and whinnying, striking out at any who attempted to control him. The Thessalian chief was praising the animal to the skies, telling the King he was worth an enormous sum. Philip said a horse which couldn't be tamed was worth nothing. Amyntas was standing beside him, his usual quiet self, observing the proceedings. Alexander was fascinated by the stallion.

'Look at that power,' he commented excitedly, 'look at that spirit. Let me try to ride him, Father,' he said.

'No chance,' replied the King with a snort. 'He'll trample you underfoot, boy.'

It was then I noticed a change on Amyntas's face. Instead of his usually inscrutable expression, he now looked animated and eager. He walked round to Alexander and whispered something in his ear. The same look now spread over Alexander's face and he turned back to his father, actually tugging at his tunic to get his attention.

'I know what to do, Father,' he said. 'I can master him. Trust me. Let me try. Please.'

Something about his son's tone of voice must have changed the King's mind. After only a moment's hesitation, he barked out:

'All right, then, boy. But don't say I didn't warn you.'

Alexander sprinted off, but then walked slowly and quietly up behind the horse, which was now standing alone in the centre of the ring. There was a hush among the onlookers as we all waited to see what would happen. Cynane made a little noise of derision, and I turned to see a malicious grin on her face. I looked back at Alexander, and had to stop myself calling out to him, begging him to come away. The horse had pricked up its ears and I closed my eyes, thinking it was going to lash out with its back legs and kick the boy to the ground. But I had to watch, willing Alexander to succeed, clenching my fists with the suspense of it all.

The prince now had his hand on the horse's flank and appeared to be whispering to it. With his other hand he was feeling for the bridle on its head. He gently gripped it and slowly turned the horse, his lips still moving. I was expecting that huge body to rear up at any moment and come crashing down on the boy, the top of whose head didn't reach the top of its flank. The silence was now total and my heart was pounding.

Suddenly Alexander sprang onto the horse's back and put his arms round its neck, clinging on as it rose into the air, trying to throw him off. It came down and reared twice again, but couldn't dislodge its burden. There was a pause, and then Alexander slowly sat up and almost imperceptibly squeezed his knees into the horse's flanks. And there it was: the great animal slowly walking across the ring, the boy sitting up straight on its back.

Suddenly there was a great guffaw.

'Well, blow me down!' boomed the King. 'But I'm not paying you more than a couple of talents for him.'

Fierce bargaining started while Alexander sat stroking Bucephalus, still whispering to him.

'Ah, now I see!' Cynane's exclamation made me jump.

'What?' I said.

'The sun,' she replied.

I looked at her completely non-plussed.

'The *sun*,' she repeated impatiently.

And she strode over to Amyntas who was still observing the horse and its young rider.

'It was the sun, wasn't it?' she demanded of her cousin.

He looked round startled, not used to being asked for his opinion. Indeed, he looked behind him to check that Cynane was really addressing him. Finally he gave a little smile and said:

'That's right.'

I was still bewildered. Cynane looked at me.

'The sun, stupid,' she said. 'The horse was afraid of its own shadow. Amyntas told Alexander to turn the horse's head into the sun so it wouldn't see its shadow any more. Then it calmed down.'

Amyntas beamed at her and she smiled back. Cynane's smile was not bestowed lightly.

'Will you help *me* choose a horse now?' she asked.

He seemed overwhelmed by her request.

'Yes... of course,' he replied hesitantly. 'Er... I saw a fine mare I think would suit you well.'

And they set off together to view the remaining horses. I decided not to follow them. Something made me think they wanted to be alone.

At that moment Alexander appeared at my side.

'Well,' he said, 'what did you think of that?'

'Very interesting,' I replied. 'I would never have thought...'

'Never have thought I could do it?' he said eagerly.

'No,' I answered, 'never have thought...' but I stopped myself just in time.

Of course Alexander wanted the praise he deserved for taming the great horse. I started again.

'Well, it was amazing!' I continued. 'The King certainly didn't think you could do it.'

'No,' he replied, rubbing his hands together, 'I suspect there're quite a few people I impressed today.'

'Wasn't it kind of Amyntas to tell you that?' I continued.

His expression changed immediately.

'Tell me what?' he challenged.

I was taken aback.

'Tell you... about the sun,' I said softly.

'I don't know what you're talking about,' he replied breezily. 'I knew exactly what to do. Amyntas had nothing to do with it.'

And he walked off.

I didn't really understand at the time why the whole episode saddened me so much. After all, Alexander had accomplished a spectacular feat, and I admired him tremendously for it. Why should it matter that he left Amyntas out of it? Of course it was unimportant. Alexander was the one who had tamed the horse! He had shown them all what he was made of. Indeed, his father appeared not long afterwards in Olympias's apartments, where Alexander was telling the tale of how he had tamed a horse no one else could. The King was all smiles, and embraced him, though he said the horse had cost him dear. It was one of the rare times I saw the royal family together, happily in harmony.

That night I was playing for the Queen after dinner. She was in a very good mood, lying on her bed, caressing a snake she had been handling earlier in the evening, showing me how to milk its venom. We had our household snake in Stagira, which I used to feed, so I had never been afraid of such creatures and had become used to their company with Olympias, who kept them as pets. I came to the end of the piece I was playing and was just about to ask if I should go on when there was a noise outside the door. I was sitting in the shadows in a corner of the room, so Philip didn't see me as he burst in. He limped unsteadily towards the Queen, his arms wide.

'Olympias, my love,' he spluttered, stumbling on a rug and being projected onto the bed beside her. I could smell the wine on his breath from where I sat, out of sight.

Suddenly there was an unearthly shriek from the King and the snake flew up into the air, landing in the corner beside me. It immediately curled itself up, hissing furiously. I stayed where I was, knowing it to be harmless. But the King was cursing and shouting, while Olympias was sitting on the edge of the bed, bent over, her head in her hands. At first I thought she was in pain, but then I saw her shoulders shaking. Suddenly she could contain herself no longer and her peal of laughter startled me with its volume. I had never heard anyone laugh so loudly.

Philip, meanwhile, managed to scramble to his feet and his face came into full view. It was purple with fury and soaked in sweat. If he had seen me, I believe he would have strangled me as a witness to his complete mortification. Instead, he turned to Olympias, who was still laughing uncontrollably. He grabbed her chin and pulled up her face. He raised his arm to strike her, but the gesture made him topple over again, resulting in renewed gales of laughter. Somehow he managed to get up on his knees, but then promptly vomited all over the rug. When he raised his head on all fours, he was luckily facing away from me; otherwise he would surely have seen me. Now there was silence. It lasted for a long time. Then there was a growling noise from the King and I could only just make out the words he spoke:

'Never again, witch, never again.'

The Queen lay back on the bed as he crawled out. She had stopped laughing. When I could no longer hear Philip's movements in the courtyard, I got up and folded the rug, taking it outside to be washed by the slaves the next day.

Between them, Olympias and Alexander healed the wounds Stagira had made in my soul. The scars remained, of course, but Olympias's care for me and her son's company filled my waking hours as the years went by in Pella.

There was always an excitement about being at court, even in the women's quarters – messengers coming and going, visitors paying their respects, gifts being exchanged, merchants offering exotic wares. I woke every day with a little shudder, a thrill about what might await me, spending the morning in fevered anticipation of perhaps seeing Alexander in the afternoon.

But I saw less and less of him. One day he came and marched me off to the forest, holding my wrist tightly, frowning and breathing heavily. Could he still be angry with me about his taming of Bucephalus a few days earlier and what I had said about Amyntas's advice? I had almost convinced myself by then that his cousin had had nothing to do with his great feat. I wanted so desperately to find no fault with Alexander.

When we arrived at our favourite spot in the grove, he let go of me and picked up a piece of dead wood. He started beating a tree with it until it finally smashed, sending fragments flying all around. If I hadn't ducked, a pointed shard would have caught me full in the face. But Alexander didn't notice. He was still seething and looking around for another instrument with which to vent his anger. I didn't seem to be its object after all, so I went over and put my hand on his arm.

'What's happened, Alexander?' I asked gently.

He didn't answer immediately, but he did appear to be trying to compose himself. Finally he spat out:

'Leonidas!'

I waited for him to say more but his chest was still heaving and his lips were set in a thin line.

'What's he done?' I finally managed to ask in a small voice.

Then Alexander exploded in a torrent of invective.

'What's he done?' he half shouted and half snarled. 'Insulted my father, that's what he's done! Stupid man! Daring to tell me how to worship my father! *Be careful with the incense,* he says, *nothing in excess.* We're talking about Father Zeus, the mightiest of the gods! But *Use the incense sparingly – it's very expensive, you know. We can't fling so much on the fire as if there's no tomorrow.* I can't bear being with that man any longer. He's an idiot.'

'My father' – this was the first time Alexander had used that title for anyone except Philip. But the moonlit scene I had witnessed on Mount Olympus had prepared me for this incarnation of the boy I loved. And I was familiar with such passionate outbursts from his mother. While I was trying to think of something appropriate to say, he turned to look at me and said in a completely different voice:

94

'And he picks his nose all the time!'

We both burst out laughing at that and suddenly he was just a naughty schoolboy, making fun of his master behind his back. Gone was the terrifying mythical demigod. He started clowning around, imitating Leonidas, until I was begging him to stop because my stomach ached so much from laughing. Of course, that was a signal for him to redouble his efforts to mimic the man. Leonidas's habit of pausing before he made an important statement, raising his right hand and wagging his forefinger at his pupils before saying: *Now mark my words...* became the preamble to any number of fatuous statements, such as... *water is wet*, or *the stars shine at night*, or *my nose really does produce tasty morsels*.

It was clear Alexander didn't value Leonidas's teaching any more. His sister Cleopatra, on the other hand, couldn't get enough knowledge. Much of what I had heard from Alexander I passed on to her. She spent more and more of her time with me. She was ten years old now and more open and confident. But she still made me sit down and tell her stories of brave maidens and goddesses. She wept for Ariadne, abandoned on Naxos by the man she had helped to find the way out of the labyrinth, the man for whom she had left home and family.

I often thought of Cleopatra later, the young widowed queen in her wild mountain kingdom, trying to protect her two-year-old son and rule those madmen who would have his throne. She must have felt stranded like Ariadne, alone and desperate, no one to defend her.

And then there was Thessalonica, the King's youngest child. She was the daughter of a sixth wife, who had died a few months before I arrived at court. I had paid no attention to her for years; she was more or less a babe in arms when I saw her first. But as she grew, the Queen began to take notice of her. One day when I came to the end of a song, little Thessalonica suddenly piped up:

'I want to play like Herpyllis, Mother. Let me, please.'

The Queen opened her arms and gave the little girl a long hug.

'And why shouldn't you?' she said.

After that I was charged with giving Thessalonica extra classes on the lyre and, by the time she was seven, she often joined Cleopatra and me in our games and lessons. She was a bright, quick child. She learnt to play her lyre far better than the rest of Philip's offspring. She had a sweet voice, too, and was a graceful dancer. Olympias came to love her most of all the girls, and Thessalonica worshipped the Queen, the only mother she had known. I couldn't understand why Olympias never showed the same affection for her own daughter.

I myself was waiting desperately for my First Blood. I wanted so much to be a real initiate of the Great Goddess, to take part in the secret ceremonies in the woods reserved only for them, to be a true Amazon. Cynane had been initiated when she was my age and seemed so much older and wiser than me. I was in awe of her and wanted to be just like her. Each time the moon waned and left the sky, I wished with all my being to find blood on my dress, on my sheet. But months and months went by with no sign of it.

Meanwhile Cynane was blossoming into womanhood. I remember being out hunting with her and her mother Audata. Cynane was breaking in the new mare the King had bought for her that day Alexander found his warhorse. We were chasing a wild boar. Cynane was taking aim at it with her bow and arrow as we cantered after it through the undergrowth in the forest. She made her shot but it fell short and I turned to look at her: it was rare for Cynane to miss. There was a look of fury on her face.

'Great Mother!' she shouted at the top of her voice, startling the new mare, which pricked up its ears in fright. 'I'm going to cut it off!'

'Cut what off?' I asked in bewilderment.

'My right breast!' Cynane shouted to the whole forest. 'That's what the Amazons did, isn't it? Now I see why! How can I shoot straight with this wretched thing in the way?'

We had lost sight of the boar by now and come to a halt. Audata caught up with us and started laughing softly.

'That's just a legend, my dear,' she commented to her daughter. 'I'll show you how to bind your breasts so they don't get in the way of your bowstring. I hadn't realised how they've grown over the last year.'

Cynane was in fact beginning to spend more of her time at court than out hunting by that time. I had witnessed the day she fell in love with her cousin Amyntas and he with her. They were complete opposites. I had always imagined only a strong hero who could equal her prowess would win her, but it turned out that the qualities she admired in a man were gentleness and kindness, and these Amyntas had in abundance. She would seek him out and I would watch his face light up when he saw her.

I was nearly thirteen years old and I would listen more carefully to the ladies talking about love. They giggled together about various men at court whom one or other of them found attractive. I had by then often experienced the startling sensation produced between my legs when I was on horseback. It made me almost groan with pleasure, but I hadn't made the connection with the act of love between a man and a woman. Though I loved Alexander, it was not of him I thought when I shut my eyes to fully enjoy that wonderful sensation.

It was about three months after Alexander's fury with Leonidas when he came to find me again in the quiet afternoon. We walked out into the deep forest around the palace. I waited for him to start telling me about his latest exploits, or something his master had told him. But he was silent.

We arrived in that little grove where we had spent so many hours together over the years. I expected Alexander to go over to the branch where we usually sat, but he pulled me to him and put his arms round me. He was the same height as me now. Suddenly he planted his lips on mine. It wasn't like his mother's kiss. There was nothing tender about it and I pulled away. Alexander's face was flushed and he was frowning. With another rough movement he put his hands on the slight mounds beginning to grow on my chest. I was startled and pushed him away. He was panting hard now and grabbed me by the shoulders, pushing me down onto the ground. It was covered in pine needles and I let out a cry as they dug into my back.

Alexander started grappling with my dress, trying to pull it up, but it was caught under my body and he couldn't move it. His red face and loud breathing were frightening me. I had never seen him like this before, and the worst thing was the look in his eyes. They weren't focussed on me but staring off into the void. I wanted to speak, to call him back from wherever he was, but my voice wouldn't work.

Then, just as abruptly as he had started his attack on me, he went completely still and sighed loudly, his head sinking down onto the ground beside my face. We lay like that for a minute or two and I began to wonder if he was all right. But he lifted his body slowly, not looking at me, and stood up. He sighed again but I couldn't see the expression on his face. I raised myself on my elbows and slowly got to my feet, brushing the pine needles off my dress and shaking my hair. Alexander still had his back to me. I reached out to touch his shoulder but he sprang away and sped out of the clearing as if competing again for the crown of oak leaves in the race under Olympus.

That was the end of our afternoon meetings, our talks, those times which were so precious to me. Alexander only came to the women's apartments to see his mother, and those occasions became fewer and further between.

Even Olympias began to complain that her son was sullen and intractable.

It was a year later when matters came to a head. The King made a rare visit to the Queen's apartment. I heard him coming and hid behind the screen. It was morning and he sounded sober, in contrast to the last time he had been there. He wasted no time on pleasantries.

'I'm sending Leonidas back to Epirus,' he said. Olympias began to say something but Philip talked over her:

'I know he's family, but your brother can pay for his upkeep for a while. He clearly has nothing to teach Alexander any more. The boy has no respect for him and I can't entirely blame him. Aristotle's agreed to be his tutor. He'll be arriving at court in a fortnight. He'll challenge the boy, make him see how much he still has to learn. All Alexander seems to care about is fighting and showing off.'

'But you can't just...' Olympias began, but again the King interrupted.

'There's nothing to discuss here. Write to your brother and tell him to expect Leonidas.'

And with that he limped out. The Queen was furious. Poor Xanthe received a resounding slap soon afterwards for no obvious reason. And now I found out that our absent philosopher neighbour in Stagira, my mother's friend Aristotle, had also been close to the King since boyhood. They had grown up and studied together.

Soon after this bad-tempered meeting between the King and Queen there were two joyful events. Two years after the taming of Bucephalus, Cynane and Amyntas were

100

married. And I celebrated my First Blood. That fateful night in the height of summer, that night of the full moon in the secret clearing in the forest.

7
INITIATION

*'Men create gods after their own image,
not only with regard to their form,
but with regard to their mode of life'*

They blindfold me long before we get to the clearing. An initiate may not know the way to that secret place until she has made her vows. It's very disorientating, that blindfold. I keep stumbling, holding back, afraid of banging into something or falling into a hole, despite a guiding hand under each arm. It's the night of the first full moon after my First Blood, as required, the hottest day of the year so far. A day when nothing has stirred in the palace except for the changing of the guard. We have eaten nothing, only drunk water in accordance with the rite. I'm wearing the new white linen dress I've sewn and embroidered so painstakingly, pricking my fingers more than once. I've always disliked sewing.

We seem to walk a long way into the forest. Just as I'm getting used to the blindfold and feeling less anxious, the hands under my arms pull me back, bring me to a halt. Silence. Where are we? Who is there?

The day I've prepared for all my young life, the day I thought might never come. Each month of waiting seemed like a year. Was I a freak of Nature, never to bleed? The relief when it happened, feeling the warm trickle down my leg! Normal at last. Now I am keen to do everything right, not shame my mother, not disappoint, be worthy of the rank of Woman. Honoured this day as fertile soil, future giver of life, part of the Earth's cycle, Daughter of the Great Mother. I jump at the sound of a lyre, strummed close behind me, then a voice:

Come, O daughter, come O dear one,
Take your place beside us.
Daughter of the Moon, Daughter of the Earth,
Today you eat the bread and drink the wine of First Blood.

The last chord resounds as the verse finishes. A pause. Just the crickets taking back the night. I gasp as two hands take mine – all my senses heightened, the touch of flesh a shock. Suddenly the Queen's voice from right in front of me, her hands in mine.

'Do you swear to keep the secrets of our Great Mother, who made the Heaven and the Earth and all Her children in it? To tend Her fruits and nurture Her legacy to you? Never to betray the rites we pay Her in praise of Her magnificence?'

I struggle to find the voice in my dry throat.

'I do.' It sounds hoarse and thin.

'Do you swear to keep Her laws: to love your sister as yourself; never knowingly to do harm to another; not to steal; not to lie; not to kill, except the creatures our Mother gives us for our sustenance?'

'I do.'

The hands removed, a fumbling at the back of my head, the blindfold pulled away. I blink hard and open my eyes. The moonlight flooding into a forest clearing, the Queen looking at me with a serious expression, dressed in the blue of the Mother, her tall cylindrical headdress resting among that still astoundingly red-gold hair. I straighten up and realise I am a little taller than her now. She touches my shoulders lightly and I know I must kneel. I do it quickly, keeping my head up, alert for what is to come next.

Then they all appear, kneeling in a line beside me. Audata, Cynane, Philylla, Hippolyta, Charis, Xanthe, Eudoxia... , the ladies of the court. Some in white, others in red, the rest in blue. Berenice comes up, holding a tray with a large loaf of bread. The Queen takes it, slowly tears it in half, in quarters, in eighths, in small pieces for the rite.

'Take and eat what our Mother provides.'

'All praise to Her who reigns above and below.'

I open my mouth and the Queen places a piece of bread in it. She smiles at me now, satisfied. Proud? I want so much to please her, this woman who has replaced my mother. She goes on to each of the ladies in turn, taking a piece of bread from the Bearer each time, intoning the instruction, waiting for the response. I look ahead, at the great stone seat in the glade. I have never been here before.

A secret place for the solemn rites of the Great Mother no man may ever see. On pain of death.

The Queen returns to stand in front of me. Now she takes the cup from the Bearer, holding it as it is carefully filled.

'Take and drink what our Mother provides.'

'All praise to Her who reigns above and below.'

I raise and incline my head. The Queen puts the cup against my lips and tips it for me to drink. I am no longer a child, often unheeded in the background, arbitrarily honoured with attention. Here I am a fellow initiate, equal to the others. A woman, a Daughter of the Mother.

One sip, a second, a third. The wine is rich and heady, full of sun and soil. The men call it the drink of Dionysos, but it belonged to the Great Goddess long before any god was invented in the minds of men. Here no man holds sway. Here we briefly taste the life of women long ago when it was not men who gave the orders, not men who ruled the world, but the Daughters of the Earth, the Daughters of the Moon. A long deep draught from the Cup of Life, that perfect vessel made of the gold from the mines of Thrace, gleaming in the moonlight. The wine flows smoothly down my throat, my lips seal the rim of the cup, my eyes close. Ripples of pleasure throughout my body, the blood turning to wine in my veins, the intoxication swift after the day's fasting.

Suddenly a trickle falling onto my breast, followed by the Queen's sharp intake of breath – a bad omen. Now I know what it portended.

The cup proceeds down the line, filled and emptied again and again, the words repeated again and again, the sips and the long draughts, but all I can think of is the trickle down my breast, clear against the white of my dress, and the Queen's reaction.

She is back in the place in front of me. The cup is filled again. She raises it high above her head.

'All praise to Her who reigns above and below.'

We all speak the words together. She quaffs the cup in one slow movement, abandoning her whole body in the act. She is magnificent. She is the Great Goddess. She is all-powerful. Slowly she lowers the cup, slowly she hands it back to the Bearer, slowly she pulls the red scarf from her bosom.

It is the signal. The lyre is struck again – long, hard ripples filling the space, a heat haze streaming through the air. The Queen raises the scarf in her left hand and takes my hand in her right. Audata takes my other hand, Cynane joins the line, then Berenice, Philylla, Hippolyta, Charis, Xanthe, Eudoxia... The dance begins. We step lightly round the glade, bending to the rhythm of the lyre, swaying gently with the beat. The others seem to float above the ground in the moonlight while I try to focus my mind on the steps, not make a mistake, not compound my bad luck.

Daughter of the Moon, Daughter of the Earth,
You have eaten the bread and drunk the wine of First Blood.
Your body ripens, your breasts swell,
Soon you will bear the fruit of your womb.

Gradually the wine takes over and I am part of it all, swept along, unthinking, ecstatic. The chords are repeated, faster now, the words repeated, faster now; our steps quicken, we give ourselves over to the senses, to that sweet enchantment of mind and spirit, abandoning thought and reason. My feet move without me – I glide, swoop, rise and fall. The line breaks up, women whirling and spinning. I am turning, gyrating, soaring; the trance is coming... now... I throw my head back – it is here! My eyes open to the stars.

Not the stars above me. Something else in the oak, among the branches. Two small points of light, reflecting the moon. A dark shape, a head, eyes in a head. A man there, watching the solemn rites of the Great Mother. On pain of death.

I swivel round, looking for help from the others. They are scattered around the clearing, all taken over by the frenzy, spinning, lurching from side to side, some holding their heads, others reaching out their arms, none looking at me, all unaware of the shape in the tree.

I turn back. It is gone. I stumble through the undergrowth to the base of the tree and into the forest beyond. What is drawing me on? Why not turn away, forget what I saw? No interloper spying on our secret rites. No man there who should pay the ultimate price for his folly. Probably a trick of the light or the shadow. Nothing there.

Blackness around me among the trees. My eyes haven't adjusted yet. I hesitate and then go on slowly, feeling my way with my arms out in front of me. I haven't gone far when something trips me. My hands break my fall and I find myself on all fours on the ground, my palms and knees smarting. I turn into a sitting position and am about to get up, but he is on me. He pins me down with his hands and thighs. I open my mouth to scream but he hisses above me:

'Herpyllis! It's me!'

I go limp, close my mouth. Alexander – my protector, my friend, my love. Now I can see his face dimly in the moonlight. Those eyes, the little pinpricks of light in the tree. There is relief on his face now he knows I won't scream, won't give him away: a man forbidden to watch the Goddess's rites, on pain of death.

We lie there for a few moments, waiting for our breathing to calm down. Then I see a change in his expression, a strange glint in his eyes. Suddenly he leans down and his lips come down on mine, like that day in the grove the year before. At the same time he hardens his grip on my wrists, and first one knee, then the other push at the inside of my thighs and part my legs.

I try to move my head but his lips are holding me down as strongly as his hands are gripping my wrists. I can't breathe. I make noises to show him he is hurting me, frightening me, but he doesn't let go. Then his body starts moving and I feel the first thrust between my legs, hitting my groin. Another thrust, just as painfully missing its mark. Another. I am desperate now. I struggle and writhe, managing to free my lips and gasp in some air.

'Stop it!' I whisper. I should be screaming, calling for help as loudly as the air in my lungs will allow. He lets go of my right wrist and puts his hand over my mouth. I grab his hair and pull hard. He seizes my hand and bites my arm. He is snarling like a wild beast and I release his hair with a yelp.

Panic overtakes me and I try to catch my breath as he brings his lips down again on mine. I have only succeeded in moving my hips a little and bringing my knees up to try to gain purchase to throw him off, but the change of position is fatal. Now when he thrusts again there is a terrific shooting pain inside me as he forces his way. He grunts with triumph and excitement. He is way beyond recall now. My protector has become my tormentor, my friend my enemy, my love my hate. I shut my eyes to see blue, red, white shooting stars in the dark, try to close my mind to escape from my body, from the searing pain spreading to every limb.

Suddenly he rears up and lets out a cry, something between a shout and a sigh. Has he been hit by an arrow between the shoulder blades? I open my eyes and lift my head to see round him but then he collapses on top of me, groaning, his body juddering again and again, his grip on my arms now loose. He is dying. The intensity of the paroxysms and moaning gradually decreases, each weaker than the last. He finally stops moving. He is dead. I lie still. My heart is beating wildly, my breathing quick and shallow, the weight on me unbearable. I am dying too. I am resigned. Nothing to live for in a world where Alexander has done this, where Alexander is no more. I close my eyes, waiting for death to take me.

But then a hand moving down my arm, a kind of caress. I open my eyes. He is alive. The great weight is removed. He is kneeling over me now, smiling. Not his kind smile – his grin. The one that says he can do what he likes. He is untouchable, unbiddable, omnipotent – the son of a god.

'Herpyllis,' he says in the soft menacing tones he uses when he is playing this part, 'don't ever tell a soul what's happened here. Swear to me now you'll never tell. Swear it in the name of the Goddess.'

I hate him now. I hate him with the same passion as I loved him. I turn my head away and stare ahead.

'Swear it!' he snarls. 'Or I'll kill you here and now!'

'Kill me then!' I say with all the disdain I can muster, but there are tears in my voice as in my eyes, and he is unmoved. He laughs his contemptuous laugh.

'I don't need to,' he scoffs. 'Look at you, snivelling like my stupid sister. If my mother had to choose between us, you wouldn't have much chance!'

And, after a quick look around, he gets up and disappears almost immediately into the forest.

I don't know how long I lay there, still somehow hoping I would die, that it was possible simply to end existence by wishing it, by repeating the words over and over in my head *Now die, die!* When I finally pulled myself up and dragged my body back to the clearing the moon had sunk almost to the horizon. I wandered around in a daze for a while, but there was nobody there. They had all deserted me, gone back to the palace without a second thought for their new initiate. I was doubly abandoned – by the Queen and her ladies as well as by my love.

Sore and aching, I hobbled down to the sea, sparkling in the distance. All I wanted now was to wash him off me, to remove that sticky, blood-streaked trickling down my legs, that stink of my betrayal. I stumbled down the hill, through the woods, onto the beach. I walked into the sea until it was above my head. But natural instinct overcame death wish. I struggled up to the surface and spluttered the salty water from my mouth and nose, bobbed up and down, finally swam back and dragged myself out. I lay down on the beach, exhausted, and somehow sleep came to put an end to that night of torment.

8
LIFE WITHOUT LOVE

'What is life without love? Love is like the sun;
without light, there is no life.'

I was in the clearing again. It was morning, the sun was rising and the birds were singing. I was feeling exhilarated, basking in a delightful warmth and glow. I started swaying happily from side to side, humming a tune to myself, the melody from my mother's favourite song. And as I looked up into the tree, there she was, my mother herself, sitting on a branch – a young girl, with a boy the same age. They were laughing and tickling each other, like Alexander and I. Then abruptly they looked down at me and they had somehow become adults, Mother as she was in the sanctuary that last day, the man serious and grey-bearded, his hair receding from his brow. I didn't recognise him. Suddenly he was the Cyclops with Philip's face, looming over me and reaching out his huge hand to grab me and devour me whole.

I woke with a piercing scream. I could hear and smell the sea and the lightening sky was above me. It must be dawn. My head was pounding and my throat was parched. My body was itching: it was covered in dry white streaks. At first I couldn't remember how I had got there, couldn't remember anything after that intoxication from the wine and the dancing, that frenzy engulfing my mind and body, nothing except the sudden shock of glimpsing a watcher in the tree above me.

But then I moved and felt the soreness inside; the memory came back like a brutal blow to the stomach. I groaned involuntarily and a surge of heat flushed through my body from toes to crown at the thought of my defilement. I – now a Daughter of the Earth, a Daughter of the Moon – violated by a man, my virginity taken without my consent. And then the sickening admission that it had been done by *him*, by the boy I'd loved, who had been my friend. I curled up and tried not to think any more. I closed my eyes tight but sleep wouldn't return. With a huge effort of will, I made myself sit up and slowly opened my eyes. The sea and the sky started spinning uncontrollably and my stomach rose into my throat. I closed my eyes again and put my head between my knees, taking deep breaths, hoping I could control the nausea.

When I finally opened my eyes again, the sun was just above the horizon. I stood up. It was difficult to walk at first, with the dizziness and the soreness. I made my way slowly back to the palace and managed to slip up the back stairs into the bedroom without waking anyone. I lay down on my bed and didn't have to wait long before Charis woke and came over to me.

'Herpyllis!' she exclaimed, 'you're back! We were so worried about you! Where did you go? We searched everywhere!'

I couldn't reply; I just burst into tears and she held me in her arms until I stopped. Then she prepared a

113

bath for me and bathed me gently as she had the day I arrived in Pella seven years earlier. We didn't speak. She just assumed the wine had made me ill and that I had no memory of what had happened.

The ceremony at the altar in the courtyard was the same. We broke our fast in the same way, though I could eat nothing. We went about our morning tasks as usual. I haltingly arranged my hair around the new gold band the Queen had given me, my head still aching as never before. I joined the ladies in the colonnade.

And then Alexander appeared. My heart somersaulted. I nearly pointed an accusing finger at him, ready to shout out: *Here he is! The man who spies on our sacred ceremony, violates the Great Goddess's initiate! Rip off his head, tear him limb from limb!* But his mother was smiling at him, he was kissing her and then, instead of sitting down beside her, he looked straight at me. I thought for one joyful moment he was going to tell her what he had done, beg my forgiveness and hers, throw himself on our mercy.

'Aristotle's going to teach us in Mieza,' he said. 'It's a few days' ride from here and he's worried about leaving his wife alone with no one to keep her company.'

As if from miles away I saw Olympias raise her eyebrows slightly as if to enquire what Aristotle's wife had to do with her. There was a pause.

'She's only got her servants and slaves. They're not much company,' Alexander continued. We waited.

'Aristotle says she needs a companion. I was thinking of Herpyllis. She doesn't really have anything to do here. She could make herself useful.'

His words bore straight into my heart. They were the same as his father's in the courtyard long ago – *make yourself useful.* A jolt, a stab, a fatal arrow. Olympias's eyes had been trained on her son but now they shot to me. I went hot and my heart started beating fast. There was a silence.

'Why did you think of Herpyllis?' the Queen asked slowly, her eyes still on me.

'As I said, she doesn't do much. You could spare her.'

The silence was now complete, the tension in the air unbearable. I looked down at the floor, the arrow through my heart. A movement, a rustle of clothing. The Queen's hand gently pulled my chin up, her eyes searched my face.

'We all love Herpyllis,' she said simply. 'There must be someone else we could send to Aristotle's wife.'

'She's a kind of princess, too,' Alexander informed us. 'An educated woman. Herpyllis is the only suitable companion for her.'

The Queen opened her mouth to reply but then closed it again. There was a long silence and then she smiled at me sadly. She cleared her throat and looked away for a few moments. She slowly kissed me on the lips and stroked my cheek before going back to her seat.

I wanted to shout out: *No! Don't let him do this! He only wants to get rid of me so I don't tell you what he did to me, what he did to us! Tell him No! No!* But not one word would emerge from my mouth. I knew I couldn't tell her. I knew Alexander was right. I knew she would choose him, not me. As I watched the Queen's retreating back, I was submerged by a colossal wave of rejection, betrayal.

The next thing I knew, Alexander was pulling me behind him as he strode quickly out of the door. I had to focus all my attention on not falling over. He said nothing as he dragged me down the hall and into the large courtyard on the other side of the men's colonnade, a part of the palace I had never seen before, a forbidden area. For one moment I looked up, away from my struggling feet, and what I saw brought renewed shock in the midst of the turmoil in my mind and the pain in my body: there, quietly strolling along the other side, deep in thought, was the man from my dream. The man with the grey beard, the grey hair receding from his large forehead, unexpectedly tall and slightly stooped now that he wasn't sitting on the branch of a tree.

Alexander ran across the courtyard, still holding my hand tightly and pulling me along behind him towards this man – the man I knew from my dream would soon turn into a Cyclops with Philip's face. But as I watched in horror, he came out of his reverie and gave me a broad smile.

'Antheia,' he said.

At my mother's name another wave hit me full on. Of course. This was Aristotle, my mother's childhood friend.

Alexander looked from Aristotle to me and back again. He had probably expected to have to sing my praises to his teacher and persuade him what a good companion I would make for his wife. He had not thought the philosopher would be so transfixed at his first sight of this inconsequential girl.

116

'Her-pyl-lis,' he said loudly and slowly, stressing each syllable as if his teacher were deaf.

Aristotle looked puzzled but then brightened up as if he'd suddenly understood something.

'Herpyllis!' he repeated. 'The wild thyme. You're named after the wild thyme.'

I swallowed hard. I couldn't speak. Would I ever emerge from the hell I had entered the night before? Alexander was losing patience.

'She's from Stagira, like you,' he added after another pause.

Aristotle's reaction was mystifying. He winced as if with sudden pain and looked away. Now there was a long silence. Finally he made a visible effort to pull himself together.

'Well, well,' he said. 'Antheia's daughter. And you have been here at court since...'

His voice trailed away. Alexander had had enough. He took charge.

'I thought she could keep your wife company – while we're in Mieza. You said you were looking for someone.'

'Yes... Yes. That would... Why not?' The great man was not as eloquent as I had expected. In fact he seemed lost for words.

'Shall we go and see her?' prompted Alexander help-fully. 'Shall we take Herpyllis to meet your wife?'

And again it was as if he were talking to a child or an old man bereft of all his faculties. He steered us both out of the courtyard, along the corridor, through the portico, down the steps and into the city. I was still struggling to reach the surface, not drown in that underwater nightmare. We arrived at a large villa near the palace. Alexander pulled the bell by the gate and it was opened quickly by a man who stepped back swiftly on seeing who the visitor was. The prince strutted into the large stone courtyard and looked around. Aristotle finally took the initiative:

'I'll go and find Pythias,' he said and disappeared through the door into the house.

In the ensuing silence Alexander leaned against a pillar, crossed his arms and looked at me with that awful grin of his. I struggled desperately with the conflicting emotions overwhelming me: the humiliation, the impotent fury, the ache from the love I had felt now turned to hurt and hate.

Aristotle soon returned with a young woman, who had an arrogant look on her face. She was my height and build, but around ten years older; her eyes were a deep violet blue. Her thick, dark brown hair was swept back from her forehead and cascaded in long curls behind her ears; it looked difficult to manage like mine, and she put her hand up to smooth it when she saw the prince.

'Good morning,' she said. Alexander greeted her and gestured in my direction.

'I've brought you someone to keep you company, Lady,' he said.

It seemed Aristotle was to have no part in this conversation and, indeed, he hung back as if *he* were the schoolboy. But Pythias looked to him and finally he stepped forward and laid a hand on my arm.

'I grew up with this young lady's mother in Stagira, Pythias. We were neighbours. She's of good family,' he added. 'She was taken in by the Queen after her parents...' – he glanced at Alexander – 'some years ago. And I believe Alexander can vouch for her.'

Pythias looked at Alexander and he nodded, a smirk on his face, the arrow sinking deeper into my heart. She looked back at me, her face a picture of scepticism. She turned back to Alexander.

'May I offer you a drink of water?' she said. 'It's already so hot.'

But my tormentor saw his task accomplished and had no further interest in the scene.

'Thank you, Lady,' he said, 'but I believe my tutor and I have work to do.'

Pythias inclined her head; master and pupil left us. Then she looked at me and sighed. She sounded exasperated. Finally she said in a flat voice:

'Nobody's told me your name.'

'Herpyllis,' I managed to mutter with a supreme effort of will, only to have to repeat it when she didn't hear me. After a long pause she motioned me to sit down in the shade of an apple tree. She sighed again and looked at me haughtily before snapping out a question:

'How old are you?'

I managed to mutter:

'Nearly fourteen, Lady.'

'So, you've been living at court,' she said, turning up her nose as if she were talking about a pigsty. 'You'll be bored to death here. We'll be quite alone. What can you do to entertain me?'

I mumbled something about playing the lyre. I must have looked very stupid that day to Pythias. She must have wondered what on earth she was to do with me. She sent me back to the palace to collect my things with barely concealed irritation. Somehow I steered myself back through the gate, along the road, up the steps and through the portico. Somehow I went to the room I shared with Charis and Xanthe. Somehow I made a bundle of my possessions. It was not much bigger than the one I had clung to on the way to Pella, seven years earlier, and there was little addition to it – just new clothing and the gold amulet. I walked back as slowly as I possibly could to my new mistress, dragging my heels, straining to hear Olympias's voice calling out to me to come back, telling me it had all been a terrible mistake.

9
FRIENDS

*'Without friends, no one would want to live,
even if he had all other goods.'*

That evening Aristotle called me to his study. As I got up
to follow him I was puzzled to see Pythias give me a cold,
sharp look and I wished for the hundredth time that I
wasn't stranded in this house where nobody wanted me.
I longed to be back with my friends.

Aristotle told me to shut the door behind me. I did
so and turned back to see the walls covered with shelf
upon shelf of rolled-up scrolls. Aristotle smiled encouragingly and pointed to a chair. It was a little like my
father's smile. A great leap of joy possessed me. I was
back home, my father showing me something, sitting me
down, explaining something earnestly, carefully, clearly.
Though I would listen attentively and take in what he
said, just being there with him was what I enjoyed most,
hearing his warm voice, seeing him look at me with that
mixture of pride and love which lit up his face when he
talked to us children. Would this man replace my father,
as Olympias had almost replaced my mother? If only
it could be so, if only I might find a place in this new
household.

'Now, child,' he said kindly, 'I must know all about you if you are to be Pythias's companion. How did you come to Pella?'

A sharp blow in the chest. Not something I wanted to talk about, especially not now when I had been uprooted from everything I knew again. I swallowed hard but couldn't find my voice.

'Come,' Aristotle continued, a trace of irritation in his voice. Not my father's voice – higher, its tone brusque.

'The Queen,' I began, '. . . the Queen had me brought to her. I mean, it was supposed to be my mother... she wanted my mother... but my mother... she only got me.'

I lapsed lamely into silence. Just mentioning my mother had brought tears to my eyes. There was a pause.

'So the Queen took you in straightaway,' Aristotle prompted.

I managed to nod.

'Has she treated you well?' he asked.

I nodded again, not trusting my voice. He sounded impatient as he posed his next question:

'What about your education? Has she prepared you for womanhood?'

What did that mean? I was non-plussed. He was looking at me with the air of a man who had no time to waste.

'I've... learnt to ride,' I stammered out, '. . . and hunt.'

Aristotle's face took on a look of horror.

'*Hunt*?' he repeated in a tone of disgust. 'Dear gods, what a barbarian that woman is!'

He turned away for a moment, as if looking for something. He sighed loudly.

'What have you learnt in terms of household management, womanly skills?'

'I can sew, sir, – and embroider,' I said meekly, hoping he wouldn't ask to see my work. He was still looking at me expectantly.

'I play the lyre,' I added, desperate to please him.

His look softened a little.

'Ah,' he sighed, 'well, that at least could be useful. Pythias likes to be accompanied on her flute. You will play for me tomorrow night. Pythias will instruct you in household duties. There will be no more riding – or *hunting*,' he added with a sarcastic emphasis, making a gesture to dismiss me with his left hand.

Pythias gave me another of her contemptuous looks when I returned to her apartment.

'What did Aristotle want with you?' she said in a peremptory tone.

'He wanted to know about my education, Lady,' I replied.

She gave a kind of snort and then dismissed me with the same gesture her husband had used. I went to my room and stared at the walls. Later I heard a muffled conversation. At first it was just a muttering but soon a voice was raised.

'... *you* certainly take a great interest in her...' It was Pythias.

I couldn't hear Aristotle's reply.

'Next you'll be saying it was Alexander's *own* idea to bring her here!' – spoken loudly with a sneer.

Aristotle had clearly lost patience.

'Yes, believe it or not, it *was*!' he bellowed.

'And why would he choose *her* in particular?' Pythias challenged. 'Wouldn't it be more appropriate to have someone my own age?'

'As I've told you,' he replied, his voice still raised, 'her parents were distinguished people. I'm sure you'll come to like her very well. Nobody will ever replace Pelagia for you, Pythias. You have to accept a woman must follow her husband wherever he goes. It's her duty. You must think of pleasing *me*, not yourself.'

There was a silence. Then Pythias said very clearly:

'Well, *she* clearly pleases you if I don't any more.'

A door opened and footsteps echoed round the balcony before another door slammed.

The following evening Aristotle called us into the courtyard and said he would like to hear me play. I hadn't touched my lyre since putting it down in my new room. I went to get it with trepidation. They said nothing while I tuned the instrument.

'Play,' Aristotle said with the air of a man who had no time to waste.

My mind raced. I knew instinctively that the songs the Queen loved would not be to his taste. I hesitated. Then my father's favourite came into my head. I replaced Aristotle's face with Father's and played it for him now, imagining his smile, always a little sad.

The vine grieves for its grapes, alas,
The tree for its leaves, all shed.
Me, I grieve for my youth, alas,

Me, I grieve for my youth.
Grapes on the vine will grow again,
The leaves on the tree will too.
My youth, alas, will ne'er return,
My youth will ne'er return.

'That's old Rhapsodos's song,' exclaimed Aristotle. 'I remember it well! But you can't have learnt it from him. He was on his last legs when *I* was a boy. You've taken me back, child,' he went on. 'Back to Stagira. It was a happy, carefree life. Sometimes I wish I could go back – live there in peace. But there's no Stagira any more. It was one of the prices we had to pay to achieve our dream.'

There was a silence.

'What dream was that?' I heard myself ask.

Aristotle looked taken aback that I had spoken, but then he smiled indulgently and answered my question.

'Why, the dream of uniting the Greeks as one people, one nation to take revenge on the Persians, who laid our country waste a century and a half ago. We must be a strong, single force to make sure they never do it again. We'll liberate the Greek cities in Asia Minor which are now under Persian rule, or, like Pythias's city of Atarneus, are threatened by them.'

'And it was for this dream that the King destroyed Stagira and put all the men and boys to death?' I asked. It was difficult to see the connection.

'Yes, child. It was politics – nothing personal. Your father might have joined the Athenians in opposing the

Macedonians when Philip's back was turned. That threat had to be eliminated.'

'But Father only wanted us to live in peace, in a democracy,' I said, repeating what I had heard round the dinner table in my family home.

'It may be hard for you to understand these things, child, but you must try to see this is all part of a much bigger picture. Stagira had to be sacrificed to a greater ideal.'

Pythias spoke up suddenly. We both turned to look at her.

'I can't imagine not having the city of my birth to go back to one day. That must be a terrible thing,' she observed. 'Why hasn't it been rebuilt?'

Aristotle raised his eyebrows and looked about to say something, but then he put his hands on his knees in the same gesture as my father's and got to his feet.

'Well,' he said, 'I'll leave you to play together. I think you have a good accompanist for your flute, Pythias. I look forward to hearing you when I return from Mieza. Good night.'

The following day we said goodbye to Aristotle before he left with Alexander and his companions. He turned back to give one last instruction to Pythias, his eyes fixed on me:

'Don't forget what I told you,' he said severely. 'Avoid the Queen and the court. That woman is a terrible influence.'

All I remember about those first days in my new home is the continuing sensation of being underwater, drowning.

I kept reliving the night of my First Blood, the dancing, the elation, then the eyes in the tree, Alexander holding me down, hurting me, humiliating me.

There were long, silent afternoons, Pythias and I sewing or embroidering. I had far too much time to keep going over and over that terrible night. I began to wonder what would have happened if I had screamed, if I had told the Queen there was someone watching us from the tree. I had waking visions of her tearing Alexander apart, his bloody torso, his arms and legs scattered about. Horror waking and sleeping. I stopped eating more than a few morsels. The very sight of food made me want to be sick.

It must have been about a fortnight later when Olympias invited us to visit her at the palace. Despite what her husband had said, Pythias could hardly ignore a direct invitation. My heart leapt at the thought of seeing the Queen and all my friends. In the event, she practically ignored me after a kiss of welcome and focussed on Pythias.

'I hear you're the daughter of the ruler of Atarneus,' she said. 'Tell me about that city. I know of the sacred hot springs of the Great Goddess, but nothing more.'

Pythias assumed that arrogant look I had seen the first time I met her with Alexander.

'Indeed, Lady,' she replied, 'people come from all around to bathe in the springs and be healed by the Mother.'

There was a pause. Then Olympias realised that Pythias wasn't going to supply any more information.

'In my homeland of Molossia is the great oracle of the Mother at Dodona,' she volunteered.

'I've heard of it, of course, Madam,' said Pythias.

Having only recently been initiated, I didn't know whether there was some kind of code in this exchange for two initiates to recognise each other. Olympias turned to a topic closer to her heart.

'You're not accompanying Aristotle to Mieza,' she observed.

Pythias inclined her head slightly but said nothing.

'Why is that?' pursued Olympias.

There was a pause; then Pythias replied:

'Aristotle believes, Lady, that young men learn best when they are not distracted by the comforts of home or by the presence of women.'

'That makes it hard for you, left here alone,' commented the Queen, looking at me. 'I hope Herpyllis will be some consolation. Come, my dear,' she said, 'play for us. I've missed you.'

And she gave me one of those unforgettable smiles of hers, so rare and so precious to those of us who loved her. Feeling light-headed, I hurried back to get my lyre and returned to find the conversation had not advanced much beyond its stilted beginning. All the ladies looked relieved to see me and I tuned the instrument quickly. But as I raised my head to begin the song, I simply collapsed onto the floor with a clatter and lost consciousness.

I don't know how long it was before I came round to find everyone fussing round me, Charis rubbing my wrists and commenting loudly how thin and pale I had become. Then she asked Pythias in an accusatory tone if

I was eating properly. My new mistress was at a loss to answer her and Charis shouted:

'Look at the state she's in! If you can't look after her, Madam, she should come back to court where she's among those who care about her!'

Charis sent Xanthe off to get some food and water. Then she sat me down in the corner and refused to let me go until I had eaten a pancake and some cheese. I had to keep sipping water to keep the food down. When I finally finished, Charis turned to Pythias and said in a challenging voice:

'Well? Can we trust you to look after her properly, Madam?'

Pythias's face was flushed, whether from embarrassment or anger at being addressed in that way by one of the Queen's ladies wasn't clear. Besides, Olympias had now come over to join us and was frowning at my new mistress. Pythias seemed to make some kind of decision. She put out her hand to me and said:

'Come, we're going home. You need to have a lie-down.'

She sounded like my mother. That was the phrase she had used when I was little and it was time for my nap in the afternoons. I took Pythias's hand as I had so often taken my mother's, and we walked back to the villa, holding hands all the way.

That day marked the beginning of a new relationship between Aristotle's wife and me. I don't know why it happened. She assumed the role of elder sister and showed a daily concern for me. At every meal she watched what I ate and insisted I could not get down from the table until I had eaten as much again. It was hard at first and I tried to conceal food in my dress, or gently drop it on the floor, but Pythias missed nothing and would gently chide me while she coaxed me into eating something more. I felt like a little girl again, a little girl loved. And I began to look at this strange woman who had adopted me with new eyes. I began to think that what I had taken for arrogance was actually sadness, mixed with a natural reserve. I started asking her questions:

'Did you marry soon after Aristotle came to Atarneus?'

First she was startled, but then she answered:

'We married not long after he came to court,' she said. 'My father was delighted with his friend's interest in me, you see, and he encouraged him immediately. And to me he praised Aristotle to the skies – his wisdom, his knowledge, the respect he had from everyone at the Academy.'

I wondered if Aristotle had fallen in love with Pythias because she looked like my mother. Had Antheia been his first love? Had he grieved for her too, far away in Athens, when he heard how she died? Had he wept for Stagira? I remembered how he winced at the mention of our city. And how did Pythias feel about Aristotle? Did she love him? He must have been at least twenty years her senior. It was impossible to tell with Pythias.

'My mother died when I was still a child,' she continued, 'and Father didn't remarry. I had no brothers or sisters and was brought up by my nurse. My father taught me to read and write, to play the flute – which he loved – but I was mainly left with servants and slaves. I had one friend, a bit older than me. She was the daughter of my father's chief adviser. We spent a lot of time together. She played the lyre like you.'

That must be the Pelagia Aristotle mentioned the night they argued about me. Pythias was silent again. Behind what she said I glimpsed the cavernous pit of loneliness and boredom which had constituted her life as a girl. Although I had lost my whole family in such terrible circumstances, I had never felt so alone as it seemed she had. Yet there was something fascinating in her solitude. I could well imagine how a man would fall in love with her aura of mystery, the depths of character to explore. She certainly admired her husband.

'As soon as we were married, Aristotle taught me how to organise a symposium. They had one every week, discussing a topic over dinner. I felt so important planning the dishes we would serve, the arrangement of the tables and couches, the entertainment. He made me feel part of something exciting and worthwhile.'

It was only after this conversation that I fully realised how hard it must be for Pythias now, in Pella, with nothing of great moment to take part in, with no husband to please. Like me, she had been left alone in a new place where she knew no one. Worst of all, it was a foreign land where people were very different from those she had known.

We were summoned to court more and more often. I would play the Queen's favourite songs whenever she asked. One day I asked permission to play some of the

131

new music from Atarneus I had learnt from Pythias. Olympias inclined her head in the way that meant *Yes*, and soon I was sent to fetch Pythias's flute so that we could play together. And with that we all became much more at ease; Pythias's strained look relaxed a little and she was persuaded to tell us about each song we played. The culmination was the tale of Antianeira, Queen of the Amazons.

'Like all Amazons,' said Pythias, 'Antianeira coupled from time to time with men she had conquered and enslaved. Her race must be continued, so men were required for that purpose. One day she found particular pleasure with a man who was crippled by a war wound in the leg. After that, she ordered all her male slaves to be crippled; she claimed the lame best perform the acts of love.'

We all involuntarily turned to look at Olympias; Philip had been lame since his leg injury. The Queen frowned but then threw her head back and began to laugh uproariously. It was the laugh I had heard that night of the snake in her bed. All the women were grinning now. Pythias was accepted in the inner circle from that day on. And I noticed that she didn't wait for an invitation to visit the Queen any longer.

But she obeyed her husband in teaching me all about household management. She included me in all the tasks she had to carry out, showing me how to keep accounts of money spent, advising me how to manage servants and slaves, explaining the duties of a wife. I listened dumbly, like a child being taught to read and failing to recognise the letters forming a word. Pythias said I would soon be of marriageable age and must get used to the idea of being a good helpmate to a husband. I dreaded the idea and tried not to think about it at all.

Besides, I wasn't sure I was a proper woman after all. I hadn't bled again since my First Blood, and Charis had told me it would happen every time the moon left the sky. Months went by with no bleeding, but gradually my body filled out a little and the bones were not so visible under my flesh. When I got up one morning there was blood on my sheet again. The relief I felt was overwhelming, and Pythias asked me why I was looking so happy. My lie nevertheless had some truth in it:

'I'm happy to be here with you,' I said, and I hugged her for the first time. She beamed at me.

10
ON DREAMS

'Most prophetic dreams are... to be classed as mere coincidences, especially all such as are extravagant, and those in the fulfilment of which the dreamers have no initiative, such as in the case of a sea-fight, or of things taking place far away.'

It was about a year after I had moved in with Pythias when I heard her screaming in the middle of the night. I jumped out of bed, lit the lamp and rushed to her room, dreading what I might find. She was sitting bolt upright in bed with a look of absolute terror on her face. I said her name softly but she didn't react. I went to her and sat down, tentatively putting my hand out and stroking her arm.

'Pythias,' I said, 'what's happened? Tell me. Did you have a bad dream?'

It took her several minutes to calm down but finally she managed to speak.

'Oh, Herpyllis,' she said, 'my father! Something terrible's happened! I saw him. They were...' and she collapsed on the bed with a great sob, covering her eyes with her hands.

I fetched some water and coaxed her into sipping a little. Then she sighed deeply and gave me such a sad look that tears came to my eyes, too, and I begged her to tell me what she had seen. She drew herself up, taking in a deep breath to control herself.

'I was back in the palace in Atarneus, Herpyllis, a child again, playing with my father,' she said in a flat voice. 'Suddenly the doors to the chamber burst open and a big ugly man in armour marched in, followed by a squad of soldiers. Not *our* soldiers but long-haired bearded Persians in felt caps, wearing loose tunics and trousers, carrying shields and spears. There was no sign of the palace guards. The man grabbed Father by the arm and shouted: *In the name of the High King, I arrest you on a charge of treason.* I clung to my father. Two of the soldiers chained his wrists and ankles and dragged him from the room, shaking me off.'

Pythias's voice had broken on the last word and she paused to collect herself again before continuing.

'Suddenly I'd become a bird, flying above the men,' she said. 'I watched them pulling and pushing my father out of the palace. It was completely deserted except for them. They flung him into a cart and all mounted their horses, riding along beside the cart across miles and miles, inland. I flew after them. Finally they came to a gate with two colossal doors, flanked by huge stone creatures. Each one had the body of a bull and the head of a bearded man. They continued through the gate and out of sight.'

A long pause. I squeezed her hand gently.

'Then I heard screaming and groaning. I was in the sky again. I could look down on a man lying inside a wooden structure. It was like an upturned boat. His head, arms

135

and legs were sticking out. I flew down until I was just above him. It was my father.'

She broke down completely and started sobbing again. I stroked her arm again and got her to sip some more water. Just when I thought she had told me the whole of her dream, she went on.

'Soldiers were poking his eyes,' she said, her voice shaking, 'forcing him to open his mouth, stuffing food into it and pouring a sticky liquid into him as well, smearing his face and limbs with it. Almost immediately he was covered with flies and wasps, buzzing loudly. The men withdrew, leaving him there. I desperately tried to shoo away the insects, but my waving arms had no effect on them. It was as if I was a ghost. They went on buzzing and stinging while my father lay helpless, pinned down by the wood. And then suddenly...'

She swallowed hard and looked away. Presently she managed to finish the story.

'. . . suddenly all the insects flew away. There were just bare bones and a skull left behind... That was when I woke up screaming... He's dead, Herpyllis. They tortured him to death. I know it.'

I was dumbfounded. What a terrible dream! What could it mean? I made a hesitant attempt to reassure her that dreams never represent actual events. That was what my father had told me when I was little. But I had seen Aristotle in my dream and then met him shortly afterwards. I didn't know what to say. We spent the morning in silence. Pythias could neither eat nor sleep again. And the terror didn't leave her face. I tried various ways of distracting her; I played to her, recited her favourite poems, but I might as well have been alone – there was no reaction.

Finally I thought of the Queen. She would know what to do. I went to her and told her the dream; I begged her to come to Pythias. She took no persuading, simply picking up her chest of herbs and potions and following me back without a word. As I had hoped, Olympias took charge, ordering me to make tea with the dried valerian she gave me, while she began to rub some oil of spikenard into Pythias's temples and wrists.

When I returned with the tea, Pythias was lying on the couch, breathing regularly, the terror gone. Olympias had put some of the oil to burn and the whole room was full of the scent. I took a long breath in and then let it out, feeling my body finally unwind. The Queen waited for the tea to cool and then she gently lifted Pythias's head and put the cup to her lips, helping her to drink as if she were a sick child. Within half an hour my mistress was calm again. Olympias gave me instructions on caring for her and told me not to hesitate to send for her if she were needed again. She smiled at me and touched my arm with the old intimacy.

It took more than a month for the news to reach Pella. Hermias, Pythias's father, the ruler of Atarneus, had been captured in his palace by a Greek mercenary in the service of the Persian King. Aristotle had advised Hermias that this man could be trusted, so he had been invited to the court. Pythias's father was taken to Susa, where he was mercilessly tortured to extract information about his alliance with the Macedonians. He revealed nothing.

His method of execution was known as 'the boats': he was made to lie in a wooden boat and another upturned boat of the same size was nailed over it, leaving his head and limbs protruding. He was made to drink milk mixed with honey. Milk and honey were smeared all over his face, arms and legs, attracting flies and wasps. Naturally, his bodily functions were performed inside the boat; worms gradually ate away all his flesh. It took fourteen days for him to die.

Aristotle returned from Mieza as soon as he heard about Hermias's death. And with him was Callisthenes.

Some people say there is no such thing as love at first sight; they say it is just lust. All I can say is that what happened to me the first time I saw Callisthenes has happened only that once. Yes, there was a little leap of ecstasy only normally evoked with the touch of a finger or on the back of a horse, but there was something much more. First of all, my heart turned over and my stomach dropped, as if from fear, but these strong physical sensations were accompanied by an overall feeling of warmth and joy, and what I can only call relief: relief at finding what I had searched for all my life without knowing it.

A sob from Pythias brought me back to the present. Aristotle was holding her in his arms; she was weeping again for her father. I felt guilty that I had completely forgotten why the men were here, had been entirely taken over by that surge of emotion towards this young man standing in front of me, his soft hazel eyes fixed on me, the waves of his dark brown hair swept back from his high forehead, his brown tunic sitting easily on his lithe tanned body.

Pythias's sob roused him, too, and he looked over at her anxiously. Aristotle was stroking her back and making sympathetic noises; Callisthenes went over and embraced her, murmuring some words. When he turned back towards me, he had a sad look on his face. Pythias calmed down and Aristotle took her hand, leading her over to the stone bench. We followed in silence. Aristotle sat his wife down and called for a servant. Tycho brought some water and cups. Finally Pythias noticed Callisthenes looking at me again.

'Ah,' she said, 'you haven't met Herpyllis yet. I don't know what I'd have done without her. Dear girl.'

And she stood up and held out her right hand to take my left, taking his right with her left. It was as if we were part of a ritual: the priestess joining us. I remember that glowing moment now as clearly as if it happened just a few days ago.

Aristotle said he would order a statue of Hermias. We would all travel to Delphi to set it up there when it was ready, and celebrate the life of a fine man and ruler. Then he excused himself to Pythias and left for the palace. Pythias went to supervise meals and accommodation, now the household was back to its former size. Callisthenes and I were alone. It was what we had both been waiting for impatiently. He was nineteen, four years older than me. After a short silence he said:

'Tell me about yourself, Herpyllis. How did you come here to us?'

I was surprised and delighted at his use of the word 'us'. When I had come to the house, he had already been in Mieza, preparing for Alexander's and his companions' arrival.

I told him in as matter-of-fact a way as I could about the sack of Stagira, the deaths of my parents and brothers, and how I had been brought to Pella and lived at court after that. My voice broke and I had to stop. He put his hand gently on mine.

'Our fates have been similar,' he said simply. 'I'm from Olynthos, you see.'

Olynthos. The hundred oxen slaughtered that day in Dion to mark the sack of another city, the year after Stagira, the steaming air, the gore, the stench – I gasped and retched at the very memory. Callisthenes poured more water for me and helped me drink, his arm around me. I was a little girl again and my big brother Theron was back, soothing me after I'd fallen over and cut my knee. A long-forgotten feeling of security overwhelmed me. It was as if I were home again. We had been drawn together by some invisible force, a bond of suffering joining us. I wanted to stay with his arm around me forever.

Slowly his own story came out as we sat together in the courtyard.

'My mother was Aristotle's niece,' he began. 'I hardly remember my father. He died when I was ten, but he'd been ill for a long time. Not long afterwards, there was talk of war. My mother's brother Nicanor came to fetch

140

us and bring us back to this house. My mother died a few months later. So I was left on my own.'

He was silent for a few moments. Then he turned to me and asked:

'You've met my Uncle Nicanor, haven't you?'

I thought back to the awkward soldier who had visited us a few months after I had gone to live with Pythias. As soon as he sat down he looked as if he couldn't wait to leave. But he had stared at me strangely when I played and sang for him, and had given me a very odd look when he rose to go. I nodded.

'Well, Nicanor was already a captain in Philip's army when my mother died. He was often away from Pella. He decided I'd receive a better education with Aristotle, so he sent me off to Asia Minor with a merchant friend of the family. I became Aristotle's ward.'

Callisthenes looked down. He didn't need to explain to me how hard it had been for him at first.

'I must have been an irritation to Aristotle,' he said with a rueful smile. 'He wasn't used to dealing with boys of my age and spent most days involved in discussion and debate with Hermias and the other men in their group. Pythias was kind to me, though. She introduced me to other boys at court and made sure I was always occupied in some kind of activity, soon joining in their classes and training. And then I was really lucky,' he added. 'Her father took a great liking to me for some reason. He had me join the philosophers' circle. Hermias gave me this gold earring,' he said, touching the metal in his right ear lobe.

'We spent a lot of time collecting specimens of wild-life for the men to dissect. I was glad to feel useful,' he went on. 'We were part of something important. Aristotle made me feel that. He was completely absorbed in creating his index of all the animals and plants in the area, discovering everything there was to know about them. *Knowledge, my boy,* he used to say, *gaining knowledge is what life's all about. To say before you die that you've added to the sum total of what we know. There's something to strive for!* He's inspiring, Aristotle, especially for a young man. I wanted nothing more than to please him.'

He smiled a little wryly, I thought.

'But as I grew up I found what interested me most was listening to the men speaking about the past. I would listen for hours to their stories and write down everything I heard. By my sixteenth birthday I had started my history of the Greek cities.'

After that first day Callisthenes and I talked like old friends, assuming an immediate familiarity with each other, as if we had grown up together and needed no small talk. The lurch in the stomach was there every time I saw him, but it didn't make me shy or unnatural. And he seemed relaxed and happy in my company. Being with him was both exciting and reassuring. He had begun to write a eulogy for Hermias, whose kindness he wanted to repay in some small measure. He sat and read us what he had written and asked for Pythias's comments, listening carefully to what she said and making additions that she requested. He returned to Mieza with Aristotle after just six days.

The months that followed were long and tedious now I was in love. Pythias and I spent a great deal of time at court. I was glad to see that Cleopatra had become closer to her mother since her First Blood and in Alexander's absence. Her confidence was growing and she would occasionally take part in discussions with the older women. Thessalonica was always at Olympias's side: she had clearly taken my place as the Queen's favourite. She played her lyre well. I taught her new music to entertain the ladies, and she, Pythias and I would often play together.

Cynane had stopped hunting. She was with child. A softer side to her was now revealed. She sat with us, sewing and embroidering as she had rarely done without complaint in the past. There was a quiet joy about her and she confided in me that she found great happiness just sitting with Amyntas and talking about nothing in particular. Had I not been in love with Callisthenes, I might have been scornful of this change in the Amazon maiden I had admired without reservation. As it was, I was relieved not to be constantly trying to compete with her and falling short. I felt closer to her, and she would seek me out. I even took pleasure in sewing some things for the unborn baby.

11
PERMANENT INTOXICATION

*'Young people are in a condition like permanent
intoxication, because life is sweet and
they are growing.'*

I'll never forget the day Pythias and I walked into the
palace about six months later and found the ladies chattering excitedly. The Queen called out to us as soon as
she saw us.

'Great news!' she said. 'Philip's recalling Alexander to
court. He's to be regent while the King goes campaigning
against Athens!'

The exhilaration I felt made me stop breathing for a
moment. Callisthenes would come back and I would see
him every day.

The week that followed dragged interminably until the
men returned. Callisthenes' face showed me he was as
thrilled as I was that he was back, but we had no chance
to be alone that day or any other that first week. He
spent most of his time at the palace with Aristotle. Even
when the men were in the house, they took their meals
separately from us. I was used to this at court, but in
Stagira we had all eaten together. There were no opportu-
nities to sit and talk to Callisthenes. The frustration and

desperation I felt were as strong and deep as my excited anticipation had been at the thought of having him back.

It was several evenings after the men had returned from Mieza when they finally came to the courtyard and Aristotle asked us to play for them. I was surprised Pythias chose the song of the Amazon Antianeira, which had amused the ladies of the court with its declaration that crippled men made the best lovers. While I was singing during a pause in the flute part she was playing, I noticed a little ironic smile on Pythias's face and realised she had chosen it deliberately. She knew perfectly well that her husband used music as an accompaniment to his thinking process and didn't listen to the lyrics attentively. The Amazon Queen spoke much of hunting, both deer and love.

While his great uncle appeared to be dozing, Callisthenes leaned forward and cradled his chin in his palm, his elbow resting on his thigh. Those hazel eyes were on me again and soon I was singing only for him, giving chase to his heart with the words of the Amazon Queen.

Hunt you down, my bow in hand, will I
Till you lie at my mercy, begging for my kiss.

When we finished, Callisthenes startled Aristotle by exclaiming loudly:

'Why have I never heard this song before, Pythias? It's wonderful.'

She smiled at him indulgently and commented:

'You heard it in Atarneus many years ago,' she said, 'but you were only a boy and the singer was much older.'

'It has a barbarian air,' Aristotle remarked, 'not much to my taste. Sing me again that song from Stagira, Herpyllis, the one about youth,' he added, sitting back in his chair.

I did as I was told. When I had finished, Aristotle gave me a look of satisfaction and turned to Callisthenes.

'*There*,' he declared with emphasis, '*that*'s proper music for you! Such songs are the essence of our Greek heritage, far superior to the music of Asia.'

He paused and sighed. Then he stood up slowly and said to Pythias:

'Come, my dear, time I saw the household accounts. I hope you've been keeping them in order while I've been away.'

Pythias's face fell and lost all the vivacity which had marked it only a moment earlier, roused by the music she loved. She was clearly not looking forward to show-ing her husband the accounts. But this household report finally gave Callisthenes and me the opportunity to be alone together for the first time since his return. I felt a thrill go through me and my heart started beating fast. I hoped we would fall straight back into the easy way of talking together we had almost immediately developed when we met, but what if we didn't? What if I said the wrong thing, something stupid? Callisthenes smiled at me a little nervously, I thought. Perhaps he was thinking the same thing.

'I'm ashamed of myself,' he began, 'when I listen to you play. I've never practised much and I've more or less given up now,' he said, giving me that long look again.

'My lyre is all I have left of my mother,' I said. 'When I play, I think of her and the way she taught me. The things she said. I want to be like her – play like her, sing like her. The Queen says I do.'

'The Queen knew your mother?' asked Callisthenes with surprise. 'I knew she'd taken you in, but I didn't realise she knew your mother.'

I told him about their friendship.

'What sort of a woman is the Queen?' he asked. 'I've only seen her from afar. Certainly a striking lady, but Aristotle says she's a complete barbarian.'

'If I were to compare her with the King,' I reflected, '*he* would be more the barbarian.'

Callisthenes looked uncomfortable.

'Why do you say that?' he asked slowly.

'You don't have to look any further than what he did to our cities, yours and mine,' I replied, returning his earnest look.

He sighed and looked down.

'Aristotle says it was all in a just cause,' he said softly. 'The King's uniting the Greeks so they can fight the Persian threat and give all our cities peace and security.'

He took my hand and squeezed it.

'It's what the philosophers want, Herpyllis,' he continued. 'It's what our cities in Asia Minor want. Look at what they did to Pythias's father, to Hermias, the wisest of rulers. He was a good man, Herpyllis, a very good man. Aristotle says we have to make sure men like him can live and rule without the fear of barbarians destroying all they have built.'

I didn't answer. He was a historian and knew what he was talking about. All I knew was what I and all Stagirans had lost – our homes, our families, our happy lives. I said nothing more. The man before me made me glow with irrepressible excitement, an urge to throw myself into his embrace, feel his lips on mine. I was in no mood to disagree with him, to change that expression on his face which told me he felt the same welling-up of emotion as I did. I smiled and looked into his eyes. He took my other hand and fondled it gently until we heard Aristotle and Pythias coming back.

The following day Charis came to tell me Cynane had gone into labour. I visited her and found her pale and bathed in sweat. The midwife said she didn't seem to be making any progress. Every few minutes she was wracked with pain but there was no sign of the baby. Audata held her hand and Amyntas was pacing the floor outside, desperate to help her but not allowed in.

I spent my time going between husband and wife, encouraging and reassuring both, though I had no experience of childbirth at all and was as terrified as they were. A night and another day went by before Cynane was finally delivered of a daughter. The midwife shook her head and said to me the princess would never have another child. She didn't explain why not.

I went to tell Amyntas he had a daughter. He almost wept with relief and would not be turned away when he rushed in to see his wife. She even managed to smile at him before falling into a long sleep. He stayed by her side until she awoke many hours later.

They called their daughter Adea. She was small and red and wrinkled, but they both doted on her immediately. Although Cynane was too weak to get up for several days, she gradually recovered from her long ordeal. But it was three weeks before we celebrated her Third Blood in the clearing in the woods. I was shocked to see the princess looking older and even thinner in the blue dress of a mother, but she was still the same Cynane beneath it all. She danced and smiled with great determination.

Not long after the birth of Adea, Pythias and I were sitting in the garden when she burst into tears. I immediately put my arm round her and asked her what was the matter.

'Oh, Herpyllis,' she said, 'I'm so unhappy.'

'Why?' I asked. 'What's happened?'

'I've been married now for nearly seven years and we still have no child,' replied Pythias. If only...' and she bit her lip to stop herself crying again.

'But Pythias,' I said. 'Aristotle's been away so much. You've had little time together.'

'I lost a child. A boy. He was born dead.' She turned away. 'Since then...' she began and then lapsed into silence.

Later that day I went to see Olympias. I remembered a rite we had held for Berenice. She was childless and desperate after four years of marriage. Her husband had taken another wife. A few months after the ceremony, she was with child and went on to give birth to a healthy boy. Perhaps the Queen and our Great Mother could help Pythias, too.

As the sun was setting on the evening of the next full moon we stood in the clearing. I had cut long thick stalks of giant fennel, wound them round with ivy and topped them with pine cones to make a thick wand for each of us. Charis had picked the pomegranates, one for each of us in the winnowing basket. Berenice had found the agnos berries for Pythias to eat. With Olympias's supervision, Cynane and I made some of the sacred potion with barley and water, adding honey when the fermentation was complete. Just before we left, the Queen carefully measured out a small amount of the nectar made from the special mushrooms of the Great Goddess. Only she knew the secret of how to make it. She stirred it into the mixture. There the Queen stood in front of the altar in her heavenly blue with that ancient headdress of the goddess, her arms stretched out as she intoned the prayers, Pythias kneeling before her and the rest of us in a line behind, facing the altar.

'O Great Mother, Mother of us all, make this woman before you a mother too. Make her womb bear fruit as your Earth bears fruit to sustain us all. Accept our offerings to you now and grant this woman fertility in return. Make her belly swell with child and her breasts with the milk of your favour. O Mother, grant our prayer.'

The Bearer passed Olympias the jug of the drink we had made and she sprinkled some of it on the stone altar. Then she poured some more of the liquid into the golden chalice and put it to Pythias's lips to drink. It was refilled and Audata drank, and so on down the line, until we had all taken a long draught. Then Pythias took the huge basket of pomegranates and laid it on the altar. The Queen made one of those slight movements of the head which so characterised her, and which we had all quickly learned to interpret. Xanthe struck the drum and I began plucking the strings of my lyre; we played while the women danced in a circle around Pythias in the centre, each brandishing her wand. They whirled and gyrated, spinning on one foot then the other, bowing, squatting, jumping.

It made me giddy just watching them, and the potion was beginning to have a strange effect on me. Everything around me was surrounded with bright white light; all the colours within it were enhanced to peacock greens and blues, goatweed yellow, poppy red. Then I glimpsed a strange creature among the trees: first I thought it was a deer, but then glimpsed the head of a lynx, the tail of a snake. Pursuing it was a sprite, flitting along the tree line, flashing golden eyes in a violet head, a shapeless, limbless body. Suddenly I was hovering above the clearing, looking down at them all, including myself, standing there playing the lyre and singing.

Much later, it seemed, I was back on the ground. Pythias was facing me; the whites of her eyes had turned up and she was swaying from side to side. A strange keening sound was coming from her mouth; slowly she bent down before throwing her body up and back. She started turning, her back bent, and soon she, too, was spinning. Olympias stepped forward and held Pythias round the waist so my friend could turn with more abandon, leaning further and further back. Finally she dropped to her knees and her head came forward; we stopped playing and the women all knelt around her.

The Bearer took the kerchief of small dark brown berries and poured them carefully into the Queen's cupped hands; Olympias held them out towards Pythias and let them fall slowly, one by one, into the other woman's upturned mouth.

'Take, eat. Our Mother gives you these drops of Her blood. Swallow them whole and feel them grow within you, making your womb a fertile field in the spring, ready for the seed to sprout there. Soon you will bear fruit and bring forth a child. All praise to Her who makes life grow within us, all praise to Her.'

'All praise to Her.'

We echoed the words three times. Pythias remained kneeling on the ground, her head now bowed. Olympias made a sign for us all to leave. I hesitated, worried about my friend, but the Queen beckoned and I followed.

'Come back in an hour,' she said, 'and help her walk home.'

I did as I was told and found Pythias still in the same position, as if in a trance. I gently touched her arm and she immediately looked up at me, a radiant smile on her face. She took my hand and we walked back in silence.

12
A SINGLE SOUL

'Love is composed of a single soul
inhabiting two bodies.'

It was about six months after our ceremony for Pythias that Aristotle called me into his study again. This time his wife didn't look concerned at his attention to me. She must have seen how Callisthenes and I felt about each other and knew I posed no threat to her marriage.

'Sit down, my dear,' Aristotle said when I entered. 'I've been thinking about your position in my household,' he went on. 'I know Pythias is happy to have you as her companion but I understand you are technically still the Queen's slave. Now, do you want to go on living with us, Herpyllis? If you...'

I was so eager to make it clear I wanted to stay that I interrupted him.

'Yes, yes,' I said quickly. 'There's nothing I want more.'

He was a little taken aback by my enthusiasm, but then he smiled and carried on.

'I'll talk to the Queen. If she has no objection, you'll become my ward. I think your mother... your parents would have liked that. Since I understand you have no relatives, no one else.'

He paused and I realised he was waiting for confirmation.

'No,' I managed to say, 'no one else.'

I was overwhelmed by Aristotle's concern, the fact that he had thought about my position and what I would want, what he could do for me.

Pythias later told me Olympias gave her consent to Aristotle becoming my guardian only grudgingly, but I had never been legally bound to her as a slave; it was just a formality to ask her permission for me to become Aristotle's ward. The document was drawn up and I became a full member of the household with my own maid.

I still remember how Callisthenes snatched the opportunity one afternoon to find me alone in the courtyard. He caught hold of my right hand and with the other gently caressed my face, a half-smile on his face. After a short while he said:

'Herpyllis, you've changed. You remind me of a flower that's been in the shade but has now been moved into the sun. You've come into full bloom,' he added.

I felt his presence as intoxicating as the wine at my First Blood. I was about to move into his embrace, to feel that beautiful, strong body next to mine, but Aristotle came bustling out of his study and we sprang apart.

A date had been set for a ceremony at Delphi to erect a statue of Pythias's father Hermias near the sacred oracle of Apollo. Two wagons were hired, one to carry Pythias and me, and the other the servants and slaves we took with us. When the day came to start our journey we settled ourselves in the wagons while Aristotle, Callisthenes and Theophrastus rode alongside.

Theophrastus had become part of our household after the men's return from Mieza. He had been Aristotle's main assistant for years, a man of medium height with curly light brown hair, receding now, his pale blue eyes slightly protruding and his lips rather full. There was nothing particularly unattractive about him and yet he evoked an almost physical repulsion in me. It was the same reaction I had that first day in the courtyard in Pella when I met the second hostage, Perdiccas. I can't really explain that feeling I had about either of those people. In both cases it was like encountering a creature of a different species masquerading as a human being, lacking the feelings and emotions the rest of us share. Anyway, I kept my dislike of Theophrastus to myself; we never had any need to address each other, or be in each other's company.

The trees were just coming into blossom as we set off on our long journey. We trundled down the coast road, stopping at Dion, where Pythias and I made offerings to the Great Mother and the men to Zeus. There followed many a day in the wagon, entertaining ourselves with music and games when the tedium reached its height. Callisthenes would often position his horse just behind the wagon and tie back the flaps of the cover so he could listen and take part when we were making up riddles. Aristotle and Theophrastus always rode ahead, endlessly debating or discussing some point of philosophy.

The best days were the ones when Callisthenes would tell us stories. Some of them were from recent history – he told us about the Sacred Wars around the possession of Delphi – but most of all I enjoyed his stories of heroes, nymphs and gods. Even the ones I knew took on a special charm and significance in his telling. He would add a minor character looking on or making jokes. But there was one myth he told with great eloquence: his version of the tale of Orpheus.

'That great poet and musician was born under Olympus,' he said.

We were not far from Dion at the time, the mountain looming ahead, its peaks in the clouds as usual.

'Orpheus roamed through Macedon and Thrace,' he continued, 'charming all mortals, animals and gods with his playing and singing. Apollo took him as his lover. But one fateful day Orpheus saw a beautiful woman dancing in the meadows with her friends. She was slim and graceful with thick black hair and spell-binding green eyes, and her voice was not of this world.'

'That's enough of that,' scolded Pythias, but she couldn't help smiling a little at his description, which he made looking straight at me. Callisthenes grinned at her and went on with his story.

'Her name was Eurydice and she couldn't hide the fact that she had fallen in love with Orpheus, as he with her. The wedding day couldn't come soon enough for either of them,' he added, giving me another meaningful look.

'But as they danced at the feast, each in the circle of their friends, a viper bit the bride in the heel and in seconds she was dead. The bridegroom was inconsolable and would have followed her into death immediately if his companions hadn't restrained him.

'In his grief Orpheus wandered from place to place in a delirium until he came to the gates of the Underworld itself. Since the gods loved him, they allowed him in, and there he played his lyre and sang his songs as sweetly as he had ever done, seeing Eurydice behind the throne of Hades and Persephone. They granted his request to take his bride back to the world above, but only on one condition: he must not look back before they were outside.

'Orpheus set off, hoping against hope that his wife was following him. As he stepped out of the gates of the Underworld, he looked back, thinking he had fulfilled the gods' condition. But Eurydice was still within the gates! He could only watch in horror as she was dragged inexorably down forever, never to be united with him in their love.'

Callisthenes paused. He had as good a sense of drama as Alexander. He looked down at the road for a few moments before resuming in a quieter voice.

'Orpheus went back to his wanderings, playing only the saddest songs and making love only to boys, for he could never love another woman. Finally, he chanced upon a dozen of the Mother Goddess's initiates, intoxicated with wine and dancing in a frenzy. They fell upon him and tore him to pieces, throwing his head into the river, where it floated along, still singing mournfully of his lost Eurydice.'

Callisthenes stopped and looked at me. But this was a different look – not playful or humorous, but deadly serious. I felt panic rising in my throat. How much did the man I loved know of women's sacred rituals? Was he just recounting the stories he had heard, the myths and poems recited, or did his look mean he knew I was an initiate of the Great Goddess and a secret opponent of the power of men? Was he trying to discern a raving madwoman in me, who might tear him apart? I wanted to tell him he had nothing to fear from me. He was my choice as I was his, and there was nothing to stop us living a happy life together.

There was a silence and then he reined in his horse, stopping by the side of the road for some minutes, his head turned away from us, as the wagon went on its way. Pythias put her hand on mine but said nothing.

The day we made our way up to Delphi seemed to last twice as long as usual. The winding road rose slowly and gradually above the plain, twisting again and again, a colossal slowworm lying on the mountainside. The horses strained and whinnied on each bend, becoming more and more exhausted as the hours went by. The wagon drivers got down and started leading them by the bridle. When we reached our destination late in the afternoon, the sun was low in the western sky and we had to shade our eyes to look back down the way we had come. My head began to spin a little and I grabbed Pythias's elbow as we stood together by the wagon. She turned to look at me, her face radiant.

'Look, Herpyllis,' she said, 'look!'

We were at the top of the world, observing it like the gods themselves. The plain below was clouded in a deep violet mist and the slope down to it was so steep that the bottom of my feet tingled uncomfortably, and my heart thumped with the fear of tumbling headlong into the void. I swayed forwards and then quickly looked away and up, only to feel my heart leap again, but this time it beat fast with elation to be so close to the azure sky above. I had to stop myself raising a hand to touch it and trace its streaks of rosy cloud.

When my neck began to ache, I slowly straightened my head and carefully looked back down the mountain to the gash in the sky where the elongated and misshapen disc of the sun was sinking towards the horizon in its setting of gold, now brass, then bronze, and finally copper, before falling away to leave dull iron.

Aristotle took Pythias's arm and they went together to supervise the unpacking of the wagons and see to our accommodation in the guest quarters. Callisthenes moved to stand beside me and took my hand. We stood there together until we saw the first stars in the translucent sky. Dinner was a quiet affair and we all had an early night.

Isn't it strange how memory works? Some events which happened decades ago still evoke clear images and strong emotions as vivid as anything in the present. What a weak, irrelevant measure of our lives time is! I remember practically every moment of that memorial day in Delphi when we celebrated the life of Pythias's father at the foot of his statue.

We emerged from the hostel soon after dawn to be confronted with thick white cloud just below us, transforming our world into a narrow space between it and the airy blue above. I can feel again the sudden unexpected sensations of cold and wet on my toes as I walked through the heavy dew on the grass, hear the goat bleating indignantly as it was untethered, see the little smiles we gave each other, which faded away as we contemplated what we had to do. I recall the simplicity of Aristotle's gesture as he held out his hand to take Pythias's and lead our slow walk to the site, accompanied by my playing, and how my fingers trembled slightly on the plectrum from the cold and the solemnity of the occasion. I can see that encouraging look on Callisthenes' face. And it's not just the sights I remember so vividly but the smells too: that fresh dankness, the reviving tang of the pines, the aroma of millennia in the stone.

When we arrived at the designated spot where the statue had been freshly erected, Pythias stepped forward and stood before it, facing us. At first she looked hesitantly at Aristotle, but he nodded at her and she started speaking. She had a calm dignity, her voice catching slightly at the beginning, but gaining strength and tone as she proceeded. A lump stuck in my throat as she spoke of her happy childhood, so like my own; how she would ride on her father's neck, walk on his feet, sit on his lap, hide under his desk, play with his hair; how he never failed in his gentle love, his infinite patience, while he taught her about the world, always following the maxims

160

there before us at Delphi, the watchwords my father had so often repeated: *Know thyself* and *Nothing in excess*.

By the end, the pride Pythias felt in her father overcame all other emotions and the tears in her eyes were those of joy, joy that such a man had given her life. I felt we were not only honouring Hermias that day but Agathias, my father, too. I finally laid his ghost to rest, though my mother's would take much longer.

Then it was Callisthenes' turn to read his eulogy. He enunciated the words simply and clearly, allowing the beauty of the language he used to emerge like perfect music, accompanied only by birdsong. Hermias had become the ideal ruler, following the precepts of the finest philosophy and setting great store by moral action and the public good. I felt proud that the self-assured and eloquent man who was speaking about Pythias's father was my love, and that he seemed to love me.

None of us had heard the poem Aristotle had composed before. Who could have imagined it would be the cause of his downfall and unhappy end? At the time it seemed a fitting tribute to his friend and wife's father. His voice rang out across the mountainside like that of a priest; he became the mouthpiece of the deity welcoming Hermias among the ranks of the Blessed, the devotees of Virtue.

Aristotle nodded to me and I played and sang the laments he had chosen. The others planted flowers around the base of the statue. Pythias was visibly moved. The ceremony was turning her grief into quiet pride and helping her forget the dreadful manner of her father's death. There was a new serenity about her as we processed to the temple and prepared to sacrifice the goat.

The priests at Delphi reminded me of the ones at Dion when the hundred oxen had been slaughtered together, as if with one stroke of one colossal knife. Apollo's celebrants were just as impressive in the elaborate gestures they made and the rites they performed that day over the one goat we had brought for our ceremony. But for me the men's rituals had none of the mystery and thrill of our women's secret religion. The sacrifice was just a succession of movements and words, going through the motions, without the depth of meaning I felt in our own ceremonies.

The following day we toured the site. Many a Greek city had built a treasury at Delphi to contain the offerings the city had made to Apollo to thank him for the advice his oracle had given them. Callisthenes managed to spend most of the day at my side, and we lagged behind the others as he stopped to tell me about each building and how most contained a tenth of the spoils of victory the city had gained in a battle. We laughed together at how each treasury vied with its neighbours to be more magnificent.

Olympias had told me how the ancient shrine and oracle of the Great Goddess here at the navel of the Earth, guarded by Her Son, Python, had been usurped by the new god Apollo. He had killed Python and set up his own temple and oracle, but his father Zeus had ordered him to hold music, poetry and theatre competitions every four years in honour of the Great Mother's Son. I was sorry this was not one of those years.

We walked on and into the woods and groves of Mount Parnassus, sacred to the Muses. I remembered my mother telling me they were daughters of our Mother Goddess long before they became daughters of Zeus in the men's myths. Callisthenes recited a poem to Clio, the muse of historians. Then he looked at me and said he needed no other muse but me. There was no trace of the strange look he had given me on the journey; we were back to our previous intimacy.

Callisthenes could have recited lists of words and numbers for all I cared that day. I just wanted to be by his side and hear his melodious voice, feel his smouldering presence next to me, emanating a kind of radiance. My sense of touch was so heightened that there was a kind of shock which ran right through my body when his hand brushed my arm. We walked on slowly in silence. To calm my senses, I asked him to explain to me about Hermias and the situation of the Greek cities in Asia Minor.

'Well,' he replied, 'you know about fifty years ago the barbarian Persians took control of the Athenian cities in Asia. But Atarneus regained its independence while the Persians were squabbling among themselves. And with Hermias, and Aristotle beside him, those lands were ruled by a philosopher as Plato had always recommended.

'But then King Artaxerxes came to the throne,' he said in a new, harder tone, 'a force to be reckoned with. Hermias could see the new Persian ruler would try to regain lost territory. But having Aristotle in his lands and the alliance with King Philip reassured him that growing Macedonian power would protect him.'

Callisthenes sighed. He paused for a moment before going on.

'Then our enemies in Athens threatened that their city would join the Persians and attack Macedon, so Philip had to withdraw his protection from Hermias. Aristotle and Pythias were desperate with worry about her father. Aristotle kept writing to Philip to plead for some help, but the King couldn't be persuaded to do anything that might provoke Athens and Persia. And we all knew he couldn't possibly fight such an alliance.'

There was a silence. I plucked up courage and stated the obvious conclusion as calmly as I could.

'So this dream of Philip's and Aristotle's of uniting Greek cities and taking on the Persians together has failed,' I commented. 'Destroying our cities, yours and mine, killing all those men and boys, was all in vain and led to the horrible death of Pythias's father.'

Callisthenes stopped. He turned towards me and his face was drawn, his eyes suddenly dull.

'There has been a big setback,' he said slowly, 'but Philip and Aristotle don't see it as the end of the dream.'

He began to walk on, but I couldn't stop myself.

'So there will be more pointless deaths and destruction,' I said loudly, swallowing hard.

He stood for a moment, his back to me, his face hidden, and I almost took back what I'd said, suddenly terrified that he approved of this mad idea, that he was another man who saw glory in the senseless violence. I desperately wanted to regain the precious exultation I felt with him, that tantalising excitement of desire suppressed. Yet how could I go on loving him if he shared the mad dream of the Macedonians, which brought nothing but slaughter and grief?

After what seemed like an infinitely long pause, Callisthenes turned and came back to me. He took my hands in his and looked straight into my eyes.

'Herpyllis,' he said in a gentle voice, 'it is all madness. We are living history. It's an endless cycle of killing and destroying, followed by triumph and rebuilding on one side – misery and suffering on the other. That's what we human animals do. I want to document it all in the hope that one day, perhaps, people will read what happened in the past, look around themselves and say *Why do we go on like this? What kind of life is this? Let's settle down as we are and live out our lives in simple contentment.* That's my dream, Herpyllis. I think it's yours, too.'

I stepped forward and he dropped my hands, putting his arms around me as I put mine around him.

'When I think back to my childhood in Olynthos,' he went on, caressing my hair with one hand, 'there's one thing I remember above everything else. Our dog. My father was given him as a puppy and we called him Kerberos as a joke. All he wanted to do was play and be stroked – he was the exact opposite of the fierce hound guarding Hades. He quickly grew into a big white furry creature, bounding around and chasing birds in the courtyard. My father despaired of him as a guard dog. When somebody came to the gate, he would jump up and lick their faces, waiting for them to play with him. He rarely barked at anything. He was my only real playmate. My father didn't let me out on the street with the other children. I spent most of my time with my tutor, who was a serious, dull man. Kerberos was my best friend. He loved me without question. Whenever he saw me, his tail wagged madly and his black eyes sparkled.

'I told you how my Uncle Nicanor came to fetch my mother and me,' Callisthenes went on. 'Aristotle had told him to get us out of Olynthos before Philip arrived to raze our city to the ground. Kerberos jumped into the wagon with us but Nicanor grabbed him by the scruff of his neck and threw him out again. *That's my dog*, I told him, *we can't leave him behind*. Nicanor didn't say anything. He just put the dog back in the courtyard and closed the gate. And that was the first time I heard him howl. He howled and howled. I could still hear him when we were already streets away from our house.

'And that's what I think of when I remember Olynthos. I don't grieve for our neighbours or friends, any of the children I barely knew. My heart aches only when I think of that big white dog, left alone in our courtyard. What happened to him? Did he starve to death? Did anyone take pity on him? Was he burnt alive when the soldiers set fire to the city? Did one of them run him through with a sword, just for a laugh? He was no more fitted for this world than you and me, Herpyllis. He only knew how to love.'

Callisthenes had stopped stroking my hair and was silent. I stepped back, reached up and turned his face towards me. He had a look of infinite sadness in his eyes. I gently pulled his head down and kissed his eyelids. No doubts were left. This was a man I could love without restraint of any kind. This was a man who shared my soul, who knew my heart, who sensed my every thought.

The weather had changed when we set off on our long journey back to Pella the next day. We awoke to steady rainfall, which continued throughout the day. The journey downhill was treacherous, the horses slipping and sliding in the mud, the wagons swaying wildly behind them. On a particularly tight bend one of the front wheels lurched off the road and landed in a hole with such a thump that it cracked and collapsed, the wagon crashing down on top of it. Pythias and I were thrown over violently, tearing through the cover, landing painfully on the stony ground and rolling downhill at terrifying speed. Fortunately, our fall was broken by a large rock; otherwise we would have been pitched headlong off the mountainside with a long drop onto the boulders of the foothills below.

We lay there bruised and panting with fright for a minute or so, before we saw the men slowly coming down to our aid. I saw the relief on their faces as I got to my feet and gave Pythias my hand to pull her up. But as she came towards me she cried out in pain and put her other hand to her stomach. A tremor of fear and panic passed through me and I went down on my knees beside her.

'What is it, Pythias?' I asked. 'Are you hurt?'

Her look was one of abject despair.

'Oh, Herpyllis,' she groaned. 'Oh no.'

And as she sank back a bright red stream ran from her into the puddle in front of the rock and a scarlet stain suddenly emerged in the lower part of her dress, quickly soaking through into the cloak she was wearing over it. A great shudder overtook my whole body as I realised what was going on. I took her in my arms and rocked her gently. Aristotle and Callisthenes came up to us in horror.

'Is she injured? Where? What can we do?' asked Callisthenes, looking hopelessly from Aristotle to me and back again.

Aristotle gave a great sigh and then told him to go back to the wagons and fetch as many clean cloths as he could find. Callisthenes climbed back up the steep slope. Aristotle bent down and kissed Pythias on the forehead, wiping her hair away from her face and stroking her cheek.

'There, there, my love. All will be well,' he said.

When Callisthenes brought the cloths, he was sent back to the wagons, and Aristotle gently wiped the blood from Pythias's thighs as I stood in front of them, blocking the view from the road. Occasionally I heard a moan or a sob. I'll never forget the great groan Pythias suddenly let out and the slithering sound I heard behind me. I turned round in panic. To my horror, I saw a tiny pink formless creature, streaked with blood, had emerged from between her legs. Aristotle was gently wiping it with a cloth soaked by the rain. When he had finished, he reverently wrapped it up. Pythias was lying with her eyes closed, her face pale and drawn. She looked much older than the day before. Aristotle pulled down her dress and covered her with the stained cloak.

'Herpyllis,' he said, 'come and sit with Pythias for a while.'

I quickly knelt down in the mud, cradling her head against my chest. She was hardly breathing and her eyes were still closed. Aristotle picked up the bundle he had made and carried it carefully into the undergrowth nearby. He began to dig a hole with a stick. The ground was muddy and the hole kept filling with water, but he went on pushing out the earth in a dull, mechanical way until it was big enough to receive its contents.

My guardian slowly got to his feet with the bundle in his hands. He raised it to the skies as carefully as if it were made of the thinnest, most fragile glass. Then I saw his lips move as he invoked some unseen power. I couldn't hear the words. I don't think he spoke them aloud. Then his lips stopped moving, but he still held the bundle high above his head for a minute longer. With the same slow, meticulous movement he lowered his arms. When he bent his knees to place the bundle in the shallow grave, he gave an involuntary grunt of pain and nearly dropped it as he collapsed onto the sodden ground. He leaned forward and it was a long time before he gently laid the helpless, lifeless little lump of flesh – his child – in the water-filled hole and covered it with the muddy soil.

After a while he got up with a painful jerk and then stood for some time staring away from the mountainside, the rain running down his face and dropping from his beard. When he walked back to us, he seemed to have shrunk in stature, hardly recognisable as the commanding priest whose voice had invoked the deity on the same mountainside only two days before. I helped him to pick Pythias up and struggle back to the road with her in his arms.

Our slaves and the driver had been busy righting the wagon and replacing the wheel. Aristotle laid Pythias inside and helped me up beside her. She was staring straight ahead, unblinking. I found some clean dry clothes and gently coaxed her into undressing and putting them on. I covered her with a blanket and changed my own muddy and sodden dress. Then I lay down beside her and stroked her hair. We made our way down the mountain with everyone else on foot, holding the horses' bridles and coaxing them at a snail's pace along the road and round the corners to reach the bottom as daylight was fading.

The rest of that journey is a blur of endless waking hours rocking from side to side in the wagon in silence and torpor. The nights were little better, as we yearned desperately for a sleep which came only briefly, and ended with nightmares which jolted us upright in the darkness.

I have often heard how one of the older generation in a family dies to be replaced soon afterwards by a new life, a gurgling babe to bring smiles again to the faces around the hearth. Hermias was gone, but so was the child which had hardly begun to stir in Pythias's womb, the child which would have brought her the joy she so mightily deserved. Had the evil spirit of Apollo, who had slaughtered the Son of our Mother, struck now at her Daughter, snatched away the prize she had been given? It was hard not to feel the male god had triumphed again.

13
PASSIONS

*'It is the nature of desire not to be satisfied, and
most men live only for the gratification of it.'*

In Pella the men were immediately called to the palace.
Callisthenes told me the reason when they returned in
the evening.

'Philip's declared war on Athens,' he said, a deep frown
between his eyebrows. I wanted to caress it away with
my hand, reach up and kiss his forehead, but Tycho was
busy in the courtyard nearby.

'They've formed a war council,' Callisthenes went on.
'Other Greek cities will join the Athenians – maybe all of
them. They can't wait to get rid of the Macedonians and
now's their chance. If they all stick together, they may
win. This is going to be the decisive battle of the King's
life. He'll either defeat the Greeks and bring them under
his leadership, or see the kingdom he's built crushed
by their united forces. The army's leaving the day after
tomorrow. My uncle's coming to say goodbye. It might
be the last time we see him.'

Sure enough, Nicanor appeared half an hour later. He
was the same height as Callisthenes and Aristotle – all tall
men. But he was bigger and more muscular than either
of them, his face and body permanently sun-tanned, his

brown hair speckled with grey at the temples. He emitted an intimidating sense of physical strength, but his hazel eyes were warm and kind like Callisthenes', without the piercing power of Aristotle's. There was a kind of shyness about Nicanor, too, which endeared him to me, and he seemed to be moved by music. He listened to Pythias and me playing with a frown on his face, as if he was completely taken up with it.

My feelings about the coming battle were mixed. I wanted Philip stopped – an end to the senseless bloodshed and suffering. But I also saw that the world men had created was never at peace, just as Callisthenes had said. Before Philip took Stagira, Athens had aspired to win the city. It was a constant cycle, only the roles of friend and foe changing over the generations. And if the Greek cities conquered Macedon, I might be taken as a slave to Athens. A woman was now a commodity exchanged among men with little say in the course of her life.

The next few weeks were tense as we waited for news. Then Callisthenes came back in the mid-afternoon, calling up to me in the women's quarters. Pythias was in the kitchen with the cook; I was alone. I ran down to join him in the courtyard. He looked at me with a sad smile.

'The King has won a great victory,' he said softly.

I turned away. Philip's 'victories' made me think of my parents lying lifeless beside me, a mound of men stoned to death, houses in flames, Melissa being raped...

'Now the Greek cities will have to join the Macedonians in an alliance against the Persians,' he continued.

'It's what Aristotle and Philip have been working towards all these years – a united Greek nation.'

I let out a bitter laugh. He sighed and took me in his arms.

'I know how you feel, Herpyllis,' he said gently. 'It's a terrible way of gaining unity. But we must both accept that this is the world we live in. It doesn't do to try to imagine another one where there are none of these crazy ideas which lead men on to war after war, an endless cycle of slaughter and destruction.'

Callisthenes was right about the world we lived in now, the one which had replaced the society my father held dear, where the good of the community was the most important goal of the city magistrates. I felt for his hand. He took mine and raised it briefly to his lips.

'We are all victims of history,' he said, still holding my hand in both of his. 'Sooner or later something happens in everyone's life which they can't control. That's why I want to write histories. I want to be close to those who make history, who in the end control our lives. Then I feel I have more control myself. And what I write is what people as yet unborn will learn. In that way I can control history, if not the events themselves. I can choose what I tell and what I leave unsaid. I can define how people see the past and how it was made.'

It still brings a lump to my throat remembering those words of his today. Little did either of us think at the time that Callisthenes' burning desire to write history and to seek to control it would come to be so decisive in his life.

Philip's triumphant return to Pella was followed by great festivities: another hundred oxen sacrificed at Dion, more games and races to celebrate the deaths of thousands of our countrymen. Alexander was once more at the King's side for the ceremony in the sanctuary of Zeus.

I thought back to the last time we had been together in that same place below Olympus eleven years earlier: he a playful, loving boy, seeking me out whenever he could, his favourite companion. Then I remembered the face I had glimpsed as he watched that first sacrifice, the wild dance he had performed later on the mountain slopes, his merciless grip as he forced himself into me. They all foreshadowed what he had now become. There was a hardness about him, a slight curl of the lip. He was what the King had wanted him to be: a cold warrior, a consummate butcher. My heart ached for the old Alexander. When I caught his eye, he looked through me as if he didn't know me – a knife in the stomach.

Soon afterwards, when we were back in Pella, Pythias and I went to the palace to visit the Queen as we so often did. Charis met us at the door and said it would be better to stay away that day. As she was speaking, we heard a crash and a scream from inside.

'What's happening?' I asked, afraid for my friends.

'Oh, Herpyllis,' Charis whispered, taking me aside. 'The King's taking a new wife. It's not good news. A Macedonian.'

Then she excused herself and went back to the Queen while we left quietly. We found out more from Aristotle. Philip was to marry yet another girl called Cleopatra, niece of his close companion and general Attalus. She was just sixteen and had not been seen at court; Philip had met her on Attalus's estates on the coast.

At the wedding feast a few days later, Aristotle sat close to the bridegroom as the King's old friend and adviser. Pythias and I were with the ladies, all Macedonians; none of Philip's other wives were invited. We only knew Berenice, but she was sitting at the other end of the table. We were not included in the conversation.

Alexander was seated near Aristotle, Callisthenes on one side of him and a young man I didn't know on the other. But I had heard of him. The replacement Alexander had found for me in Mieza: Hephaestion, his best friend, his love, Patroclus to his Achilles. Hephaestion's fine features were framed by his dark wavy hair and his pale blue eyes were striking, the colour of forget-me-nots growing by a woodland stream. I felt a kinship with him rather than jealousy. Now I had my own love.

The bride was a pretty girl, small and delicate. She looked terrified sitting between her husband and her uncle, both middle-aged and battle-scarred. Attalus had no doubt dangled his poor niece in front of the King to further his ambitions; the ploy had worked. Philip's passion for both young boys and girls was well known. I remembered his evil eye leering at me a few summers earlier and reflected how lucky it was I had been removed from the court before it alighted on me again. There had been several times I had only just managed to hide when he appeared unexpectedly in the ladies' apartments. My heart beat in sympathy with the trembling bride, shuddering at the thought of being at the mercy of the Cyclops.

The drinking and dancing were reaching a climax when Philip got to his feet and boomed:

'Silence!' The room went quiet immediately.

'Today is a happy day for me, my friends!' he said, swaying slightly as he held his cup in one hand. 'My new queen is from an ancient noble family of Macedon,' he continued, 'like my mother. And today I give her a new name in honour of that great lady who bore me. From henceforth Cleopatra shall be known as Eurydice!'

He raised his glass and shouted *Eurydice!* and all the men rose, echoing the toast and draining their glasses – all except Alexander and Hephaestion beside him. I could see the prince's scowl and his flushed face quite clearly, but he was sitting out of Philip's sight line, so his hostility had not been noticed. As the others sat down again, Attalus stood and hushed the guests again.

'We thank you, Lord, for the supreme honour you do our family. Long may you live and long may we serve such a great and generous king!'

There was cheering and shouting, but Attalus had not finished.

'I raise my cup now, I again invoke the gods to look favourably on this marriage. May they bless this royal couple. May this bride of pure Macedonian blood bear the King a fine son, a lawful heir to the throne of Macedon!'

But before the men could take up the toast, there was a loud thump as Alexander sprang to his feet, knocking over his stool. His face was the image of Olympias, the foreign Queen, erupting with fury.

'Does that mean I'm a bastard?' he stormed in a threatening voice.

Attalus was struck dumb but Philip was now on his feet, unsheathing his sword.

'Why, you little...' he blustered, waving his weapon and staggering towards Alexander. We all gasped in horror but nobody dared move. The King took one more step, lost his balance and landed sprawling on the floor. The ensuing silence was broken by Alexander's mocking laughter and his loud comment:

'Look at this man who wants to cross from Europe into Asia – he can't even cross from one seat to another!'

Out of the corner of my eye I saw a movement near the King and, before anyone else could say or do anything, Aristotle appeared at Alexander's side. He nodded to Callisthenes, and they each took one of the prince's arms and hustled him out of the room, helped by Hephaestion. Alexander was caught off guard and put up little resistance. Philip was now struggling to his feet, shouting and swearing.

'I'll kill him!' he kept repeating.

The room was in uproar and Pythias and I took the opportunity of escaping to the Queen's quarters. That was where we found Alexander, still with Aristotle and Callisthenes. He was furiously recounting Attalus's speech to his mother, who was pacing up and down as he talked, her face a study for a statue of Hera, Queen of the Heavens, about to inflict some terrible punishment on mankind.

Had the situation not been so grave it would have struck me as comic that she was repeating *I'll kill her!* over and over again, a slightly altered echo of her husband's fulminations in the courtyard nearby. It was then that Aristotle intervened.

'Alexander, Lady,' he said urgently. 'You must waste no time. I know Philip in his rages. He may do something he'll regret for the rest of his life. You've humiliated him, Alexander. He can't let that pass.'

Alexander was bristling.

'What about me?' he fumed. 'Do you think *I* can let it pass? Did you hear how Attalus insulted me? How could my father allow that? I want him executed!'

'Of course, it was wrong of him,' Aristotle conceded quickly. 'He should never have said what he did. Unforgivable. But your father isn't himself. He could order *your* death at the moment. And your mother's. You must leave court. Now. Immediately. Go to your uncle. We'll make your father see sense, but he's like a raging bull. He could charge and finish you in that state. You must get away. *Now!*'

Aristotle had spoken in a commanding way. He took Alexander by the arm again and barked at the Queen:

'Come, Lady! Your women will gather your things together and follow. Callisthenes, go to the stables and meet us by the gate.'

At that Callisthenes sprinted out. Charis beckoned to the others and they hurried into the Queen's apartment. Pythias and I were left alone and I looked at her for the first time. She was pale and trembling. I put my arm around her and steered her outside, down the steps to safety at home.

'Oh, Herpyllis,' she kept saying. 'What if the King... ?'

She didn't finish her sentence, but I knew she was afraid that Philip might turn against Aristotle for helping Alexander and Olympias escape his wrath. I also knew Aristotle would not thank me for leaving his wife in the King's path if he set out to find them. It seemed hours before the men came back, looking worn and anxious.

'Did they get away?' I asked at once.

'Yes, yes,' replied Aristotle. 'I'm sure they'll be back soon enough when the King calms down. It's just best to keep them out of his way for the present.'

'Have all the ladies joined them?' I asked, thinking of Charis. Aristotle nodded.

'Thessalonica's gone, too,' he said. 'She wouldn't leave the Queen.'

'And what about Cleopatra?' I asked, in a sudden panic about my little sister. 'She must be with them?'

'No,' said Callisthenes, with a quick look at Aristotle. 'Her mother decided she should stay. She could be useful as a go-between with her father. But for the moment she's going to keep out of his way.'

'I must go to her,' I said, going to get my cloak.

They all looked at me in surprise.

'She's still just a girl – she'll be frightened,' I continued.

Aristotle looked as if he was about to forbid me to go, but something stopped him. I think it was the look on my face. I was so sure what I had to do.

'I'll go with her,' said Callisthenes. 'There's pandemonium at the palace. It could be dangerous.'

Aristotle hesitated again, but then he nodded. He told Callisthenes to bring me straight back if there was any disturbance in the women's apartments, or threats of violence. We hurried up the slope to the palace and, indeed, there were flaming torches everywhere and people rushing about in the darkness. My heart started beating fast and a sense of foreboding overtook me; I started running towards the main portico to reach Cleopatra as quickly as I could. Callisthenes grabbed my arm.

'Herpyllis,' he said. 'Don't draw attention to yourself. There're guards everywhere. Be careful. Let's go in the side entrance.'

We made a long circle round to the side of the palace, creeping along in the darkness. There were no guards on the door to the servants' quarters, so we darted in that way and made our way to Olympias's rooms. They were deserted.

'Where can she be?' I whispered, the panic rising.

Callisthenes steered me back the way we had come. Something told me to go to the old room I had shared with Charis and Xanthe. I ran upstairs leaving him on guard. The room was dark and empty. I whispered:

'Charis. Are you here? It's me, Herpyllis.'

There was a slight movement behind the screen.

'Herpyllis, is it you?' said a small voice, and Cleopatra emerged, throwing herself into my arms. She was trembling.

'I'm so afraid,' she said. 'Alexander said the King might...'

'Sssh,' I said. 'It's all right. Come with me.'

I led her quietly down the stairs and found Callisthenes, who looked relieved to see us.

'I think we should take her away from here tonight. Until things have calmed down,' I said.

'You mean, take her home?' he asked.

'Yes,' I replied. 'Nobody will look for her there... if indeed they're looking for her at all,' I added, to reassure the poor girl.

'I don't know if Aristotle...' Callisthenes began, but I interrupted him.

'On my head be it,' I said and set off quickly the way we had come before he had a chance to stop me.

When Aristotle saw the princess his first question was whether anyone had seen us. We assured him we had not been observed. I could see him quickly weighing up the options, always the politician. I don't know what swayed the decision in our favour.

'Sit down, my lady,' he said to Cleopatra, and told Pythias to fetch a cloak for her. He had sent all the servants and slaves to bed. The girl was shaking so much that her teeth were chattering. We sat down together, my arm still round her.

'Your father's a good man,' Aristotle went on. 'He just says and does things sometimes on the spur of the moment which he heartily regrets later. You'll be our guest tonight. Tomorrow we'll see what's best to be done. But I think now we all need a good night's sleep. Would you like something to eat or drink first?'

Pythias had put a cloak round Cleopatra's shoulders and her trembling was less pronounced now. She even managed to straighten up.

'No, thank you,' she said. And then, as if surprised to hear her own voice come out without shaking, she added calmly: 'I'm grateful for your hospitality.'

Aristotle and Pythias conferred briefly and then asked the princess if she would like to share my room. She shyly nodded her head. So it was that Cleopatra stayed with me in Aristotle's house for a few days after that dreadful night. Her maids came out of hiding, and Audata and Cynane were kind, promising to take care of her while her mother was away. Pythias and I spent even more time at court, playing and singing to keep Cleopatra's spirits up.

We were never able to establish whether the King had actually ordered his daughter's arrest after he discovered Olympias and Alexander had fled. I doubt that he would have put her to death, but at least we had spared her anguish alone in the hours and days of uncertainty that followed.

It turned out that Cleopatra's mother and brother had arrived at Olympias's brother's court in Epirus, but that Alexander had stayed only a week. He had gone on with his companions to Illyria to receive hospitality from the King he had only recently defeated in battle. Men are strange creatures; it appears the respect they gain from fighting bravely and winning can overcome thoughts of revenge in those they subdue. No doubt Alexander promised his hosts some future territorial advantage if they supported him against his father, although few men would have thought it wise to oppose Philip at that time. Whatever their reasons, the Illyrians didn't send Alexander's head in a sack to Pella.

Not long afterwards Callisthenes sought me out and we went to sit under the apple tree in the courtyard as the last rays of the evening sun lit its branches.

'Aristotle's sending me secretly to the Illyrian court,' he whispered, that frown on his forehead again. My heart beat faster at this news and I was gripped with fear.

'Why?' I asked. 'Why should you go there? It's dangerous.'

Callisthenes looked down and took my hand.

'Aristotle says Alexander likes and respects me,' he said, almost to himself, 'and I can work with Ptolemy to persuade him to write to the King and find a way of being invited back to court.'

'Who's Ptolemy?' I asked.

'Don't you know?' Callisthenes sounded surprised. 'They call him Philip's bastard.'

'Oh,' I replied, 'is that his name? Olympias has only ever called him The Bastard in my hearing. I never knew what his name was.'

'Well, Ptolemy and I are good friends,' he explained, 'and Alexander admires him. He's proved his worth on the battlefield many a time. Aristotle thinks he and I can have a good influence on Alexander and bring about a reconciliation with the King.'

Callisthenes took my face in his hands and looked at me with such intensity I wanted to cry out. But the gate opened and he jumped up and disappeared into the men's quarters.

We said goodbye the next day and Pythias looked as worried as I was at seeing him go. A letter came within a week, though, and Aristotle read us most of what his great-nephew wrote over the following months.

Presumably because Callisthenes had grown up among philosophers, he lacked the usual male posturing I had seen in Pella. It was Pythias's father Hermias who had named him for the beautiful physical strength he had attained in the gymnasium in Atarneus. But he spent little time now on physical activity, and disliked hunting and riding. His military training had been minimal and he gave us amusing accounts of how terrifying the warlike women of Illyria were with their scanty clothing and bows and arrows, let alone the savage-looking tattooed men who had escorted him to the court.

Callisthenes had a natural authority which made it unnecessary for him to prove his worth in fighting, and this quality was accompanied by a facility for saying exactly the right thing with an eloquence which convinced men it was what they themselves had thought all along and wanted to hear. I had already experienced that for myself many a time. Men quickly grew to love and respect him. Alexander had been as glad to see him as Ptolemy was, and he had been a welcome reinforcement to those around the prince who were earnest and serious-minded. Other friends of Philip's also interceded, and eventually, after several months had elapsed, Alexander was invited back without either him or his father losing face, an important point for them both. Olympias remained in Epirus, however, trying to incite her brother, King Alexander, to attack Macedon.

Callisthenes' return was greeted with great joy in our house. The very next day he managed to find a few moments alone with me.

'Herpyllis,' he said, 'these months away from you have convinced me I don't want us to be parted again. Indeed, I want us to be as close as a man and a woman can be. I want to marry you.'

I need hardly say my heart leapt. I was truly loved – and by the man I loved myself! What greater fulfilment could there be in life? My soul soared as I told him I had no greater desire than to be his wife. We embraced and then he kissed me, several times. Different kisses from those gentle, tender ones the Queen gave me, but different again from those hard lips of Alexander's pressed down on mine. They excited me and made me want him to go on, kiss me on my neck, my shoulders... When we finally parted, he said he would speak to Aristotle the following day.

I kept waking that night, each time thinking I could see the beginnings of the dawn, only to realise it was as dark as before. In the end, the sun was above the treetops when I awoke and jumped out of bed. I went to Pythias to tell her my wonderful news. She clapped her hands together with pleasure. It was the first time I had seen her smile since that terrible day in the rain and mud below Delphi. We kept going to the gate to see if the men were coming back from the palace, looking forward to planning the wedding together.

But the sun had set when they came and I could immediately see from Callisthenes' face that all was not well. Aristotle told us to sit down.

'Callisthenes has told me he's asked you to marry him, Herpyllis, and that you have consented. He should have spoken to me before he spoke to you. You must both see it's impossible. Callisthenes is only twenty-three, much too young to marry. He still has so much to learn. He can't possibly think of having his own household and teaching his own children. The best age for a man to marry is around forty, when he knows the ways of the world and has formed his own views on all aspects of life.'

He paused, but he had not finished. He fixed his cold stare on me and asked:

'How old are you now, Herpyllis?'

I didn't answer. I couldn't really take in what he was saying. I felt as if I'd fallen down and hit my head. Aristotle repeated his question impatiently.

'Nineteen,' I finally managed to whisper.

'Well, it's high time you were married then,' Aristotle went on. 'I would have seen to it long ago if I hadn't been so busy with other things. I've been remiss on that score. But I've had a fine man in mind for you for some time and we'll see to it very soon. I know you two young people are fond of each other. I'd thought it was in the manner of brother and sister. Had I realised the truth, I would have parted you sooner. Now this forces my hand.'

He turned to look at his great-nephew. Callisthenes was pale and he was looking at the ground.

'I've been thinking that you need to be properly apprenticed to a historian, Callisthenes, since that's the way your aspirations lean. You're like a son to me, lad, and I'm loath to see you go, but you need to develop your writing with an expert in these matters.

'I blame myself for allowing this to happen, but I'm sure your feelings will soon fade. You're both young and such affections pass quickly. You mustn't let your hearts rule your heads. It will be best for both of you to be parted now. Come, Callisthenes,' he said, and they went to have their dinner with Theophrastus, apart from us as usual.

I was dimly aware of Pythias taking my arm and leading me away. She sat me down in her apartment. I couldn't make a sound. It was the tightly-fitting cage again. Inside was a tumult of emotion but no way of expressing it. I could only stare ahead of me while Pythias became more and more distressed.

The thwarting of love, it turned out, caused as strong a physical reaction as grief. We think of love for a parent as being completely different from that for a lover, but the despair I felt at losing Callisthenes was of the same intensity as that of losing my mother and father. I was in a nightmare world where there could be no thought of a future, only a gaping wound in the soul which would never heal, and which made my life feel pointless.

14
BECOMING BRAVE

'We become brave by doing brave acts.'

I don't know how long I spent in that hopeless state but it must have been several weeks. I have tried to forget it and think of happier times. And friendship is a tie that binds as close as the other forms of love: Pythias didn't leave my side. We had both learned a great deal from Olympias about the care of the sick of soul as well as of body, and she quickly went about preparing tea from valerian and rubbing oil of spikenard into my wrists and temples. Gradually she brought me out of the cage, out of the abyss.

Aristotle was as good as his word; he parted Callisthenes and me as soon as he could. Callisthenes went to live with Theopompus, a renowned historian who was writing a history of Philip's reign and so spent much of his time at court in Pella. We never saw him. Life took on a kind of grey dullness and the days, weeks and months dragged by.

It must have been about three months after Callisthenes had left that Pythias sat down with me, a frown on her face and a sad look in her eyes.

'Aristotle's asked me to talk to you, Herpyllis. I told him it's too early, but he insists. You remember he said he had a fine man in mind for you to marry.'

She paused, searching my face. I expect she was afraid I might go into that cage again.

'It's all right, Pythias,' I said. 'I'm resigned to my fate now. You can tell me.'

She looked relieved.

'Well, you may have guessed who he meant... It's Theophrastus.'

Pythias was right. I should have guessed. Probably because I had so excluded Aristotle's assistant as a husband in my own mind, it came as a shock. I took a deep breath and got up so she wouldn't see my expression.

'Aaah,' I managed to say, 'Theophrastus.'

'He is a fine man, Herpyllis. A good man. Like Aristotle. I'm sure you would come to love him. He loves you.'

'Loves me?' I sneered, unintentionally, 'I don't think he's ever looked at me properly.'

'No, you're wrong there, my dear. I've seen his looks. He admires you very much.'

'I'm sorry, Pythias,' I replied. 'I know you've been given a hard task to persuade me. But I just... The man... I couldn't bear the thought of...'

'Oh, Herpyllis, it takes time. At first I... Aristotle wasn't a young girl's dream, but I've come to love him very much. It'd be the same for you with Theophrastus.'

I turned on her with a venom I must, on reflection, have learnt from Olympias.

'No,' I spat out, 'I can't stand the man. He disgusts me. I'm sorry, but there it is.'

Pythias stared at me open-mouthed. I had never before spoken like that, and it surprised us both. But I was a woman in love, brought up in the Goddess's ways, an Amazon who would choose her own man like Cynane, or have none at all. For most of the world this was now a thing of the past. Men laid down the law and women had to submit to their will. Almost all the women I knew since leaving Stagira as a child had come to terms with this reality and made the best of it, leading a secret, parallel life to that of good wife. Pythias clearly thought I should do the same. Perhaps if I had been offered any other man I would have accepted that fate, but I felt such a physical antipathy to Theophrastus that the idea of spending my life at his side was tantamount to being condemned to daily torture.

Pythias finally found her voice again.

'Please, my dear, take some time to consider. Aristotle is your guardian. He might...'

She didn't have to finish the sentence. He might indeed. I would have to leave his house penniless and in disgrace. But rather that than share the bed of a man I could not even respect, let alone love. I had gained tremendous strength from somewhere. In this situation, at least, I wasn't a coward.

'I'll talk to him, Pythias,' I said. 'I'll tell him you did your best to persuade me. I'll explain the fault is mine. He's not a vindictive man. He won't separate us.'

I tried to sound more confident than I was. I hardly knew my guardian. I had been touched by his kindness in taking me on as his ward, and yet the way he had parted Callisthenes and me had been cold and callous. He saw our love for each other simply as an irritant in his plans for me to marry Theophrastus. The happiness of his wards was not considered.

That evening I knocked on the door of his study in great trepidation. I was determined to refuse Aristotle's choice for me, but couldn't begin to imagine what I would do if I was thrown out of my guardian's house, if I had to leave Pythias, the only friend I had now. My guardian didn't disguise his irritation at seeing me.

'Well?' he said impatiently.

My heart started racing and my palms sweating. I almost turned round and left. But then I thought of Theophrastus, imagined him touching me. I shuddered and summoned up the courage I knew was there, somewhere inside, the right I had as a Daughter of the Earth to decide my fate for myself. I had planned what I was going to say. Now I had to take to the stage, convince my audience, sway their feelings. But I knew the audience I had was the least open to persuasion I could possibly have had. I was to address the master of rhetoric and logic himself, who could dissect and destroy any argument in seconds. What hope did I have? Only that he was capable of pity, that somehow I might touch his feelings.

'Pythias has told me of your wish that I marry Theophrastus,' I began, my voice audibly quavering on the name. I took a deep breath. 'As your ward, I have obeyed you in everything, sir,' I continued, 'and I believe you have had no cause to be dissatisfied with me. But, in this one matter, I cannot comply with your wishes. The union between a man and a woman depends on respect and affection between the two. These are feelings I can never have for Theophrastus. Forgive me.'

I can only describe Aristotle's initial response as a bark. He looked at me indignantly, then got up and walked around the room. He stopped in front of me and stuck his face out at me aggressively.

'What can you possibly have against him?' he blustered. 'One of the finest men I know. I'm sure he would have been your father's choice as well. Would you defy your father?' he challenged.

'My father would have consulted me before there was any talk of marriage,' I retorted. 'He would never have made me marry a man I found repugnant.'

'Repugnant?' Aristotle pounced on the word. 'Theo-phrastus can hardly be described as re-*pug*-nant!' he said, emphasising the word sarcastically. 'I suppose you still fancy yourself in love with Callisthenes,' he pursued. 'Marriage isn't about love, Herpyllis. It's about a woman gratefully serving a man's needs, a man who magnani-mously shares his wealth and status with her, who gives her a place in society and a purpose in life. Theophrastus is a well-respected man of substance who will provide well for you. You can't reasonably object. In time you will realise how fortunate you are in having such a husband.'

'I regret I can't share your view, sir,' I said. My panic had been overcome. I didn't care what happened to me any more. I knew he could not force me into the marriage bed and I considered any fate better than that. I looked Aristotle straight in the eye.

'In this alone I cannot obey you, sir,' I said in a level voice. 'Ask anything else of me, but not this.'

'You're my ward, Herpyllis,' he retorted severely. 'You can't pick and choose in your obedience. As your guardian, I have your best interests at heart. It's enough that I wish you to marry Theophrastus. If you defy me, I'll be wholly justified in turning you out on the street. You wouldn't wish to be disgraced and lose Pythias's friendship, would you? Nobody else would take you in. Where would you go? What would you do?'

'I came to your house as Pythias's companion,' I reminded my guardian. 'She has been more than kind to me and treated me as a sister. I have loved her in return and carried out her household duties when she could not, when she was grieving for her father and... when we came back from Delphi. I cannot imagine life without her. But I don't think she could do without me, either.'

I was still looking straight at Aristotle. I wanted to make him aware that the happy life of his household would change irrevocably if Pythias had no friend beside her to pass the days. He depended on her running the house perfectly for him and knew that I had been indispensable in maintaining that smooth operation in the bad times. I could see him weighing up the pros and cons of punishing me for my defiance.

'I want you to go away and reflect on your duty, Herpyllis,' he said after a long pause, turning away from me. 'I'll give you two days to come to your senses and tell me you will obey me. That will be all.'

I left the study. I hardly slept for the next two days and every waking hour was filled with anxiety. I kept looking at Pythias and wondering how I could live without her. But I forced myself to put those thoughts out of my mind and concentrate on the impossibility of intimacy with Theophrastus: my mind and body recoiled at the very idea and I felt physically sick. I couldn't marry him, even for Pythias's sake. On the third day Aristotle called me into his study.

'Well?' he began in an echo of our first interview, the same look of irritation on his face.

I wasn't nervous or intimidated this time. I knew I could make no other choice, whatever the consequences.

'Do as you wish with me, sir,' I said. 'I cannot marry Theophrastus.'

He sighed with exasperation. There was a long pause while I awaited my sentence. Finally he looked down at his desk and said quietly:

'I'm extremely displeased with you, Herpyllis. Get out of my sight!'

I quickly retreated, closing the door behind me. I was trembling. Pythias was waiting nearby. She flung her arms round me and stroked my hair.

'If he says you have to leave, I'll tell him I'm leaving, too,' she whispered in my ear.

I was touched and hugged her hard. I had come to see that the relationship between Aristotle and Pythias was quite different from how my parents had behaved towards each other. Mother and Father had been like friends and partners, sharing their thoughts and feelings, discussing everything together, giving each other advice, laughing and singing after dinner. When I was little and had been put to bed, I remembered lying there on light summer evenings, happily listening to their voices until I fell asleep.

But Aristotle rarely talked for long with Pythias and seldom smiled at her. I always knew when he was displeased with her for some reason; she would keep knitting her brow and biting her lip afterwards, anxious and worried. Often she would then find fault with me, where there had been none before. Once she actually ripped my sewing apart, telling me it was hopeless. I had to start again. Even though I didn't manage to achieve any better stitches the second time, the finished garment was then approved without comment.

Yet now Pythias was ready to throw in her lot with me and take my part against her husband. We spent the following days in trepidation, afraid Aristotle might order me out of the house at any moment, but, as time went by without retribution for my defiance, Pythias and I settled back into our routines, running the household, doing the accounts, visiting friends, playing music together, sewing and weaving. I began to hope Aristotle's punishment would consist of never offering me another husband. Life as an old maid wouldn't be so bad – certainly infinitely preferable to being wife to a man I strongly disliked.

A few months later Theophrastus invited us all to his wedding. He married the daughter of a wealthy merchant. She was just fifteen. We performed the Second Blood ceremony in the woods the evening after her wedding night. Pythias and I prepared the mead, which we boiled with rosehips to make it red. Both of us drank a great deal of it. In my case it was because I felt sorry for the bride, and wanted to rid myself of the notion that she was a kind of sacrifice to the Great Goddess, offered in my stead. I did my best to raise her spirits by clowning around with a carrot between my legs.

She died a few months later of an unspecified illness. She seemed to shrink and fade into nothingness. Theophrastus didn't marry again.

15
POLITICS

'Man perfected by society is the best of all animals;
he is the most terrible of all when he lives without
law, and without justice.'

A few weeks later we were invited to another wedding, a
far grander affair. Philip had decided to marry his daughter Cleopatra to her uncle, Olympias's brother Alexander,
whose first letter to his sister had led to me teaching the
Queen to read. I dreaded to think what Olympias would
make of this match between her daughter and her brother.
She was still at her brother's court in Epirus, trying to
persuade him to attack Macedon on her behalf. No doubt
Philip thought the wedding would remove the threat of
rebellion on his borders once and for all.

Cleopatra was eighteen now and confided her mixed
feelings to me about the marriage. She liked her uncle,
but she dreaded seeing her mother again and going to a
land she had been told was wild and uncivilised. Rightly
or wrongly, the princess had never forgiven Olympias
for abandoning her in Pella; she believed her brother's
warning that her father would have her killed now he
had a new Macedonian wife. I had first-hand knowledge
of her terror at that time. But since Olympias had left

court, Cleopatra had developed a new self-assurance and become close to her father the King.

'Father's been to Delphi,' she told me excitedly. 'He asked the oracle about invading Persia. You know that's what he's been planning for years. Now he has an alliance with all the Greek city states, there's nothing stopping him. But, of course, he wants to be sure he'll be successful, so he went to Delphi. You know Apollo's oracle is always right.'

'What did the oracle tell him?' I asked, expecting it to be favourable, considering Philip's power and wealth.

Cleopatra looked triumphant.

'The priestess said: *The bull is garlanded for sacrifice. All is ready and the sacrificer is at hand.* The bull's the King of Persia, Herpyllis, and Father's the sacrificer, so he's going to invade Persia as soon as I'm married.'

I was given the honour of participating in the wedding ceremonies as one of the bride's companions; there would also be the secret rites to perform after the wedding night. We guests all had to hire wagons as the event was to take place in the ancient Macedonian capital of Aegae, a two-day ride to the south.

It was only when we arrived there that I realised quite how lavish an event Philip had planned. He clearly wanted to display his wealth and the magnificence of his kingdom to all and sundry. There were dignitaries from all the Greek city states, as well as from distant Scythia, neighbouring Paeonia and Thrace, not to mention the bridegroom's large delegation from Epirus, all the Macedonian nobles and Philip's numerous friends, including

Aristotle. But Olympias was not invited to her daughter's wedding.

As the day dawned we gave the princess the ritual bath and decked her out in the fine embroidered clothes she and her ladies had sewn. We put on the heavy gold jewellery she was to wear and covered her with the red veil. Then we led her down to the banqueting hall. The King took her hand and gave her to his brother-in-law, saying the customary words of betrothal in his booming voice. The banquet began and there was much singing and dancing.

Cleopatra and Cynane had become close since Olympias had left court. My Amazon hunting companion was now a wife and mother and behaved in a protective and loving way to Cleopatra. At one point during the banquet Cynane walked over and whispered something in King Alexander's ear, making him turn to look at her in horror.

'What do you think Cynane said?' I asked Cleopatra.

'Probably that she'll come after him with her bow and arrows if he treats me badly,' she replied, smiling. 'Don't forget how she led an army against the Illyrians that time they rebelled while Father was away in the south. I'm sure my husband will remember how she killed their Queen and came back triumphant.'

Cynane was still renowned far and wide as a warrior, and most people found it hard to believe she loved and respected her husband Amyntas. He remained a quiet, gentle man in the background. I think he was glad not to be king and didn't want anyone to remember that he had once been monarch when he was a small boy, with

Uncle Philip as regent. His hereditary right was of course stronger than Philip's: he was the son of the previous king, Philip only the brother. But it seemed the King recognised Amyntas was no threat and left him to live happily with Cynane and four-year-old Adea. I saw father and daughter that day in the courtyard playing together, he carrying her around on his neck and neighing like a horse while she shrieked with delight. Amyntas seemed to prefer this simple activity to the feasting and drinking going on in the hall.

I knew it was inevitable that I would see Callisthenes somewhere in Aegae. I couldn't help feeling huge excitement at the thought, accompanied by an equal dread. What if he looked at me with complete indifference? On my way back inside I glimpsed him sitting with some of Alexander's companions, but he wasn't looking in my direction and didn't see me.

The next day I was at Cleopatra's side again. When we arrived to dress her for the first day of the games after her wedding night, she gave me a little smile and embraced me, but said not a word. That night we would dance in the woods to celebrate her Second Blood and drink the red mead. She would be at the centre of our ceremonies and we women would be exultant, forgetting for a few hours the male world we lived in.

My parents had brought me up as equal to my brothers and I had gone on fancying myself the Amazon with Olympias and Cynane, regardless of the fact that I had daily proof of the rule of men at the court. Our life worshipping the Goddess was more real to me than the intrusions of men into our lives. But Alexander's brutal victory over me and Aristotle's view of me as someone who must be prepared for the role of grateful wife to the man he chose had had their effect on me. I was beginning to see my life was to be a lesson in humility, from childish centre of the universe to insignificant being in the background, someone whose death would be an inconvenience rather than an event to mourn.

I tried to think of something else as I followed Cleopatra in the procession into the theatre from the palace. Alexander and his companions followed our wedding party. I saw Hephaestion next to him, more than a head taller than the prince, still the favourite. We all took our places in the front two rows, the King's marble throne and surrounding seats empty in the centre. Then Philip's advisers and captains entered and took their places beside the throne. Antipater was chief among them and I smiled ruefully when I remembered Olympias's words to me about my good fortune in being found by this man in Stagira. I could finally accept that she was right. Whatever he was like in that world of the court where he had risen to be the King's closest adviser, he always had a smile for me and some kind words.

It was clear that Philip was going to appear last, to great acclaim from the crowd, many of whom had been seated since before dawn. A hush had fallen in expectation of his arrival. Suddenly there was the raw sound of horns coming from the right entrance. A new procession started: statue after statue of the Olympian gods was carried in, each garlanded with gold. They were paraded around the stage and placed at intervals on the perimeter. But then the statue of a thirteenth god appeared with an even louder fanfare – who was this supposed to be? I quickly searched my knowledge of Macedonian religion, failing to find an answer. It was given by the whispers all around me – *The King!* Philip had made himself a god? So all the pomp and circumstance had been in aid of this: the celebration of a new living god among us! There really were no limits to the man's conceit.

And suddenly there he was, Philip the god himself, limping into the theatre alone, a dazzling white mantle over his tunic, pinned at the shoulder with a great gold brooch, a magnificent gold wreath on his head. He raised his arms to elicit a colossal roar from his assembled subjects. But just as he turned to face the other side of the theatre, a bodyguard standing to his right darted forward, pulled out a dagger and stabbed the King in the chest.

Philip had scarcely hit the ground before the assassin sped out of the theatre. There was uproar. Some of the men on the front row dashed across the orchestra and sprinted after him, while others surrounded the King. Cleopatra was beside herself, sitting with her head in her hands and moaning. King Alexander was clearly in two minds whether he should stay and comfort her or join the other men around Philip. Finally he ordered us to take his bride back to the palace and ran across to where Philip lay. I caught a glimpse of another red-gold head beside the King. Alexander was there, too. Was Philip dead?

But there was no time to sit and ponder. I helped the other ladies lift Cleopatra from her seat and guide her along the row and out the other side, avoiding the place where her father had collapsed. And looking back, I saw them raise him onto their shoulders and march slowly out, son and new son-in-law at the front. At that moment Callisthenes appeared at my side, Aristotle and Pythias behind him, and some of the men of Epirus surrounded us, guarding their new Queen. As we hurried along, we passed a knot of women beside the outer wall of the theatre. The sound of sobbing came from among them. I watched Callisthenes go over to them and saw them shrink from him in terror.

'It's all right,' he said, 'I'm not going to hurt you. Come with us. We'll take care of you.'

And then they parted. Eurydice was the one sobbing. Philip's queen looked even younger than her seventeen years, her face red and swollen with weeping, her nose running. She had given birth to a daughter a year earlier and then to a son only the previous week, the true Macedonian heir desired by her Uncle Attalus. But he was far away with the army in Asia Minor. Who would protect her now if Philip was gone? We hustled her and her ladies into our midst and headed for the palace. The men delivered us to the royal apartments and made sure guards were posted at the entrance; then they left us to go to the King. Pythias and I did our best to calm the two queens left in our charge.

It must have been a few hours later when little Adea, Cynane and Amyntas's daughter, wandered in, looking lost and bewildered. She took my hand and pulled me up, clearly wanting me to follow her. We went out across the courtyard and she led me through a side gate into a secret garden. It was still and fragrant in the afternoon sun, narrow paths running in different directions among the trees and bushes. She hesitated and then took me down the left-hand path. It opened up into a grassy area with statues of nymphs on either side. She pointed.

And there lying on his back, his hand on his chest as if taking a short nap, was her father, Amyntas. He looked so peaceful I put my finger up to my mouth in case Adea was going to say something, but she pulled on my hand and pointed again. Finally she said in a frightened little voice:

'Daddy won't wake up. Wake him up.'

'Well, he must be tired. Let's leave him to sleep,' I replied, trying to lead her back to the path.

'No,' she said, cross now, pulling her hand away. 'I hided, I hided for ages and Daddy didn't find me. Wake Daddy up. Daddy come and find me.'

I looked at Amyntas again. Then I noticed the pool of dark liquid under his body.

'Oh, Great Mother,' I groaned and went over to kneel beside him. I took away his hand and saw the scarlet gash in his chest. Panic was rising inside me, but Adea came up behind me and pushed me:

'Wake Daddy up!' she repeated impatiently, three or four times.

I got up and took her hand resolutely.

'No, Adea,' I said firmly. 'Poor Daddy isn't very well. He needs to sleep. We'll go and tell Mummy.'

She seemed to like that idea and started running ahead of me back down the path. I ran after her, suddenly afraid that the murderer might still be in the garden. Was Adea in danger too? What about her mother? Had they killed Cynane as well? I caught up with the little girl and picked her up, looking around in terror. I crept to the end of the path, convinced that a man would jump out at any moment from behind a bush and slaughter us both. But we reached the gate without incident.

I had to summon up all my courage to peep out into the courtyard to see if anyone was there. It was deserted. I looked down at the child in my arms. She had her thumb in her mouth and was looking at me trustingly. I smiled and kissed her forehead. My heart was thumping so loudly I thought anyone in the palace could hear it. I stood for a minute or two, breathing deeply, and then checked the courtyard again. Still no one. I darted out the gate and walked swiftly back to Cleopatra's apartment. All the ladies were still there, together with the children and their nurses. Adea's nurse came to greet us and took the girl from my arms, taking her thumb from her mouth and scolding her.

'Where's her mother?' I asked urgently. 'Have you seen her?'

The nurse shook her head and continued fussing over her charge. Pythias came over. I took her outside with me and told her what I had seen in the garden. Her hand went up to her mouth.

'Oh, Herpyllis,' she said, 'what madness is this?'

Indeed, what madness? And whose madness? Who else would be stabbed through the heart before the day was over?

'We must find Aristotle,' she added suddenly. 'He'll know what to do.'

I nodded and we ran back through the courtyard to the guards at the entrance. I recognised one of them. He had been Xanthe's sweetheart for a summer. He had my brother's name.

'Please, Theron,' I said. 'Do you know where Aristotle is?'

He looked at me suspiciously.

'You should stay here,' he said. 'Those are the orders.'

'I know,' I replied. 'But something's happened. We must talk to him.'

'He's with the prince,' he said, 'and the King's advisers. Can't interrupt them. More than my life's worth.'

I drew myself up and found that decisive part of me which had surprised both myself and Pythias before.

'It's more than your life's worth *not* to interrupt them, Theron,' I said as forcefully as I could. 'If you don't go and get him, *I* will.'

Theron looked from me to Pythias to his fellow officer. Luckily, the other man seemed impressed.

'You go,' he said.

Theron hesitated for a moment longer, but then sighed and set off down the corridor. He turned out of view at the end. We waited in silence. After some minutes we saw Aristotle coming back down the corridor with the guard. He looked sternly at Pythias.

'What's the matter?' he asked, not hiding his irritation.

Pythias took his arm and led him into the courtyard out of hearing.

'Tell him, Herpyllis,' she said.

So I related as briefly as I could the scene in the garden, adding that we couldn't find Cynane. Aristotle furrowed his brow.

'You're sure he's dead?' he asked.

I nodded. He let out a long sigh and shook his head. I heard him mutter something under his breath. I think he said *Was that really necessary?* but he wasn't speaking to us. Then he looked at me and patted my arm.

'You did the right thing, Herpyllis,' he said. 'Go back to the ladies. Look for the princess in the apartments but don't leave this area. You're safe here. Wait here till I come for you.'

'Is the King dead?' I managed to get out.

'Yes,' he sighed, 'Philip's gone. Hard to believe.'

And with that he turned on his heel and was about to leave us when another thought struck him.

'The King's body,' he said. 'The women should be preparing it for cremation tomorrow. I'll send guards to bring it to you with due ceremony. Everything must be done in accordance with the customs.'

He went back to the crisis talks. Pythias and I searched the apartments around the courtyard. They were all deserted. Just as we were about to rejoin the others, Cynane came striding through from the outer corridor.

'I'm looking for Amyntas,' she said peremptorily, looking at us both accusingly.

While I was searching for what to say, Pythias took her arm gently and led her to a stone bench, sitting down with her.

'I'm afraid we have bad news,' she said in as level a tone as she could muster.

Cynane said nothing but her face suddenly emptied of colour and expression. Pythias looked up at me, unsure how to go on. I took my cue from her.

'Adea took me to him,' I began. 'They were in the garden together playing hide-and-seek. She was hiding but he didn't come and find her. She found him lying on the grass. She thought he was asleep. I told her he wasn't well and we should come and get you to look after him. I didn't know what else to say.'

She understood immediately and turned her face aside. A kind of involuntary moan came from her and her head and shoulders crumpled. I stepped forward to embrace her but she pulled herself together, jumped up and pushed past me as she marched off towards the garden gate. I went to follow her but Pythias held me back.

'No,' she said. 'She wants to be alone.'

In late afternoon a procession brought the King's body to the royal apartments. I remembered the words of the oracle at Delphi Cleopatra had quoted to me. So *the bull* garlanded for sacrifice was not the King of Persia after all, but Philip himself, the gold wreath of oak leaves on his head and his white ceremonial tunic slashed and blood-stained over his heart. His queen Eurydice became hysterical when she saw the deep knife wound which had killed her husband, and her ladies took her back to her apartment. Cynane had not reappeared, so Pythias and I helped Cleopatra to supervise the washing and preparation of the body.

It was disturbing to see the number of scars on Philip's body. The physical cost of the kingdom he had carved out for himself was there for all to see. I tried to imagine what kind of mentality it took to spend so much of a life on the battlefield, but it was beyond me. The men I knew best, like my father and Aristotle, lived for the life of the mind and would have been out of place on a battlefield. But that had not stopped either of them advocating force when they considered it necessary. Aristotle encouraged Philip to lead the Greeks in a war of revenge against the Persians, and had clearly thought battle justified in first uniting them. My father had only led his city in fighting when he knew there was no alternative.

As soon as Philip was prepared for his funeral, we sat round the body to start our vigil. It was only then that I realised we had not celebrated Cleopatra's Second Blood as required. There was no question of slipping out into the forest unnoticed. I hoped the Great Goddess would forgive this lapse and that the ceremony could take place in Epirus with Olympias, although I knew the daughter's resentment towards her mother. I tried to convince myself that all would turn out well.

During the night the men came to see the King laid out. When they had paid their respects, they sat down with us. Just before dawn we lined up and followed the bier out of the palace. It was placed on a brightly painted funeral cart, drawn by four black horses. The hired mourners were wailing and the veiled royal ladies joined in the lamentations. As we came down the hill I saw another grim sight ahead of us: three men pinned to wooden boards by the side of the road. The one in the middle was covered in gashes; his genitalia had been cut off and stuffed into his mouth.

We walked on to the cemetery, where the tombs of the Kings and Queens of Macedon lay in their mounds, and stopped at a great pile of wood next to a platform on one of them. Four soldiers carefully removed the bier from the cart and mounted the platform to lay it on top of the wood. All the dignitaries and guests from the wedding gradually spread out around the site while the laments, the keening and wailing went on around us.

The horses were uncoupled from the cart, their nostrils flaring as they were shackled to the ground, one at each corner of the pyre, their whinnies drowning out the prayers offered up as the libations were poured over them. Their throats were slit as one. It took me back to Dion, the dumb creatures sacrificed in another male ritual. I was glad Amyntas wasn't there to see those beautiful animals pointlessly slaughtered. As I turned away from the sight, I saw Cleopatra flinch as the knives were raised again to the heavens and remembered how she had whimpered that day long ago. She had grown up now, but could still not look on impassively as her mother would have done.

Antipater, Alexander and his half-brother Arrhidaeus, the simpleton, slowly climbed onto the platform and Antipater began the funeral oration. He praised the dead man and listed all his achievements, exhorting his relatives to emulate him and finally consoling them for their loss. Antipater had a fine voice and spoke movingly; only someone who hated Philip as much as I did was not touched by his words.

We all threw flowers on the pyre and then a torch was passed to Alexander, who threw it onto the bier. As the wood caught fire, the men descended from the platform and we all watched the body gradually consumed in the flames. We then returned to the palace for the funeral feast.

Callisthenes and I managed to slip away and meet in a corner of the courtyard.

'Are you ill?' he asked me in a worried voice.

'I'm fine,' I replied.

'You look so pale and drawn,' he said, caressing my face. A shiver of pleasure went through me and I closed my eyes. We stood like that for a while and then Callisthenes sighed.

'I've missed you so much,' he whispered. 'I hate the life at court – the drinking, the petty squabbling. I'll talk to Aristotle again. I'll beg him to let us marry.'

'He'll never agree,' I told the man I loved. 'He wanted me to marry Theophrastus but I refused. He's very angry with me. He'll make sure I stay an old maid.'

'Oh, my love,' he murmured and took me in his arms. My whole body ached with the joy of that embrace.

'I must get back to Aristotle,' he said, stroking my hair and moving his hands to my shoulders. 'He's told me to keep notes of the meetings they're having with the delegates from the city states. Everything's on a knife edge.

Alexander has to convince them all he'll be the new king, a strong leader, show them nothing's changed, that he'll continue his father's invasion of Persia.'

'Did he have Amyntas killed?' I asked.

Callisthenes put his finger to his lips and looked around to check there was no one else in the courtyard. Then he said quietly:

'Cynane burst into the room where the King's advisers were speaking to Alexander. She had her bow and arrows and shot straight at her brother. Luckily he ducked and the arrow missed him. She started cursing him, screaming *Murderer!* at him, reaching into her quiver for another arrow. Perdiccas and Ptolemy grabbed hold of her and took her away, still shouting at the top of her voice.'

'So it was Alexander who had Amyntas killed,' I said, a feeling of complete hopelessness overwhelming me. I kept thinking of Amyntas happily playing with Adea the day before, neighing like a horse and trotting around with his daughter on his back.

'We don't know that,' Callisthenes replied.

'But Amyntas had more right to the throne than he does,' I went on.

'Possibly,' he conceded. 'We mustn't talk about these things, Herpyllis,' he whispered. 'This is a dangerous time. The sooner we leave this place the better.'

Tears came to my eyes. I could only see and talk to the man I loved because of these terrible events, because men had been murdered, because the world was falling apart around us. He took my face in his hands and kissed me. Then he was gone.

We had long been up and broken our fast the next morning when Aristotle sent for us. We gathered our belongings and said our farewells. I took Cleopatra aside and told her how important it was to have her Second Blood ceremony as soon as she reached Epirus. She had achieved some composure overnight and she promised me solemnly that it would be done. Then she relapsed for a moment into the state of fear and anxiety of the previous day.

'Oh, Herpyllis,' she said tearfully, 'my father's dead. The King is dead. What will happen now?'

'Everything will be all right,' I said, smiling with determination. 'You have a new life ahead of you with a good husband. You're a queen now. You must act like one.'

She looked at me as if I had told her a great secret.

'Yes,' she answered, drawing herself up, 'now I'm a queen.'

And there before me I saw again a young Olympias, ready to face the world, ready to fight. I left her with a new confidence that everything would, after all, be well. It was the last time I saw her.

16
HOPING AGAINST HOPE

'Hope is a waking dream.'

We returned to Pella and Aristotle spent every day for months closeted with Antipater and other advisers, trying to ensure a smooth transition of power to Alexander. But there were rebellions in the south and news came of trouble in Thrace. The new King was pitched into battle after battle.

Aristotle's nephew Nicanor, Callisthenes' uncle, came to see us the day before the army left yet again to fight an insurgency. He had survived the terrible battle against the Athenians and Thebans two years earlier, but had broken his leg in an accident on the way back. Now he was off again to fight for his new King.

That afternoon I was sitting in the courtyard and Nicanor sauntered out, looking embarrassed when he saw me. I tried to put him at his ease.

'How's your leg now?' I asked. 'Does it still give you any trouble?'

He mumbled something. I think he said it didn't bother him most of the time, only when the weather changed. We were both silent for a few moments but he sat down with me, so I tried to think of something else to say. I knew he was a man of few words.

'I hear you command an infantry division now,' I said. 'What's it like having Alexander as your general?'

He smiled shyly.

'Well, I've known him all his life, you know,' he began. 'We trained him to use a spear, wrestle and fight. We think of him as one of our own,' he said proudly. 'Alexander's much more reckless than his father,' Nicanor went on. 'Most of the time we think he's attacking too soon, taking huge risks, but so far he's always had surprise on his side and Fortune has smiled on him.'

'But you think his luck'll run out one day?' I asked.

'Well,' he replied, 'I do wonder how long it'll last.'

I hoped it wouldn't last much longer. I hoped the army would be defeated, humiliated. I hoped Alexander would get his comeuppance and all the Greek cities would be free again to rule themselves as they had before Philip had started his campaigning, obsessed with Aristotle's dream. I still believed in my father's teaching on politics and longed to live in a community where everyone's views might count for something, even though a woman's voice could only be heard through a man. It was a much better world than the one where kings and princes murdered and destroyed at will.

Suddenly Nicanor brought me back from my reverie.

'Not married yet, Herpyllis?' he asked.

I felt as if he had stabbed me. The desolation I felt about my future welled up inside me.

'No,' I managed to get out. 'I don't suppose I ever shall be.'

After a long silence Nicanor got up and went back inside. It was only years later I discovered why he had asked me that question.

The long months of insecurity came to an end one day when Pythias told me Aristotle had said we should prepare for a move. We would be going to live in Athens, where he would head his own school.

'And I have some other news,' Pythias went on, looking uncomfortable. 'Alexander's invited another historian to court, and Theopompus is going back to his home on Chios. Callisthenes is asking if he can come to live with us in Athens rather than going with his tutor.'

I just stared at Pythias, searching her face for signs of what was coming next. I couldn't utter a word.

'Aristotle says he's going to send him to Delphi first,' she went on. 'Apparently, when we were there Aristotle promised to draw up a list of the victors in the Pythian Games. It was part of the deal he made for my father's memorial. All their documents are in a hopeless mess and must be sorted out. So Aristotle thinks it'd be an ideal job for Callisthenes to do while he decides whether he should live with us again. But I must warn you, my dear. Aristotle doesn't think it's a good idea to have you two under the same roof for both your sakes.'

My mind was racing. Just the thought that perhaps... The infinite human capacity for hope against hope had a hold of me. It's what keeps us going from day to day – we never *quite* give up. The thought of possibly seeing Callisthenes made me count the days until we left Pella, replacing reluctance to leave my friends at the palace with excitement and anticipation.

Pythias and I went to say our farewells. Olympias had returned to Macedon ten days after Philip's assassination. She must have passed her brother and daughter on the road going the other way. We heard she had gone straight to Aegae and laid flowers at the feet of the rotting body of the King's assassin. She had him taken down and a mound built for his burial. She made sure he had a costly funeral. Everyone now assumed it was Olympias who had engineered the terrible events we had witnessed in Aegae. The assassin had relatives in Epirus, and the rumour was that it was through them that the Queen had influenced him.

They say it was Alexander who had Philip's baby son killed, but that his last wife and her young daughter were murdered on Olympias's orders. Burned to death. Although I had already known there was a hard, even cruel side to her nature, I had never imagined her capable of such ruthlessness.

Things had certainly changed at court. There were guards everywhere who challenged us at the foot of the steps and at the entrance to the women's colonnade, even though they knew us. We had to wait while they asked the Queen's permission for us to enter. Inside, the atmosphere was always subdued and strained now, like the times when Olympias had erupted earlier in the day and was still seething. But Charis greeted us near the door as usual and we embraced warmly, all smiles.

That day Olympias was reading a report; I couldn't help smiling with satisfaction to see she no longer pretended to be illiterate. Her brow was knitted with concentration and she put up a hand to show us she was aware of our presence but wanted to finish reading. Finally the Queen turned to us and acknowledged our presence.

'My dear ladies,' she said, 'I hear you're leaving us.'

She kissed us both and was gracious but remote: a different woman altogether. Conversation was stilted; we had little of interest to report and there were few subjects at court that could be discussed in a neutral fashion. The only thing which awoke any real animation in the Queen was our opinion on a bride for her son. Apparently he intended to set off for Asia as soon as he had subdued all rebellions in 'his lands' (this was how Olympias referred to the kingdoms and city states defeated by Philip), and she was keen that he should leave an heir. I reflected that this would, of course, ensure her position should anything happen to Alexander. But it was clear from what Olympias said about the various candidates that the new king's wife must be malleable and pose no threat to his mother. We politely discussed the merits of these ladies, most of whom we scarcely knew.

When we said our goodbyes I little thought it would be many long years before I saw any of those ladies again – Olympias, my second mother; Charis, my dear old friend; Thessalonica, the girl who shared my love of music. The next time we met they would look on me as an enemy.

And the unassuming, earnest lad of fifteen who joined us on our journey south that day would be instrumental in the way they saw me – Cassander, one of Antipater's sons. How could we have guessed the role this boy would play in all our lives, how important those years in Athens as Aristotle's pupil would prove to be for him, and for the history of the world as we knew it?

Antipater came to see us off, bringing Cassander with him. The boy was already the same height as his father and had the same blue eyes, but in his case they shone bright and hopeful, not yet dulled by pragmatic considerations and moral dilemmas in the service of the state. He had a pleasant face under his brown curls but there was nothing remarkable about it until Antipater introduced us. Cassander's smile transformed him. It showed a warmth and intelligence quite unexpected in one so young. Every time I see that smile again now, so many years later, it takes me back to that first day; I remember the youth who was not yet a man, his promise only manifest in that glimpse of his soul through his eyes and lips.

'Be kind to him, Herpyllis,' Antipater said. 'I can see he's already fallen in love with you like the rest of us.'

I laughed at this, but catching sight of Aristotle's irritated expression and Theophrastus scowling beside him put paid to my light-heartedness.

'We'll make him feel part of the family in no time,' I quickly assured Antipater, and Pythias broke her usual reserve in front of the men to add:

'Indeed we will.'

We mounted the wagon and Cassander positioned himself on his horse behind us, much as Callisthenes had on the way to Delphi, Aristotle and Theophrastus leading the way in front.

Over the following days I discovered from Pythias that Antipater had made Cassander's education part of their agreement for Aristotle to go to Athens. My guardian had wanted to delay the boy's coming to the school until he was seventeen, but Antipater had insisted his friend would find the lad a quick learner and a willing assistant. Theophrastus's eyesight was going now and both the older men needed a young man constantly at their side to read and write for them. The role Callisthenes had once played was to be taken over by Cassander. The boy was eager and excited.

'My father wants me to learn about the world first from Aristotle,' he commented, 'not from intrigues around the court.'

He told us this openly and trustingly, accepting without question that he was now part of the family. Cassander had two elder sisters – the younger of whom looked a little like me, he said – and another younger sister and brother. He didn't seem awkward or shy with us as many boys of his age would have been.

'My tutor has taught me what he can of philosophy,' he told us, 'but Father says Aristotle was behind every decision King Philip made, and it will be the same with our new king. Alexander learnt from Aristotle and I want to do the same, so one day I can be as good an adviser to him as my father is now.'

Antipater was making provision for his succession, just as Philip had. He was in his sixties and Aristotle nearly fifty. It was doubtful either of them would be there to advise Alexander for many years longer. Antipater had selected the ablest of his sons to be at the Macedonian king's side after his death and that of his friend. I tried to imagine Cassander in twenty years' time, as trusted at court as his father. Then I remembered I had first met Antipater as an army commander. The Macedonians valued military prowess highly; perhaps it was a prerequisite to gaining a king's trust.

'Have you done any military training?' I asked Cassander.

'Oh, yes,' he replied, 'but I'm not really cut out for it. I find the square bashing and the discipline boring. Father says I'm the brains in the family and I'm to replace him at court. My brother Philip is the soldier. He's been on campaign with the King.'

I decided I liked this young man, who could be so honest about his feelings and not feel he had to stress his great virility. Alexander's constant talk of his fighting skills as a boy came back to me, how he made brutality and slaughter sound heroic, the stuff of poetry and myth, glorifying all the violence as a noble quest. Like Callisthenes, Cassander seemed refreshingly free from that kind of illusion.

We continued on the same road as we had to Delphi: Pydna, Dion, Larissa and on through Thessaly to the pass at Thermopylae, the site where the Spartan King Leonidas and his three hundred men had all died in the rearguard of the Greek army, holding the narrow pass between the sea and the cliffs against the Persian hordes a century and a half earlier. Callisthenes' voice was fresh in my head, recounting the events in his own inimitable way. And my heart ached again.

We all stood around the stone lion commemorating Leonidas's sacrifice while Aristotle read out the inscription:

Go tell the Spartans, thou who passest by,
That here, obedient to their laws, we lie.

He told us with great satisfaction how Alexander would now take revenge on the barbarians who had invaded our brave, free land, the same tyrannical despots who had tortured and murdered Pythias's father Hermias. I reached out and held Pythias's hand and we all stood there in silence for some time.

17
ON HAPPINESS

*'Happiness is the meaning and the purpose of life,
the whole aim and end of human existence.'*

It was early summer when we arrived in Athens, that renowned city of the south of which Aristotle had told us so much. He spoke with great affection of the years he had lived there, and I realised he had spent more than half his life in the city. He was clearly overjoyed to be back and his enthusiasm was infectious. As we approached, he stopped the wagons and we got out to stare up at the citadel where we could see the back of the great bronze statue of Athene dwarfing everything else. The tip of her out-thrust spear and the crest of her helmet glinted in the setting sun as we looked up. What a terrifying protector goddess the city had!

We returned to the wagons and followed the road round the city walls to our new home by the Lyceum. The area was full of foreign residents, those who couldn't take part in political life because their parents weren't Athenian citizens. None of them could own property, so all had to rent. We moved into the spacious villa Antipater had leased for Macedonians. It was next to a large park with tree-lined avenues converging on the main Lyceum building – that was where rooms were to be rented out to the new school. There was a magnificent old plane tree to the left of the central avenue. Apollo's sanctuary lay in the grove on the other side of the park and there was another sanctuary to the Muses nearer the river, close to the springhouse. The running tracks and military exercise yard were behind the main building. The colonnades on either side were lined with maps on stone tablets.

My guardian now took up the serious business of opening his school and finding students. He and Theophrastus had planned a special programme, dealing with more complex problems in the mornings and giving public lectures on popular themes in the afternoons. Despite the anti-Macedonian feelings of most Athenians, their curiosity and Aristotle's fame won the day, and it wasn't long before the school was buzzing with activity; those who frequented the gymnasium next door were soon dropping in to hear the great man and take part in discussions. On the lengthening sunny days, I often saw Aristotle and Theophrastus strolling with students along the avenues or sitting in the shade on the marble seats. After a few months, young men were being sent from all the Greek cities to study under Aristotle, and large crowds were coming to attend the public lectures.

Our days took on a recognisable routine. I helped Pythias to run the large household and arrange the weekly symposiums for distinguished guests. Every afternoon, while the older men were resting, Cassander would come and tell me about the day's lessons; I would ask questions to see how well he had understood them.

Cassander became the little brother I had never had, to be teased and spoilt and loved, and he returned that love with an almost dog-like devotion. Whenever he was not with Aristotle, he would be hanging around the courtyard asking if he could run any errands for me; sometimes he sat with us and played the lyre. He had great musical sensitivity. Occasionally I fancied him Orpheus, charming the gods, and then I would think of Callisthenes telling us the tale on the way to Delphi. I would wonder for the tenth time that day when we would have news of him, what he was doing in Apollo's city, whether he might come to Athens soon, perhaps live with us again.

It must have been about six months after we arrived when my guardian started on a major project at the Lyceum: setting up a library. Oh, dear library, what cause I have to value you! Aristotle was determined to create the greatest and finest collection of works in the world, but he couldn't do it single-handed, especially when he and Theophrastus were so occupied with teaching.

Aristotle told Pythias to expect Callisthenes in a few days and to have a room prepared. So those days were full of conflicting emotions: joy – such joy that I would see him again – alongside anguish that we would be kept apart; and somewhere in my heart was still the fear that he might have changed towards me. I remember the complete upheaval of soul, the endless days, sleepless nights, inability to eat more than a few morsels of food without feeling terrible nausea. Pythias later told me how worried she was on my account and how she had spoken to Aristotle about it, but he had told her nothing of an agreement he had made with Callisthenes.

How much a look can say! Even though I tried to reason with myself that it might mean nothing, Callisthenes' eyes told me I was still loved, and he couldn't have been in any doubt about my feelings for him from my own reaction on seeing him. There followed two days of misery, when I didn't even catch sight of him. Aristotle seemed to have imprisoned him in the library. The torment I felt was far worse than when he had been living far away: to know that he was there across a courtyard and beyond the avenue of trees but I was never to see him, never to talk to him, never to feel his touch or his kiss.

But on the evening of the second day suddenly there he was, knocking at my door. I flung it open. He rushed in and took me in his arms, his lips on mine. I thought my heart would burst with the ecstasy of it. When he finally drew back, he looked into my eyes and said simply:

'We can be married, Herpyllis. If you still wish it as I do, we can be married.'

I erupted with a kind of shout – something between a cry of joy and a sob. The emotion was so powerful I couldn't control it. When I had managed to calm down all I could say was:

'However did you persuade him?'

'Is that a Yes?' he responded, with a laugh.

'Yes, yes, yes,' I said, throwing my arms around him again and hugging him close.

When we could talk again, I asked for a full account of his dealings with Aristotle.

'I don't know what it was that finally weighed in our favour,' he replied pensively. 'He needs me here for the library, and I made it clear I wouldn't come back unless we could marry. Aristotle isn't one to stand on his pride if it would work against his own interests. And he's also one for peace in his house. He could never stand tension and bad feeling around him. He's not a great one for bearing a grudge, either.'

Our betrothal was a simple affair since the guardian of the bride and of the bridegroom was the same person, but Aristotle still gave Callisthenes a dowry for me and Pythias presented me with some exquisite gold jewellery, which I wore for the ceremony. I still have it in its alabaster box. The delicate filigree flowers in the earring discs, an intricate crescent-moon boat hanging inside the pendant suspended from them, surrounded by more flowers, thirteen long gold chains attached to them, each ending in an elegant gold pendant; charms attached to the middle section, images of the Great Mother. The matching bracelet and necklace in the same fine gold, the same design. Work of the goldsmiths of Atarneus, city of the Goddess. Still gleaming and wondrous, as on the day they were given all those years ago in Athens, in that mansion we shared with Aristotle and Pythias, in our home by the Lyceum.

My wedding day began with the ritual bath. It was midwinter and the day was cold but sunny. I gasped at the shock of the spring water on my body, but then felt a tremendous glow, as if my old skin had been shed and a new one had taken its place. Pythias and the Macedonian ladies who lived in the compound dressed me in the new red dress we had made and decked me out in the gold jewellery, finally placing the veil over my head. We proceeded to the courtyard where Callisthenes and I sacrificed to Hymen and Hera; then the wedding feast began.

I kept thinking of my parents. They would have approved of Callisthenes, although no doubt I would have been married at a much younger age if life had gone on as usual in Stagira, so my husband would have been an older man. It was my mother I missed most; she would have given me her wise advice and carried out all the rituals for the Second Blood; her smile would have accompanied me to the bridal chamber.

When Aristotle took my hand and joined me with Callisthenes, he reminded me a little of my father. That same sad look when he was serious. He performed the ceremony with a good grace and I realised that Callisthenes was right about him. He was a politician in whatever he did, and turned everything to his own advantage. Show was extremely important to him. That was why he hadn't thrown me out of the house when I refused to marry Theophrastus, avoiding a scandal in front of the court. Now with Callisthenes and me, Aristotle wanted to make it seem that he was a benevolent guardian, who had deliberately brought his two wards together, grooming them for each other.

As for Pythias, she was mother, sister and friend to me that day. She had clearly determined that everything would be perfect and it was she who led the proceedings from morning till night, when I finally lay in the arms of the man I loved.

I'm an old woman now. There is only a vague memory of that overwhelming passion, that hunger, appetite, call it what you will. It was thrilling, a little frightening, that giving over of control, allowing myself to be lost in the pleasure sweeping through my body. Then lying there, another body wrapped around me, warmth and comfort beside me. It really was as if we had become one.

When we woke the next morning, our arms had gone numb and we laughed as we rubbed them hard to get the feeling back. And that produced more touching, caressing and stroking. Soon we were moaning in each other's arms again.

After Callisthenes had finally gone to join the men, Pythias came into our room to strip the bedclothes to look at the sheet we had been lying on, as was the custom. There was no blood. My heart jumped into my throat. The memory of Alexander groaning over me in the dark, his weight almost suffocating me, my feeling of despair, the hopelessness and shame flooding through my whole body – I shivered and gave a great sigh.

Pythias must have seen the sudden look of horror on my face. There was a long silence before she spoke.

'I've heard this happens sometimes,' she said in a matter-of-fact voice. She went quickly over to my sewing basket and picked out a needle. Before I had understood what she was going to do, she grabbed my finger and pricked it. I started and jumped back as the red bead appeared.

'Here,' she said, snatching up the sheet in the middle and grabbing my bleeding finger with her other hand. 'Just smear that here,' she went on, squeezing my finger and rubbing it against the linen. 'Just so people don't think anything bad about you,' she explained, reassuringly.

I didn't say a word and she never asked me why there had been no blood. I had buried the memory of what Alexander had done deep inside me. I hadn't consented to it and it wasn't part of my life. I really had considered myself a virgin on my wedding night and I'd given myself to the man I'd chosen.

That night Pythias showed the sheet triumphantly to all the women at my Second Blood ceremony. We all drank the red mead and danced wildly in the woods near that temple of the male god. I could hardly believe it was really me whose wedding we were celebrating, me at the centre of the circle, me whooping and careering around triumphantly, waving the sheet and laughing hysterically at the crude antics of those usually sedate Macedonian ladies in the City of the South. The men were at the weekly symposium; we were all back in our beds before they came to join us.

It wasn't long after my wedding day that Pythias confided in me: she was with child again. I was torn between alarm caused by the outcome of her last pregnancy and delight that her dearest wish might at last be fulfilled. We discussed the dangers together and decided that she should spend the next few months resting and doing as little as possible. Although she was loath to be treated like an invalid, Pythias reluctantly agreed that it would be sensible to lie down most of the time and handed over all household tasks to me.

So it was that I had my hands full every day and was as busy in the house as Callisthenes was in the library. My new husband still ate with the men and I with Pythias; we were only alone together for a few happy hours in the evenings. And once a week he was required to attend the symposium with Aristotle and Theophrastus, eating and discussing with the guests and pupils until late at night. The Lyceum was becoming the place to be seen and heard in Athens.

I mustn't complain. Those evenings together were the perfect end to each day. He would join me in our apartment, his face shining as he greeted me, and we would embrace, just stand there clasped in each other's arms for long minutes. Then we would sit and exchange news of our day. Callisthenes would tell me about his work in the library, something he had been writing, some incident during a public lecture that afternoon. He would pass on messages from Aristotle about household matters that needed attending to, and I would report on plans for the next symposium to be relayed back to our guardian.

We often spoke of our childhoods, our parents; Callisthenes would talk about his mother, recall something Hermias had once said; I would speak of Olympias, of Cleopatra, Cynane or Thessalonica. We were easy in each other's company. It was what I had always thought marriage should be. And we were still young. Occasionally we would romp around like children, chasing and dodging each other. Once when he had caught me and pinned me down, he was disappointed when I didn't react to his tickling.

'Why aren't you ticklish?' he asked indignantly.

'Alexander tickled all the tickle out of me long ago,' I replied without thinking.

He pulled back from me and asked in surprise: 'Alexander?'

I sat up quickly, all the gaiety gone from us both.

'When we were little,' I explained urgently, 'when I first arrived at court. All the children played together. It was completely innocent.'

'You didn't tell me that before,' he replied. 'You didn't say he played with you like that.'

'I told you we grew up together,' I replied. 'You know what children are like. I saw little of him when he started his proper education.'

This wasn't strictly true, but I was talking to the man I loved and I didn't want him to think there had been anything between Alexander and me, anything other than childish high spirits. We said no more, but Callisthenes withdrew into himself for the rest of the evening. I was desperate, furious with myself for ever mentioning Alexander and our childhood games. They meant nothing to me now except as a sweet but painful memory of a boy who no longer existed.

Otherwise those winter months were a good time. As the weeks went by, my husband was happy and content, his moments of solitary moodiness rare. Pythias was putting on weight and looking healthier every day. As for Aristotle, he was at the peak of his powers, idolised for his wise words and insight into all aspects of life. Theophrastus glowed in his orbit, and young Cassander was wide-eyed and dreamy, as if he believed himself on the heights of Olympus. Far from being jealous of Callisthenes, my husband became the joint object of the boy's worship. When he wasn't with Aristotle, he liked nothing better than fetching and carrying for Callisthenes, sitting in a corner of the library at his beck and call, or relaying messages between us.

It was easy to forget that we depended on what was happening ten days' ride away, at Pella. The world of the court, Alexander's hopes and dreams – all that belonged to another time, another life. Messengers came and went, but I paid them little heed. How could they affect the idyll we were living? We were all safe and secure in our beautiful home. I was beginning to believe that history had decided to ignore us here in the south, and that my husband could concentrate on writing of events long gone and unremembered, focus on bringing them to life again, showing what they could teach us.

But it wasn't our destiny to be forgotten. The ambitions that Aristotle himself had fostered in Philip and in his son were coming to fruition. It was in the spring that the call came from Alexander. A letter in the King's own hand to Callisthenes. The order to be part of the greatest campaign Greece had ever seen, to be official historian of the invasion of the Persian Empire, to record the exploits of the finest army ever assembled. Refusal was not an option.

18
FARAWAY WARS

'We make war that we may live in peace.'

Sometimes I sit and read my husband's *Deeds of Alexander*, his account of the Asian campaign. I remember a conversation we had one evening before he left. Aristotle and Pythias were there. Callisthenes was saying that he would soon see Troy itself. I remembered Alexander's tragedian face in the grove that day when he recited those fateful lines of Achilles about his mother's prophecy. My childhood love was off to Asia to seek glory and death, and my husband would be by his side.

'It will be quite an experience,' Callisthenes exclaimed, 'to see the ruins of that great city with our new Achilles!'

I couldn't stop myself. All my animosity to the whole enterprise spilled out.

'I'm glad to see Alexander will have a true believer writing his history,' I said sarcastically. 'You do realise you'll have to record everything that happens as part of the legend of the second Achilles, don't you? Anything that doesn't fit will have to be jettisoned!'

Callisthenes laughed and then looked serious again.

'Don't worry, Herpyllis' he said. 'I'll record what really happens. I'll give a true picture of the campaign and its leader, faults and all.'

'That's certainly what Theopompus did,' remarked Aristotle.

In his history of Philip's reign, Callisthenes' tutor had written the truth about Alexander's father, his heavy drinking and debauchery, as well as his brilliance as a strategist and his prowess in battle.

'But Theopompus is a rich man,' continued our guardian. 'He wasn't dependent on the King or anyone else to feed and house him. He was just an observer at court. I doubt if Philip ever saw anything of what he wrote. You, on the other hand, will be in Alexander's pay, part of his travelling court, far away from home. You'll have to read him what you've written; you might even have to write what he dictates. You may end up wishing you'd never been chosen to be his historian.'

Callisthenes was subdued now, but he said:

'I know I'll have to weave a history to the King's liking, not necessarily tell the whole truth, Uncle. But there's something about Alexander. You and I know he's not a great scholar, but even his father recognised his brilliance in battle. Herpyllis has told me he believed his destiny was to be a great hero when she met him, when he was only seven years old. That single-mindedness of purpose must count for something. There isn't a scintilla of doubt about him. Complete confidence. And that makes the men around him trust him to lead them to victory. They can all achieve superhuman feats with a man like that at their head. And *I'll* be writing their story. The world will hear it from *me*.'

Now, of course, that sounds like hubris. At the time it was thrilling. Even I, who was losing the man I loved to this dream, felt a shiver of excitement go through me, elation at the thought of my husband having this supreme role in a great story. And, although I could never forgive Alexander for what he had done to me, I was swept up in Callisthenes' enthusiasm for Alexander the hero, Alexander the charmed king who would crush the long-feared barbarian foe, removing the constant threat of a second invasion by those hated foreigners. My husband had a way with words. And he *wanted* the history he wrote to be magnificent, he *wanted* Alexander to equal Achilles. At the time I didn't realise how much.

I prepared everything Callisthenes would need on campaign. I quickly sewed him tunics of the finest linen for the heat of the deserts, cloaks of the finest wool for the cold nights of which Aristotle warned him. Somehow my stitches were close to perfect and I hardly pricked my fingers at all. I bought sandals of the finest leather and boots lined with fur, caps to shade his head, and beautiful calf-skin gloves to keep his hands warm, yet allow him to write while wearing them.

The day he left I hung the special amulet I had made for him around his neck. It was the little gold box I had been given to wear by Olympias, containing the single ear of corn sacred to the Great Mother. I carefully removed the dried grain and kept it safe; in its place I put a tiny sprig of the wild thyme I was named after and a small lock of my hair. I suppose what I did was blasphemous. It didn't even occur to me at the time – I just wanted to give Callisthenes something he could wear close to his heart to remind him of me in the months ahead.

A great sadness suddenly came across his face when he raised his head again after I had hung the amulet round his neck. He held me close for a long while, just as my mother and father had done all those years ago in that other life in Stagira. He kissed me and smiled again, and then he was gone. It was spring. We had had less than four months of married life together, and it seemed hard that he must go. But we thought he would be gone a year at most and would win renown in his own right as Alexander's chosen historian. Then he would be able to write the kind of history he wanted to write.

And it was a year full of happy events to occupy us. Three special children came into the world. In the first month Queen Cleopatra gave birth to a son, named after his ancestor Neoptolemus, son of Achilles. At the beginning of autumn Pythias was delivered of a healthy daughter. What relief and boundless joy there was on that day! And the birth relatively quick and easy. Aristotle's daughter was named after her mother. None of us had ever seen a more beautiful baby, delicate and dainty.

Then in the early winter, three months after the birth of Little Pythy as we soon came to call her, my own son was born, eight months after his father had left for Asia. My pregnancy went smoothly, which was fortunate as I was looking after Pythias and the rest of the household, so I had to be strong and healthy for them. And I was. The last months after Little Pythy was born were much harder. I felt so cumbersome and awkward. How strange not to

238

be able to see my feet when I walked! I couldn't wait to be back to normal with a child of my own, Callisthenes' child, to nurse and cherish.

Childbirth involved the greatest pain I have ever known, but that's not what remains, not how I think of it. No, it felt more as if Nature simply took over my body to produce Her greatest wonder, and I was swept along by the process, not consciously doing anything but provide the vessel from which new life would fight its way out. And after those seemingly endless waves of agony, those involuntary moans and cries, suddenly there he was – a little man born of love, perfect in every miniature detail. It was the most stupendous event of my life. I shall never forget Pythias's beaming smile as she gave me my baby wrapped in freshly washed linen, never forget the smell of the fabric, of that new, raw-looking skin and those little tufts of hair, astonishing in their softness. I knew immediately that this small creature now commanded my heart and there was nothing I would not do for him, nothing I would not sacrifice for his sake, even my life itself.

Callisthenes had asked Aristotle's permission to call the baby after our guardian if it was a boy, so our son was named for the man who had given both his parents a home and a family. Life was good. Pythias and I both mothers, both now wearing blue after our Third Blood ceremonies, both having brought new life into the world. All of us healthy and happy, though anxious about the great army heading into Persia. Alexander had resisted his mother's efforts to marry him off and beget an heir, so there was no royal baby in Pella as there was in Epirus.

Every month dramatic news came from Callisthenes, recounting how our young King threw his spear into Asian soil at the Hellespont and said Asia was his gift from the gods, how they had reached Troy and seen the ruined city of King Priam. Alexander had sacrificed before the tomb of Achilles and all those young would-be heroes around him had stood enthralled as Callisthenes told them his calculations proved that the sack of Troy had taken place exactly one thousand years before a Greek army had again returned to Asian soil.

Soon after Little Aristotle's birth we attended a great ceremony at the goddess Athene's temple of the Parthenon to celebrate the first victory over the Persians. With countless others, we walked in procession through the streets up to that superb temple on the cliff above us. The throng parted to allow three hundred men to pass, each carrying a suit of Persian armour to place as an offering at the feet of an awe-inspiring statue of the goddess in gold and ivory looking down on us. Then a proclamation echoed around the space:

Alexander, son of Philip, and the Greeks, except the Spartans, from the barbarians who live in Asia.

Despite my opposition to the campaign, I couldn't help but feel proud. Alexander was fulfilling his destiny, defeating the Persians, and Callisthenes was there, creating the legend. Cassander cheered loudly and Aristotle was beaming beside me. He even chuckled softly at the reference to the fact that Spartan soldiers had taken no part in the glorious victory at the Granicus.

But just a few months later Aristotle was smiling no longer. Cassander told me why. I could always rely on him to tell me what was going on. Otherwise I would have known little of the great events unfolding.

'The Athenians still haven't sent their fleet to Asia Minor to support the King along the coast,' Cassander told me, with a grave expression and a little frown on his face. 'And the Greek cities there are not opening their gates to us as expected. My father even says there are more Greeks fighting on the side of the Persians than for us,' he said indignantly. 'I don't understand how they could join our enemies, those barbarians who looted our temples and laid our country waste.'

I couldn't resist explaining how they might feel.

'That was more than a hundred and fifty years ago, Little Brother,' I said, 'and the enemy who has most recently destroyed their cities and killed their finest men is Alexander, or his father before him.'

Cassander looked at me in astonishment.

'But we were uniting our people to lead them against the barbarians,' he said simply. It was the lesson he had been learning since he was a small boy. It was the only version of reality he knew.

'Well,' I replied, 'try to put yourself in their shoes for a moment. If someone kills your father, rapes your sister and sells your mother into slavery you might not feel very well disposed towards them, even if they tell you it's somehow in your own interests.'

Cassander's blue eyes were now trained on me as if he wanted to see through to my soul.

'So you think they're wrong?' he asked.

'I lived a happy life,' I told him, 'in a fine city with fine people until I was seven years old. Simply because that city might one day have joined his enemies, Philip razed it to the ground, killing all the men and boys, taking all the women and small children away to a life of slavery. You shouldn't ask *me* about the rights and wrongs of Aristotle's ideas or how Greek cities feel about them,' I commented drily.

Cassander said no more, but he never again mentioned the Greeks fighting against Alexander. He went on reporting the news to me, soon telling me the army had had to retreat north to Phrygia to await reinforcements from Macedon. Cassander's father Antipater was regent while Alexander was away. He was surrounded by enemies just waiting for the opportune moment to attack, but he obeyed his king and dispatched the required troops so Alexander's campaign could resume in the spring. By the time news came of the defeat of the Persian King himself at the Battle of Issus, little Aristotle was taking his first tottering steps alongside a slightly more confident little Pythy.

The children were our constant preoccupation. The first smiles, the first sounds, the coming of each tooth, a sneeze, a cough – all these were major events in the lives of the whole household. Aristotle followed the babies' progress with particular interest, asking for a daily report on both and taking notes. First and foremost, it was the observation of a philosopher, a man who was never bored or inactive. Nothing was too minor or insignificant to merit his attention. He would get up in the night if either of them cried, and Ambracis, their nurse, would be angrily interrogated about their needs until they fell asleep again. None of us was allowed to make a potion or a poultice for them without his supervision. A new side to him was revealed.

It was a particularly prolific time in Aristotle's life. Apart from the daily classes and lectures, he wrote long letters to Alexander on every subject under the sun. The Macedonian King responded by sending him exotic plants and animals from Asia, much to the philosopher's delight. I remember in particular the strange little white desert fox with its enormous ears. It made a variety of noises, including blood-curdling shrieks which had all of us springing from our beds in horror in the middle of the night, believing one of our children in terrible pain or under attack. In the end, the fox met the fate of most of Alexander's gifts: it was dissected in the interests of science.

Young Cassander had little stomach for that side of his studies with Aristotle. He was one for tales of distant lands and customs and spent many an hour looking at the maps on the walls of the Lyceum. Whenever I had a free moment, he would take me there and show me the route Alexander was taking, the places Callisthenes was seeing. He infected me with his own fascination and we began to examine together the scrolls in the library.

I particularly loved the maps of the night sky; Cassander would try to imagine which stars my husband was seeing where he was, and in which part of the sky they lay for him. Then in the evening we would sit outside and view the heavens together. I felt that by staring hard at the same stars which shone down on Callisthenes far away I was sending him a message, reassuring him that I was thinking of him, letting him know he was loved.

I remember the evening when Cassander came with news about the army in Egypt, where they had been greeted as liberators. He said that Callisthenes and Ptolemy had persuaded Alexander to let them travel further up the Nile.

'They want to find out why the great river floods in the summer,' he said excitedly. 'Aristotle's been telling us about the Nile,' he continued. 'It floods every summer and brings fertility to the soil on its banks. Otherwise Egypt's a desert country. Apparently they know when the flood's coming because the Dog Star returns to the eastern sky at dawn just before it starts. When they see that, they know they must harvest all the corn from the fields to save it from the waters. So the Egyptians look forward to the dog days of summer, unlike us! It's the beginning of the new year for them, too,' he added.

'Are they going to follow the river to its source?' I asked him.

'Nobody knows where it is,' pursued Cassander. 'There are all kinds of legends about it. But Aristotle says the floods must be caused by heavy summer rains in the south. It's the wrong time of year to see that, of course, but Callisthenes is going to talk to the southerners to find out if it's true. Then he's going to try to follow the river back to where it springs from the earth.'

That evening I took Little Aristotle by the hand and went to sit in the courtyard with him. He was walking well by then, although he'd tried to run before he could walk and would revert to crawling, which he did at such speed he could cross the room in the wink of an eye, much faster than he could do it on two legs. He wanted to explore everything and we couldn't let him out of our sight for an instant. Once he pulled a jar over on himself and had a big cut on his forehead; another time he burnt his fingers on the cooking pot. That evening he was getting sleepy, so he was content just to sit on my knee.

'Look up there,' I said, pointing his little hand up at the Dog Star. 'A long long way away Daddy's journeying along a great river under that star. He's looking up at it now as he sits by his tent and he's waving at it. *Hello, Stotty*, he's saying, *Hello, Mummy*. Let's wave back.'

And we sat there waving at the Dog Star together. After that, every evening when the stars came out Little Aristotle would wave at the stars and shout *Hello, Daddy* and *Hello, Stotty* at the top of his voice. 'Stotty' was the closest Little Pythy could come to pronouncing my son's name; we all came to call him that.

I've just been reading what Stotty's Daddy wrote about Alexander's expedition to the famous oracle of the Egyptian Zeus in the desert. He says the scouts got lost in the sandstorms on the way to the oasis but then Alexander led them, following the birds. Is this true, or is it another example of my husband showing the second Achilles as superior to everyone in everything? But he does state they all nearly ran out of water six days from the coast before they sighted the oracle buildings. He continues that the priests greeted the King as *Son of God* and admitted him immediately to the inner sanctuary. Alexander emerged triumphant, declaring he would only share the secrets he had been told with Olympias and no other. But he gave Callisthenes instructions to declare him Pharaoh of Egypt and, as such, Son of Zeus.

Today no one knows what the oracle told Alexander, though rumours abound. Did the priests *really* tell him he was a god? Had his mother *really* told him Zeus came to her as a snake and fathered him? These were not questions anyone could ever have asked Olympias. But a mother dreams great things for her children; a queen can quite rationally have the most inflated fantasies, especially for her son. As soon as my little Stotty could talk, I imagined him becoming a historian as eloquent as his father, a philosopher as all-knowing as his namesake, a man as kind and wise as his grandfather. Finer than all of them, worthy of the highest praise. And Olympias remembers a son who more than fulfilled her wildest dreams.

One evening Aristotle told me Alexander sent a cartload of incense to his old teacher Leonidas in Epirus.

'Apparently,' he said, 'the driver had a message for the old man: *May you never stint the gods again.*'

My mind flew back to Alexander's tirade against his master in the grove twelve years earlier, his fury about Leonidas telling him to use incense sparingly in his sacrifices. I remembered his comic apeing of the man and my own helpless laughter; I smiled in spite of myself.

Somewhere in the King's soul was the clowning schoolboy after all, somewhere was the boy I had loved.

19
ONE BRIEF TIME OF HAPPINESS

'One swallow does not make a summer,
neither does one fine day; similarly one day or
brief time of happiness does not make a
person entirely happy.'

In his letter from the ancient city of Babylon, Callisthenes sounded like his little son, brimming over with
enthusiasm. He was an honoured guest in the home of
the Babylonian Chief Astronomer, who had shown him
detailed maps of constellations, together with records of
the movements of the stars stretching back thousands
of years. These were being translated and would be
dispatched to Aristotle as soon as they were ready. The
news had our philosophers practically dancing for joy.

From Babylon the army marched towards Persepolis,
the Persians' capital, and the barbarian foe was finally
defeated. I still have vivid memories of the great ceremony we attended at the Parthenon that year. The statues
and gold objects taken back to Persia from the temple by
Xerxes' army a century and a half earlier were reinstalled
with great pomp. The priests extolled Alexander's name
and virtues many times. It seemed his luck had held and

he had won a decisive victory. I was convinced that the army would soon be marching home and Callisthenes would be back with us in Athens before long.

My days were filled with my four-year-old son. That summer we went as usual to Aristotle's villa at Chalcis. It was a Macedonian protectorate. Aristotle inherited the land from his mother's family and built a fine house on it. It was a relief to escape there from the heat when it was at its most extreme in Athens. Stotty was quite a handful even in the hottest weather and the children's nurse Ambracis often looked worn out chasing after him. I decided it was time for him to learn to swim as my brothers and I had all done at his age. Surrounded by the sea as Stagira was, it was wise to have children feel at home in the water and not to fear it. The same applied at Chalcis.

We made our way down to the nearby beach, hand in hand; I knew Stotty would run down the cliff at breakneck speed if I let go of him. When we reached the flat sand, I released his hand to take off my sandals and put down the linen sheet I was carrying to dry him after he had been in the sea. When I turned to take off my son's sandals, I was shocked to find he had run off towards the shoreline. There he was, almost at the point where the waves were gently lapping the sand.

I shouted: 'Stotty, stop!' but he didn't even pause in his mad rush towards the sparkling water. I sprinted after him, watching in horror as he ran on into the sea. My dress was getting bunched up between my legs, slowing me down. I stopped to pull it up and tuck it into my belt, thinking of Cynane that day I met her in the courtyard at the palace.

'*STOP!*' I shouted, anxious now. I watched as Stotty's splashing feet disappeared under the water and he raised his arms as it came up to his waist, wading on unafraid of the white crests of the waves breaking just ahead of him.

'Stotty, Stotty, wait for Mummy!' I shouted, cursing my own stupidity in coming down to the beach alone with him. I started running again, seeing only his little light brown head above the water. My heart was pounding hard and I was panting loudly. It seemed as if the shoreline was receding from me instead of getting nearer. Then suddenly I was splashing towards the little head, just as a wave broke over it and it vanished.

'*STOTTY!*' I screamed as I waded in, beside myself with panic.

And suddenly there he was in the water in front of me, spluttering and coughing, before giving me one of his big grins.

'Stotty swimming,' he declared, as another wave broke over him.

I swept him up in my arms and held him close.

'That's not swimming,' I said, 'that's drowning. You can't breathe underwater.'

'Why not?' he demanded after another fit of coughing.

'Because you're not a fish,' I replied, walking out of the sea.

'No, no,' he said, pummelling my chest with both his little fists. 'Stotty swim!'

So back we went into the water and I held his little body under his tummy while he flailed around with his arms and legs, giggling most of the time. His apparent lack of fear worried me, but even so I was smiling when he finally tired of learning to swim for that day.

Stotty's energy and curiosity knew no bounds. They made you see the world afresh as an exciting place to explore and wonder at. My son also had great tenacity, never giving up on things he had decided to do. Swimming turned out to be one of them and, sure enough, he was swimming impressively for a four-year-old by the end of that summer when we returned to Athens.

Climbing trees was another favourite pursuit of Stotty's. Aristotle told me he should be allowed to do this and that children learnt quickly how to find footholds and feel at ease above the ground. As he was speaking, I had a vivid image from my dream, thirteen years before, when I had seen him and my mother sitting in a tree and tickling each other. I wondered for the hundredth time if he had really looked like that as a boy, if dreams really show pictures of how things were or will be. Pythias's dream of Hermias's torture certainly seemed to have been accurate.

Stotty was so sure-footed in climbing that we began to pay him little attention when he was up a tree in the courtyard. But I'll never forget the day Little Pythy came rushing in saying:

'Stotty fallen down! Ouch!'

Pythias and I dropped our sewing and tore into the garden where we saw Stotty lying motionless, crumpled up on the ground. I screamed and fell to my knees beside him, already wailing. I lifted his little head onto my lap and stroked his cheek, trying to revive him. Pythias leaned over to see if he was breathing and whispered:

'He's all right! He's alive!'

With great presence of mind, Simon had run to the Lyceum to fetch Aristotle, who arrived breathless beside us to hear Pythias's pronouncement.

'Don't move him!' he ordered, and set about gently lifting each of the boy's limbs to see if they were broken while I looked on in terrible suspense.

'Nothing broken,' he finally declared, and gave me a little smile. 'Pick him up,' he said 'and let's take him inside.'

When I laid Stotty down on his bed, I realised Aristotle had not followed us. I kept on desperately stroking my little boy's cheek, willing him to come round. After what seemed like an age, my guardian reappeared with a little bottle, which he put under Stotty's nose. I looked questioningly at him and he said simply:

'Frankincense.'

Gradually my son's eyelids moved and then his hazel eyes were open again. Callisthenes's eyes. Oh, how I missed him! How much longer would it be before Stotty's father was back home with us, here to play with his little boy, here to share such moments of anxiety with me and all the moments of joy?

'Where am I?' Stotty asked unsteadily.

'Here, here you are in your own little room!' I replied, stroking his brow.

'Head hurts,' he declared, closing his eyes.

'Where?' Aristotle asked, frowning.

'Everywhere,' was the reply as Stotty closed his eyes again.

Aristotle gently lifted my child's head and felt around the back, stopping when he found a large bump. He turned it towards me to see. Then he left the room and I sat there, still stroking Stotty's brow and murmuring to him how everything would be all right. Little Pythy came up and held his hand, looking worried, while her mother repeated that her playmate would soon be back on his feet.

My guardian returned with a poultice, which he put on the patient's bump. He made one twice a day for Stotty over the next week, reassuring me that he would be fine. He had shaken his brain, apparently, and needed rest and quiet. When I still looked worried, Aristotle gave a little laugh.

'I know,' he said, 'Stotty's so unlike himself, you think he must be very ill. But believe me, he'll be back to normal in no time. Take the opportunity of having some rest yourself,' he added, squeezing my arm gently.

He was right. Stotty was back to rushing around like a whirlwind after a week or so, but it had been a chastening experience for us and even he started to be a little more careful. Our interrogation about his fall revealed the fact that he had been startled by a bird suddenly flying out of the nest he was poking in the tree he had climbed, and that was why he had lost his grip on the branch.

'What kind of bird was it?' Aristotle asked him.

And that was the beginning of Stotty's studies of the natural world around him. He still loved climbing, digging holes and running races, but he would also take great care collecting samples of all kinds of flora and fauna to present to his great-great-uncle, who seemed to find pleasure in sitting down and explaining everything to him patiently in the evening before bedtime. Aristotle told me Stotty reminded him of Callisthenes when he was a lad.

Still no news came of the army returning from Asia and no messages from Callisthenes. And then there was trouble closer to home. Cassander told me how his father Antipater had had to march his army down to the south to fight an uprising. Aristotle and Cassander spent many sleepless nights worrying about Antipater's fate. Nearly nine thousand men were killed in the final battle; Antipater emerged victorious to great relief at the Lyceum, though my heart sank to hear of more pointless slaughter.

Shortly afterwards Aristotle was summoned to Delphi for a great ceremony honouring him and Callisthenes for their work on the *List of Victors of the Pythian Games*, the importance of which had been recognised far and wide. Apparently, it was of inestimable value in corroborating the dating of historical events. This time my guardian made the journey alone; Pythias was with child again and confined to her bed most of the time, so I was in charge of the household and the children. Stotty was six years old by then.

The two children filled our lives, and their education was becoming our chief concern. Both had learnt to read and were writing their letters better and better each day, although my son was still more interested in exploring his surroundings, curious to know everything about the world around us. The only thing that would keep Stotty sitting still for long was a story about Perseus, Theseus or a hero of Troy. He persuaded me to make wings out of cloth to attach to his sandals and would jump off a rock so he could fly like Perseus with Hermes' winged sandals. I would catch him in my arms and run along with him lying there, legs outstretched, feet moving up and down as he swam through the air.

'Will I grow up to be like Perseus?' he asked one day when I sat down exhausted.

'No,' I said. 'You'll be a historian like your father.'

'But I don't want to sit and write all day,' he replied, looking crestfallen.

'You'll be far more important than the heroes,' I said, holding his puckered little chin in my hand. 'Without a historian, nobody knows about them and all the things they do. They die unknown. You'll write down their stories so their names will live forever, like Daddy and Alexander.'

He looked a little mollified but was soon begging me to catch him again and fly him around. Pythy would often just sit and watch us. She was much less active and enjoyed looking at the world from further away. She liked talking to her dolls and carrying out little rituals. But her greatest pleasure, too, was in listening to stories; she could never get enough of them.

It was a month after Aristotle's return from Delphi when the fever struck. One morning Pythy was off her food and listless. At first we thought it was just an upset stomach which would quickly pass, but she developed a fever which made her forehead hot to the touch. She became delirious, crying out about plants growing on her bed, their tentacles stretching out to strangle her. Then the same symptoms appeared in Stotty, and my guardian spent the days going between his study, where he prepared potions, and the children's bedside, ordering the servants to fumigate the house with various herbs. Next he sent most of them away and confined Theophrastus and Cassander to the Lyceum.

Soon our lives became a nightmare vigil over two small, writhing, sweating bodies, each of us locked into a private hell of our worst imaginings. Anything we managed to feed them came up minutes later in paroxysms of vomiting; even Aristotle's potions could not be digested. Then Pythy was wracked with foul-smelling, green diarrhoea; her mother and I were driven to distraction with our inability to stop the torture inflicted on her by the disease. Scenes from Pythias's dream of her father haunted me, but instead of a grown man, it was our helpless children who were being mercilessly tormented in that wooden structure. Those were weeks of agony; I will never forget the little girl's parents looking half-dead with exhaustion and lack of sleep. I must have looked the same.

It was around the twentieth day when hope slowly returned to the household. Pythy's little body became still and she slept through the night, waking the next day pale and thin but at last calm, taking untroubled breaths in and out. She even managed to keep down the broth we gave her. The relief we felt showed in all our haggard faces, and I sat beside my son's bed with new courage, convinced that he would soon recover in the same way.

I could hardly bear to look at little Stotty's body. He had become so thin his ribs and shoulder bones were sticking out, and his arms and legs had lost all the sturdy strength they had gained from his climbing, swimming and running around. Worst of all, his stomach was swollen and painful. My little boy was no longer twisting and writhing in bed, but he was gasping for breath.

Aristotle kept preparing potions for Stotty to take. I would coax my son into swallowing each one, only to have to watch him vomiting and retching soon afterwards, that small body almost torn apart by convulsions. It was after one of these episodes that I laid his little head back on the pillow and saw those hazel eyes wide and staring. He had stopped struggling for breath. His heart had stopped beating.

I barricaded myself in the room with him; I couldn't bear the thought of him buried in the earth, or burnt and become ash. I just sat there cradling him in my arms. I was dimly aware of Aristotle banging on the door and begging me to let him in to see his namesake. Somehow he managed to open the door enough to push past the heavy chest I had put there. He came and took us both in his arms and wept with me.

I was dimly aware of Pythias coming to us. She was supposed to be lying down until the birth, as she had before. Her distress brought Aristotle back to reality. He carried her back to bed and gave me a potion to drink when he returned. It must have been poppy because I fell into a dream-like state. As I prepared my son's lifeless body for his funeral, the ritual mechanical washing soothed me, passing the linen of his old swaddling clothes over his beautiful limbs, taking his little hand in mine to bathe under his arm, parting each perfect toe to wash and dry between them – it was all done in a strange trance. I spent hours washing my boy and then dressing him as if for a special feast.

My guardian gave me more of the potion so I remember nothing of the funeral. I was in a world where my little son was laughing and feasting, dancing around with a little smile on his lips, his happy face glowing and grubby. He kept dodging away from me as I tried to wipe it clean with a napkin.

A week must have passed with me on the edge of sanity. Aristotle finally took me aside and told me I must be strong for Pythias's sake; they both needed me to run the household in her stead. I forced myself to take charge again. At least for a few hours each day my mind was on other things, and my little boy's face could fade into the background.

Days became weeks, weeks became months. Still there was no letter from Callisthenes. I needed his words of consolation, needed to feel we were mourning our boy together. Every evening I would look at our stars and talk to him in my head, remind him of things Stotty had said and done. Aristotle commissioned a beautiful tombstone.

It is still there near the Lyceum, a little head with wavy hair, bent over a writing tablet at precisely the right angle. When Callisthenes came home he would at least have a faithful picture of what his son had looked like.

The time came for Pythias to give birth. She was pale and lethargic before the labour pains began, and the delivery took much longer than before. The midwife tried various ways of hastening it, but kept shaking her head when they failed. I sat beside my friend and held her hand throughout. She seemed to lack the energy to push at all. I wiped her brow with cool spring water and whispered in her ear that all was well and the baby would appear any time now. Just when we were beginning to give up hope, Pythias suddenly reacted to a great wave of pain that swept through her body, and a little head appeared between her legs. Another huge effort produced the rest of the body, expelled in a great pool of blood. Pythias gave an enormous sigh and closed her eyes.

Meanwhile the midwife was holding up the baby and shouting excitedly:

'It's a boy!'

My heart gave a leap and my throat was blocked with a lump. A son. Stotty had come back to us. I squeezed Pythias's hand tight and wept with a mixture of grief and joy. She responded with a weak smile and a little squeeze back, but she didn't open her eyes. Aristotle had taken the baby and smacked him to start the breath coming; a surprisingly loud cry emerged from the blood-soaked little body. The philosopher busied himself washing his son, trying to hide the tears rolling down his cheeks from the midwife, who was waiting to take the baby from him.

But Pythias didn't recover as fast as she had with her first child, and seven days later she had a high fever and a putrid discharge from her womb. Aristotle exhausted his own considerable medical knowledge of remedies with no change in her condition. Other physicians and wise women were consulted but none of them could help her. We looked on helplessly as my friend, my sister, slipped into unconsciousness and crossed to the other side.

The funeral was a desperate affair. Aristotle's oration was full of pauses; the almost inaudible voice was unrecognisable as the one which had rung out at Delphi. Little Pythy now understood death and would not let go of her mother. Her father reluctantly pulled her away and carried her struggling back home. I couldn't turn my back on my friend and walk away. I just stood there at a loss. I couldn't conceive of a life without the woman who had been my close companion through so many of the key events of our lives, good and bad. She had become an extension of myself. Cassander finally took my arm and gently led me back to the Lyceum. I felt no connection with the body I inhabited.

Aristotle's son was named Nicomachus after his grandfather. He was a quiet baby. It was almost as if he didn't dare to distract us from our grief with his crying. Ambracis found him a wet nurse and the household gradually went about its tasks again, though now I would catch sight of Aristotle sitting alone in the courtyard, staring into space. Not reading, not writing, not recording the movements of the stars. Just sitting.

20
JUSTICE

'People want justice to mean this:
If a man suffers what he did, justice will be done.'

It was Antipater who ended the mystery of my husband's lack of communication. His letter came two weeks after Pythias's death. He wrote that Callisthenes had been found guilty of involvement in a plot to kill Alexander. He had been executed.

When Aristotle told me my husband was dead, my knees gave way. How does that happen, I wonder? Why does it happen? I was suddenly on the floor, groaning, my useless legs under me – much as I had been at the age of seven, there in the square in Stagira, my parents' bodies beside me. Somehow I had made a new life after that, gradually found new friends and family. And now the three I loved as much as my parents were dead – all of them – within the space of a few months. Son, closest friend, husband.

Mourning for Stotty and Pythias had left me numb and empty. I had no tears left for the husband whose happy, excited face I could barely remember as he turned to wave goodbye seven long years earlier. All the tears cried out, as the tickle had been tickled out. I just rocked myself there on the floor, moaning, my arms crossed tight across my chest, trying to keep my heart from breaking. Aristotle just stood there, holding the tablet, looking at me. Then Cassander came and knelt opposite me, putting his arms around me and moving to and fro as I did.

I took to staring into nothingness like Aristotle. Him I never saw smile properly again – only wry, ironic upturnings of the mouth with no humour or tenderness behind them. Theophrastus wept openly and wrote *Callisthenes or On Grief* for his companion. Cassander shut himself away in the library.

Somehow everyday life went on. Aristotle took no pleasure in watching the new baby grow and develop. When he referred to his son, which was rarely, he called him 'the boy'. I, too, could find little love in my heart for Nicomachus, this creature who had taken away my dear friend. Luckily, Little Pythy seemed to enjoy playing big sister. She helped Ambracis and the new nurse care for the otherwise unwanted addition to the family.

Theophrastus took over many of Aristotle's classes and lectures; my guardian spent most of his time in his study, dictating his conclusions on a wide variety of subjects he had dealt with over the years. Cassander acted as secretary to him. He had become an indispensable member of the household.

I went on with all the tasks I had taken over from Pythias during her pregnancy and was thankfully kept busy. It was a dull, mechanical time. Avoiding thinking and feeling, focussing on getting through each day.

It was a couple of months later when Palaephatus came to the Lyceum. He was from Abydos; it was the place where Alexander had thrown his spear onto the beach from the ship when crossing the Hellespont into Asia Minor – in that other life of excited anticipation and hope long ago.

Palaephatus was the most beautiful young man I have ever seen. The skin on his perfectly formed limbs seemed to shine of its own accord, and his eyes made him look as if he came from another world. They were of a colour between the blue of the deep sea and the green of the cypress trees, the iris surrounded by a deep charcoal ring. His hair was a glossy reddish brown; it reminded me of the coat of Cynane's mare, the one Amyntas chose for her. When Palaephatus entered a room, it would go quiet as all those present turned to enjoy the sight of him.

Many were those who fell in love with him, but it was Aristotle who fell the hardest and whom he loved in return. I would sometimes see them sitting together with my guardian's hands simply cupping his face and staring at him, or stroking his arms slowly and gently. It reminded me of how Olympias had often treated me: a kind of awe in the face of youth, of perfection, of the glorious, transient bloom of Adonis, of the red anemone.

We live such separate lives, men and women. We have little understanding of each other. It is lust that brings us together, and fear of the unknown which keeps us apart. But with those of our own sex we know what gives pleasure, we understand each other's wishes and desires without words. It is an uncomplicated relationship. I envied Aristotle his complete absorption in that beautiful youth.

Meanwhile Alexander had been to the highest mountains in the world and down into India. It was more of the stuff of legend, but with no one to write about it any longer. I heard that Ptolemy, Callisthenes' friend and the man Olympias always called 'Philip's bastard', kept a diary; I wonder how he felt about Callisthenes' fate.

We heard everything that happened at the Ends of the Earth from Uncle Nicanor. Alexander sent him to make an announcement to all the Greeks at the Olympic Games. He arrived by sea and came to stay with us in Athens first. It was a subdued reunion with Aristotle's sole remaining relative, apart from his children. Although he was my guardian's adopted son, they had lived in the same house together for only a few years and, since Aristotle was ten years older than him, they had had little to do with each other. And Nicanor had chosen a life in the army and shown no interest in his father's and adoptive father's careers in philosophy.

My first sight of him now was quite a shock. He looked much older than his forty years, much older than when we had seen him last, eleven years earlier in Pella. We had heard how Alexander had murdered Nicanor's best friend, Cleitus, at a drunken dinner. The murder had marked my final reluctant acceptance that the little boy I loved had died after all in the king who now ruled. It had also extinguished Nicanor's sparks of humour and warmth, glimpsed behind the awkward, slightly truculent exterior he displayed before our guardian. The old soldier had many more battle scars and a bad limp from a spear wound to the leg.

Before Nicanor left ten days later to attend the Games we went to the Theatre of Dionysos, which we had visited regularly before Pythias died but had not attended since. It had been refurbished after we arrived in Athens and now the seats and stage were stone. My friend and I had loved sitting there entranced by the strutting actors, their voices resounding in that perfect space as they recited the fine verse of great plays we came to know well.

But that night they were performing a work by Euripides which I had never seen. It was *The Bacchae*. The story of the Queen and her women followers, celebrating their secret rites, who catch a man watching them and tear him to pieces for profaning their sacred law. It is only when the Queen is showing the head of her victim to her husband that she slowly comes out of her wine-induced frenzy and realises she has murdered her own son.

I was sitting next to Aristotle and we had good seats in the front row. The actors were very close. I became more and more agitated as the action played out. When the Queen suddenly raised the severed head of her son with a blood-curdling scream, I could do nothing to suppress a loud gasp as my hands went up to my face and I half rose out of my seat, only to slump to the ground in a faint. I was back in the grove outside Pella, that night, nearly twenty years earlier, those eyes in the tree above me.

And I saw the watcher's face, clearly now, bathed in light. Alexander watching the Goddess's secret rites. Death the penalty. One word to Olympias, one word and I could have changed the course of history. All those men and women who would be alive today if I had betrayed Alexander to the Queen, if she had carried out the punishment due: Callisthenes – my Callisthenes, Amyntas, Attalus's pretty young niece and her children. Not to mention the thousands upon thousands killed and executed during the relentless years of conquest. Let alone those whose lives have been irrevocably destroyed by his campaigns. If I had only screamed, shouted to the others, brought them running... The shock and recognition were so strong I lost consciousness.

When I came round it was to see Aristotle's worried face. But as I blinked and became aware of my surroundings, his expression suddenly changed. He looked excited and slowly enunciated just one word:

'Ca-thar-sis!'

A few days later I plucked up courage to approach Nicanor when I saw him sitting in the courtyard with Cassander. I had to know about Callisthenes, whether he had really hatched a plot to kill Alexander, whether he had tried to make history rather than just writing about it, whether he had finally accepted that Alexander's quest was madness. When I joined them, Cassander was asking Nicanor about the lands east of Babylon.

'The further east we went the more savage were the tribes we met,' commented the old soldier and then stopped when he saw me.

'Please go on, Nicanor,' I said. 'I want to hear everything. Most of my life I've been a victim of this great idea of uniting the Greeks and leading them against the Persian foe. I think I have a right to know if it was worth it.'

Nicanor gave me one of his strange looks. Then he looked down and slowly nodded. Finally he said:

'Yes, Herpyllis, you're right. I think Callisthenes would have wanted you to know – most of it, anyway,' he added.

Cassander looked impatiently from him to me and back again. Nicanor continued.

'We carried on,' Nicanor said with a long sigh, 'on and on into the wilds. A long succession of vicious skirmishes followed by drunken dinners in the evenings. By then we veterans were sitting in our own corner, in each new encampment further away from Alexander and his favourites. Alexander seemed to like the company of the Persians better than ours. He loved the way they bowed and scraped to him. He started dressing like them. He surrounded himself with them. Hephaestion, Perdiccas and the rest saw the only way they could stay close to him was to ape everything he did and said. So they sat around in those ridiculous trousers, too, looking much the same as the women dancing in front of them.

'One day the order came for all the King's subjects to bow down before him, not just the barbarians. He wanted his new Persian subjects to see due respect paid to their King of Kings by everyone around him. Macedonians and Greeks to treat him as if he were a god! All of us saw him as one of us – we veterans had watched him grow up and trained him. And we'd made him king. We could just as easily unmake him. I told Callisthenes this. I was surprised by his reaction.'

Nicanor looked down for a moment. I could hardly contain myself. I nearly shouted *What? What did he say?* But I didn't have long to wait. Nicanor looked me in the eye and went on as if he'd heard me:

'Callisthenes said: *Enough is enough. I boasted to Aristotle and Herpyllis that Alexander's fame would depend on what Callisthenes wrote. And look what I've written! I wanted to create a myth of the second Achilles, be a second Homer in prose. At first I thought a little exaggeration of the truth could do no harm. But now it's turned into full-blown and abject lying, worshipping a god who can do no wrong. I've become the worst kind of court flatterer. I'm thoroughly ashamed of myself, Uncle. We must finally stand up against tyranny and falsehood.'*

I was so overjoyed at this that I gave a little clap of my hands. Nicanor gave me a sad smile and went on:

'The following day your husband got up before the King, Herpyllis, in front of the whole army, and presented a reasoned argument about why Macedonians and Greeks could not give to a man the honours reserved only for a god. When he finished we all applauded loudly. Alexander looked furious. But he managed to control himself. He turned and left. A little later Perdiccas announced that only barbarians would be required to bow to their King in the Persian manner.'

This time Cassander said 'Yes!' out loud. 'What a triumph! What a man Callisthenes was!' he added. But Nicanor didn't smile this time.

'Alexander never forgives, Cassander,' he observed. 'I've learnt that about him by now. It was the beginning of the end for Callisthenes. The King was out for revenge. He called for a proper symposium like the ones Aristotle had arranged at Pella. And it was, of course, Callisthenes who was entrusted with the organisation. I've never enjoyed such occasions, being so tongue-tied myself, but my nephew always shone. He was brilliant that evening, displaying his famous eloquence. He listed and exemplified all the Macedonian virtues, much to the delight of the assembled men. But then Alexander commented: *That's all very well, Callisthenes, but you had an easy subject. How much greater a challenge it would be to speak so elegantly on the subject of Macedonian vices.*'

Nicanor paused and shook his head.

'I expected my nephew to make some clever excuse, Herpyllis, but I'd forgotten how ashamed he felt of his former flattery. He launched into a new exposition, this time on all the faults of Macedonians. I dimly remember something of rhetorical devices my father tried to teach us. And Callisthenes used them. The trouble was, most of the men listening didn't have much education. They didn't appreciate the niceties of Callisthenes' oratorical style and took his words as unpardonable insults. Alexander had given Callisthenes enough rope to hang himself. In one fell swoop he lost all the respect the men felt for him. They suddenly remembered he wasn't Macedonian and that I wasn't either. I felt more alone than ever.'

Nicanor gave a great sigh before continuing:

'It wasn't long afterwards another plot to kill the King was discovered. This time the culprits were supposed to be the pages who'd recently come out from Macedon to join the campaign. Callisthenes was their tutor. The poor boys were tortured and none of them accused him, but Alexander decided my nephew was responsible for putting the idea into their heads. He was brought before the King and army commanders under armed guard, his face grey. Perdiccas read out the charges. Callisthenes denied them. But his voice was dull and flat – no sign of his usual eloquence. I think they'd already tortured him. He knew this trial was just for show. He'd seen so many like it by then.'

Nicanor stopped and gave me a searching look. I met his gaze, trying not to show my dread of what he would say next. After a short silence he went on.

'It was The Little Rat who passed sentence – Perdiccas, I mean. It was to be death at a time and in a manner of the King's pleasing. The guards bound Callisthenes' hands like a criminal's and hustled him out of the room.

'I don't know if there was ever a plot in the first place, Herpyllis. It was probably just Alexander's twisted way of getting his revenge. Or perhaps Callisthenes had really tried to have him killed. I never got a chance to ask him. But I think he would have included me in the plot. I lead several divisions of the army now and Alexander had killed my best friend. My nephew could have relied on me to bring the men with me.'

There was a long pause.

271

'You haven't told us,' I said as calmly as I could, 'how Callisthenes was executed.'

'That's not something you need to know, Herpyllis,' Nicanor replied, averting his eyes from mine now.

'I must know everything, Nicanor. You said you'd tell me.'

'Forgive me,' he replied, 'there are some things that don't bear talking about.'

I waited. Then I said gently:

'You promised me.'

'No, Herpyllis,' – he was almost pleading with me now – 'there are some things you don't want to know.'

'On the contrary, Nicanor,' I retorted, sure now, 'I can never come to terms with what happened to Callisthenes if I don't know the whole truth.'

'Very well,' he said, looking right at me again. But now there was a kind of hardness in his eyes. 'Don't say I didn't warn you. I'll tell you how it happened but there's something you need to know first.'

He paused, breathing heavily. Then he took up his story again.

'Before Perdiccas passed sentence,' he said, 'Alexander intervened. He didn't usually. He liked to pretend others were bringing crimes to his attention while he played the just ruler, saddened by the behaviour of wicked, ungrateful men. *How was your wedding night, Callisthenes?* he asked in a clear, loud voice, that nasty grin on his face. We all stared at him as if he'd gone mad. But Callisthenes' face went from grey to white. He said nothing. Alexander continued in the same mocking tone: *I had*

Herpyllis long before you did. It's me she loves, you know.
Callisthenes swayed on his feet and the guards reached out to steady him. He still said nothing but he looked completely crushed.'

The shock I was feeling can't have been obvious on my face. Nicanor glared at me and asked:

'Why did Alexander say that, Herpyllis? Why?'

I felt my whole body go cold and my heart almost stop. Then from somewhere inside me I felt a deep resolve, a liberation. I stood up and fixed my eyes on Nicanor's, hesitating for only a moment.

'Alexander raped me,' I said clearly. 'And the next day he took me to Aristotle, to get me away from his mother,' I continued.

Nicanor and Cassander were struck dumb. They just stared at me. But then a voice suddenly spoke from behind me.

'Why did he do that?'

It was Aristotle. I turned round. I would tell him. I would tell them all. I hardly hesitated.

'Because he didn't want his mother to know what he had done in a sacred place on a sacred night,' I said loudly and clearly. 'Alexander shouldn't have been there. He should have paid the ultimate price then, that night.'

I drew myself up. Suddenly I felt the power of the Great Goddess, as if I was towering over the men, though they were all so much taller than me. For one brief moment I felt that raw, elemental rivalry, that struggle for sovereignty over the other, that eternal battle of the sexes. And for one brief moment I saw fear in the philosopher's eyes,

273

fear of a primeval force, the fear of Orpheus before the Great Goddess's followers.

'Now Alexander must die,' I declared, 'it's just a matter of how.'

There was a silence. Then Cassander sprang up.

'I'm ready,' he said softly. 'Let me go to him. I'll do it. I'm not afraid of that madman. I'll run him through. I'll slit his throat. I'll...'

But at this point Aristotle boomed:

'Enough, Cassander. Enough of your hot-headedness. Shame on you! Have you learnt nothing in all these years here? It must be done subtly, not out in the open. How many have tried to kill him and suffered terrible deaths, all their relatives too! This needs careful planning and complete secrecy.'

I could hardly believe my ears. Aristotle had accepted the sentence I had passed on the man I now hated above all others, the man who had raped me and killed my husband. And suddenly inspiration came. I knew how Alexander must die. I heard myself speak as if I were under some kind of enchantment.

'The Styx,' I said. 'If he is a god, the son of Zeus, he must be punished by his father as he punishes all the gods. He must drink the water of the River Styx to stop his lying, deceitful tongue. And if he is not a god, that same water will kill him with its deadly poison.'

Aristotle gave me his intense stare. We all waited.

'There is great poetic justice in that, Herpyllis,' he said, nodding approvingly, 'worthy of Euripides. But such a thing could never be achieved.'

Cassander suddenly exploded:

'Iollas!' he exclaimed. 'My brother Iollas is now the King's cup-bearer! He was sent out as a hostage for my father's good behaviour last month. It can all be done so simply and easily!'

Aristotle frowned.

'Well,' he said, 'we'll think this over. None of you must speak of it, even among yourselves. Do you have any idea what the King is capable of? Nicanor, have you told this young man what happened to Callisthenes?'

Nicanor shook his head.

'Tell him,' urged Aristotle, 'tell him what could happen to his brother if Alexander hasn't thought of something even worse by the time he comes to execute his next would-be assassin.'

Nicanor hesitated. And now he was looking at me. It was hard to decipher his feelings.

'In front of Herpyllis?' he asked his uncle.

'Yes,' replied Aristotle, 'Herpyllis has a right to know.'

He was echoing my own words. He saw it in the same way as I did.

Nicanor sighed and started talking, his eyes fixed on the distance as if he was seeing it all again, happening far away in Asia.

'Alexander ordered the most terrible torment for Callisthenes he had yet devised. First they cut off his nose, ears and lips. Then they put him in a cage with a rabid dog.'

I shivered with horror and suddenly found it hard to breathe. Nicanor went on relentlessly.

'The dog attacked him again and again, biting him and tearing his flesh. The cage was placed on a cart which was pulled behind the wagons for days and days. Nobody was allowed to go near him.'

I thought I was going to faint. Cassander caught me as I swayed and helped me sit down. Nicanor turned to Aristotle, a desperate look on his face, but my guardian put up his hand and said simply:

'Go on.'

After a short pause Nicanor continued, his eyes fixed on a point in the distance again. He was almost whispering now.

'The last time I glimpsed Callisthenes alive it was by the light of a campfire one freezing cold night. The dog was asleep. My nephew was naked and so pitifully thin all his bones were poking out. His cheeks had sunk into his skull. He looked nothing like a man – more like some strange creature captured in the mountains, shivering, whimpering and slavering. But he reached a trembling hand through the cage when he saw me. His guards were occupied with their game of chequers. I went up to the cage out of their line of sight. Callisthenes couldn't speak, of course, not without his lips. I'll never forget the look he gave me. My sister's brilliant boy, the King's teacher and friend, the man people treated with respect, almost awe, reduced to this stinking, repulsive creature with only those eyes to hint at his humanity and express his anguish.'

I let out a sob. Nicanor came and squatted beside me.

'I didn't believe Alexander,' he said urgently. 'I thought he just said he'd had you to hurt Callisthenes. There by the cage I told my nephew it wasn't true, but he slowly shook his head, the tears on his cheek briefly catching the light from the campfire. One of the guards got up and looked towards us. I quickly shrank back and walked away. The following day they found Callisthenes dead on the floor of the cage. They slit the dog's throat. It had outlived its usefulness.'

There was a long silence. Then I felt my grief turn to anger. It was as sudden as a burn from the cooking pot. I turned to Nicanor and gave him a grim smile.

'You were right,' I said, touching his arm. 'Alexander never had me. It meant nothing. It was the last of our childhood fights that he won. But it made me hate him. Before that I had loved him in a childish way, closed my eyes to his selfishness and his callousness. I had told myself he still loved me as he had when he was a boy. That night he simply managed to make me realise how little he deserved to be loved. And now he must be punished as he was not that night. All the good men and women he has wronged and killed must be avenged now.'

Aristotle nodded but made it clear that the conversation was ended for that day. I doubt any of us slept well that night. No more planning was done in my hearing, and Nicanor left two days later to attend the Games.

21
PERCEIVING THE TRUTH

'To perceive is to suffer.'

When Nicanor set off for Olympia, Aristotle and Cassander accompanied him for part of the way. Then their paths diverged. It was some time before I discovered where they went. It was to the source of the River Styx. They carefully collected some of that black water and stored it well.

A few weeks after their return, Cassander set out for Pella. His father had recalled him. He hadn't seen Antipater for ten years; he was part of our own family by then. Yet another one leaving us, never to return. The boy who was now a man, still loved as he had been from the beginning – my link to the outside world, who had shared all the latest news and rumours with me, traced the path of Alexander's army across mountains, plains and deserts on those maps in the library and on the walls of the Lyceum colonnades, charted the stars for me in the courtyard, held me close and stopped the cage closing around me, the one who had always been at my side through all that the Fates had given and taken away over the years in Athens. I tried not to think how life would be without him. The last of them gone. As he embraced me he whispered in my ear:

278

'You will soon be avenged, Herpyllis, I promise. You and all the others.'

He stepped back and took my right hand in his. He slowly raised it to his lips and kissed it. Then he gave me a long look with those clear blue eyes of his. He seemed to want to inscribe my face on his memory as he inscribed his own on mine. To me he is still first and foremost my little brother, regardless of what he has become.

It wasn't long afterwards Aristotle had a letter from Cassander's father. He only told me Alexander had removed Antipater as regent and that Antipater was to take yet more reinforcements to Babylon and face the charges against him in the King's new capital.

Meanwhile in Greece Nicanor had made his announcement at Olympia. All exiles who had fought for Alexander were to be welcomed back to their cities and have their property returned. The Athenians were outraged. They began preparing for war. It was no time for Antipater to leave Macedon and remove troops which would be badly needed in dealing with the situation. In the spring he sent Cassander to Babylon to plead his case with the King. Cassander facing Alexander – I was terrified for him. The following months waiting for news were full of anxiety and trepidation while we tried to distract ourselves from what might be happening far away in Asia.

I took to slipping into Aristotle's study when I knew he was occupied elsewhere. I read what he had written about tragedy. Pity and fear were the emotions I should have experienced that night at the theatre watching *The Bacchae*. I should have been purged of those emotions through watching that mythical tragedy unfold. Catharsis. Pity and fear I could feel for Oedipus or Antigone, but they were not my feelings as far as the man who had watched the secret rites of the Great Mother was concerned.

I read on. Aristotle wrote that women were inferior to men. I began looking at another scroll in the study and found more statements about my sex.

Females are weaker and colder in nature, and we must look upon the female character as being a sort of natural deficiency.

That was what I was reading one memorable day. I was so absorbed and incredulous that I didn't hear footsteps approaching. I only looked up when the door was opened to see my guardian standing looking at me behind his desk, surprise and growing anger clear on his face. But my own fury was now ready to erupt. I forestalled his rebuke by going on the attack.

'What evidence do you have for what you say about women?' I asked. '*Weaker and colder in nature, a sort of natural deficiency*? It seems to me it's the other way round! Men are the ones who are lacking in something. Men don't feel things as women do. *They* are the cold ones.'

Aristotle was certainly taken aback. He struggled to compose himself.

'Herpyllis, you know very well you shouldn't be in here reading those scrolls.'

I was not to be deflected. 'That's beside the point,' I dared to say. 'You've always told us to come to you with our observations about the world. You've clearly never troubled to ask a woman how she feels or you wouldn't have written any of this.'

'Those are my observations of women and they are based on a great deal of experience,' he replied rather primly.

'Really?' I said in a voice I was having difficulty controlling. 'You spend most of your time with men. Pythias was the only woman you knew at all, and she rarely ventured to express an opinion in front of you. But she felt things very strongly, you may be sure. How hurt she was at the slight attention you paid her! How often she would have liked to sit with you and talk about anything that came into her head. But with you it was always instruction and improvement, or silent disapproval. Nit-picking over her accounts, comments about over-spending on the symposiums, her management of the servants. You rarely smiled at her, showed her little affection. You quickly found consolation with Palaephatus!'

'How dare you criticise my behaviour as a husband?' stormed Aristotle. 'I always showed her respect, I hardly ever raised my voice to her. Pythias was a good wife. She knew her place. Unlike you, Herpyllis! What is it in you makes you think you have the right to speak to me like this?'

'Because you've always encouraged people to think, to learn, to seek knowledge. I always thought that applied to everyone. But now I see it doesn't apply to me or any other woman. We're inferior, defective. That means we have no right to think for ourselves, to express any opinion which differs from yours!'

I was breathing heavily now, on the verge of tears. I knew he would make some withering comment and I wouldn't be able to counter it. Even though I didn't consider women inferior to men, I certainly knew my intellect was inferior to Aristotle's. What's more, I didn't have his lifelong practice in debating issues and arguing a case.

But Aristotle did something completely unexpected. He came round the desk, grabbed my shoulders, pulled me up and kissed me. It was a hard and violent kiss, like Alexander's all those years ago. I squirmed and struggled to get out of his grip, pushing my fists against his chest. At first he tightened his hold and I felt a wave of hopelessness, but when he tried to lay me down on the couch I finally found the strength to push him away as he changed his position.

I ran out of the room and took refuge in my apartment. I tried to quell the shaking taking over my body, the involuntary whimpering sound I was making. I felt betrayed. In spite of Aristotle's sometimes callous behaviour towards me in the past, I had come to see him as a substitute for my father, whom he resembled physically in several ways. I had constantly reminded myself of small acts of kindness he had shown at different times. But now he had shattered my illusions. I had aroused his lust and no other consideration had stopped him from trying to satisfy it. I was completely alone now. All those who loved me had gone.

After that I avoided my guardian as much as possible. I stopped reading the scrolls in his study, but I couldn't live without reading. I had to occupy my mind with something other than thoughts of loneliness and despair. I visited the library when I knew there was no one else there – during the public afternoon lectures.

I started working my way through everything in the room, and one day Callisthenes came and showed me where to find a scroll that interested me. But when I turned to look at him he was gone. Another day he was sitting with his elbows on a desk, his fingers on his temples. When I leaned down to see his face, he disappeared. Once he was moving around silently, seeking the right place for a new item. But the closer I approached the more the image faded. I thought of Orpheus and Eurydice. Our roles were reversed. I was the one who had to watch in despair as my love was dragged back into the Underworld.

To try to avoid my own company I started listening in on the symposiums I arranged each week. Some months after my encounter with Aristotle in his study I was eavesdropping on a symposium on how to be a good man. The debate was following a predictable pattern, similar to the works I had read on ethics. My guardian was elaborating on the duty of a good man to be a good citizen. He was interrupted by a voice I didn't recognise. It must have been one of the Athenians from outside the Lyceum.

'What you say is all very fine, Aristotle,' he commented, 'but one might wonder whether you yourself have been a good citizen – of Stagira, I mean, for you don't qualify to be a citizen of Athens. One hears you were less than a good citizen of *that* city.'

My heart jumped at the mention of Stagira. What did this man mean? There was a hush and I wondered what had caused it. What expression did Aristotle have on his face? I was hidden behind the door and had no view of anyone round the table. Finally I heard my guardian's voice. It sounded quieter and more strained than before; it took me a moment to realise it was him speaking.

'I'm at a loss to know what you're referring to,' Aristotle said.

'Why, the sack of the city,' the man replied. 'Some twenty-five years ago now, isn't it?'

Aristotle didn't respond. Perhaps he had nodded his head. The Athenian went on:

'It's common knowledge you betrayed the city to your friend, King Philip. Told him where the weak point in the walls was.'

This was met with a murmuring of voices and some louder exclamations. I heard Theophrastus objecting vociferously. Aristotle must have put up his hand for silence because they suddenly went quiet.

'As you see,' he said, 'that is certainly *not* common knowledge, and there's no truth to it whatsoever.'

'So how do you explain how quickly the Macedonians overran Stagira?' continued the Athenian. 'It was certainly common knowledge that the walls were thick and high. They'd served the city well for centuries. Yet Philip found his way in on the second day of the siege.'

'I wasn't present at the siege of Stagira, and nor, I believe, were you, sir,' Aristotle retorted. 'It was a sad day indeed when it was taken.'

The Athenian must have been about to respond because Theophrastus now intervened.

'We have strayed some distance from our subject, gentlemen,' he observed. 'Let us now move on to the other duties of a good man...'

My mind was in complete turmoil and my heart was pounding. It took me a long time to calm down. I went on listening, hoping – yet dreading – that they would mention Stagira again. And the longer I listened in vain the more convinced I became that the unknown Athenian had told the truth. It explained the mysteries surrounding what had happened that dreadful day and since.

When the symposium ended, I waited for all the guests to depart and then confronted Aristotle. He looked startled as I entered but I didn't give him a chance to say anything. I launched straight into my accusation.

'It's true, isn't it? I remember how you winced that first time Stagira was mentioned, when Alexander said I was from Stagira, when you thought I was my mother. I thought it was because you loved her. It wasn't just that, was it? Her death was *your* fault. That's why you took me on as your ward. You felt guilty. You didn't throw me out when I refused to marry Theophrastus. You were trying to make up for what you'd done, trying to salve your conscience. How does betraying your home city fit with being a good man? Condemning your neighbours and their families to death or slavery? How can you talk about being a good man?'

Aristotle had gone very pale. I didn't know if it was from anger or remorse. I didn't care. Finally he spoke. His voice was thick and almost unrecognisable.

'You can't understand this, Herpyllis,' he said. 'Being good has to do with civic responsibility as well as obligations to family and friends. Philip was going to attack Stagira. There was nothing I could do about that. It was part of his plan to unite the Greeks and eventually take revenge on the Persians. I supported him in that. We had to be strong, never allow the barbarians to invade us again, never have them lay waste to our cities, steal our treasures, destroy our culture again. Stagira had to be sacrificed. Your father would have allied himself with the Athenians, as the Olynthians did. Philip would have had the enemy at his back. It was a terrible decision for me. Knowing he was going to attack Stagira, I thought it best to make sure it was quick. So as few men would be killed as possible.'

'As few as possible!' I repeated in a voice which was more like a croak. 'They rounded them all up. Both my brothers were there. Aristion was only thirteen. They stoned them all to death! Theron – he was coming to Athens to study with you in a few months. He was so excited. Not to mention my father, the best man I've ever known!'

'I never expected Philip to have so many killed' Aristotle said softly. 'I knew your father would have to be executed. The chief magistrate could never have been

286

left alive. He defied the King. I wrote to him months before. I told him to take you all away. You could have gone to Pella.'

'Pella?' I choked on the word. 'My father would never have been a friend to the Macedonians! And how could he have left Stagira? He was chief magistrate. It was his duty to defend the city. Wasn't that part of being a good man?'

'It's much more complicated than that, Herpyllis,' Aristotle replied in an irritated tone. He started stressing parts of words as if speaking to a particularly dim-witted servant. 'He would have been a better Sta*gi*ran if he'd allied himself with the Mace*do*nians. I tried to persuade him in Athens. I told him he should be their *al*ly. Your father wouldn't *lis*ten. He called them bar*ba*rians. Said we Sta*gi*rans were civilised *Greeks* who should have nothing to *do* with a bunch of *mur*derous *war*riors who wanted a king at their head. He wouldn't *see sense*. He was no politician. He didn't see that Philip couldn't have a *de*mocrat in league with the Macedonians' strongest enemy so *close* to *home*. You must try to understand, Herpyllis. It was all *po*litics. Nothing *per*sonal. Your father understood that.'

I was so taken aback and humiliated by the way Aristotle had spoken that it took me a few moments to recover. Then the core of my anger re-emerged and I managed to control my voice better as I continued more quietly:

'So you're saying uniting the Greeks against their will under a barbarian king is worth the lives of countless good men like my father and brothers.'

There was a glimpse of something resembling shame on his face before he resumed his usual expression and commented coldly:

'I said you couldn't understand.'

The sting of his disdain was still driving me on:

'Because I'm a woman? Because I'm inferior? Because your precious politics is something higher than human life? Having revenge on the Persians is more important than living a peaceful, happy life?'

Aristotle's face was now expressionless. He turned and walked out of the room, leaving me alone to give full vent to my anger and grief.

After that night Aristotle asked one of his students to prepare the symposiums. We lived as strangers in the same house. I couldn't condone his betrayal of Stagira. I could never forgive him. He was right: I could never understand. I went about my daily tasks like an automaton. I spent little time with the children. The nightmares came back: Philip's command, my father stabbed in the back, my mother reaching out to me before she died, saying my name. My guilt again. Aristotle hadn't killed my mother, neither had Philip. That was *my* fault. That was *my* guilt. The rest would have happened sooner or later. Aristotle was right. Perhaps we would all have starved to death. Perhaps it would have been much worse – long and lingering.

My loneliness reached a peak in the following weeks. The women around me – the servants and slaves – were kind but I knew they saw me as unnatural. They thought

I should be satisfied with running the household, supervising the children. There was no one with whom I could share my sense of betrayal by Aristotle, my longing for love and companionship. I missed Pythias even more than I had in the months after she died, and wished Cassander had been there to distract me with his enthusiasm for the latest thing he had learnt or read in the library.

In the end it was ten-year-old Pythy who saved me. One day she came into the room where I was sitting and staring at nothing.

'Why don't you want to be with me any more, Auntie?' she asked with such a hurt look on her face that it jolted me into action and I took her in my arms and hugged and kissed her.

'I'm sorry, Pythy,' I said. 'I'm in a terrible place where I feel so completely alone.'

She drew back and gave me a serious look:

'I'm here, Auntie,' she said reassuringly, 'I love you. Don't forget me.'

I began spending most of my time with the children again, not just playing the lyre together but taking up Pythy's education where Aristotle had left off. He took little interest in his daughter any more, and his son might as well not have existed. It was strange thinking back to the early years in Athens when our children had been an inexhaustible source of fascination for him. That seemed to be characteristic of the man. He would pitch himself into the study of something and find out all he could about it, but then move on to something else and pay it little attention any longer, unless some new and startling information came to light.

Pythy was still a girl, but it wouldn't be long before her breasts filled out and she gained a waist and hips – we would celebrate her First Blood in a few years now. She had her mother's clear skin and dark hair, but her eyes were grey, like Aristotle's. I had always regarded her as my daughter; it was a kind of joint enterprise of motherhood that Pythias and I had with our children – they were so close in age. Now that my friend was no more, I was her daughter's mother. And it was a great comfort to find that was how she looked on me. She gave me back a role in life.

Pythy was a sweet child, shy and retiring like her mother, but mature and efficient when it came to looking after her little brother. He had replaced her dolls. She hugged him and scolded him in equal measure; I told his nurse to let the girl take care of him as much as she wished. And she would come to me whenever she wanted to be hugged herself. She reminded me of Cleopatra in her love of myths and legends, and it was the same ones she asked me to tell her again and again. Andromeda, Ariadne, Atalanta – women with different fates: one a passive victim saved by a man whose wife she became; the second an active helper of the man she loved, forsaking everything she knew to follow him, only to be abandoned but then partnered by a god; and the third a proud virgin warrior, feared and despised by men, but finally finding love. Pythy didn't know which woman she should resemble, which fate she should desire. In the end she had a little of all of them.

As Nicomachus grew and started to explore the world around him I took the place of mother to him, too. There was something of my own son in him, something so dear that it wasn't long before he had his corner of my heart. But he was a solemn little lad, wide-eyed and timid like a fawn.

As I lived from day to day, trying to build my world around the children, I had almost forgotten about Cassander going to Babylon, almost stopped worrying about him and dreading what terrible fate might be his. Then one unforgettable day a messenger came to the gate. I thought nothing of it. There was frequent correspondence between Aristotle and his former students, not to mention between him and Antipater. But ten minutes later he came to me in the apartment where I was sewing. It was weeks since we had spoken to each other. He simply held out the tablet to me. It was hard to read his face. Was it sorrow? Was it resignation? I took the tablet. I immediately recognised Cassander's hand. It contained simple facts without comment:

I have to report that the King has died of a strange fever which lasted twelve days. None of the doctors could say what caused it. None of their remedies worked.

I looked at Aristotle. Catharsis at last! I started sobbing uncontrollably. Grief for the boy I had played with and come to love, who had loved me. Grief for what he had become. Grief for Callisthenes, killed at his command. Grief for how the world is. Aristotle put his arms round me and stroked my hair. I didn't pull away. I knew there was no desire in it. It was a reconciliation. A joint relief that Alexander could do no more harm and that Cassander was alive and well. But there was no joy in it. Neither of us found revenge held any pleasure or satisfaction.

22
DESTINY

'Choice, not chance, determines your destiny.'

When the Athenians heard Alexander was dead, they rose up in revolt against Macedonian rule. Aristotle had often commented that Athens was a dangerous place for Macedonians, or anyone who had anything to do with them. And, soon after this new war started, he was proved right. His fame and status as the most celebrated philosopher in Greece were no protection. On the contrary, they were probably his downfall. Other philosophers from less prestigious schools accused my guardian of impiety. They raked up his hymn to Pythias's father Hermias, the one he had recited so movingly that day in Delphi in front of his friend's statue, where it was inscribed for all to read. His detractors claimed that it placed a man on the same level as the gods. They were calling for Aristotle to be tried and face the penalty which awaited all blasphemers – death.

My guardian decided it was not worth defending himself against this accusation, spurious though it was. After all, the Athenians had condemned Socrates himself, Plato's teacher, and forced him to take his own life for the same alleged offence.

'No point in allowing them to commit a second crime against philosophy,' he commented drily.

We packed our belongings into some wagons and left the city of Athene in the middle of the night. Theophrastus stayed behind to lead the Lyceum school. It was over twelve years since I had arrived in the City of the South, the longest time I had lived anywhere. In Athens I had experienced my greatest joys and my greatest griefs. The main reason I was loath to leave was Stotty's grave. I often used to visit it; it was my only connection with my husband and our son.

Our journey was mainly silent except for the sounds of the horses' hooves and the creaking of the wagons. Most of the time I sat with Pythy under one arm and Nicky under the other. In four days we reached the narrowest point of the strait dividing the island of Euboea from the mainland: Aulis, where Agamemnon sacrificed his daughter to get fair winds for the fleet to sail to Troy – the act which set in train so many others, down to this day. We crossed the sea on a misty morning and went to the villa in Chalcis. Aristotle's face was set in a grim expression. I wondered if we would ever go back to Athens, if I would ever sit beside Stotty's grave again.

My guardian retreated into his study as soon as we arrived. I supervised the unpacking of the wagons, the airing of the rooms, the cleaning and making up of the beds, the preparation of a light supper. Aristotle didn't emerge that evening or the next. Simon took him all his meals and we lived separate lives across a courtyard for two days, three, a week, two weeks... I organised small repairs to the buildings, the weeding and pruning of the garden, the purchase and cooking of food, the collection of water, the washing of clothes. Various citizens came to our gate to pay their respects to their famous neighbour; all were sent away.

Simon kept me informed about his master's health: he was pale and losing weight, hardly eating or even working. The shock of having so many of his former colleagues and friends turn against him and seek his death had clearly brought on that blackness of the soul he suffered from periodically; this time he couldn't seem to shake it off. I told Simon to encourage Aristotle at least to go out for a walk, but he said his master didn't seem to hear him if he spoke; most of the time he just sat staring blankly or lay on his bed. I tried to believe that the physician would heal himself, but, as the weeks went on, the likelihood of this decreased.

It was a shock to realise that I had forgiven him for Stagira. My anger had gone. It had been a terrifying experience watching Aristotle's transformation from a master of politics into its victim. He had lost everything because he had chosen the Macedonians over the Greeks. And then it struck me: choice had not come into it. He had been placed on their side from childhood and had played the role he had been assigned. I could have gloated but I didn't. It was like Alexander's death. I couldn't rejoice at it. My feelings for both of those men who had shaped my life were too complicated.

Gradually I came to feel Pythias showing me my duty. I saw her face, looking sad and disappointed in me. No matter how much I rehearsed the reasons I had to hate my guardian, I ended up feeling pity. Finally, I decided the worst thing that could happen if I went into Aristotle's study uninvited was that he would shout at me and forbid me ever to do so again. It seemed a small risk to take.

There was no answer to my knock. I knocked again and waited. I wanted to turn on my heel and go away but Pythias's face was still there in my mind's eye; she looked at me full of reproach now. I felt the handle and opened the door – softly, slowly. Aristotle was sitting at his desk. There was nothing on it. The room was bare except for the scrolls we had brought with us on the shelf, the ones he had been working on in the last few months. No specimens – we had left them all at the Lyceum. He didn't seem to have noticed me come in. I moved towards him and spoke his name. It sounded tender, it sounded like Pythias's voice. I knew my role now.

'Aristotle,' I said again, more loudly this time, 'are you all right? I'm worried about you.'

His head turned slowly, as if it hurt him to move his neck. He looked at me, blankly at first. Then his face collapsed into a desperate expression.

'Herpyllis.'

His voice was weak and hoarse, but I didn't hesitate. I knew what I had to do. I went up to him and took his head in my arms and held him close. He gave a great sigh. We stayed like that for several minutes, not moving. Then I took his hand and led him out into the courtyard. The sun came out from behind a cloud at that moment; he closed his eyes and let it warm his face. I sat him down on a stone bench and went to get the herbs we had used to calm Pythias. I massaged Aristotle's temples and wrists with the oil of spikenard and Simon brought the valerian tea I asked him to prepare. My guardian drank from the cup I held without demur. When it was empty, I took him to his bedroom and helped him lie down. He slept like a baby all afternoon and I watched over him.

In the evening when he woke I took his hand again. We went out of the gate down to the cliffs to look over the sea. There was a slight breeze and the waves had little white crests. The sunset was magnificent – all crimsons and golds. We stood and watched, hand in hand. Then we walked back and sat down to dinner together, the first time ever at home. Neither of us said a word.

When dinner was over, I asked him to show me the stars and we stood in the courtyard until my neck ached while he showed me the different constellations and indicated their paths across the skies. I thought of Cassander far away and in danger in Babylon. I thought of Callisthenes looking at the stars, thinking of me, me thinking of him. Stotty pointing, his sweet, pure voice. As we retired to bed my guardian lightly patted my arm and gave a feeble smile. A feeling of warmth and relief spread through me.

Aristotle slowly resumed his old routine of work in the study. I had to be his eyes, of course. It had been many years since his eyesight had weakened so that he needed others to read and write for him. Now I was the only one left. And I had to run the household as well, so I often had to leave him alone. But every evening he would come and find me if I wasn't already with him. We would walk down to the cliffs and watch the sun set together.

One day there was a seal bobbing about in the water. Then it flopped onto the beach below and lay there as if exhausted. Aristotle pointed to it.

'You see that creature,' he said. 'Both a sea animal and a land animal. Both and neither. Like me. I'm both a Greek and a Macedonian, and neither. An Athenian and an exile, and neither. An insider and an outsider, and neither. Something in between. I spent more than half my life in Athens. I studied every article of the constitution, wrote about how to be a good citizen. Yet I could take no part in the life of the city, own no property, cast no vote. Then they hounded me out. But I'm not an exile – it was never my city. I'm like the seal – of the sea and of the land, of both and neither. My fate is to belong nowhere.

'Theophrastus was right. Life is ruled by fortune, not wisdom. What good did it do me to seek to know every-thing, to tell others what I knew? They saw me as Philip's man, Alexander's teacher. That is how the world will always see me. That is my curse, my fate. My search to live the good life and show the ultimate path to know-ledge and happiness has been in vain. They don't want me in the sea or on the land.'

I looked at the seal lumbering across the sand, dragging itself along as if it had lost a limb. I thought Aristotle was more like a chameleon, adapting to its environment, changing colour, fitting in wherever it found itself. He had played the game at court much better than Callis-thenes; in Pella he would wear fine linen, have his hair curled, put a ring on each finger. But this was a point not worth arguing about.

'Tell me,' I said, 'what will be left of Philip's kingdom or Alexander's empire in a hundred years' time? Your works will be there forever; you've written them down – all the fruits of your research, the results of your observations, the essence of your wisdom. You'll leave a library of the sum total of human knowledge. Your work will last for as long as people inhabit the earth.'

He squeezed my hand and neither of us said any more that evening. The next morning he commented:

'I think I know why you're called Herpyllis. Your mother and I had our favourite place to sit and talk. It was by the old sanctuary. The ground there was covered with wild thyme. We used to love the smell of it – that's why we sat there. And you're named after it.

'Whenever I look at you, I think of that place, those carefree years before I became Fortune's plaything. I thought I was carving out my path in life, but in fact I was simply following the way laid out for me by chance. I only see that clearly now. We never cease to be the slaves of random events, however much we think we control our destinies. If my father hadn't died when I was still a boy, if I hadn't gone to Pella with my sister's husband, if my guardian hadn't been Philip's teacher, if I had never met Philip, if my guardian hadn't been from Atarneus, if I hadn't been from Stagira, if I had never lived in Athens... Better not to think about these things, Herpyllis. But that doesn't mean they don't rule our lives.'

He stopped. I could see he was hesitating about telling me something. Finally he said, not looking at me:

'The time has come to tell you about an agreement I made with the King,' he said. 'I went to Mieza and taught Alexander on condition that Stagira was rebuilt at the King's expense.'

'Rebuilt?' I repeated in disbelief.

'Yes,' he said softly, 'I fulfilled my half of the bargain and now I hear the rebuilding has been completed. I thought you'd like to know.'

We had weeks of complete harmony when Aristotle seemed resigned to his fate, almost back to his old self, inquiring into everything, working hard. And Fortune brought us Myrmex. He was a bright lad. He reminded me a little of Cassander when he first came to us – earnest, eager, respectful. He was the orphaned son of a distant cousin of Aristotle's. According to his tutor, he showed great promise, and my guardian had not needed too much persuading to take the boy on as a pupil, mainly to be his eyes when I could not be.

It was good having the boy there at Aristotle's side all day, a successor to Callisthenes and Cassander, requiring his attention and hanging on his every word. They often went down to the beach together or walked along the cliffs, describing the creatures they saw and talking about their habits. The boy had lived in the area since birth and was an observant youth. He was just what Aristotle needed. But some days my guardian would sink into blackness again and shut himself up in his study. None of us would disturb him. In the evening, though, I would collect him for our sunset walk.

Aristotle became fascinated by the strong tides in the strait between Chalcis and the mainland. Even local sailors had been known to get caught out by them; a father and son had recently drowned when their boat hit a vortex as the tide turned and they were thrown overboard.

'Appropriate,' remarked my guardian one evening, as we watched just such a whirlpool forming, 'that I should end up here where everything goes up and down all the time. Nothing stable, nothing constant. Like our lives. Ah, Plato, Plato. At least the soul is immortal, unchanging, isn't it?'

I wasn't sure that this was a rhetorical question. Although there was a falling intonation at the end of the sentence, the furrowing of the brow that accompanied it was usually a sign that Aristotle was seriously considering an issue, weighing the pros and cons. He was silent for a moment. Then he gave me his wry smile.

'I used to think the myths were simply stories, Herpyllis, that we just invented them and played them out on the stage to provide a way of purging ourselves of irrational emotions, that they had nothing to do with reality. But I was wrong. Life *is* like the myths; it's just that we don't know which myth we're living until the telling is nearly done. And it's our very own myth we live. I'm not Oedipus, Odysseus, or Tiresias. I'm all of them and none. My fate is mine alone.

'But now I know which myth is closest to mine, Herpyllis. Prometheus. Punished for having the temerity to seek knowledge for the good of mankind. Having his liver pecked out, only to find it intact the following day, so he can go through the same agony again and again. Suffer the same excruciating pain every day for the rest of his life.'

He turned away then and soon we returned to the house in silence. It was a few days later I discovered the pain he was talking about wasn't metaphorical. As I took his hand for the evening walk, he snatched it away and put it to his stomach with a groan.

'What is it?' I asked, taking him round the waist as he doubled over. He groaned again. I shouted for Simon and together we supported him as he hobbled to the study, where we laid him down on the couch. He still had his hand clutched to his stomach. Then suddenly he leaned over and vomited onto the floor. He was wracked with spasms of retching, between which he was breathing fast. I put my hand on his forehead and felt it hot and sweaty. Simon tried to lift his master into a sitting position, but Aristotle seemed to be completely rigid and gasping.

'Please, please, try to calm yourself,' I said, making a tremendous effort to make my voice sound soothing despite my rising panic. 'Try to sit up and breathe deeply.'

Suddenly Aristotle's body started shaking uncontrollably and he threw his head back, lurching sideways. Fortunately, Simon had a grip on his waist, so he didn't fall on the floor. The whites of his eyes had rolled back and looked yellow, as did his face. We managed to put a pillow under his head and straighten out his body. The shaking decreased a little but his breathing was still rapid and shallow. I sent Simon to get some spikenard and stroked Aristotle's head gently, making the same shushing noises I had used to calm his little namesake during those terrible weeks in Athens. I again found myself praying in my head to an unknown deity to save this man: *Please, please, don't let him die.* I needed him, the last 'family' I had.

Slowly Aristotle started breathing more deeply and stopped shaking. He closed his eyes. I massaged the spikenard into his temples and wrists, but he moaned again and pulled both hands away to lay them on his stomach. It wasn't long before he was vomiting again and shaking. Simon and I looked at each other in desperation. The best physician in the area was the man who lay on the bed, but we sent Philo to get help in the city.

That night and all of the next two days were spent helplessly watching as Aristotle writhed in agony, unable to keep down any of the potions the local physicians prepared. He gradually slipped into unconsciousness on the fourth day. I sat by his bedside all the time, occasionally nodding off and waking to find my head next to his.

The philosopher was declared dead of a stomach complaint, but I knew the real cause of death. Disillusion. Despair that his influence in all fields of philosophy, whether politics, metaphysics, or any of the other forms of scientific inquiry in which he had spent his life, had come to nothing. In the end he had been ignored, disdained, hated.

23
BEARING WITH COMPOSURE

'The beauty of the soul shines out when a man
bears with composure one heavy mischance after
another, not because he does not feel them, but
because he is a man of high and heroic temper.'

'The executors and Nicanor, in memory of me and of
the steady affection which Herpyllis has borne towards
me, shall take care of her in every respect and, if she
desires to be married, shall see that she be given to
one not unworthy; and, besides what she has already
received, they shall give her a talent of silver out of
the estate and three handmaids whomsoever she shall
choose, besides the maid she has at present and the
man-servant Pyrrhaeus; and if she chooses to remain
at Chalcis, the lodge by the garden, if in Stagira, my
father's house. Whichever of these two houses she chooses,
the executors shall furnish with such furniture as they
think proper and as Herpyllis herself shall approve.'

When the local executor read out these generous provisions Aristotle made for me in his will, I was struck by the mention of my *steady affection* for him. Then I thought back over the last months in Chalcis and realised that affection was indeed what I had come to feel for him. Later I allowed myself a rueful smile at my guardian's considering I might want to marry again. In his eyes I must still have been the girl he had mistaken one day in Pella for his childhood friend Antheia. Twenty years had gone by since then. I was thirty-four years old now.

Aristotle named Antipater as the chief executor of his will. When Nicanor returned, he was to become guardian to the children and me, and Pythy was to be his bride as soon as she was of age. The local executors asked me to make a decision where I would live, but I told them we should wait for Nicanor. The will specified that if he didn't return, Theophrastus would be our guardian and Pythy should marry him, if he wished it. I remembered the pallid, frightened girl who had been Aristotle's assistant's short-lived wife. Fortunately, he was fully occupied with the Lyceum school and wouldn't be visiting us soon.

I spent my days carrying on as usual for the children's sake, and willing Nicanor to arrive or send word. We had not yet celebrated Pythy's First Blood; it seemed hard that she should marry a man more than four times her age, but such was the tradition, and Nicanor would not be a bad husband from what I had seen of him.

Just when it seemed we would have to give up hope and bow to the inevitable, Aristotle's nephew and adopted son appeared at the end of a short winter's day. We all embraced him joyfully and ushered him in excitedly. His hair was completely white and he had a large, livid scar down the left side of his face. His limp was much worse.

He sat down heavily with a suppressed groan. He seemed exhausted. I quickly had the servants bring food and drink, and then occupied myself with the children until he had come to himself.

Nicanor said little that evening, simply that he had spent months in a shepherd's hut in Thessaly, being nursed back to health after being left for dead in a skirmish. Over the following days we heard the rest of the story. He had cautiously found his way back to civilisation and discovered the war was over, the Macedonians again in charge. He decided to join us in Athens. While he was spending the night in Aulis on his way down the coast, the locals told him Aristotle had moved to Chalcis but had recently died. They found him the ferryman the following day to bring him across the straits to us.

We soon slipped into a daily routine with the new man of the house. Every morning Nicanor would swim and afterwards Pyrrhaeus massaged him. My man-servant had come to us from the gymnasium at the Lyceum and the skills he had acquired there came in useful. I had the table laid for all our meals to eat together, the children included, and Nicanor accepted the arrangement without comment. He was clearly still in a great deal of pain, but as time went on he began to walk with less difficulty.

We fell into the habit of evening walks just as Aristotle and I had. Somehow it was easier to discuss matters in the open air. Once he said to me with his usual hesitation and look of embarrassment as we walked along:

'I should thank you, Herpyllis, for looking after the children on your own since my uncle died.'

'Oh no, Nicanor,' I replied, 'don't thank me. It's always been as if they were my own children. I hope you won't ask me to part from them now.'

He stopped and looked at the ground. He clearly didn't know how to say what he wanted to. My heart sank. I dreaded what was coming. Finally it came out, while his eyes remained on the ground.

'Herpyllis, I'd like you to remain with us more than anything else. Indeed, I don't know what I'd do without you.'

So I stayed in Chalcis and, despite my protestations, the lodge was furnished for me and the servants moved in, though I spent most of my day in the main house, organising the household. I took care to keep Pythy by my side at all times, to watch and learn how to carry out the responsibilities which would soon fall to her as a wife. I often heard myself using exactly the same phrases her mother had uttered in her early lectures to me on the same subject. And then I would give her daughter a hug and tell her they were her mother's words.

Meanwhile, I continued Little Nicky's education; his seventh birthday when he would be given his own tutor was two years away. He was still a quiet boy without much apparent liking for anything in particular, except his lyre. He had always loved me to play to him from infancy and was now quite proficient himself. I was afraid that Nicanor would be disappointed at his ineptitude at archery and find him unwilling to follow male pursuits like wrestling and hunting.

Antipater wrote to suggest that Aristotle's bones should find a resting-place in the city of his birth, now that it had been rebuilt. Nicanor considered this a fitting memorial to his uncle and wrote to the city magistrates. The Stagirans agreed on the proposal, and the plans for the Aristoteleion began to take shape. Clearly they had never heard what was said in Athens of their famous son's betrayal. And I had long since accepted the truth of what he had told me, of the impossibility of his position. What's more, I knew it had tormented him all his life.

Towards the end of the year, news came that the Aristoteleion would soon be ready. We were asked to bring the philosopher's bones to Stagira and be present at the memorial ceremony. Nicanor read the letter to me and then looked very serious. I waited.

'I've been thinking,' he said. 'You know I was born in Stagira and I've always thought I'd go back there one day when I got pensioned off from the army. Well, now that day's arrived. I don't feel any connection to Chalcis, though this is a beautiful property my uncle left me. But my grandfather's house in Stagira was left to you in my uncle's will. How would you feel about us all moving to Stagira and living there? I'll have a new house built for me and Pythy to live in when we marry. But it'd be good to go back to the old house now, if you allow it.'

'Allow it?' I exclaimed. 'Please, Nicanor, you have far more right to the house than I do. I'd just be content to live there with you all for as long as you'd have me.'

He smiled.

308

'Well,' he said, 'we won't argue about rights here. As far as I'm concerned, we're all family and should stay together. I'll make arrangements for our move as soon as possible.'

I was delighted. It was the best I could hope for: to live with the children back in Stagira, to be home again after all these years. Like Nicanor, I wanted to end my days where I had begun them. We sailed two weeks later and the straits were kind to us. In fact the sea was calm for the whole voyage, and we arrived in the city of my birth without incident.

At the dock there was a welcoming party with the whole city present. The chief magistrate greeted us. He was a tall, slim man, with little grey in his black hair but his skin lined, especially down his cheeks and between his brows. When he turned his brown eyes towards me I let out a cry of joy. It was Linos, our steward, that same proud smile on his face he had given me when I landed the fish all those years ago in that other life.

I embraced him and we all walked up into the city. I was overcome by a feeling of warmth and comfort, safety and security, which I suppose only the act of coming home produces. It seemed my mind was able to erase all the horror of my last day in the city and only to evoke happy childhood memories of playing here, swimming there, hiding behind this tree, walking along that wall, sitting there on the sand, picking herbs from this bush, running along that path.

Aristotle had insisted that all citizens of Stagira who had been enslaved or had gone into exile be returned to their homes, and all buildings be reconstructed as before. Everything was more or less as it had been. Our house had been rebuilt and Linos was living there with his wife Chloe and two children.

As a child, I had idolised Chloe for her simple grace and goodness, as well as her devotion to the Great Goddess. Her mother had been one of the assistants in the sanctuary rites until she had become ill and bedridden, and Chloe was much praised by all the women as a model to which every girl should aspire. I had loved her and been envious of her.

Not long after we arrived in Stagira, Linos and Chloe invited us to the old house and we sat down together. I asked them how they had come back to our city.

'We've been here most of the time, in fact,' Linos said. 'When the mistress took you to the sanctuary, Herpyllis, I didn't know what to do. I couldn't protect the house from the soldiers on my own. In the end, I decided to hide in the trees and watch what happened. I climbed the cherry over there – it was full of blossom. Nobody could see me from below.'

I nodded.

'What did you see?' I asked.

'You know what I saw. From there I had a good view of the square; I saw the King, I heard the orders. After a while I looked away. There's only so much killing you can watch...' and his voice trailed off.

'So you waited in the tree for them all to leave?'

'Actually, I sat there all night. I was too afraid and shocked to come down. It was only when I saw Chloe wandering into the square that I stirred myself and found my way down.'

I looked at Chloe with renewed interest.

'But you were in the sanctuary with us. I remember you there.'

I didn't say I remembered because she had been so brave, singing beside me and fastening her eyes on the Great Mother in fervent prayer, unlike me, quaking in panic.

'Yes,' she said, 'You're right. But I stayed inside when you all went into the courtyard. I felt safest with our Mother. I went on praying. I only realised what had happened when I heard the crackle of flames and turned to see the doors burning. I looked around for some other way out, but, of course, there wasn't one. By then the roof had caught fire and beams were crashing down in front of me. I crawled between the Goddess's feet and curled up in the space beneath her robe. It sheltered me from the fire. Just when I thought I would choke to death from the smoke, the rest of the roof collapsed and the building was open to the sky. The stone of the statue didn't catch fire, and soon I could breathe a little. The Goddess saved me. The flames died down quite quickly but I waited till morning to venture out. I came down and saw...'

She swallowed and looked away. Linos put his hand on hers and took over.

'By the time I arrived,' he said, 'she was on the ground, weeping and wailing. I took her in my arms to hide her face from the awful spectacle. We sat like that for a long time. Then I led her away and into our courtyard. I sat her down on the stone bench. The house was in smoking ruins but I managed to find some dried figs and cheese still intact on the tiles in the pantry. I brought some water and we made ourselves eat and drink a little.

'I sat there thinking hard about what to do with the dead bodies in the square. I couldn't bury them all in the manner required, and that thought haunted me. Finally I decided I should prepare the bodies of our dead magistrates, your father and mother, for proper burial in the cemetery, but I realised I would have to burn the others where they lay. So that's what I did. I buried your parents with all the dignity I could. I spoke of the love and respect felt by all of Stagira for them both, and of my own gratitude for making me a free man and educating me.'

I reached out and hugged Linos. It was a great relief to know that my parents had been buried with due cere-mony and my heart was touched by this simple man, who had endured such mental suffering and physical labour in dealing with the horror left by the Macedonian soldiers. Single-handedly, he had managed to restore some honour to Stagira.

Chloe took up the story of how they had salvaged what they could from the houses, though that was precious little after the burning and looting that had taken place, and stored it under the colonnade in the square, part of which was still standing. They had gone to live with an uncle of Chloe's in a village in the foothills, unaffected by the fighting. There, six months later, they had made their vows to each other and married.

'So when did you come back to Stagira?' I asked them.

'It's almost twenty years ago now,' Linos replied. 'News came to Chloe's uncle's village that Stagira was to be rebuilt and they were looking for men to work here. I volunteered immediately.'

'They made Linos chief foreman of the site,' Chloe broke in to say. 'He could remember what every building looked like and he helped the architects. They were really surprised how well he could draw,' she added with pride.

Nicanor and I both commented on how Stagira seemed to be exactly as we remembered it.

Pythy and Nicky were greeted with such warmth and treated with such respect and interest by all our neighbours that they soon felt far more at home than they ever had in Chalcis or Athens. After a few months Nicky had a string of friends and was quite changed. He was always laughing and running, and soon discovered a love of swimming, encouraged by Nicanor. I remembered my own little boy's enjoyment of the sea and I ached to see him there, splashing about with Nicky.

I am lucky, I had to remind myself, *lucky that I have a son and daughter to replace him.*

A month after our arrival, we celebrated Pythy's First Blood in the woods one moonlit night; I tried not to think about the one twenty years earlier when Olympias officiated and I was the one blindfolded. Chloe was our chief priestess; the Goddess had saved her in the burning sanctuary and the women of Stagira had taken this as a sign that she should lead them. I played my lyre and sang, feeling my friend Pythias beside me all the time, seeing her smile, sensing her pride and happiness. She lives on in me as much as she does in her daughter.

The more public ceremony in Stagira at that time was the dedication of the Aristoteleion. It replaced the colonnade in the centre of the city, and the council was to meet there from that day on. All the citizens had assembled and the magistrates headed the procession. Nicanor and Nicky followed, carrying the casket with Aristotle's bones, and I had the honour of carrying Pythias's behind them, alongside her daughter. All the young men and girls, wearing white and carrying flowers, lined the route.

First we climbed the hill to the Temple of Zeus and sacrificed a bull in the god's honour. We passed the statues of Zeus and Athene which had been set up nearby in accordance with Aristotle's will when Nicanor returned safely. Then we went back to the square and entered the brightly coloured building of the Aristoteleion. It was supported on soaring columns and was much higher and more grandiose than the old colonnade it replaced. There, in a simple ceremony, we placed the bones of my guardian and my friend in the shrine at the centre of the space. The fine, larger-than-life statue of Aristotle was then placed over the top with its simple inscription beneath: *Here lie Aristotle the Stagiran and his wife Pythias*. All the citizens processed past the statue and laid their flowers beneath it.

Looking at that building across the square sparkling in the sunlight every day, I feel satisfied that Aristotle will not be forgotten as he clearly feared in those last few months of his life. And I trust no Stagiran but I will ever know he betrayed this city of his birth. What makes me happiest is that he will be remembered for his philosophy and not for his connections with the Macedonian kings.

His closest friend, Antipater, however, will never escape those associations. News of his death came in a rare letter from Cassander. I hadn't seen my saviour since the day he entrusted his son to us when we set off for Athens. Now the man who had taken me out of the smoking ruins of Stagira was gone too.

The wars started up again and we heard snippets of news from time to time. It was all very complicated as there were two Kings of Macedon: Alexander's simpleton half-brother Arrhidaeus and Alexander's infant son, born after his death. I was relieved that Nicanor showed no signs of wishing to re-enter the fray on anyone's side. He seemed content to live a quiet life in Stagira, spending hours with Nicky or sitting with the men in the square, occasionally adding his comments to the discussion, always listened to with great respect by the others.

One day I asked him to tell me about Callisthenes on the campaign with Alexander, whether they had seen much of each other. An expression of pain crossed his face. I started to say it didn't matter, but he interrupted me:

'No, it's all right,' he said. 'I should think back to the better times, not try to block it all out of my mind. Callisthenes and I didn't spend much time together, but I was proud to see him with Alexander so often, the King listening to him with respect and attention. My companions would often tease me,' he went on. 'They'd nudge each other and say: *That's Nicanor's nephew, you know*. They could see my breast swelling to think that this man who had the King's attention, who spoke so rousingly, who said such wise things, was my sister's boy. And sometimes he would take me aside and talk about you all, wondering aloud what his son looked like, whether he was a good boy worthy of his name.'

There was a long pause. Nicanor was looking at the floor. Finally he started speaking again, but his voice was quiet and strangely hoarse.

'Callisthenes would go quiet when he mentioned you, Herpyllis,' he said. 'He would look up at the stars, or touch that amulet you gave him and stroke it with his fingers.'

He paused again. He looked up and saw the tears in my eyes, but I gave him a kind of nod and he went on, hesitantly now.

'We were crossing the mountains into India when he was killed... There was nowhere to bury him. But... my friends helped me carry his body to a cave. I washed him and laid him out in a fresh tunic. . . I put his copies of *The Iliad* and *The Odyssey* at his side... I put on his hands those special calf-skin gloves you gave him, Herpyllis.'

He looked at me and then back down at his sandals. He went on.

'One frosty night, long before that, I saw him writing in his tent while we were all huddling round the fire. *What a wife I have, Uncle!* he said. *She gave me these*

*gloves so I could go on writing while everyone else is hugging
themselves inside their cloak to try and warm their hands.'*

There was something I wanted to know. I cleared my
throat first. I didn't know if my voice would work.

'And the amulet?' I managed to ask. 'Do you know
what happened to that?'

Nicanor shifted his feet. There was silence again.

'It doesn't matter,' I said. 'I just wondered...'

'Yes,' he suddenly interrupted. 'Callisthenes... gave it
to me for safekeeping. I... I put it back round his neck
in the cave.'

Nicanor stopped talking but still didn't look up. Then
abruptly he added:

'I tried to speak an oration. It was a very poor attempt.
I'm sorry. You know I've never been a man of words.'

I reached out and held his arm. He patted it with his
other hand and fell silent.

Not long afterwards we had another public ceremony in
Stagira. I had commissioned monuments to my parents
to be erected in the cemetery and the whole of the city
came to see them dedicated. Many Stagirans told me it
had helped them find some peace of mind; they could
finally look to the future rather than dwelling on the
past. As for me, I was glad to have restored our dignity
and reminded everyone of the virtues of my mother and
father, but I could still not be reconciled to the futility
of my mother's death.

After the ceremony at the temple I went down the
hill to the sanctuary alone. I thought somehow I might

feel Mother there, that she might talk to me through the Goddess. I sat and stared at that huge lump of cold stone for hours and a kind of resentment grew within me. My mother had appealed to the Great Goddess for her protection and She had failed to come to our aid in our darkest hour. I could forgive neither Her nor myself for causing my mother's death.

I ran out of the sanctuary, trying to escape the awful realisation which was sweeping through me. I came to the edge of the cliff, the waves crashing onto the rocks beneath me. Suddenly my body was engulfed in great sobs; I fell to my knees, shaking. I had been invaded by a vengeful spirit, controlling every movement I made, forming the moans that erupted from my mouth. There was a gaping emptiness inside me, in the place where the Goddess had lived, comforting me when I needed it, reassuring me there was a presence greater than myself, guiding me, giving meaning and purpose to my existence. Now there was a void. It was unbearable. Worst of all, there was no link left with my mother. I was no longer true to her. *Promise me you'll never forget what I've taught you,* she had said. *Whatever happens, you'll always be true in your heart.* I couldn't stop those terrible sobs. There was no longer any point to my life. I had nothing left now.

It was Chloe who found me. She just held me in her arms until I finally stopped sobbing. She didn't ask me anything and I didn't tell her anything. She walked home with me, arm in arm. In the following days I kept going to that place above the rocks. I would sit there for long hours doing nothing, trying not to think about anything.

I was numb. I was hoping my faith would come back, that I would find that warm centre of my being again.

Pythy was fifteen when Nicanor asked me if it was time they married. I had prepared her well for this event and she seemed completely reconciled to it. Her friends were sensible girls who didn't spend their time eyeing the young men whenever possible. Pythy had much of her mother's balanced pragmatism and sharp intelligence. She was beginning to be a friend as well as a daughter to me. I had managed to persuade Nicanor that there was no need to build another house for him and Pythy on my account. I told him now I thought she was ready to be his wife. He looked down and then turned to me, an ironic smile on his face.

'You did know, Herpyllis, didn't you,' he asked, 'that it was you I wanted to marry?'

'Me?' I queried. 'You never said anything.'

'Twice I spoke to Aristotle,' he went on, 'twice I asked for your hand. The first time he said you were to marry someone else. Soon afterwards Callisthenes came to me in despair, saying he wanted to marry you but my uncle had refused to allow it. Months went by and you were still unmarried. I began to hate Aristotle. I believed he had lied to me, that he wanted to have you himself.'

'It was Theophrastus he wanted me to marry,' I admitted with a shudder. 'I told him he could do what he liked with me but I would never marry that man. He disgusted me.'

'You were very brave,' he said, giving me an appreciative look. 'I never dared to cross Aristotle. When I asked him the second time if I could marry you – that time I came to Athens on my way to Olympia – he told me I must marry his daughter when she was old enough, continue the family line. I wanted to strangle him. It was the thought of coming back to you that had kept me alive in the years after Callisthenes was killed. It was your face I held in my mind when we crossed the desert on the way back to Babylon and most of my men were dying of thirst around me. I was coming home to you.'

I leaned across and kissed his cheek. I had never once suspected how he felt about me. It was a genuine surprise. But we had lived together like an old married couple to all intents and purposes for three years, except that we had never shared a bed. When he and Pythy were finally married, nothing really changed. We all continued living in the old house after the wedding in much the same way.

It was only three months later when Nicanor's wounded leg started causing him a great deal of pain again and he had a swelling which wouldn't go down. No treatment seemed to alleviate it and he began to lose weight. Most days he had to sit with his leg up, his face grim from suffering. Pythy would sit and play to him, or just sew, looking up and smiling at him from time to time. It was terrible to see his efforts to smile back. Usually they emerged as a macabre grimace. There was little respite at night; the pain was worse and sleep came only rarely.

We awoke one day to find him dead, his face finally at peace, the hint of a happy smile on his lips. I had come to love him. He had been such an easy companion; there had never been anger or tension between us and we had lived together as if it were the most natural thing in the world.

Nicanor had been a soldier all his life and must have killed countless men, seen unspeakable atrocities, yet he appeared mentally untouched by this experience, though the physical scars were plain for all to see. He somehow managed to keep that life separate from his family role. He was a man who asked nothing; unlike Aristotle and Callisthenes, he didn't question existence or the nature of reality, the foundations of virtue or vice. He was part of Nature, as integral as a bird in the air or a fish in the sea. A rare beast indeed.

Yet he left me a puzzle. A few days after he died, I was sorting through the few things he kept in the chest in his room. Under the armour and the greaves I found a familiar object: the amulet Olympias had given me all those years ago and which I had given to Callisthenes. I opened it to find the sprig of wild thyme, grey with age, still there, and the lock of my hair.

Years later Cassander told me his father had given him more details of my husband's execution. His body had been left by the roadside and Alexander had expressly forbidden anyone to bury him on pain of as excruciating a death as Callisthenes himself had experienced.

I decided Nicanor must have made up the whole story about Callisthenes' funeral to comfort me.

24
VOCATION

*'Where your talents and the needs of the world
cross – there lies your vocation.'*

As chief executor of Nicanor's will, Linos put off writing to Theophrastus for as long as he could. In accordance with Aristotle's wishes, the Head of the Lyceum was now our guardian. Two weeks after my friend Linos finally wrote to inform Theophrastus of Nicanor's death, Eumares appeared on our doorstep. He was Theophrastus's personal servant, devoted to his master, a stout self-satisfied man in his late forties now. Our dislike was reciprocal. He greeted me in a perfunctory manner, handed me a tablet and walked past me into the house. Theophrastus's message was brief and succinct:

Pythias and Nicomachus are to come to me in Athens. You will pack all their belongings and entrust them to Eumares, who will accompany them. You will stay in Stagira.

My whole body started shaking and I dropped the tablet. I don't know which emotion was uppermost – anger or grief – but I completely lost control of myself. I just kept repeating *What right...? What right...?* over and over again.

Pythy and Nicky were staring at me in horror. Eumares had sat down at the table and was nonchalantly biting into a pear.

'Get out!' I shouted at him in a fury. 'Get out of my house – *now*!'

At first he gave me an ironic smile but, when I picked up the tablet to throw at him, he jumped up surprisingly quickly for a man of his age and made for the door. We heard the gate in the courtyard bang behind him a few seconds later. I grabbed the children and held them close.

'It's all right,' I said as calmly as I could, 'I'm not letting him take you away.'

'Is that what he wants?' Pythy asked in a small voice. 'To take us away?'

'Don't worry,' I replied, hugging her close. 'I won't let him.'

Nicky buried his face in my chest. My mind raced back to that day in Dion, Cleopatra doing the same thing while the nauseating stink of the slaughtered oxen polluted the air around us. I must protect him as I had her. I was still shaking. I forced myself to take some deep breaths and sit down with the children so as not to frighten them too much. We were still at the table holding hands when Linos and Chloe came in. Chloe sat down with us, putting her arm round me. Linos couldn't look at us. He stood there for a long time without saying anything. We all just stared at him. Finally he spoke, still contemplating the floor:

'Herpyllis,' he said, his voice hoarse as if he'd been shouting for hours, 'you must know there's nothing we can do. Theophrastus is completely within his rights. He is guardian to all of you now. Eumares has appealed to me as chief magistrate. I have no choice but to enforce a guardian's wishes.'

I couldn't believe my ears. Linos was my oldest friend.

'What kind of friendship is this?' I whispered incredulously. 'I thought I could trust *you* at least to be on my side!'

Linos winced as if I had slapped his face.

'Linos,' I begged, 'you must help us! I can't let them go. Not to that awful cold fish of a man! These children are mine – they look on me as their mother. You can't let him take them, Linos! Linos!' I repeated his name desperately now.

And then at last he looked up at me. I can still see his expression. It was the same one he had when he recounted to me how he had hidden in our cherry tree and watched the slaughter and destruction of our city, thirty years earlier.

'My dear Herpyllis,' he said in a voice thick with emotion, 'you know I would give my life for you and the children if it would help. But in this case I'm completely powerless. If we refuse to send the children to Theophrastus, he'll demand the magistrates not only carry out his wishes but also throw you out of this house. Who knows what else he might do? Fighting him over this will only bring you even more pain and suffering.'

'But, Linos,' I went on, though I knew it was hopeless, 'he doesn't care for them, he doesn't love them! This is his way of causing *me* pain, taking his revenge for my refusal to marry him all those years ago. We can't let him do this!'

'If there were any means of thwarting his wishes, you may be sure I'd use it, Herpyllis. But a guardian's word is final. And many would say he has their best interests at heart. Nicky is of an age to start his education in Athens. To be at the Lyceum. You must admit, it's what his father would have wanted. And Theophrastus has a new husband for Pythy in mind, a man in her father's image.'

I jumped up and shielded Pythy with my body.

'Not him!' I shouted. 'Not Theophrastus! She can't marry him!'

Linos came and held my arms.

'No, Herpyllis,' he said soothingly, 'a man who studied under Aristotle. He was one of his favourite pupils. He'll make Pythy a fine husband.'

I could hear the girl's sobs behind me. I turned and embraced her, stroking her hair. Chloe gently parted us after a while and sat me down again. She coaxed us both into drinking some water. I was still trembling and the water spilled onto my chest. I looked down at the wet mark and saw again the dark splash of wine on my white dress in the moonlight, all those years ago. Another bad omen.

Chloe took charge. She made us both drink a potion and slowly I stopped shaking, Pythy stopped sobbing. Nicky had said nothing to anyone since Eumares' arrival. He was in a state of shock.

That afternoon a delegation of little boys arrived in the courtyard. One at a time they came in and presented Nicky with their farewell gifts: knucklebones, shells, fish hooks. The young women of Stagira came to say goodbye to Pythy. They gave her combs, pieces of embroidery, charms. And that day the Daughters of the Earth came and sat with me. Some of them busied themselves packing the children's belongings, adding delicacies for them to eat on their long journey south. We all sat together that night as if holding a vigil, and the next morning they were at my side as we watched the wagon trundle down the road and out of the city gates at dawn.

That day and every day afterwards the women of Stagira stayed with me. There was always one of them sitting at my side, sewing, talking of this and that. Linos came and told me what was happening in the world beyond our gates. He asked my advice though he received none. We would just sit in silence.

One day when Chloe was sewing while I sat at the table, I could stand it no longer.

'I know you mean well,' I said to her, 'but I'd like to be alone. I don't want everyone coming here, keeping an eye on me. Please leave me alone.'

Chloe looked up and smiled.

'Ah, Herpyllis,' she replied. 'We can't leave you alone. Look at you. You might do something stupid.'

'No, Chloe,' I countered. 'I might do something perfectly sensible in the circumstances.'

Then she came across and hugged me, just as I had held Aristotle in his study in Chalcis when he had been in the depths of the blackness. And finally I wept, my face in her stomach, my tears wetting her dress as she went on holding me until I had vented my grief. Then she sat down beside me and held my hand. Finally I turned to her.

'Look,' I said slowly, 'there's nothing left for me now. I am of no use to anyone. Have pity on me, Chloe. Let me go.'

'No, Herpyllis,' she replied. 'You're being selfish, so full of self-pity. Your parents would be ashamed to see you give up like this. Is that what they taught you? To feel sorry for yourself? You are their daughter, brought up by our chief magistrate and high priestess. You were with Aristotle all those years. Teach us what you know. Give us your knowledge. Do something for your city.'

Chloe spoke with indignation and I was shocked into silence. I don't know if she had prepared that speech, perhaps together with Linos, or whether the idea came to her that day. Whatever the case, I could find no arguments to counter her. She had made me feel guilty and at the same time given me back a reason for living.

I started teaching just a few neighbours' children at first, then over the years my house developed into a little school. I taught all the boys and girls to read and write, to play the lyre, to sing and recite. And those men and women who wanted to learn I helped too. Stagirans have become the most educated of citizens.

Pythy wrote to me often. Within a month Theophrastus had married her to the man Linos had mentioned: a Spartan. Her second husband was a nobleman, thoroughly inculcated in the civilising views of the Lyceum, but life in Sparta was quite shocking for Pythy at first.

Women wore short tunics, revealing much more of their bodies in public than she was used to, and indeed they walked around the city freely on their own. Much to Aristotle's disapproval in his writings, Spartan women were all educated. Although Pythy had a prickly reception from them at first, they came to provide Aristotle's daughter with much better company than had been available in Athens. Within a year she had borne a healthy son.

I heard nothing from Nicky. He was at the Lyceum, strictly under Theophrastus's control and, as Pythy was no longer in Athens, I had no news of him. I hoped he had found friends and not retreated into himself again. As a boy, he had already shown signs of the recurring sickness that had affected both his father and Callisthenes, that withdrawal into self which dimmed the world into uninviting greyness, made company of any kind an undesirable irritation, eating and drinking disagreeable chores.

I redoubled my efforts to be loving and caring to all the little boys in Stagira, as if this would somehow be mysteriously transferred to that one little boy so far away to the south, as if it would inspire a woman there to keep him close to her, give him the affection he needed, the smiles and encouragement his mother and I would have lavished on him.

Life in Stagira went on quietly, far away from the turmoil beyond. I was busy with my school and the months rushed by. At the end of the year a letter came from Pythy with the news that she was with child again. I was worried about her, remembering her mother's second pregnancy and how that had ended. But another letter eventually came, telling me her second son had been born and that the birth had gone more easily than the first time.

Pythy soon wrote asking me to visit her. I was preparing to take up her invitation when she wrote again. Sparta was fortifying itself against invasion after rebelling against the Macedonians. Cassander was now regent for King Arrhidaeus, Alexander's brother, but Alexander's son, the joint King, and his mother had joined Olympias in Epirus. Pythy knew that Cassander was leading an army south to quell the uprising in Sparta. Poor girl. Her husband commanded a unit of the Spartan army. It looked as if he would soon be facing her 'big brother'.

News then came that Olympias had taken the opportunity of Cassander's absence to march on Pella, planning to install her grandson as sole King of Macedon. The Macedonians refused to fight Alexander's mother and she was successful. King Arrhidaeus was executed and scores of Cassander's relatives and friends were then murdered on Olympias's orders. Meanwhile Cassander was victorious, and Pythy widowed for a second time in her short life.

25
VICTORY OVER SELF

'I count him braver who overcomes his desires than him who overcomes his enemies, for the hardest victory is over self.'

So it was that my life tended towards its culmination. I saw it stretched out behind me, leading inexorably towards a vital point in the near future when I might finally have a clear view of it.

My second mother and my little brother were to confront each other on different sides of a battlefield. I envisaged Olympias's forces marching south while Cassander's moved north to meet them, converging at Pydna on the sea between Pella and Dion. The news came quickly to Stagira: the battle went badly for Olympias and she withdrew into the city, which Cassander then besieged.

A vivid memory came back to me of a day in Athens when I was sitting exhausted after flying Stotty through the air with his cloth-winged sandals for the twentieth time. Cassander saw me and asked if I was all right.

'Why do little boys want to be like Perseus?' I asked him in exasperation. 'Why can't they want to be wise philosophers who sit still and read all day?'

He laughed.

'Boys and young men are all the same,' he replied. 'We dream of fighting monsters and saving beautiful maidens. I myself am really looking for a Gorgon to slay and free a grateful lady.'

At the time, Cassander's words had brought a smile to my face. But now he had found his Gorgon and I remembered them with foreboding. We had not been in communication since he had written to tell me of Antipater's death. Cassander was not a great letter-writer like his father, but I had followed his movements and his rise to power through the reports of merchants and soldiers visiting Stagira, as well as from Pythy's letters, which were full of politics and showed her torn between her feelings for her husband on the one hand and her 'big brother' on the other. It was a relief to know that she was surrounded by in-laws who would love and console her, although she could, of course, never tell them of her divided loyalties.

I decided to write to Cassander at Pydna. It was the most difficult letter I have ever had to compose. I could barely understand or analyse my emotions where Olympias was concerned, let alone convey them to this man who was as much 'family' as she was. And here they were in a final confrontation where retribution must be meted out for all the blood spilt.

My dear Cassander,

I have thought long and hard about writing to you. You have already avenged me and many others; I have no right to ask any more of you, if indeed I ever had any rights at all, though you were kind enough to imply that I did.

The woman you now have in your power deserves your hatred and contempt for ordering the deaths of many who were close to you; this much is clear and indisputable. But she is also a queen, destined to be the mother and grandmother of kings. She is fighting to preserve her dynasty, as have all her family before her. And though once she loved your father and valued his counsel, she came to see him as one who would usurp her son's throne. She sees you now as posing the same threat to her grandson, and to herself as the protector of the rightful succession.

How can this possibly concern me, who am so completely inconsequential in such matters of state? My mother was mentor to Olympias when she was a young princess and they became very close. The Queen ordered your father to save us, my mother and me, when Stagira fell to King Philip's army. Both my parents were killed that day, but your father found me and took me to Olympias. She made me part of her household and treated me in many ways as a daughter rather than a slave.

You will appreciate that I have a duty to try to save her now, as she once saved me. When Pydna falls, which I am sure it will, I beg you to allow the Queen to retire to Stagira under armed guard. The people here have no reason to support her or to oppose her. They are indifferent to her cause, and I personally guarantee that she will never have the opportunity to trouble you again.

I ask this favour of you, my dear brother, in the name of the civilised behaviour which Aristotle urged you to adopt, and which I know is close to your heart and your nature.

Show mercy to one who shows none to others for the sake of your own goodness and happiness.

Your loving sister, Herpyllis

The weeks dragged by with no word from Cassander or news of the siege of Pydna. I could bear it no longer and went to see Linos. I told him what I had written to Cassander and that I must see him to plead the Queen's case in person. I informed Linos I wanted to bring Olympias to Stagira. He looked grim.

'I couldn't possibly allow you to go there,' he said. 'Chloe would never forgive me, I would never forgive myself if something happened to you. And there are thieves and bandits everywhere. The road isn't safe. No, Herpyllis. It's impossible, you must see that.'

We argued for hours. I wished I had never approached Linos – just left without a word. But that would have been cruel after all he and Chloe had done for me. I stood my ground. Finally he agreed to let me go, but insisted on leading a guard of twenty Stagirans to accompany me. Many of the men he chose had been my pupils. He said they loved and respected me.

'Don't test their loyalty,' he said 'They would die for you, as would I.'

I thought of Cynane and Olympias, women at the head of armies. Now I sat on a horse for the first time in many years, leading my own troops. How strangely life was turning out! It was early spring, a day much like the one when Philip's army appeared at the gates of Stagira.

The old ache was there in my heart as we set off, the hole where my parents were, my brothers, the old city we had known. And there was a new anxiety – for those around me: my old friend Linos and those young men with no experience of war, but confused dreams of glory, perhaps, as my brother Aristion had had. What if I was leading them to their deaths? How would I ever face their parents, and Chloe? I would never be able to come back. Yet at the core of it all was a conviction. A certainty that I must speak to Cassander, face to face, must prevent him from taking his revenge on Olympias, stop the cycle of murder.

Our journey was uneventful at first. The wars had not touched our region of Chalcidice, the claw with three fingers on the map my father had drawn in the sand all those years ago. We had been fortunate during the blood-letting between Greeks and Macedonians and in this latest round between the Macedonians themselves. Stagira was an outpost of the kingdom and we were mostly left to ourselves, though Linos had to send a report to the governor of Chalcidice in Pella once a month.

As we skirted the swampland near the ruined city of Therma and headed south, we began to see scenes of devastation everywhere. Crops and houses burnt, villages deserted. We rationed out the food and drink we had brought, and slept fitfully at night in makeshift shelters. I kept thinking of Nicanor, spending most of his life like this, facing many a night in cold and discomfort, always alert for danger, constantly aware that today might be his last on Earth. How had he managed to remain so apparently sane and decent?

On the fourth day we could see city walls on a hill above the plain and the smoke of campfires ahead. Pydna. The young men around me fell silent. I raised my hand to stop them and turned my horse. Now it was again Cynane I thought of, teaching me how to do that. She always looked part of her mount, like a centaur. How I had admired her! How I had wished to be like her!

'Linos is your commander,' I said. 'If they take me away, if... whatever happens to me, Linos will decide what to do. We Stagirans have no quarrel with the Macedonians. We are neutral in their war. Keep your heads and follow orders.'

They looked at me gravely, much as they had when they were learning to read, write, play the lyre or recite. Linos had not explained why we were here. He had said it was enough for them that I needed them. I was touched, seeing those solemn faces. I had lost my son and then Pythy and Nicky, but I had gained fifty other sons and as many daughters. All of Stagira was my family.

We rode on slowly and it wasn't long before we were met by a unit of Macedonians twice our size. They all looked battle-hardened, their faces lined despite their youthful bodies. Their leader addressed Linos beside me.

'Who are you and what is your business?' he asked curtly.

'This lady is sister to Lord Cassander and wishes to speak to him urgently,' Linos replied.

The captain turned to me.

'What is your name, Lady?'

I spoke my name as loudly and bravely as I could. I was surprised to hear myself. It was as if someone else had used the voice in my body. The captain said something to his lieutenant, who rode back towards the camp. We spent a tense quarter of an hour before we saw the man riding back towards us. He whispered something to his captain, who then addressed me again.

'My lord Cassander says he received your letter, my lady, but can be of no assistance.'

'I am here on another matter,' I lied, facing him down. 'I must see him. I will be brief.'

There was a stand-off. The captain was staring at me and I at him. Linos's horse was restless beside mine. I still felt as if some other person inhabited my body, governed my voice and my actions. Finally the captain spoke:

'You have your answer, Lady. My lord will not see you.'

I was just about to say again that there was an urgent matter on which I must speak to him when the Macedonians parted. And there was Cassander in full armour, a sword at his side. It took me a moment to recognise him; I remembered his confession on the road to Athens as a lad of fifteen that he had little liking for military matters. Yet he had spent the last seven years on the battlefield. His head was bare, his brown curls much shorter than they had been, his face marked with frown lines and a scar on his cheek; but his blue eyes were as bright as ever. My heart leapt for joy to see him and I spoke his name, smiling, expecting his own brilliant smile in return. But he looked cold and hard.

'I cannot do as you wish, Herpyllis. You should not have come,' he said in a voice I didn't recognise. Then he looked at the men around me.

'Who are you?' he asked Linos.

'My name is Linos,' my old friend answered, 'chief magistrate of Stagira, my lord. These are all men of that city. We came to protect our lady on the road,' he added with a kind of pride.

Cassander looked away. He seemed to need a moment to master whatever emotion had overtaken him. When he spoke to the captain, his voice was the one I knew.

'Take these Stagirans to your camp and feed them well,' he said. 'They have come a long way.' Then he looked at me. 'My sister will come to my tent. It's been too long since last I saw her.'

And then he smiled. But it wasn't the old smile that transformed his face. It was sad and crooked, one side of his lips turning down. I finally realised the full force of the grief he had had to endure. The scores of men, women and children slaughtered on Olympias's orders – every last relative of Antipater's she could lay her hands on. Like me, Cassander had no family left. Perhaps that was why he called me sister, repeating the title I had claimed for myself in my letter. I was now the closest thing he had to a relation, the only one left he had grown up with. I rode over to him and he leaned across and kissed my cheek. We didn't speak until we were inside his tent. He sat me down on a couch and gestured to his page to pour water for us both. Then he sent the boy away.

'I'm sorry, Herpyllis,' he said with a long sigh when we were alone. 'I was afraid of seeing you again. Afraid of having feelings, afraid of hearing you argue for pity. There is no room for pity here. That woman behaves like a wild animal. Worse than that. Most wild animals kill other creatures for food. She kills indiscriminately. Women and girls, as well as men and boys. They can never be a threat to her, but she wants them all dead – anyone who has the slightest amount of blood shared with me. You cannot justify her. You cannot ask me to show pity to her, who shows none to any, even babes in arms.'

I said nothing. I just put my hand on his and held it. Then the tears came. He wept with great sobs that shook his whole body. It must have been the first time he had wept since childhood, or perhaps since we heard what happened to Callisthenes. He had shut himself in the library then, alone. I put my arm around him as he sat, his head in his hands. When the weeping subsided, he stood up and walked away from me. Then he came back, sat down again and poured himself some wine. He took a long draught. He offered me some and I drank, too. He spoke again, his voice calm now and gentle.

'She must die, Herpyllis. You must see that. She and all those around her. It's the only way to stop the cycle. Then there will be peace.'

'Peace at what price, Cassander?' I burst out. 'Peace at the price of behaving like wild animals? That won't put an end to the cycle.'

'It will if I finish off all of Philip's house!' he retorted angrily.

'And leave no rightful heir to the throne?' I asked. 'That'll just lead to an even bigger free-for-all among you and the other generals. Olympias is the problem. Her son was her whole life. She knows you killed him. Don't ask me how, but that must be the case. That's why she's behaved as she has. And the only aim she has left in life is to keep Alexander's son on the throne and protect him for as long as she can. All you have to do is remove her from the scene and become regent until the king is of age. You can pass on to him all your learning from Aristotle, make him a wise and good ruler. I swear to you, Olympias will cause you no further trouble. Your soldiers can accompany her to Stagira. She has few supporters now. You'll be left in peace.'

'Ah, Herpyllis, Herpyllis,' he sighed again. 'Always the peacemaker. But it could all go horribly wrong.'

'What were you thinking of doing with Thessalonica?' I asked. 'She's still with the Queen, isn't she?'

'Yes,' he replied. 'And yes, I have thought of marrying her. Yes, it would give me legitimacy with the army. But I wonder if I could stand to have her in my bed. And, if she's anything like her stepmother, she'll slit my throat while I sleep.'

I laughed in spite of myself. I thought of Thessalonica's earnest expression while she played her lyre, of how she would close her eyes and let the music take her over.

'No,' I said. 'Unless she's changed out of all recognition, she'll make you a fine wife. But if you kill the only mother she's ever known, she'll never forgive you, she'll never love you. If you show generosity to Olympias, you'll earn Thessalonica's eternal gratitude. It'd be worth it, I'm sure.'

Cassander got up again and paced around.

'Tell me about her, Herpyllis,' he said as he came to a halt again in front of me.

'The last time I saw her, Cassander, she was ten years old. I taught her some new songs on the lyre. She was fiercely loyal to Olympias, as I was. That woman inspires such feelings. She's passionate and extreme, yes, but her generosity to those she loves is boundless. We all fell under her spell. But I expect Thessalonica, like me, sees her faults and grieves for the terrible things she's done as well. Olympias must have told her you're a monster. If you're merciful, Cassander, she may well start to look on you with new eyes. She's highly intelligent. She can think for herself. She'll need time; she's been with Olympias all her life, known no other family. But if you treat her well, I think she'll come round. If you show her your true self, she cannot but fall in love with you.'

It was Cassander's turn to give a rueful laugh. But I could see I was winning him round. He strode outside and gave an order. He came back in and sat down next to me, refilling our cups. Soon afterwards Linos was ushered into the tent. He stood up straight, looking composed and authoritative.

'Tell me, chief magistrate,' Cassander began, 'how you could guarantee security for the Queen if I were to consent to her coming to Stagira.'

'Well, my lord,' replied Linos, as if he was used to speaking to Macedonian generals every day of his life,

'I think I've found the answer. Ever since Herpyllis told me of her request to you I've been considering the problem. There's an island off Stagira. It was once inhabited by a fisherman, who kept his wife there in a large house surrounded by a high wall. Nobody has lived there for years, but I visited it recently and found it still in a good state of repair. It wouldn't take us many days to make it a suitable place for the Queen to live, completely isolated from the mainland. The only access to the island is by boat from the bay, and the crossing can be treacherous for any who don't know the waters. The only landing place is a small beach, which can easily be guarded by just a few men.'

Of course! Kapros! As I looked at Linos, I had a piercing memory of how he had looked that day as a young man when we had gone to the island with my father and met the poor madman in his sea-god costume, still protecting the woman whose skeleton sat at table in the house. And my father's face came back to me, speaking the words I still remembered about moderation in love, as in all things.

'What do you think, Herpyllis?' Cassander asked, turning to me.

'It's perfect! A brilliant idea!' I exclaimed, grinning at Linos, who couldn't restrain himself from half smiling at my enthusiastic reaction, despite the seriousness of the situation.

Cassander sat for a further five minutes, his right elbow on his thigh, supporting his chin with his fist. I hardly dared breathe. Finally he dismissed Linos, sprang up and went out to give more orders. Men started running in all directions. In a short time the tent was filled with all Cassander's lieutenants.

'It's time to send Olympias our terms,' he said. 'She's already sued for peace, as you know. The situation inside those walls is desperate. I intend to be generous. I will take the King and his mother under my protection and exile his grandmother to a place where none will seek her or find her. The princess Thessalonica will be my bride.

'We will negotiate with the captains of Olympias's army separately. If I marry Philip's daughter, our troops should be happy to see me as regent for Alexander's son. They long served my father. What say you?'

There was silence. In the end one of them said:

'If you, Cassander, find it in your heart to give such merciful terms to that she-wolf, we will not gainsay you.'

The others nodded. They looked from their general to me and back again. His terms had clearly changed completely overnight. It was only then that I realised it would have been too late to save Olympias if I had stayed in Stagira for one more day. Somehow I had sensed the moment. It also came to me that I might regret what I had so wished for. How would I talk to Olympias now? How could I communicate with this woman who had crossed the boundaries of all civilised behaviour? A snarling she-wolf.

A messenger was sent to read the terms before the walls of Pydna. He waited an hour for his reply. Olympias acceded. She would surrender the city the following day. Cassander sent Linos and half of our men back to Stagira to ready the island for the Queen's imprisonment. He said she would be kept in isolation under heavy guard in the camp until Linos sent word they were ready. But he asked me to stay and greet Thessalonica, to prepare her for her wedding, to convince her that Cassander would make her a good husband. I was also to see that Alexander's widow, Roxana, and her son the King had everything they needed.

Thessalonica made a sorry sight. It was true that the citizens of Pydna had been brought to the point of starvation, and even the royal party had nothing to eat by the end of the siege. The princess looked gaunt, her face prematurely lined, her cheeks hollow. But it gave her an ethereal beauty; her black hair and deep brown eyes stood out in sharp contrast to her pale face. She greeted me with incomprehension.

'Herpyllis?' she whispered. 'What are you...? Why...?'

'Thessalonica,' I said, as warmly as I could. 'You must sit, eat. I've prepared everything for you. Come.'

I kissed her cheek and she allowed me to lead her to the table and sit her down. Then Roxana and her son came in. I was taken aback by my first sight of Alexander's queen. She had his mother's colouring, his mother's presence, her flashing eyes, her arrogance. It was difficult not to feel cowed before her. But I went up and presented myself.

'I'm Herpyllis, Lady,' I said. 'Thessalonica knows me,' I continued. 'I was once one of Olympias's ladies.' *I was once*, I thought to myself, *Alexander's love. But that was a long time ago. That was a different Alexander from the one you knew.*

She said nothing and stood holding her son's hand, looking slowly around the tent. It must also have been some time since she had eaten, but she wore Persian clothes and headdress, swathing her whole body in layers of fabric, hiding her doubtless emaciated figure. She had a dignity to match her mother-in-law's; I wondered how they got on. I couldn't imagine it was a friendly relationship, but something must have stopped Olympias eliminating this woman. Perhaps it was to do with the link she had with Alexander, the continuity she provided in the eyes of the army.

Alexander's son was the same age his father had been when I first saw him in the garden at Pella. The resemblance was striking. It was uncanny. For a few moments I was back there standing with Olympias, Alexander on her other hand, she explaining to him why he should be kind to me. But Alexander IV had his mother's eyes, not the arrestingly mismatched ones of his father.

I came to myself and invited mother and son to sit down and eat. Roxana took her time to walk slowly over. What self-control the woman had – not to throw herself on the food like a starving beggar! She was definitely the equal of Olympias. The two ladies started eating with restraint, but the boy couldn't stuff enough into his mouth at once. His mother did nothing to stop him, and it wasn't long before he vomited it all up. He wept with frustration. Roxana barked out a name. A harassed woman appeared in the tent entrance. The guard let her in and she rushed over to the little boy and took him in her arms. He started pummelling her hard but she seemed not to feel it. She went on hushing him and stroking him, whispering to him in Macedonian. He gradually calmed down. I joined the ladies and called the slave over to fill our drinking cups.

Nothing was said until they had eaten their fill. Then Roxana rose and said with a heavy accent:

'I wish to rest now.'

I nodded to the guard and he called a man over to show the King and his mother to their tent. Thessalonica and I were left alone together.

'Are you feeling better now, my dear?' I asked her.

'Yes,' she replied quietly, 'the dizziness has gone.'

Suddenly she looked me straight in the eye.

'They won't execute her, Herpyllis, will they? Please tell me Cassander will keep his word.'

'He will,' I answered. 'He's a fine man, Thessalonica. You couldn't find a better husband among the Macedonians. I've known him since he was a lad of fifteen. He studied with Aristotle for ten years in Athens, you know. He's honourable. I expect Olympias has told you terrible things about him; she hates him because he's Antipater's son, and Antipater became her worst enemy. But she ordered all his family killed – not just the men, the women and children too.

'You and I lost our mothers when we were very young,' I went on, 'Olympias adopted us both and was kind to us. Perhaps it's hard for you to imagine what it must be like to have your whole family murdered, those closest and

345

dearest to you gone in one fell swoop. Cassander's grief has been unbearable. He wanted to have you all killed in revenge, but his better nature's won through. He wants to put an end to this awful cycle. He wants peace.'

'I wish I could believe you, Herpyllis,' she said, 'but you're one of them now, aren't you? Olympias says you're as bad a traitor as they are.'

'Traitor?' I repeated in disbelief. 'What do you mean?'

'You were Callisthenes' wife. He led those pages on to kill Alexander. And Aristotle was behind it all. When that plot failed, he sent Cassander to kill the King. And he succeeded. Oh, Herpyllis, what a terrible thing to do! Alexander gave Macedon the greatest empire the world has ever seen! He made our people great!'

I was stunned. I had come to think of Alexander as a madman who had to be stopped from destroying cities and killing innocent people all over the known world and beyond, stopped from murdering those around him who made the slightest criticism. Here was a woman who had seen him as his mother did – a hero who could do no wrong.

'Oh, Thessalonica,' I said, 'let's not argue about Alexander. He's dead and now his son is king. Cassander will be a good regent until the boy comes of age. And you will be Cassander's wife and bear his children.'

Her face had little colour but now it drained away and she looked as if she was going to be sick. I stroked her arm.

'What's the matter?' I asked. 'Are you all right?'

'The very thought of it makes my stomach heave,' Thessalonica whispered.

'The thought of what?' I asked.

'*It*,' she said with disgust. 'You know.'

I had worked out that Thessalonica was thirty-five now, a couple of years older than Cassander. I presumed she was still a virgin. It was only natural she should dread marriage.

'Why didn't you marry earlier?' I asked her gently. 'As Philip's daughter, you must have had any number of proposals.'

'No,' she said quietly, 'I never have.'

'I find that hard to believe,' I continued. 'Perhaps Olympias hid them from you. You've been closer to her than anyone else, much closer than Cleopatra. You've been her real daughter. She wouldn't have wanted you to leave her side.'

She looked at me earnestly.

'You might be right,' she said after a while. 'But Cleopatra's the one they want. She's Alexander's only true sister.'

Yes, poor Cleopatra. She had been captured by one of Alexander's generals but had refused to marry him. He had been keeping her prisoner in Sardis, deep in Asia, for years, far away from her son and all of us who loved her. Thessalonica and I lapsed into silence, our thoughts in Sardis.

Meanwhile the men were striking bargains. Cassander was to make Cleopatra's son king in Epirus and the army Olympias had brought from there was to return under his banner. The Macedonians united under the boy I had just seen, Alexander's son, Cassander ruling as his regent. The future looked brighter than it had for some time, though there were still generals to rival my little brother for power. I reflected that, if Thessalonica could have a son, that would put him in a much stronger position.

I prepared her for her wedding a few days later – the bath, the red dress, the gold, the veil. We went to the sacrifices. She looked for all the world as if she were the creature to be slaughtered, but Cassander treated her gently and smiled at her kindly. I even began to hope her wedding night would not be just an ordeal, might indeed bring her pleasure. The following day she was subdued but not unhappy. There were no other initiates with whom to celebrate her Second Blood and no sacred space for the ceremony, so our womanly rituals were not performed. Olympias had been conveyed to Kapros by armed guard under cover of darkness. It was time for me to go and face her, though now I knew from Thessalonica I would not be welcomed. I could expect no gratitude for saving the Queen's life. I took my leave.

'Herpyllis, stay with me,' she said. 'Be one of my ladies. Come to court with me. You know Cassander. You can advise me.'

I politely declined. She had several ladies who had been with her from childhood. I felt she was well looked after and I had told her everything I knew of her husband. What I knew, of course, was how he had been before war had taken him, made him into a man who thought first of survival, killing the enemy, avenging a friend, a brother, a sister. I thought about what it had done to Philip, to Alexander.

But I had seen the old Cassander emerge in that camp, I had seen him come back from the brink, I had seen him dig deep into his soul to retrieve the teachings of his master. He gave me a long embrace when I took my leave. Standing beside Thessalonica, he gave me an open invitation to Pella whenever I wished to go. Seeing them together like that, both smiling, they made a good couple. They were physically similar. I don't think I was deceiving myself into believing they might even be happy together one day.

Cassander insisted it should never be known that Olympias was living in exile on Kapros. Her general Polyperchon had escaped Pydna with some of his troops and was regrouping in the south, where he controlled some territory. Alexander's mother could still be used by him to evoke powerful loyalties in his men; they would fight to liberate her.

Cassander let it be known that Olympias was executed at Pydna.

26
HOME TRUTHS

*'The educated differ from the uneducated as much
as the living differ from the dead.'*

I made my way back to Stagira with the ten men Linos
had left with me. On the road we met Cassander's trusted
band of soldiers who had accompanied the Queen. They
had left a small unit behind to guard the exile in her
new home. Olympias had been allowed to keep only
two of her ladies. They were transported by boat from
the harbour outside the city walls to the little island of
Kapros off the bay. She and her small entourage were to
be the only inhabitants, with just three servants to see
to their needs.

Two days after I got back, I myself took a boat over to
the island. I had hardly slept since my return. Now that I
had the opportunity to speak to the Queen openly about
that long past event which had overshadowed my life, I
found that I could wait, that I was reluctant to broach
the subject, afraid of receiving a definitive answer to the
question I had asked her a hundred times in my head.

It was a breezy day and the boat lurched from side to
side unnervingly with the swell. I thought of Aristotle
and that day on the cliffs above the straits when he had
watched the turning tide and remarked how nothing was

stable in our lives. The statue in the Aristoteleion was an excellent likeness, so he was often in my thoughts.

It was a great relief to arrive safely on the little beach. I found my hands had been gripping the side of the boat so tightly that they were completely numb, and I had to open and close them several times before any feeling came back. Two soldiers had already appeared from the woods which came down to the shoreline. The boatman and I approached them and they demanded to know our business. They insisted that the Prisoner, as they referred to her, was to have no visitors. I tried argument and persuasion, but nothing worked. I was becoming desperate at the thought that I would be prevented from seeing Olympias, in spite of having brought her to my doorstep.

Just as I was about to accept defeat, a woman came bustling down the path between the trees towards us. To my great delight, I recognised Charis, the lady who had adopted me that first day at court and taken care of me. Now she was grey-haired, plump and wrinkled, but that jolly face I would have known anywhere! We threw ourselves into each other's arms like a pair of young lovers, much to the embarrassment of the soldiers. In her inimitable way, Charis had clearly got them eating out of her hand. They stood aside respectfully and said nothing as she steered me up the slope, our arms entwined. When we got to the top and the house came into view, she stopped to catch her breath. Then she held me at arms' length and looked at me, a little frown on her face.

'You've been through a lot, my dear one,' she said. 'But you've obviously gained great strength from it. How good it is to see you again! They've all gone now. Even Thessalonica. She was some comfort to the Queen. Now there's just me and Helene. You don't know her. She's a distant cousin from Epirus. The poor girl didn't bargain for spending her best years stuck on an island in the middle of nowhere!'

Charis paused to breathe in and out a few times again. Then she went on:

'But I must warn you, Herpyllis. The Queen won't be happy to see you. She's got it into her head that Aristotle had Alexander murdered. She won't believe he died of that Persian sickness. And, of course, Alexander told her your Callisthenes got those pages to try and kill him, too. I don't know the truth of any of it, and perhaps you don't either, but whatever you say, look her straight in the eye if she asks you about it. Otherwise she'll believe you're lying.

'Oh, Herpyllis,' she went on, 'can you stay with us for a while? *Will* you stay with us? How often I've wanted to have you back in the bed beside me, chatting about this and that till late into the night. What times we had! Do you remember?'

Of course I remembered. Had it not been for Charis, who knows what might have become of me in those first days in Pella? I hugged her again. Then I braced myself for the coming meeting and we walked in together.

Olympias was sitting in the courtyard, her back to us. A frightened girl was hovering nearby, anxious not to miss one of those slight inclines of the head I had been so familiar with, each one a signal for a different action required: *Come here*, *Bring me that*, *Play me a song*,

Stop playing, Go away... I had learnt them all quickly. No doubt this girl had, too. Helene, Charis had said.

'Who is it?' the Queen asked, not turning her head.

'Herpyllis, my lady,' replied Charis.

Olympias visibly straightened but said nothing. After a long silence I walked round to face her. Alexander's mother was hardly recognisable as the imperious woman with the billowing mane who had made such an impression on me the first time I saw her in the palace at Pella. A small lock of white hair was visible on her forehead, the rest pulled back off her face under her headdress. Those clear green eyes were now dull and tired, her neck, chin and cheeks wrinkled. She scowled at me but I felt a rush of love for her, mixed with pity. I stepped forward and lightly kissed her dry cheek.

'My lady,' I said.

I kissed her hand with its swollen, distorted knuckles and brown spots. She looked surprised and gave me a searching look. She still said nothing. Finally I managed to find my voice and spoke:

'I wish I could have welcomed you to Stagira under different circumstances.'

Another silence, during which she continued staring at me, as if daring me to look away first. Then she spoke.

'You've aged badly,' she said.

I smiled. She was just as I remembered – something hurtful to put you in your place if necessary. She was right. I looked older than my forty years, but I didn't care. Vanity had never been one of my failings. She looked disappointed at my reaction. She tried again.

'You went over to *them*. Traitors, the lot of them.'

'I've had little to do with men's affairs, Madam,' I replied.

Thessalonica and Charis had prepared me, and I was ready to deflect any references to Alexander's death. I hoped to remind her I was a Daughter of the Earth, that we were first and foremost women together in a world of men. Part of me wanted to shout: *Yes, we killed him, killed your mad son! He thought he was a god! He had the finest man I ever knew executed because he refused to bow down to him. He was out of his mind, out of control. He had to be stopped.*

But this I kept to myself and sought to be reconciled with the woman I still associated first and foremost with my mother. And my whole body ached. How I had missed Mother over all these years! How I missed her still! Stagira in flames was only yesterday, the pain overwhelming.

'He didn't dare to have me killed,' Olympias said suddenly. 'That boy couldn't even look me in the face. Too ashamed. A miserable milksop like all the others. Polyperchon's regrouping our forces as we speak. I'll be back in Pella soon enough, just you wait and see! And that boy will be hanging upside down on a board beside the road, the crows picking at him.'

I tried to suppress the image she was evoking of Cassander. I thought of him smiling at me as I left Pydna and kept that image in my head. Olympias gave up expecting a comment from me.

'Well,' she said. 'What are you doing here?'

'I wanted to see you, Madam,' I replied. 'I'm in your debt. Had it not been for you...' My voice trailed off.

Her face had softened slightly.

'So you're all alone now,' she commented.

I nodded.

'Where's your lyre?' she asked. 'Play for me. Play that song again.'

I knew the song she meant. I looked at Charis and she sent Helene to fetch an instrument for me. I tuned it quickly and gathered my thoughts. I was back in Pella, a little girl, playing for the kind Queen who had taken me in.

Awake, fair maid, come follow me,
Leave childhood things behind.
Your life awaits you here today
Come grasp it by the reins.
The springtime calls you, hear its voice,
The blossom fills your hair.
Choose worthy swain to take your hand,
To bring you joy unbound.
Your body aches, your heart leaps up,
The blood within you pounds.
Come join the round of Gaia's dance
Surrender to Her power.

The moment had come. I put down the lyre. I waited for the Queen to look up.

'My lady,' I said softly. 'Do you remember that night in the woods? My First Blood?'

An incline of the head. Yes.

'I saw something in the tree above me, during our dance.'

No movement. No reaction. But she held my gaze.

'A man spying on the Goddess's rites,' I said. 'Watching us from the tree. Two eyes catching the moonlight, one blue, one brown. I couldn't see the colours then, of course. But I know it was him.'

She looked away.

'Alexander,' she whispered, the way she used to when he was sitting beside her and she was stroking his hair. I felt with a pang the same tenderness, the quiet joy of my son's head on my shoulder as he sat on my lap, the softness of his hair, the clean smell of him.

'I knew something had happened the next day,' she said with a long sigh. 'When he came and took you away, took you to Aristotle.'

She was silent for a moment, but her tone had changed when she gave me a sharp look and asked:

'Why didn't you tell me what you'd seen?'

'It's pretty obvious,' I snapped. 'Make you harm Alexander? Your precious son? Destroy what you loved most in all the world?'

I spat out the words. All the resentment I felt against the boy I had once loved myself more than anything else in the world spilt out at that moment in a voice I didn't recognise as my own. Olympias looked startled. I had never spoken to her like that before. I don't suppose many had, certainly not her ladies. There was a long silence during which I caught sight of Charis's horrified face. Then a sly smile slowly came to Olympias's lips.

'Finally she reacts,' she said. 'Well, better late than never, I suppose! You disappointed me growing up. So meek and mild. I thought your mother's daughter would have more spirit.'

Was this true? Had she wanted me to become as fearless and proud as Cynane? Is that why she had let me go riding and hunting with her? I decided to ignore the Queen's last comments, made to hurt again. I must bring her back to that night in the woods.

'Tell me then, Madam,' I said as calmly as I could. 'What would you have done that night if I'd told you what I'd seen? If we'd caught him?'

She looked away. A much longer silence. I thought she wouldn't answer. Slowly she got up from the bench. Although she bore herself with the same dignity as always, it clearly pained her to hold herself erect as she walked a few steps forward, her back to me. Now I could also see with a shock how thin she was.

'You know the punishment for men who spy on our secret rites,' she said softly.

I waited. Finally she turned to look at me and the imperious Queen was back.

'You think I wouldn't have done it?' she challenged in the old, commanding voice. 'Think I wouldn't have killed my own son? In that state the Goddess inspires, I wouldn't have recognised him! Did you never experience that frenzy, that intoxication? Not in your music, the wine coursing through your veins? Don't lie to me, Herpyllis! I saw your face!'

Again she was trying to deflect me, make me question my soul instead of hers. But for a brief moment I relived the intense sensation of that night, just before I saw the eyes in the tree, that ecstasy of letting go, the abandon of the trance. I had been so close. A moment later and I would have dragged Alexander down from the tree myself and torn him to pieces. I remembered the exultation I felt at *The Bacchae*. But I would not be satisfied.

'Had you reached the frenzy then, Madam, if you remember *my* face so clearly? I thought in that state one remembers nothing, sees nothing for what it is,' I commented in that same hard, cold voice I had discovered in myself again.

'We were all in a trance, weren't we?' she said exultantly, looking at Charis.

'Indeed we were, my lady,' said Charis, with hardly any hesitation – enough, though, to make me realise she was the one who could tell me what Olympias never would.

And then I looked at the old woman before me in a new light. All her life she had carefully cultivated that idea of herself as dangerous, seductive sorceress and ruler – irrational, unpredictable, terrifying. It had served her well; few had dared to cross her, and those who did were lucky to escape alive. All those who posed any threat to her power had been eliminated: Philip's young queen and her children, Arrhidaeus, all Cassander's friends and relations.

She would never admit to me now that she would have stayed her hand that night in the clearing. She needed to believe in her own myth. I went and took her arm. She didn't resist. We walked out of the grove, through the woods till we could see the promontory of Stagira. She looked across.

'So you've built him a memorial,' she said sarcastically. 'An Aristoteleion.'

I nodded.

'My boy lies far away across that sea, down by the Nile, with the bulls of his father Zeus. Philip's bastard took him and put him there. But one day we'll bring him back to Aegae, to lie near his father and me in a magnificent royal tomb. They've excavated it. Soon we'll bring him home. Yes, we'll bring him home...'

I looked sideways at her. How did she imagine Alexander's two fathers? Did she believe Zeus had lain with her in the guise of her husband? How exactly had she explained it to Alexander? I could never hope to understand her thinking. Olympias was the kind of woman Aristotle had so despised and feared. She had been brought up in mysticism and fanatical belief. In her turn, she viewed with contempt the educated reasoning and thirst for knowledge I had learnt. She had only seen the priestess in my mother, she had only loved one side of her, whereas I had adored the wise and tender woman, the intense and inspiring teacher. I pointed to the cemetery by the temple on the hill.

'My mother is there,' I said. 'We've given her a fine monument, with my father.'

She squinted, straining to look across the strait. I wondered how much she could see nowadays. No doubt her eyes were duller than mine.

'Poor Antheia!' she commented. 'Two boys and not one of them to have made anything of himself. I had a son who was the greatest king the world has ever seen!'

She looked at me with a mixture of disdain and triumph. I had to fight hard to resist the urge to hit her. How dare she mention my brothers, murdered on her husband's orders before they had a chance to achieve anything in life? Theron would have been chief magistrate of Stagira now, a wise, good man like my father, and Aristion his commander-in-chief. Before I had a chance to reply, she continued:

'And look at you, her daughter! One dead child to show for her womanhood! A good thing he died, too! He'd have grown up to be a useless scribbler like his father. Antheia's daughter, wife of a weak and snivelling coward, whore of a bitter, scheming traitor. A dried-up husk of a woman with nothing to justify her pointless existence. Alone and rejected. Why did you come here? Did you expect to gloat over me? I'm twenty times the woman you are! Men have quaked at my command, adored me, worshipped me. What have they done for you? Used you and thrown you aside! You have nothing now and nothing is what you deserve!'

I had heard the Queen speak with such venom on many occasions in the past, but this was the first time I had been her target. I was in shock. I stood there looking at her, not a thought in my head. But the phrase *whore of a bitter, scheming traitor* had particularly struck home. Was this how I was seen? Did everyone think I had been Aristotle's mistress? It took me some time to realise the Queen was shaking violently and about to collapse.

'Let's go back,' I heard myself say. The old instincts took over and I put my arm round her to hold her steady. We slowly turned and walked the way we had come. Charis was waiting anxiously nearby; she had followed us to the edge of the woods. Together we helped Olympias back to the house and laid her on a bed. She closed her eyes, breathing fast and wheezing. Charis led me out of the room.

'She's dying,' she said. 'I don't know how much longer she'll last. What am I going to do without her?'

I patted Charis's hand and we sat down together in the courtyard. Helene was nowhere to be seen.

'Is there anything we can give her?' I asked.

'Nothing that will cure her,' she replied. 'She's lost the will to live now. She pretends the army will come and rescue her, that the Macedonians still love her, the mother of Alexander, that they'll turn on Cassander. But I can see doubt's crept in. She only half believes herself. That's fatal.'

I sent the boatman back to tell Linos I would stay on the island for a while. Over the following days and weeks the Queen became less and less coherent. I had arrived on a 'good' day when she was more in touch with reality, but those days became rare. In her lucid moments she and I talked about our happy memories; I think my presence made her regress to better times when she had her little boy with her and I was constantly at her side. Neither of us ever referred to her outburst on the cliff; I kept it in my heart and it lay there quiet while she lived. Charis had been right. She died two months later. On Cassander's instructions, her body was secretly buried on the island.

The harbour people who served the mysterious captive on Kapros, bringing her food and drink every day, were in no doubt about her identity. They call their village Olympiada now, proud as they are of their association with the renowned Macedonian Queen.

27
THE BEGINNING OF ALL
WISDOM

'Knowing yourself is the beginning of all wisdom.'

Charis came to live with me in Stagira. She had first arrived at the Macedonian court more than forty years earlier. Olympias had been good to her in her way and Charis, for her part, had served the Queen well and loyally. She was quite bereft now. I tried to involve her in my little school, but she found the children quickly tired her. In the evenings we would sit in the courtyard, talking together about the old times.

She told me about the stormy years of Antipater's regency and the impossible demands Olympias made on him. The Queen could never accept that Alexander had not given her absolute power in Macedon, and spent several days a week writing to him about perceived slights, wrong decisions, bad judgements. Charis said she felt sorry for the King having to read it all and give some kind of answer. Instead he would often send yet another gift of gold, jewels, or exotic cloth, but his mother couldn't be silenced with such things. She would write yet another letter listing the same complaints and adding new ones. It was rare for her to send her son any good news.

Over the years Charis had become a go-between for Cleopatra in Epirus. Mother and daughter didn't communicate directly. It saddened us both that they had never been reconciled. They were probably too much alike, Charis said. I remembered the shy girl I had known, her face buried in my chest at Dion, the way she clung to me that night in Pella when her mother and brother had fled the court. It seemed the day after her wedding and her father's assassination in Aegae had changed her life; she became a queen and took her mother's example for the role. She was still captive in Sardis; it had been five years now. Even though she was past child-bearing, Alexander's sister was an important prize for any of the rival generals, warring over his empire. At least her son had finally become King of Epirus with Cassander's support. He was eighteen years old, ten months older than my own Stotty would have been.

Soon after Olympias's death, I finally plucked up courage to ask Charis the question which had remained unanswered on Kapros. Did she believe the Queen had really been in a state of frenzy the night of my First Blood? Did she believe any male intruder would have suffered instant death at her hands? To my amazement, she nodded.

'Even Alexander?' I queried.

She nodded again. And she added:

'Nobody knew the Queen better than I did, Herpyllis. She would have killed him in the frenzy. I swear it in the name of the Goddess.'

That phrase sent a shiver through me. Alexander's words: *Swear it in the name of the Goddess*. At that moment in the clearing he had been the male god witnessing female supremacy; he had to punish, assert his superiority, rejoice in a woman's defeat, in her degradation.

And now I also understood that the opportunity I had missed to give life back to all those the man in the tree would murder, to restore homes and loved ones to all those he would dispossess and enslave – that chance to influence history so profoundly – never really existed. I had already known at the age of seven that I wasn't the Amazon maiden I had imagined myself to be. I wasn't made of the stuff of those women of Epirus and Illyria I had so admired – Olympias, Audata, Cynane. Nor, now, did I wish to be. I didn't want to surrender to my passions, let them take me over. I had no need to suppress the Amazon inside me – she had never been there. I was who I was, my mother's daughter, taught with love and kindness, taught to love and be kind. I had been true to Mother after all. It didn't enter my head to betray the boy I still loved, tell what I knew would cause a terrible act of violence, destroy the Queen's life.

Life in Stagira with Charis was peaceful and happy. Chloe and the other women accepted her without question and gave her a place of honour in our ceremonies. But Charis was not well. The shortest walk uphill left her panting and breathless, her face flushed and her eyes bloodshot. She spent more and more time resting, increasingly lethargic. She was also putting on a lot of weight; she loved eating, especially delicacies with honey and nuts. When I tried to dissuade her, she would say she needed to have some pleasures in life.

One day we were indulging ourselves, imagining how life would have turned out if I had never left the court, if Philip hadn't been murdered, if Alexander had never gone to Asia.

'Life is full of might have beens, could have beens and should have beens,' she mused. 'If the man I was to have married hadn't been killed, I would never have gone to court in Pella and we would never have met. If Olympias had agreed to it, you would have been Antipater's wife.'

I had to ask her to repeat that last sentence. She chuckled.

'Of course,' she said, 'I'd forgotten we never told you. Antipater wanted you. He was quite insistent. First the Queen said you were too young – you were not yet thirteen, I think. Then, when he asked the following year, she said she couldn't spare you. Did you never notice how he looked at you? She was jealous. She wanted him to be totally devoted to her. He had ten wives, you know, and goodness knows how many children. She had them all killed, as many as she could find. Dangerous to be loved by that woman; such love turns into a terrible hatred.'

I was still stunned by what she had said about Antipater wanting to marry me. He had always been a father figure for me, like Aristotle. But a husband? What a different fate might have been mine as Antipater's wife: any children of ours and I myself would have been murdered on Olympias's orders. Better not to think about such things, as Aristotle advised that evening at sunset on our cliff together.

Meanwhile Antipater's son Cassander was busy as ruler of Macedon. Later that year he founded the city of Cassandreia on the site of the ancient city of Potidaea, on the westernmost peninsula of Chalcidice, the first finger of the claw. He had a canal dug from coast to coast, with two harbours – one on the east side and one on the west. These were to be the chief bases for the Macedonian navy.

The following year Thessalonica gave birth to a son. The proud parents called him Philip and the new mother was honoured with a city named after her on the swampland in the gulf near the old city of Therma. It was to be a port to replace Pella, which was becoming silted up. It seemed my little brother had brought peace and prosperity to Macedon at last.

But I was glad I hadn't accepted Thessalonica's invitation to stay with her at court. My life in Stagira gave me contentment and fulfilment, and it was good to have a companion in the house again. Yet Charis and I were to have just two years together. She withdrew more and more often when the children came, or stayed at home when we had our ceremonies at the sanctuary. In the end she spent most of the day and night in bed, her face drawn. She was always tired but slept little. One day I came home to find her cold and lifeless. It was a few hours before I could calm myself and call Chloe.

We prepared Charis's body together and all the women came for the vigil. I was surprised to find how long it took me to grow accustomed to living alone again. I missed having someone to care for, someone to worry about, someone to tempt with the confections she had always loved. It was almost like having the children taken away again.

And the man who had inflicted that heavy blow on me was active in his guardianship. Theophrastus found a new husband for Pythy: a physician. That would have pleased Aristotle. One of the last things my guardian did was commission a statue to be placed in Stagira of his elder brother, Arimnestus, who had been trained in the medical arts by his father. He died at the age of nineteen of the same fever and vomiting which took his twin sister and little Stotty, and there had been no children to raise a memorial to him. Perhaps one day these physicians will find a cure for that terrible sickness, continuing Aristotle's lifelong quest for knowledge, the human quest, the burning desire to know. Perhaps in one insignificant detail of Nature they will find what they are looking for. Aristotle said no fact was unworthy of attention. Everything was to be noted and studied.

Pythy writes that she will leave her two sons with her second husband's family in Sparta. That will be hard. No woman should have to do that. It isn't right that she should return to Theophrastus's guardianship, to one who knows nothing of the love of children, the one overruling force in a woman's life. I still miss Pythy and Nicky, not to mention my own little Stotty. 'Miss' is an inadequate word. Language has no way of conveying that constant ache, that emptiness, that gaping pit which can suddenly open up when you least expect it.

Pythy's new husband lives in Athens and studied at the Lyceum, so at least she will be going home to where she was born, to where she was loved and brought up by her two mothers. But her brother will not be there. Nicky spent fifteen years studying at the Lyceum, helping in the library, expanding his father's lecture notes with Theophrastus, guarding his father's legacy. Then, in these endless wars over Alexander's empire, a fleet sailed to take Athens from Cassander's allies. At first the Athenians were tricked into thinking they were friendly ships, but when their true purpose emerged, the young men scrambled to grab weapons and man the walls. Nicky was swept up and fought alongside them. He was killed in the defence of the city which had wanted to kill his father. The irony would not have been lost on Aristotle. I wonder which myth he would have found as a parallel.

Perhaps the new King of Macedon will think of one. Cassander. Alexander's son and widow are dead, buried at Aegae with full honours. The King is coming to Stagira to visit the Aristoteleion, to honour his old teacher, his second father. I am impatient to see my little brother again; it has been eleven years. He is a man in his prime and I am an old lady. His life has been little other than wars since that fateful day in Babylon, that day which was a turning point in all our lives. I wonder how much of Aristotle's teaching still informs his actions, helps him rule, make wise decisions.

It was a sunny spring day when he came, again much like the one when that other King of Macedon arrived at our gates to destroy everything we had. Just politics, you remember, nothing personal. The cherry by the old house was white with blossom, and Linos, who had hidden in its branches that dreadful day so long ago, now stood before it, his full head of hair as white as the flowers, his chief magistrate's silver headband hardly visible against it. The other magistrates stood on his right, and I was on his left. Cassander rode in at the head of his guard.

And for a moment I was back at the sanctuary gate, a young girl, the same man on a horse at the head of his troops. Antipater. Cassander's face had changed, grown wider, stronger. This man could have been *my* son, Antipater my husband. Some small part of him was what I had made him during those ten years in Athens when he was coming to manhood. Something of him was mine. He greeted Linos formally and was welcomed in return, but then those blue eyes were on me and his arms were around me; he embraced me long and hard.

Cassander sacrificed a bull at the altar on the hill and spoke a eulogy to Aristotle. I am not versed in rhetoric; for one sad moment my mind went back to Alexander strutting up and down before me as I sat on our branch in the clearing, trying to sound like a man with a voice as high as mine. But he made me giggle and clap with his imitation of Leonidas expounding the rules of rhetoric. So many things now trigger an unexpected memory, moments I had thought passed forever, suddenly alive, suddenly present and arresting, like that sharp pain in the side I get from time to time.

After the sacrifice, King Cassander met the magistrates in the Aristoteleion and discussed city matters. But while the bull was being turned on the spit in the square he came to my house, and we sat and talked, just as we had every evening at the Lyceum.

'Aristotle was counsellor or teacher to three Kings of Macedon,' I commented, 'but the first two didn't seem to follow his philosophy on ethics. Is it so hard for a king to live a good life?'

He laughed.

'Ah, my dear Herpyllis,' he said. 'How I've missed you! Straight to the heart of the matter!'

'And you playing for time again!' I teased. 'Not answering the question.'

'Very well,' he replied, serious now. 'Yes, it's hard. It's almost impossible when your enemies behave like your Queen. It wasn't just the fact that she had so many killed, it was the *way* she had them killed! My family were butchered, some burnt alive, some mutilated and hanged. If you hadn't come to Pydna, I would certainly have had Olympias executed; I would have driven a spear through her heart myself and felt great pleasure.'

'But you had pity on her for my sake,' I countered. 'That was a noble feeling. In the end you probably punished her far more than if you had executed her on the spot. She couldn't bear the isolation, the lack of power. It ate her up inside. Her final months were full of pain and suffering.'

He had a hard look in his eyes but said nothing.

'And what of her grandson and his mother?' I asked. 'Did you have them killed?'

'I did,' he answered simply. 'Roxana was another Olympias. Alexander married a woman just like his mother.

371

She was filling her son's ears with the same madness. Telling him he was a son of Zeus, born to rule the world. I couldn't let him be king. He would have brought down more death and destruction on all our heads, fought to restore the whole empire to his rule and then gone on to make it bigger than his father's.

'Macedon needs peace, Herpyllis!' he said with emphasis. 'It's been thirty years of war. Aristotle wanted the Persians defeated, the Greek cities in Asia Minor liberated, but he didn't want Macedonians to rule there like barbarian potentates. It was enough to neutralise the threat from beyond the Hellespont. We never had enough troops to carry out Alexander's crazy plans. All of Greece rebelled as soon as his back was turned. They allied themselves with the Persians, most of them. My father spent all his time trying to subdue them while having to send reinforcements to Asia every year. Macedon was stretched to breaking point. The last thing we need now is another Alexander.'

'So you had them killed for the sake of Macedon.'

'Yes,' he said. 'I think Aristotle would have approved. He knew a king doesn't have the luxury of maintaining the high ethics of an ordinary man. And Macedon must have a king. It isn't Athens and I can't make it so in my lifetime. But if we have peace, perhaps I can bring people a better life and they'll slowly tire of being ruled by the army. Our soldiers will retire to their farms and we'll only need a small force to defend our borders. Then people could lead good lives as Aristotle taught. We could restrict the blood and guts to the theatres.'

'So you hope one day to have democracy in Macedon?' I asked.

'It was the system Aristotle thought best,' he said, 'at least until he experienced for himself how one or two men can manipulate the rest and perpetrate the same kinds of injustice and crime as a despot. It depends on electing good men. But even Aristotle didn't find a way of ensuring that.'

If only his teacher could have been there to hear him! Finally a king who wanted nothing but a good life for his subjects, who was not obsessed with power and glory.

And he had given us peace at last. I had nothing more to wish for in life. Stagira was now as it had been when my father was alive; though nominally part of the Macedonian kingdom, we were left to organise our city as we wished. Linos no longer reported to the governor in Pella.

Our conversation turned to Cassander's wife and children. He spoke of Thessalonica with quiet affection. She had already borne him three sons: Philip, Antipater and Alexander. I smiled ruefully at the names and he shrugged.

'There are many things I have to do as King of Macedon because they are expected,' he mused. 'My men are proud of their land and their achievements. My wife is Philip's daughter. Such things provide continuity, legitimacy. That's what they want.'

And then Cassander told me Thessalonica was now the only surviving member of the house of King Philip. Cleopatra had finally managed to escape from her guards and leave Sardis in disguise. But she was betrayed and recaptured. Her captor concluded that Alexander's sister still posed a serious threat to his power. She was found suffocated in her bed not long after her return to imprisonment. Reports had come to Macedon of Cleopatra's elaborate funeral where she was eulogised as *the most beautiful nymph that ever graced the palace of Pella*.

So I would never see my little sister again, she would never come and sit with me in Stagira as Cassander was doing.

We talked on, mainly about the old days, avoiding the bad times, focussing on the good, until Linos came to take us to the feast. Cassander found himself among friends and visibly relaxed. He chatted and joked with many. What a contrast he was to his two predecessors! It still brings a warm smile to my face remembering that day.

And that's what I'm doing now, a year later, sitting here beside the sanctuary, alone. I'm watching the sun go down over the sea and waiting for that brief moment when the sky and the sea are the same, that limpid blue which makes you feel a sweet and gentle elation – peace. The same thing anyone can see, the same feelings anyone can have, whether man or woman, slave or free. A short, magical time between light and dark when the sky is transparent and you feel you might see through it to the secrets that lie beyond – might discover something new, know something more.

AFTERWORD

Very little is known about the protagonists in this novel and most of it is disputed. The usually accepted facts of Aristotle's life are drawn from *Lives of Eminent Philosophers* by Diogenes Laërtius, written some time between the 3rd and 6th centuries CE, but Herbert S. Long in his *Introduction to the Loeb Classical Library* 1972 reprint of this work states that '*Diogenes has acquired an importance out of all proportion to his merits because the loss of many primary sources and of the earlier secondary compilations has accidentally left him the chief continuous source for the history of Greek philosophy.*'

Readers who know something of the orthodox version of the philosopher's life will probably be surprised that in this novel Herpyllis does not become Aristotle's wife or concubine, or bear his son, Nicomachus. This scenario has a long tradition and is usually accepted in biographies today. I follow H. B. Gottschalk in his 'Notes on the Wills of the Peripatetic Scholars' (*Hermes*, 100, H3, 1972). Aristotle's will is the only source for Herpyllis and a close reading of it makes it much more likely that she was a ward of the philosopher, a woman from his own birthplace of Stagira with no surviving family. She is bequeathed a great deal of money for the time and a household of her own in Chalcis or Stagira, as befits a woman who had run her guardian's household and cared for him and his children for some years. Were she the mother of Nicomachus, it would have been cruel to propose in the will that she could choose to go to Stagira while the boy remained in Chalcis under the guardianship of Nicanor, who is also appointed her guardian.

It has been proposed that Herpyllis was a slave of low birth because she was named after a plant (wild thyme). This argument does not seem quite tenable when we remember that Olympias – the Molossian Princess Polyxena – was given the name Myrtale, the name of another plant (myrtle), just before becoming Queen of Macedon.

Olympias's exile to Stagira is a tradition of the people of Olympiada in explaining the name of their village, which lies on the mainland next to the peninsula on which Ancient Stagira stands. Most historians believe the Queen was executed on Cassander's orders, in spite of his promise to spare her during negotiations before the surrender of Pydna.

I have completely invented Herpyllis's parents, but not the accusation that Aristotle was involved in betraying Stagira to Philip II. However, the first record we have of this accusation dates from forty years after the event in a speech by the Athenian statesman Demochares, nephew of the anti-Macedonian orator, Demosthenes. He claimed to be quoting letters between the philosopher and Antipater. Aristotle was a prolific letter-writer in regular correspondence with many contemporaries, but the collection of his letters has long been lost.

My invention of the First, Second and Third Blood ceremonies associated with the cult of the Mother Goddess is based on my own experience of a wedding many years ago in the Republic of Macedonia. After the wedding night, the bride's women relatives and friends sent all the men out of the house and celebrated together drinking *topla rakia*. This is made by heating sugar until it caramelises and adding clear grape brandy. The resulting hot liquid represents the blood shed by the virgin bride on consummation of her marriage, displayed for all to see on the bed sheets. There were a large number of 'dirty' jokes told as the evening went on and much cavorting by women waving carrots, both of which I was informed were age-old rituals. I might add that when my own daughter menstruated for the first time, I felt the need to mark the occasion by having the whole family drink red wine in celebration of her womanhood.

I make no apology for the similarity of the wording of the Great Goddess ceremonies with Christian phraseology. Many readers will be aware that Pope Gregory I actually exhorted his missionaries in the sixth and seventh centuries to take over pagan shrines and adapt them to the needs of the new religion; days which already marked important points in the calendar were chosen for the celebration of Christian holy days, together with the figures associated with them, such as Odin/Santa Claus/St Nicholas, Brigid/Brigantia/St Bridget, etc. I imagine the kind of language used in pagan rituals was also adopted by the Christians.

The picture of women we have from researchers of the Classical Greek world is that they were meek creatures mainly restricted to the home, rarely seen or heard. However, on visits to sites in what used to be Ancient Macedon it is hard not to be struck by the frequency of the depiction of the defeat of the Amazon women, most notably in the large central image on Philip II's shield in his tomb at Vergina (Ancient Aegae). This would seem to indicate that the victory of male warriors over females was especially prized, and was constantly held up as a reminder to the women of the time that they must submit to men. It appears to have been futile in the case of several of them: Olympias has the reputation of being an imperious woman who came to lead an army, as did Philip's daughter Cynane and her own daughter Eurydice II (Adea). It cannot be too far from the truth to believe that matriarchal traditions lay close to the surface in the Balkans in Antiquity.

When it comes to education, it is probably true that most women were uneducated in Ancient Greece and Macedon. Yet there are two women in the roll call of Plato's Academy – Axiothea of Phlius and Lasthenia of Mantinea – and Plato advocated the education of girls alongside boys. Aristotle, however, is not beloved of feminists. He believed that women were inferior to men and should not be educated in the same way, only receiving training in gymnastics and household economics. A wife should be in charge of the household but '*it is fitting that a woman of a well-ordered life should consider that her husband's wishes are as laws appointed for her by divine will, along with the marriage state and the fortune she shares.*' Nevertheless, the philosopher did set great store by virtue and fidelity in both marriage partners and believed that women's happiness was as vital to a society as men's.

As for Aristotle's close involvement in Macedonian politics, rulers in the fourth century BCE sought out philosophers as political advisers, preferring them over local noblemen. They took Plato's *Republic* seriously in its declaration that only philosophers were fit to rule in the ideal state. When Aristotle arrived in Athens to begin his studies in 367BCE, Plato had gone to Syracuse, where he stayed for over two years, teaching the young tyrant, Dionysius II, and attempting to improve the political system.

In c. 365 Plato's pupil Euphraeus was invited to the court of Macedon by the young king Perdiccas III, Philip II's elder brother and predecessor, Amyntas's father. Euphraeus appears to have enjoyed equal status with the King and inspired loathing among many noblemen, who didn't share his view that a knowledge of geometry and of philosophy were necessary to be part of the King's entourage and sit down with him to dinner. When Philip II acceded to the throne, the philosopher left court; the new king in fact made a point of seeking out Euphraeus eighteen years later on Euboea in order to ensure his death for anti-Macedonian activities. The bad relationship between the two may have affected Philip's views on Plato, whom he censured and held in low regard. This might also reflect Aristotle's influence on the King, as Plato's views are often criticised in Aristotle's work, although it is usually thought that he respected his teacher.

There was even speculation in the mid-fourth century BCE that philosophers would actually seize power in city states: two of Plato's students, Python and Heraclides of

Aenus, assassinated the Odrysian king Cotys I in 359. It was another philosopher, Isocrates, who urged Philip in an open letter of c. 344 to unite the Greeks and lead them in a war of revenge against the Persians. When Philip achieved the first part of this policy by defeating Athens and Thebes at the Battle of Chaeronea in 338, the philosopher, then aged 98, starved himself to death in horror at how it had come about.

I cite these examples to underline the fact that philosophers were expected to have political influence and that this was considered desirable and beneficial. Pythias's father Hermias wished it to be known that he had not betrayed philosophy, despite undergoing excruciating torture by the Persians. Clearly, philosophy to him did not mean metaphysics but politics, and his relations with Aristotle and Philip II of Macedon.

Several ancient historians claimed Hermias was a eunuch, unable to father children. Thus Pythias was said to be his adopted daughter, niece, or both, rather than his natural daughter. It is now generally thought that this claim was simply a ploy to blacken Hermias's name by Greeks, who considered him a barbarian. He was from Bithynia and had been the slave of a rich banker who ruled Atarneus, but later earned his freedom. Hermias was clearly a valued and respected member of the household, sent to Plato's Academy to study there at a young age. Owing to his undoubted merits, he returned to rule jointly with his former owner, becoming sole ruler after the latter's death. He gradually transformed the despotic form of government into a Platonic one.

Readers who are surprised by my championing the idea that Alexander was poisoned by water from the River Styx might be interested in a paper, first published in 2010, which examines the theory and finds it a distinct possibility. The river in question was the Mavroneri, or Black Water, which springs from mountains on the Peloponnesian peninsula. It harboured a killer bacterium which can occur on limestone rock deposits. ('The Deadly Styx River and the Death of Alexander' by Adrienne Mayor, Stanford University, and Antoinette Hayes, Pfizer Pharmaceuticals, *Princeton/Stanford Working Papers in Classics* 051101, May 2011.)

Aristotle's monologue on myths in this novel was inspired by a comment he made in a letter to Antipater from Chalcis: '*the more I am by myself, and alone, the fonder I have become of myths.*' For the comparison of himself to dualisers (*epamphoterizein*), which cross normal dividing lines between plants and animals, bipeds and quadrupeds, etc., I am indebted to Mary G. Dietz of the University of Chicago's article 'Between Polis and Empire: Aristotle's Politics' (*American Political Science Review*, 106, pp 275-293, doi:10.1017/S0003055412000184).

The excerpt from Homer's *Iliad* quoted in the novel is an amalgam of various translations and the author's own rendering. The translation of the excerpt from Aristotle's will is by Robert Drew Hicks (Diogenes Laërtius, *Lives of the Eminent Philosophers*, Book V, 13-14, Loeb Classical Library, 1925).

ACKNOWLEDGEMENTS

I am extremely grateful to family and friends for taking the trouble to read versions of this novel at various stages when I no longer had an objective view, and for making comments and suggestions which inspired me to renew work on it.

My late friend Peggy Reid followed the development of *Alexander, Aristotle and Me* (the original title) from the beginning and had the patience to read every fumbling chapter until I had found my voice, created some plausible characters and stopped sounding too much like a history book. She never failed with her discerning and constructive observations from first to last. It was all much appreciated and now a cause of great sadness that she is not here to hold the finished book in her hand.

Thanks go particularly to my husband, Goran Stefanovski, for running his expert eye over two drafts at important stages and advising me how to make the story more immediate and dramatic.

Erica Jarnes, formerly an editor for Bloomsbury, gave me extensive and highly perceptive notes, influencing in particular the structure of the novel.

Many useful and enlightening comments came along the way from other readers and advisers: Maggie Anwell, Dragana Josifova, Pam Taylor, Jana Stefanovska, Joanna Labon, Ljubica Arsovska and Igor Stefanovski.

This novel would never have reached its current form, however, without the confidence my literary agent, James

Essinger, showed in me from our first meeting and without his coaching. Thank you, James, for making me believe in myself as a writer.

Patricia Marsh